MW01247191

THIS CUP

PAUL FABIAN

RISING
WINDS

For all inquiries, please address Rising Winds Press, 220 Fortune Boulevard #1021, Milford, MA 01757, or email business@risingwindspress.com.

Publisher's Cataloging-in-Publication
(Provided by Cassidy Cataloguing Services, Inc.)

Names: Fabian, Paul, 1999- author.
Title: This cup / Paul Fabian.
Description: Milford, MA : Rising Winds Press, [2023]
Identifiers: ISBN: 979-8-9878031-3-4 (Paperback) | 979-8-9878031-1-0 (Hardback) | 979-8-9878031-0-3 (eBook) | LCCN: 2023903501
Subjects: LCSH: World War, 1939-1945--Fiction. | Women college students--France--Paris--Fiction. | Grail--Fiction. | Relics--Fiction. | Palestine--Fiction. | Germany. Geheime Staatspolizei-- Fiction. | Nazis--Fiction. | Germany--History--1833-1945--Fiction. | Conspiracy--Fiction. | Cults--Fiction. | Abrahamic religions--Fiction. | Historical fiction--Religious aspects-- Christianity. | LCGFT: Adventure fiction. | Historical fiction. | BISAC: FICTION / Historical / 20th Century / World War II. | FICTION / Historical / Medieval. | FICTION / Christian / Historical.
Classification: LCC: PS3606.A242 T45 2023 | DDC: 813/.6--dc2

Para mi Tia "Galleta" Arcelia

*Your God is of your flesh, He lives in
your nearest neighbor, in every man.*

— SAINT FRANCIS OF ASSISI

*The most delightful and choicest pleasure
is that which is hinted at, but never told.*

— CHRÉTIEN DE TROYES

THIS CUP

PART I

SIEGE PERILOUS

CHAPTER 1

Glastonbury Tor
Somerset, England
September 14th, 1938

T he pale white sunlight of dawn peaked over the clouds and kissed the patchwork of sheep pastures and enclosed bocages of England's Somerset Levels; verdant growths of rush and bracken were sparkling with the brisk morning's foggy dew; amid the lush tree lines, the sails of stone tower mills spun over boggy mires while shepherds herded their free-roaming droves of livestock down the drovers' byways along the Levels' hedgerows and split-rail fences for the seasonal transhumance.

For 19-year-old ingénue Psalmodie Vingt-Trois visiting from Paris, Glastonbury's bucolic landscape was a far cry from the skyline of London: A grimy crucible of commerce, finance, and industry, where smokestacks and derricks vied against steeples and clock towers for the soul of the metropolitan city. Though London's atmosphere was always choked with smog the color of dirty cotton wool, Glastonbury's was humid and sweet with an emanating earthy scent.

Psalmodie lay on her back, lost in the shade inside the lone looming tower of the ancient Church of Saint Michael, which surmounted a cloud-cutting hillock and overlooked the slighted ruins of the enormous

Benedictine Glastonbury Abbey. Resting on her abdomen was a wooden mazer filled with fresh water; the magical cup so valued and desperately sought out by the locals. In that moment, only two things mattered: Her own knightly conviction, and the cup in her hands, all brought together upon this legendary Isle of Avalon—the very resting place of King Arthur himself—, as the gods seemed to have quietly fated upon her.

To drink from it for a chance at eternal life, as her father had always told her.

All around her, a vast and blanketing oceanic cloud flooded through the landscape and swallowed the horizon. Psalmodie felt the cool air of this panoramic void sweep over her chapped lips and her fair, faintly freckled face. She closed her blue eyes and inhaled the placid solitude of the enchanted Isle deep into herself.

Psalmodie knew it was not always this peaceful. Even in Arthur's time, when the Roman Empire still ruled over the Britons, the pagan Celtic druids convoked festivals where large wickerwork idols were stuffed with humans and animals before being set ablaze, burning the sacrificial victims alive. Such legends, she recalled, were written by Roman chroniclers, perhaps with the aim to smear Celtic culture. Such a ritual was a far cry from the Celtic motif of the enchanted cauldron, capable of resurrecting dead warriors; one of many inspirations for the Holy Grail itself.

Death became life and became death and life again.

As she reflected on this eternal cycle of existence, an odd blend of dread and relief made its way into her heart when she heard the sound of footfalls crunching over saturated macadam; the sound called her eyes to the Gothic archway of the tower, and she saw that standing under it was her friend, an olive-skinned Afro-Arab woman. Psalmodie's shoulders softened once she recognized the concern and disappointment in her friend's face.

"*Comment ça va,* Shiloh?" Psalmodie said; her soft voice was a thick, but dainty Anglo-Aquitaine accent.

Psalmodie saw the dark blue kerchief loosely tied over Shiloh's tousled, blunt cut brown hair, with some small wisps curling from her brow and temples, framing the sensitive features of her gamine face. Her soulful eyes were hazel, but they glowed a limpid amber color in the white dawn sunlight. Psalmodie also noticed that Shiloh had been wearing her usual attire: Calf-high cuffed boots over loose green harem pants along with a quilted burnt sienna jerkin over a muslin-sleeved pullover undershirt. Shiloh never did fit in with the traditional Parisian decorum, but to Psalmodie's pity, no one ever seemed to have expected much from an outcast foreigner anyway.

"How's your spiritual retreat up in Whitby going for you?" Shiloh asked with a weary cadence. "It seems like you're a hair off course. Or was it that you got off at London before your train left for York?" She stepped closer into Psalmodie's view, forcing a wan smile before dropping it back to that same emotionally exhausted countenance... almost as if she wanted to hurt.

Shiloh's presence atop the hill obviously presaged what Psalmodie knew would have been a caravan of uniformed goons and suits making its way up the hill's concrete path to apprehend her. Psalmodie pushed herself to standing and rushed to the archway to scan the foot of the hill. Just as she expected, she saw the straggling procession rising from the cruel world that lay beneath the cloud. The West Mercia constabulary and the curators from the National Trust, all there for the medieval mazer she had stolen from the Powell Estate all the way back in Wales.

The *Cwpan Nanteos,* otherwise known as the Nanteos Cup.

"I can't sleep," Psalmodie said. She turned to face her friend, although she couldn't have brought herself to fully look at her. "I can't eat. I can't breathe. Everywhere I go, I can't stop seeing him."

"Your father?" Shiloh asked.

A silence befell them as they stole uneasy glances at each other. Psalmodie fixed her dark blonde hair behind her ear, though her plait had already been unfurled. Then her eyes finally met her friend's gaze. "So how did you know where to find me?"

Shiloh shrugged. "Well, I *am* your roommate, and you don't do a very good job keeping your bucket list from me; you've hardly been quiet about this place."

"I know," Psalmodie said with a resigned chuckle. Her smile was short-lived and her abashed regard towards Shiloh turned more curious. Though Shiloh had enough self-control for two, she wasn't quite as headstrong as Psalmodie. Even so, since the day they had met, Psalmodie knew that there was always something underlying Shiloh's reserved demeanor. "You know..." Psalmodie started, "I read somewhere that there actually used to be an ancient Roman temple in Londinium dedicated to the mystery cult of the Egyptian goddess of rebirth, Isis."

Shiloh nodded indifferently. "And you're mentioning this to me because...?"

Psalmodie ventured, "For all your talk of God and religion and all that other stuff, you've always seemed too awkward with everyone on campus, but I'm sure there's nothing you can say about yourself that will really surprise me. Why don't you just talk to me?"

"About what?"

"About your parents in Egypt or wherever you're from. About you. About *anything*." Psalmodie saw her friend's face had again turned downcast and distant. Without another word, Shiloh held out her hand to receive the cup that Psalmodie had stolen. Instead, she noticed Psalmodie reaching for something in her pocket. With shaking fingers, she produced a ripped piece of paper. "My father sent me this," Psalmodie said, handing it to Shiloh.

The paper read:

OVXSVNRMVHGFMVILHVZOVKVVWZMHOZKRVIIV
LECHEMINESTUNEROSEALEPEEDANSLAPIERRE

Shiloh recognized it was a French-annotated Atbash telegram. An ancient Judaic substitution cipher made up of a reversely mapped alphabet that corresponded to their opposite letters; A is Z, B is Y, and so on.

Translated, it read, *Le chemin est une rose à l'épée dans la pierre.*

Shiloh's face shifted. "What is this?"

Psalmodie engaged her friend and read verbatim, "'The way is a rose to the sword in the stone.' He's definitely trying to tell me something about *this cup!*" Her wild eyes leveled on Shiloh's. "Shiloh, listen to me. This Nanteos Cup, it has to be the best candidate for the legendary relic."

"Psalmodie, how do you know it isn't just another hoax?" Shiloh asked.

"It's not a hoax!" Psalmodie protested. "It can't be! My father said so!"

"Maybe his message meant something else?"

"How? This civil parish lies along the same ley line as the city of Lancaster, whose medieval crest was a red Tudor rose! And if this place is indeed the Isle of Avalon, then this ought to have been where King Arthur forged his sword Excalib—" Psalmodie caught herself and shrank back from what she saw in Shiloh's eyes.

"Just give me the cup," Shiloh begged, "and let's just go home. I've already spoken to the Trust; I told them not to press any charges if they saw that the cup was safe."

Stroking the wych elm grain of the mazer one last time, Psalmodie sighed and surrendered it to her companion. It was in Shiloh's hand, but Psalmodie did not let go. The two locked eyes, and she read the same sadness in Shiloh's gaze. When Psalmodie saw this, her face fell small and she nodded subtly in defeat. Then, with her tongue in her cheek, Psalmodie deferred the barren relic to Shiloh. Psalmodie paused for thought, but then broke away and brushed past Shiloh's shoulder.

"Psalmodie?" Shiloh called, following shortly after her before stopping at the terrace outside the tower. Some uniforms received Psalmodie while two others leisurely converged on Shiloh to receive the priceless artifact.

"We thank you, Mademoiselle al-Ahad," one of the men said. "May we have the mazer now, please?"

Shiloh responded with a sigh, "So you will keep your word?"

He presented his outstretched hand and responded, "We'll place her under arrest in the meantime, but as we agreed, my dear, so long as there's no lasting damage to it, we will not pursue any charges or fines and no one else will ever have to know. In any case, however, I should be frank with you: I don't think your friend will be able to come back to our museum establishments for quite some time now, if ever."

Shiloh looked away and nodded at this. She looked down at the

mazer and turned it over to make sure that there was no lasting damage
to it. Once she handed it over to them, she saw the small Coptic cross
tattoo on her right wrist: The seal of her echoing past.

"*A'udhu billahi,*" she whispered in Arabic.

The clouds parted, and she saw that the many market towns and
hamlet settlements of King Arthur's fallen kingdom had come into
striking relief.

CHAPTER 2

Wewelsburg Castle
Büren, Germany
September 18th, 1938

T he Court of Legion had been convened...
Through the choir's disoriented chanting—the morbid, depraved moans of possessed men being tortured in an uncanny darkness—, the clamor of the infamous Schutzstaffel police force resounded through the halls of the secluded, mansard-roofed Renaissance fortress of Wewelsburg; the mystical center of the world destined to reign beyond the countryside of North Rhine-Westphalia.

"Oh du, dem Unrecht geschah, grüßt dich!"

The conclave where the cry echoed from was known as the "Hall of the Dead," a dark and circular crypt of flagstone adorned top to bottom with chiseled Armanen Runic symbols that immortalized the Schutzstaffel's contrived heritage, from the spiraling black sun emblazoned on the walls and floors of the castle to the golden, square-hooked swastika affixed to the room's zenith. At the very center of the room, however, was a large circular pool of a viscous, molasses-like liquid that was black as onyx and sin.

Around the pool's ledges were torches of blue and yellow flames from which a rose-scented attar incense permeated the air like a thick smoke; a testament to the fortuitous spirit of their völkisch suprema-cism. Surrounding the pool were twelve members of the Reichsführer's Personal Staff sitting on pedestals along the perimeter of the crypt in the very manner of the Arthurian Round Table legends.

Entering through the doors on the other end of the crypt was a portly septuagenarian Austrian man, holding an ivory-handled crozier and donning a bishop's pontifical headdress with ecclesiastical vest-ments. Though he donned clerical regalia, he wore a tab collar with two rhombus-shaped lightning bolts: The SS acronym of the Schutzstaffel. His chubby, sagging jowls, gibbous eyes, and the Führer's same, short toothbrush mustache bespoke his mystical and romantic devotion to blood and soil rather than faith and doctrine.

Brigadeführer Karl Maria Wiligut Weisthor.

A folk esotericist known to all branches of the SS as the "secret King of Germany." After fighting for the Austro-Hungarian Empire in the Great War and spending three years incarcerated in an asylum in Salz-burg for psychotic schizophrenia, he rose to become the patriarchal hierophant for the National Socialist New European Order based in their new occult cathedral.

Accompanying him was a chief dignitary of the Waffen-SS, anxious to find his own son in his liminal occasion of rebirth from the Earth into the light. Processing behind him were the patriarch's three acolytes, wearing ceremonial black hooded cloaks and ominously androgynous volto masks. They rocked their bowed heads, silently commemorating the Neopagan sacrament as if possessed by a single mind.

The father stepped forth before the pool while his wife—who was herself newly indoctrinated with this new Nordic truth—reluctantly awaited by his side. Wiligut Weisthor mounted a pulpit at the far end of the crypt for his sermon; a benediction of this Irministic baptism by fire was necessary before officiating in the presence of their most glorious imperator.

The high priest's eyes rolled up in his entranced state. His lips and gums were smeared with tar-black soot, and his mouth hung open like a gaping maw, exposing within a tongue that poked out from crooked incisors like an awl. Then he elevated his hands, as if to praise the unconquered sun of Valhalla, and formally commenced the Irministic paternoster prayer in the Gothic liturgical language for his council of shadows.

He gibbered hideously, *"Vater unsar. Gib uns Deinen Geist und Deine Kraft im Stoffe..."*—Our Father. Give us your spirit and your strength in matter...

With this prayer, there came the thick sound of churning and gurgling from the center of the pool's surface. The father and Wiligut Weisthor watched in joyous reverence as the glossy tar bulged, and a black, bulbous shape rose up and stretched into a humanoid form, the dark sin completely coating his body like a mucous membrane, giving the wiry creature the appearance of a faceless clay sculpture. After this rejuvenating fermentation of his Being, the boy held still, surrendering himself to a joy until now known only to the insane.

And then, in synchrony with the high priest's circular prayers, he coiled and flailed his arms through the air; erratic gyrations of ritual lamentation for the one they all knew in their hearts to have been the one true God amidst the Æsir, the vast pantheon of true gods...

Overwhelmed by the horrific sight, the mother looked away and sobbed quietly into her overjoyed husband's chest.

As the sermon went on in the Hall of the Dead, the gaunt silhouette of the 34-year-old, half-Jewish Obersturmführer Otto Wilhelm Rahn paced restively outside the doors. His neurotic eyes shot from one thing to another, from floor tile to brick to window. He then glanced out the window to scan the distant Teutoburg Forest, the legendary site of the Germanic tribes' unified triumph over the Roman legions in the time of Christ.

But off in the distance, he saw an oval-shaped blemish hovering over the cityscape of Dortmund; it was the fortress-sized Graf Zeppelin that Rahn heard the Reich Ministry of Propaganda was testing to fly over the Sudetenland... that is, if Adolf Hitler somehow managed to wrest the land under his control. Only the day before, the Führer had established the Sudetendeutsches Freikorps, a covert paramilitary in Czechoslovakia with the express purpose of fanning political instability. Apparently, the Ministry of Propaganda had high hopes for them, already preparing for a celebration despite the infamous Hindenburg disaster over a year prior.

But to Rahn, the Graf Zeppelin's droning propellers rumbled through the landscape like a thundering plague of locusts.

He rubbed the angular cheekbones and aquiline nose of his weasel-like face before looking down at his chewed fingertips; his hands were bony and delicate, like those of a pianist, although he used them more for typewriting and, as of late, nibbling off nail cuticles. Trying to distract himself from this vice, he turned to another by lighting one of his cigars in his mouth. He waited anxiously, repeatedly looking towards the light at the end of the dark, torch-lit corridor; he felt the corridor become something of an antechamber to an operating room.

It was when Rahn briefly removed his fedora to fix his slicked-back, receding hairline that he heard two men's voices and footsteps approaching, but for a man such as the one he anticipated, he recognized his sharp, authoritative accent. Rahn cocked his eyes towards the silhouetted uniforms approaching from the light. The man on the left looked up from a pile of papers and grinned passively at Rahn. From the man's square jawline and neat comb over, the Obersturmführer recognized that it was his fellow comrade, the SS poet and radio broadcaster Kurt Eggers.

But to Eggers' right was the man Rahn so dreaded. He looked at the man's black and heavily decorated paramilitary dress uniform with the crimson armband and the golden aiguillette looping over his breast pocket and shoulder. He then saw the man's round face with an unusually weak chin and the pince-nez glasses over his monotonous glare. When Rahn realized that he couldn't stop staring at the spectral apparition, he quickly stood at attention and threw up the salute of the mass party with a rigid obeisance to him.

The man who co-founded the Ahnenerbe e.V. think tank and secret society with the express intention of setting the pure ones upon their rightful destiny for *Lebensraum,* the conquest for new living space for the Aryan race. The man who, through the eclectic racial theories of his SS, was helping to realize the Führer's vision for yet another unified triumph of the Germanic peoples. The man who consistently sponsored Rahn's right-guided quest all these years.

"Herr Rahn!" Eggers greeted. "How nice of you to join us for our good friend's fledging son."

"Yes, I try to be present at every moment the gods and valkyries of the Æsir redeliver their true chosen people," Rahn remarked, looking to evoke some reaction from his unamused superior, Reichsführer Heinrich Himmler.

As Eggers shuffled through his papers one last time, Himmler's piercing, chillingly resentful eyes considered Rahn and the remark he made, as if trying to decide whether it was punishable for being too much. He then focused towards Rahn's mouth and said pointedly, "I see that some of us are still not without the commonplace vices."

It took Rahn a moment to figure out what Himmler meant, but once he realized it, he promptly tossed his cigar out the window next to him. "I am still working through this problem, sir. I am, however, still sober." A long silence persisted after Rahn's remark. Himmler's eyes bored into him, and Rahn found it difficult returning his gaze.

"Herr Eggers," Himmler started. "I see that you have already made Herr Rahn's acquaintance."

Eggers looked up with an arched brow between Himmler and Rahn. "Well, certainly! He and I share the same publicist. What's more is that we also actually worked together earlier this year at a club I organized for the Dietrich Eckart Haus back in Dortmund. Herr Rahn here gave a *riveting* lecture on the problem of Lucifer's fall." Eggers then looked at Rahn and smirked. "Hey, did you like the salute I closed your lecture with? Of course, I meant it as a joke, but word spread to high priest Wiligut Weisthor and I think he took quite a liking to it; looking back, I find it quite suitable for the spirit of his liturgy."

"Of course," Rahn assented, "it does capture the spirit of our nation's savior, the light-bearer; only now, there will be no more 'Messiah' to exorcize and demonize him... *'for we are many...'*"

Himmler placed the quote from Christian Scripture. "*'For we are many...'* That is what 'Legion' said, as the so-called 'Gospels' of Mark and Luke referred to him as, correct?"

"Indeed," Rahn said, flashing a nervous smile. "Legion is the light-bearer's other name, although as Herr Eggers can attest, I still prefer to refer to him as..." Rahn trailed off when he saw Eggers' grin drop.

Eggers turned to face Himmler with grave concern. "Our Führer's speech in Nuremberg twelve days ago is proof enough that he might denounce your Ahnenerbe's mission as merely occult, having no place in the National Socialist Programme."

Himmler looked down and licked his lips as he deliberated over Eggers' words. "Quite so, quite so. The Führer was right to profess our post-Christian völkisch spirit, although he has yet to understand that the Aryan solidarity of our party line can only go so far without a more... transcendent sense of accountability."

"Certainly, one that goes beyond the Jewish monopoly on faith," Rahn interjected in a doting vein. Himmler and Eggers stared at Rahn for a moment, almost as if he offended them somehow with a distasteful comment. Rahn withdrew his gaze and kept quiet.

Eggers sighed and looked back at Himmler. "My Reichsführer, I have studied theology, archeology, and the Sanskrit language of our Indo-Aryan forerunners; I was also a Lutheran minister before Christ eventually led me to our Führer for the promise of a new Reformation. I still believe that we can yet appropriate more Christian trappings in our quest for the conversion of the Aryan peoples' national spirit. If there is anything I can contribute to that end, my Reichsführer, please, let me help you—"

Himmler gestured towards the Hall of the Dead. "Go forth and share in our fellow comrade's glory. I shall have Officer Günter d'Alquen nominate you as his replacement as editor-in-chief of *Das Schwarze Korps* should he decide to step down in the foreseeable future."

Both Rahn and Eggers gaped at Himmler in disbelief. "Our SS's official newspaper?" Eggers exclaimed.

Himmler smiled. "Bolshevik, Papist, Freemason; no apologist or moral authority can ever match the great spirit of our new knighthood... *'for we are many...'*"

Barely able to contain his delight, Eggers straightened, clicked his heels, and gave Himmler a short bow before starting for the Hall's door. Himmler's pleased gaze followed him, and when he turned back to face the skeletal figure still standing before him, his smile faded immediately. Rahn tried holding Himmler's glare, but his terrified eyes kept blinking and returning to the tiled floor.

"Come," Himmler said. "I have been meaning to review something with you."

Rahn grimaced. "Sir?"

Himmler beckoned him again towards the end of the corridor. Rahn looked back towards the ceremony one last time before following the Reichsführer. Rahn turned the corner and saw the Reichsführer standing by an archway not too different from the entrance to the Hall of the Dead. With apprehensive deliberation, Rahn approached his superior, who, to his disquiet, fixated his unblinking eyes on the locked door before him.

"Is there a problem, sir?" Rahn asked.

"Do you have Wewelsburg's keys?" Himmler asked, still not breaking away from the door's handle. "Or does high priest Wiligut Weisthor have them?"

Staving his hesitation, Rahn rushed into the pockets of his soutane-like overcoat, but in his panicked haste, he dropped the keys. After scrambling his fingers over the floor, he picked up the keys and fidgeted through them before finding the one that locked into the door's hole. As Rahn stood back up, he noticed Himmler looking down his nose at him.

They stepped in and found themselves in the Gralsraum, a heptagonal room not too different from the crypt. The walls in this one, however, were lined with shelves stacked with tomes and grimoires on the occult, alchemical wisdom of the forgotten, ancient mystery schools: Gnosticism, Neoplatonism, Hermeticism, and Rosicrucianism, among countless others.

Across the room from the door was a statuette niche in the wall housing a shadow box display with an inscription on the bottom frame: *V.I.T.R.I.O.L.* The acronym for the alchemical motto of the Rosicrucian Order's allegorical founder, Christian Rosenkreuz: *Visita Interiora Terrae Rectificando Invenies Occultum Lapidem*—Visit the interior of the Earth; by rectification thou shalt find the hidden stone.

Inside the display were two small black stones; haematite meteorites of pure iron that Rahn found while caving the prehistoric Lombrives Cave of Ussat-les-Bains in Southern France. Known as the *Lapis Exilis,* they were meant to replicate the object of Himmler and Rahn's aspirations; the sacred panacea of all philosophies and mythologies. The meteorites' purpose as a stop-gap for the actual stone that fell from the heavens, however, was sterile of the true power Himmler and Rahn had hoped it would imitate.

"How goes your quest for the treasure?" Himmler asked.

"It is quite illusive, sir," Rahn said uneasily, carefully measuring each word, "but I am confident that it is within our grasp."

Himmler clenched his jaw but kept silent, absorbing Rahn's words. After another clamor from the crypt sounded through the corridors, Himmler asked, "Run through it for me again, will you? How is it that you intend to find it?"

Rahn's throat tensed as he gulped. "Do you want me to restate everything? Surely, you haven't forgo—"

"You should know by now, Herr Rahn, that I never forget," Himmler said, crossing towards the shadow box and removing the meteorites from their place; with a man like the Reichsführer, Rahn sensed an incident coming on. "I am, however, concerned that *you* have. So please, Herr Rahn, if you will indulge my question?"

Rahn took two steps back and nodded. "So, do you recall the famed archaeologist, Dr. Heinrich Schliemann?"

"Do tell, Herr Rahn: Why is that name so important here?" Himmler responded crisply, holding one of the meteorites close to his mouth and spitting on it before rubbing it against the other.

Though Rahn sensed derision, he cleared his throat and went on, "Back in 1873, he found the lost mythical city of Troy in Asia Minor by following clues embedded in Homer's *Odyssey* and *Iliad*. A truly astounding method, not to say deemed highly unorthodox by academia since it practically converted historical myth into fact. But I have great faith that if I applied it to the legends of King Arthur, we will most certainly substantiate our claim to the—"

"Herr Rahn," Himmler cut off, pausing again to hear the valorous clamoring of his chosen people reverberating through the walls of the castle. "Did I ever tell you how our regime came about?"

Rahn's voice faltered a moment. "I-I believe not, sir. No."

"Before our Führer was at the vanguard of this new movement, you may find it hard to believe that it was founded on the principles of this very treasure you seek now."

Rahn wiped away the sweat on his lip and held his elbows. "I beg your pardon?"

"The Deusch Arbeiterpartei, which as you may well know served as the scaffolding for our great Reich, was itself substantially scaffolded by an underground society known as the Thule-Gesellschaft."

"The Thule-Gesellschaft?" Rahn responded. "Did they not themselves draw from the Order of the New Templars, who were the first to profess our Aryan swastika?"

Himmler went on, "It is little known among our fellow comrades—and unfortunately, even some among my own ranks—that this 'Thule-Gesellschaft' was founded by Rudolf von Sebottendorf, the Ordensmeister of one noble brotherhood before his eventual conversion to Mohammedanism."

Rahn felt Himmler's foreboding aspect pressing him further against the wall. He saw on Himmler's face that his appraisal of the precious stones in his hands had ashened with contempt... for his saliva had caused the meteorites to weep a sanguine iron oxidation; the mineral property that Rahn understood was eventually foolishly mistaken for the blood of Jesus Christ.

Himmler declared, "The Munich lodge of the *Germanenorden Walvater von Heiligen Gral.*"—The Teutonic Order of the Triune god Wotan and the Holy Grail. Then his contempt burst out and he threw the meteorites down before Rahn's feet; the stones' red fragments flecked across the floor like spattered liquid. Himmler drew closer to Rahn's agitated face. "Our revolution, under the leadership of our Führer, was inaugurated by a prophecy of the Holy Grail; a prophecy that, despite his own disbelief, came to him in his moment of triumph over his own struggle. Do you understand what I am telling you?"

Rahn's teeth were clenched inside his shut mouth; he could only mumble, "Yes, sir."

Having reminded Rahn of their mission, Himmler walked over the blood-stained floor and tried to imagine Germany's uncertain future. "Our people's need for *Lebensraum* encompasses not only their need for physical space, but spiritual as well. I have just spoken with Reichsleiter

Alfred Rosenberg and Hanns Kerrl, who is our Reichsminister of
Church Affairs, on the sensitive nature of the Christian question.

"These men are both trying their best to wean our people away from
this mongrel desert religion through our German Faith Movement so
that they may come home to their true blood and soil, and yet, virtually
the entirety of the Aryan race insists on enslaving itself to this Nazarene
Judaism such like the *untermensch*. It doesn't help that Pope Pius XI,
despite the Führer's concordat with him, denounced our nation's pagan
destiny in his encyclical last year. Although for the moment, we
continue to share a greater enemy in the Jewish functionaries of the
Soviet Union.

"But be that as it may, our *Kirchenkampf*—our struggle with the
Roman Church in the fatherland—does not appear to have an end in
sight. While I and some of my fellow devotees in the party have a great
appreciation for how Jesus Christ has incubated our peoples' religious
instincts all these centuries, the Roman Church in particular continues
to make inroads into our party's efforts to reveal the final Aryan Gospel.
Our Führer spoke of a 'the brotherhood of Templars around the Holy
Grail of pure blood.' We have a sacred obligation to that honor! We
need the purified Grail *now*, for the sake of our peoples' continued
devotion."

Rahn started to respond, but he instead trailed Himmler's raised
finger towards the window in the hallway outside the Gralsraum's archway. He made his way to the window sill and beheld a prophecy of
his own.

A piercing whistle shrilled outside, and Rahn saw, beyond the
midsommar maypoles, a procession of emaciated laborers—mostly Jews
and Jehovah's Witnesses—filing in from the tipples and quarries
surrounding Wewelsburg Castle to the barracks and watchtowers of the
neighboring Niederhagen *konzentrationslager*. After the whistle came
the silence, and in such silence, Rahn saw that the muddy ground was
strewn with stiffened corpses reduced to skin and bone.

Oddly, it was the chirping of birds that transfixed Rahn; the
perpetual and unaffected stillness of nature—no different from his time
in Southern France—that muted the sounds of the distant butchery. To
Rahn's horror, such silence almost made it feel banal and inconsequen-

tial... almost as though it were simply an extension of the serene nature surrounding it.

"The Holy Grail," Himmler continued, punching his fist into his palm. "It gave our Führer the necessary inspiration to bring us out of the infamy of Versailles all the way to the Enabling Act in less than fifteen years; the power to stir and convert the masses to his cause. That power brought us to this. And mind you that, in all of this time, the Grail had merely *spoken* to him. Imagine, now, what power would come of all this if he could actually touch it. Now you—*you*—have brought the Grail within reach.

"I have granted you 1,000 Reichsmarks a month to wander Italy, France, Spain, Scotland, Denmark, Iceland. You were meant to be the final panel of our people's triptych; in yourself, you summarized the next becoming of our Führer, the Third Reich, and all of our people, and yet... every time, you return empty-handed. What have you to say for yourself?"

Rahn tensely reached for his breast pocket and adjusted his collar before holding his hands over his waist. On his ring finger, he felt his manacle: The Totenkopf ring, or the Death's Head Ring. A brass signet ring much like the ones used by the Vikings, crafted for each member of the Ahnenerbe with the emblem engraved in its head. Rahn, however, had his ring custom made: An Occitan variant of the German Iron Cross centered by a rosy-red swastika. The Rose Cross of alchemical tradition. The crest, as Rahn believed it in his heart, of the ancient guardians of the Grail; a crest he once believed this order of new knights rightfully inherited.

"Despite everything," Rahn started, "it is my hope that one day, Europe will be free of *all* Jewish mythology, for we are the people of Nordic blood who call ourselves 'the Cathari,' who were Christian only in name, contrary to what history stubbornly insists to us; in truth, they were our prophets to the primeval truth of the Holy Grail: The stone from Lucifer's heavenly diadem." Rahn's voice faded upon noticing the ire on Himmler's face.

The Reichsführer snarled, "You wandered through the whole of Europe for the Ahnenerbe with a long list of theories attached to every single nation, and you still say you need more time?"

A desperation charged in Rahn's voice. "Were it so easy, it would have been found long ago."

Himmler interrupted with a reciting timbre to his voice. "'It lies in a cave in the Tabor Forest. And the treasure itself is guarded by hundreds of vipers.' In the Tabor Forest? Those were *your* words, Herr Rahn! *Your* words in your latest work, *Luzifer's Hofgesind!*"

Rahn held in his next words. He shut his eyes, and when he felt the chill of Himmler's minty breath on his face, he knew that Himmler's presence loomed close. The long quiet that followed was pierced again by the SS's proud and sovereign cry. While Rahn silently awaited the sting of his superior's back hand, nothing came.

Instead, Himmler's voice softened. "I heard that you couldn't bear the rigors of the training regimen at the Buchenwald *konzentrationslager.*" As Himmler spoke, Rahn opened his eyes and saw him digging through his breast pocket and taking out a crumpled assortment of papers. "But you were seconded as an auxiliary troop to the SS's Death's Head Units in Dachau last year for four months, yes?"

"Sir?" Rahn responded.

"Your former associate in your quest," Himmler went on, "Professor Vingt-Trois? The scholar of Arthurian semiotics on sabbatical from Paris? The one you met at that academic conference in Gießen." Himmler shot a confounded glare at Rahn. "I reviewed his records. You yourself actually charged him and some other member of the Luftwaffe with vulgar displays of homosexuality, and yet, you also filed a request that he be kept alive since you claimed he still serves a purpose to find the treasure. Why?"

Rahn's gaze turned abstract. "For his Catholic upbringing; for my understanding of what it is about the faulty Christian claim to the Grail that persists throughout the centuries that could have lent a great deal of insight as to how to reconstruct our own rightful claim to it. While he subscribed to Chrétien de Troyes' Arthurian romances, I follow the truth that is the Cathari legacy and—"

"Rahn!" Himmler barked.

Startled, Rahn collected himself once more before Himmler. "Right," he said. "In essence, my Reichsführer, you have to untangle the

confusion of our own history by untangling the history of our tres-
passers."

"Well, then, you can begin by untangling *this* trespasser," Himmler
said, dashing the ruffled papers against Rahn's chest.

"What is this?" Rahn gathered them and perused its contents.
Under the smudges of black soot was an insensate assortment of
characters.

"These are telegrams," Himmler said. "After the Abwehr intelligence service intercepted an unsanctioned telegraph channel, they inves-
tigated the camp and found these in a cache in block 15 of the priest
barracks of Dachau, where, as you well know by now, the insubordinate
clergymen and legates of the Church in Germany are installed.

"Your associate frequented block 17 for his weekly Act of Contrition with a priest." Himmler stabbed his finger down on the papers'
swastika letterhead. "And you will notice up here by the stamps, *all of
them* came in from Paris in the last couple of months." Himmler paused
to search Rahn's face. "Is he not from Paris as well?"

Rahn swallowed and found his own voice. "I am sure many people
in there could be as well for that matter. What would make you think it
is indeed him?"

"This is a Jewish cipher," Himmler responded, his voice rising in
rage. "We've seen them many times before. It really isn't that difficult to
decrypt, but our French cryptologists verified that the encrypted
messages were written in dulcet tones. We believe it is his daughter; the
one you watched grow up, yes?" He cut another glare at Rahn. "How he
continuously broke into the commandant's office is beyond any of us,
but *someone* could have learned of our operation by now!"

Rahn's eyes swam over the German annotations of the telegrams'
Jewish code once more before looking to his superior.

"You understand that this could be worse than Arthur Zimmermann's
Telegram," Himmler said. "How many times have I told you that this is why
your associate *needed* to die? I have the code clerks at the Abwehr intelligence
service closely monitoring Dachau's communiques after the most recent
breach in its security. I will appoint the SS-Standarte Kurt Eggers to you;
they may be a propaganda unit, but they are sufficiently trained to fight in

whatever situation demands it. Still, I am going to hold you personally accountable for *all* of your partner's actions and failures. And so long as you give me progress, you will continue to be of use to me. Is that understood?"

"Yes, sir," the Obersturmführer nodded, doing well to hide his conflict from Himmler.

Another clamor echoed from Wiligut Weisthor's ritual chamber. Himmler started in that direction but stopped midway through the room's entrance.

"There is a great danger, Herr Rahn," Himmler said, looking at the blood on the floor with a passive regard. Rahn remained petrified, not facing him once. "The Grail will be lost to history once again if we allow the Christians to hoard its legacy. I would like for you to kill this child, but dead or alive, I'll expect to see a comprehensive after-action report on my desk." Himmler let the silence hang there for a moment before he clicked his heels, saluted, swiveled, and started back for the Hall of the Dead.

When Rahn heard Himmler's footsteps recede, Rahn released a breath he didn't even realize he was holding. The halls of Wewelsburg Castle fell cold, and the haunting echoes of that infernal baptismal vow that Kurt Eggers himself prescribed for the new knighthood resonated deeply into his mind.

"Oh du, Luzifer, dem Unrecht geschah, grüßt dich!"—Oh you, Lucifer, who has been done wrong to, we salute you!

PART II
THE ROUND TABLE

CHAPTER 3

Drifting leaves chased after the soft wind through the lonely street, with the only light coming from the constellations in the dusk skies above and the golden light cast from an old gas streetlamp. Some parked cars lined the sidewalks in front of the stoops of several brick row homes and flats, adjoined end-to-end up and down the street.

An irresolute Shiloh Ma'idah al-Ahad leaned back against the perimeter garden railing of the park behind her. Her eyes were fast on the Grand Mosquée de Paris directly across the street from her; a building inaugurated in 1926 in commemoration of the French and Muslim blood shed in solidarity during the Great War. Shiloh found that the green Spanish-Moorish scroll masonry and floral motifs of the mosque's front entrance were a much-needed retreat from the innumerable Flamboyant Gothic and Baroque cathedrals of European Catholicism.

Yet something else manifested itself to her; something remote, always there, sealed away beneath some hermetic vacuum of silence. She shut her eyes as a faint susurration haunted the silence until it slowly emerged louder and louder and louder into the scandalous whisperings of spirits, all judging her. The sounds were unintelligible and overlapping, but the resentful disgust in them was unmistakable. Shiloh heard one word in particular interspersed among their hissed words: *Heretic.*

There were more whisperings. *Infidel.* More whisperings. *Infidel.* More, louder. *Infidel.* Louder. *Infidel. Infidel. Infidel!*

With a gasp, Shiloh stirred from this waking nightmare and darted her eyes in all directions, finding herself back in the original silence of the street before the mosque. Not knowing who or where else to turn to for her demons, she turned inwardly, still searching and praying, *Holy Mary, Mother of God, pray for us sinners, now and at the hour of our death. Amen.*

Just as she finished her prayer, she heard gritty footsteps approaching and looked up to see the tall and sinewy 21-year-old Manchurian-born man perching himself on the railing next to her. She immediately recognized the greasy waves of his raven-black, mid-length mane; the square, smooth-shaven jawline; the chiseled cheekbones of an Adonis; the nonchalant East Asian eyes. Most notable about him, however, was his distinctive clothing: A Mandarin hat with a sable fur brim and brass finial, complemented by a dark red Chinese hanfu robe over the belted cassock and white tab collar of a Catholic clergyman.

"Bonsoir, my dear *huli xiangtou,"* he greeted in his rich, warm voice before sharing in the mosque's Moorish artwork with her.

"I'm sorry—*Brother* Francis," Shiloh rejoined half-heartedly. "There you go; I said it. Are you happy now?"

"I'm only teasing you," Francis said before blowing out his breath and trying his new name over on his tongue. *"Brother* Francis Gaiwan, S.J.... I know it's been a while now, but I'm actually still having trouble getting used to the idea myself."

Shiloh gave him an arch look and spoke with a mildly sarcastic tone that sprang from her own embarrassment. "So, you *weren't* really bothered I forgot your title then? I called you by your courtesy name in front of your fellow Jesuit novitiates!"

"Well, *I'll* certainly get over their ragging," he said with an offhand chuckle before tossing his chin towards the mosque's front doors, "but I imagined I'd find you feeling sorry for it in *there.*"

Shiloh's grin faded and she dipped her head away from him. "Don't you have that Jesuit gathering at La Dame de Fer tonight?" she asked passively.

The Jesuit Brother sighed. "Yes, well, I just had to get away from all of that. I also wasn't really expecting anyone there to get a rush out of some petty apprentice treasurer for a missionary society they have unfortunately heard little of."

Shiloh smiled, but again, she came back to herself and persisted in her reserve.

Francis cast sidelong to her. "Did you, uh... Did you dream about her again?" he prompted. Shiloh kept quiet, but Francis probed a little further, trying to be mindful of her boundaries. "What did she say to you this time?"

Shiloh shrugged and shook her head with uncertainty. Before Francis went on, he was distracted by the creaking turnstile behind the mosque's main oak doors. A Moroccan intendant stepped out and left a sign holder on the steps listing the scheduled times for *tahajjud,* the voluntary night prayer. Francis looked back at Shiloh; her gaze still looked dissociated, although her eyes seemed precariously near tears.

Francis' considerate tone changed for another note. "How is Psalmodie doing?"

Shiloh idly crunched the grains of concrete under her heel. "She, uh... She said something about going to her old home tonight. I don't know what she's doing there."

"Shiloh, can I ask you something?" Francis asked.

She looked at him with a half-turned face before responding, "Sure."

"I don't mean to pry, but I'm getting a little concerned now; has she been acting differently to you lately?"

Shiloh scoffed under her breath, "'Lately.'"

Francis sighed. "You know her better than I do, so it isn't really my place to tell you what to do, but Monsignor Jean-Patmos, the Society's procurator training me, lends his help to the bursar at your university from time to time. Yesterday, he told me that she ran out of his office crying when she finished reading her loan promissory note. I told Monsignor that he had no business telling me this, but he did say her financial status was perfectly fine."

Shiloh looked down and nodded at the ground as an unsurprised look of exasperation swept over her face. "Ever since what happened in England, there has been a lot of gossip about us; that I'm converting her to..." As she was speaking, she caught the distracted expression on Francis' face, immersed in the mosque's splendid architecture. She faced forward and sighed out, "I'm not sure I'll get anywhere with her, but I'll bring it up after fencing club tomorrow."

Francis looked down at Shiloh. "I'm not a swordsman, but did you get a chance to practice those *kendo* techniques I mentioned on Psalmodie?"

Shiloh answered, "Thank you, but I think my parrying dagger is faring pretty well against her knightly bravado."

After Francis chuckled at this, the Islamic star and crescent over the mosque turned alight with a green radiance. A voice suddenly cried out in Arabic to them from across the street. Standing at the mosque's stilted archway was the same intendant, shooing the two away while muddling through his broken French vocabulary. "Hey! Uh-um—away! Loitering is no here! Or the police, I will call them to this place here very soon!"

Then, to the man's surprise, Shiloh replied back in perfect Arabic and raised one hand apologetically. His look was still cynical but regarded Shiloh with a new impression. He returned the gesture in a milder manner before retreating back into the sanctuary.

"Don't mind him," Shiloh said to Francis. "He's had to deal with some rabble-rousers around here recently."

"Then I guess there's my friendly reminder that I'm still a Jesuit, huh?" Francis quipped. "Eh, just as well. I have some paperwork to review back at the office. Are you going back to your apartment?"

"I have to," Shiloh groaned, reaching for her red jacket hanging from a rail finial and folding it over her forearms. "I have that thesis on Saint Francis for the Missions Society due tomorrow. I might need to polish it up a little."

"Saint Francis of Assisi," Francis marveled, starting away before looking back to add, "Finally, you're finally putting that story to good use."

"Of course," Shiloh remarked. "You know me."

"I do," Francis said, "and I am sure my fellow Franciscans at the Society will find the paper to be quite the read."

Once the two parted company, Shiloh eyed the ground ahead of her, smiling her amusement for her friend. Another warm and gentle wind brushed over her face before the stillness of the night finally overtook what was left of the twilight.

Then a heaviness gripped Shiloh, and what little relief she had found with Francis gave itself back to her first dread. Her steps slowed to a halt as she again felt something get in the way. Despite herself, she looked back at him and found herself blurting out, "'Do whatever He tells you!'"

Francis whirled back in Shiloh's direction and stepped closer into the crescent's green light. "What?" he shouted over the distance.

She opened up a little more. "'Do whatever He tells you!' That's what she said to me!"

A winsome smile grew on Francis' face. Shiloh smiled back, humoring a fleeting whim before continuing on her journey back home.

CHAPTER 4

Institut Catholique de Paris
6th arrondissement

M idnight. The undergraduate university offered off-campus housing for Shiloh and Psalmodie, and although their scholarships and grants braced their academic curriculum, their modest one-bedroom brick apartment met only the bare-minimum necessities for a student to carry them through their under-graduate career: a roof, running water, and crude ventilation.

The room around Shiloh's cheveret desk was strewn with research papers and massive volumes of Aristotelian treatises on numerous corpuses of Scripture and oral tradition dating back to the Israelite patri-archs. Such works were written by great jurists and scholastic theolo-gians in the Jewish, Islamic, and Catholic traditions, such as Maimonides, Averroes, Duns Scotus, and Saint Thomas Aquinas. On her desk, however, were her typewriter and two open books on the spiri-tual unfolding of Being through the shifting tides of history: Martin Heidegger's *Being and Time* and Edith Stein's *On the Problem of Empathy*.

The walls fared no better. While Shiloh's side only had a small, inor-nate wooden plaque of the Arabic *Basmala*—the blessing recitation for good deeds—, Psalmodie's side was plastered with crumpled pages ripped out from library books and interconnected by a network of red thread; some of the papers even spilled into Shiloh's side of the room.

It appeared, however, that she wasn't home yet.

Shiloh made her way through the stacked columns of texts to her scriptorium. There was no electricity, so she used a tealight candle to illuminate her typewriter when it came to working late nights such as this one. She rummaged through her desk drawers for her box of matches. When she found it, she drew one from the container, struck its tip along the box, and held it over the candle's wick before placing the candle dish by a book cover. But before Shiloh concentrated on her paper, the words on the book's spine distracted her; the book that summarized the whole of Psalmodie's reality.

It was an English-translated compendium of the medieval *Matter of Britain,* which included King Arthur's greatest legends. From his triumph over the Germanic Anglo-Saxon kingdoms at the Battle of Badon to his achievement of the mystical sword Excalibur with the help of his wizard, Merlin, and his chivalrous Knights of the Round Table at the fairytale castle fortress of Camelot. Shiloh knew little and cared less, but as she understood it from Psalmodie, the fabled *Dux Bellorum* seemed to have been the Romano-Celtic mythological equivalent to King David from England's Dark Ages.

Shiloh thought back to when she first met Psalmodie; it was during first-year orientation in a private reading seminar analyzing the Christian anti-Semitic threads in a courtly poem written during the time of the Black Plague. During the discussion, when Shiloh had only briefly mentioned her interest in medieval Islamic civilization, somehow, Psalmodie had somehow shifted the topic to the gallant exploits of the English King Richard the Lionheart in Aquitaine and the Holy Land. Shiloh remembered nodding politely at Psalmodie's nagging passion, listening with only half of herself while her other half kept wandering back to her own fruitless quest for her truth.

Though they were only roommates for roughly two or three years, in that time, they had come to learn things about each other that flowered into a bond that Shiloh felt seemed almost sororal. When they weren't engaged in offhand religious riposte in between seminars, their favorite pastime was the fencing club. When they weren't fencing,

Psalmodie would drag Shiloh to see the city's lively venues and occasional exhibits.

Only lately, for whatever reason, Shiloh felt that they had been slowly estranging themselves from one another.

Typical, Shiloh thought, both irked and tickled at Psalmodie's lack of organization spilling into her own workspace. Her monomaniacal bibliophile of a roommate had an entire library of books lined in the cubbies in her large secretary desk next to Shiloh's. Shiloh had found the compendium most often on her desk, as if it had always been propped up against Psalmodie's favorite work and she always had to move it somewhere—Shiloh's desk—to get to it.

Another thing to talk about, she further noted. *Bien entendu.*

She grabbed the heavy volume and moved over to Psalmodie's corner. She found an empty slot for the large book, but when she looked through it, she saw the spine of the other works around which Psalmodie defined her whole life.

~ *PERCEVAL: LE CONTE DU GRAAL* ~
Chrétien de Troyes, c.1191

~ *LE QUESTE DEL SAINT GRAAL* ~
The Cistercian Order, c.1225

These ones, Shiloh knew almost nothing about; only that they had particularly tormented her roommate's conscience since her incident in England only a few days prior. It seemed to Shiloh that every conversation she had with Psalmodie lately had always come back to the quest for the Holy Grail, a mythical object borne from mythical tales.

Still, Shiloh recalled her favorite part of Arthurian legend. In *Le Queste del Saint Graal,* supposedly written by a Cistercian monk in the Middle Ages, the noble knight Sir Lancelot was said to have become unworthy of witnessing the Holy Grail after he could not bring himself to experience true contrition for his forbidden desire of King Arthur's wife, Queen Guinevere. When Psalmodie explained the romance to Shiloh, she found the sentiment so endlessly touching and captivating.

What is it to love or desire another?

What is God?

Shiloh then noticed the pile of clothes on Psalmodie's bed: Her usual day dress and shrug cardigan. Shiloh wondered why they were sprawled in such a careless, even chaotic manner; she imagined Psalmodie must have come to the apartment earlier to change into some other wear, perhaps more suitable for Paris' fast-paced nightlife. While Shiloh stood eying the pile, she heard the faint thump of a car door outside somewhere.

She went over to the window and scanned the streets below, half-expecting to find Psalmodie stumbling out of a taxi in a drunk stupor. If not her, then some of those same delinquent school children who kept wearing those unsettling plastic masks that bore the caricatured likeness of the bellicose German chancellor.

It was neither.

Instead, Shiloh saw a black car parked under a dim streetlight. Discharging from either side of the vehicle were four silhouettes, walking abreast of one another and melting in and out from the flickering cones of light cast from the gas streetlights. Shiloh couldn't have seen them clearly, but they wore all-black clothes; trench coats and fedoras. One among them carried a drawstring duffle bag. He split from the group and faded into the shadow of the tenement building across the street from her. The other three figures walked out of view, into the shadows below. She searched the building's many windows and waited for one to light up, but everything remained ominously still.

The man was nowhere to be seen.

She waited by the window one moment longer to give him another chance to reappear before finally stepping away. After taking off her jacket and setting it over her chair, she sat back down at her scriptorium and her mind kept wandering back to what Psalmodie's condition might have been if she was out that late.

Shiloh's attention focused back down on her paper; a thesis on Saint Francis of Assisi for her Abrahamic cosmopolitanism concentration that was to be submitted for the university's collaborative volunteer work with the Paris Foreign Missions Society. Though she had sieved through her draft at least five times already, she resisted a sixth revision, though not for ignorance.

In her implacable longing to forget her own past, the eidetic memory she earned from her precocious youth as a hafiza—a memorizer of the Holy Qur'an—had also cursed her with every single doctrine, prophecy, and grace she had ever heard and read from those saints and prophets who, she had convinced herself, had sustained far more desolation than her. Thrown into an existence of perpetual constellations to and within the world and its exhausted history, she concluded that the past was her only hope to ever compensate for the lingering blind spots of ignorance in her present reality.

But she also felt that the more she learned about those saints and prophets, the less she seemed to understand about herself. The more she studied the history of human faith, the more she feared carving away the useless fragments of herself until there was nothing left. Reading her thesis again would have only shown her just how pathetic her endless search to simply "Be" really was.

As her mind labored with this fear, another sound disrupted her. Normally, she would not have paid any mind to the many soirées her *bon vivant* neighbors held; she expected as much in this, the sensual "City of Light" on certain nights. But this one came from the corridor outside. It was the faint sound of nails squawking within wood, growing louder with each passing moment before finally ending in a splintering *snap!*

Shiloh dropped her project once more and made her way to the front entrance. She peeked through the door's peephole. The door across from her room was open, but all she saw was a consistent pitch black. She heard a sound murmuring from the black void, but as far as she could have known, they did not speak French or Arabic.

Yet the tongue indeed *sounded* familiar, as if she had just heard it through a recent seminar discussion of the Orthodox Jewish community in Vienna. The walls of her reality closed in on her. She backed away from the door, making no movements that would give her away to the specters haunting the other apartment. Her efforts were in vain.

Someone had come up from behind and seized her.

A hand had clamped down on her mouth and an arm tightened itself across her chest, pulling her back against the assailant's body. Shiloh twisted frenziedly to break free from their faltering hold. However, upon gripping her attacker's forearm, Shiloh's eyes widened in realization and her struggling gave way to them. She loosened her grip, and they, in turn, eased their hold. She turned around and immediately recognized her.

"Psalmodie?" Shiloh rasped.

"*Tsssh,*" Psalmodie hushed through her teeth, cringing as she tried her best to keep her shivering breath quiet and steady. Her petrified eyes remained fixed on the door, willing it to stay closed.

Shiloh noticed that her roommate wasn't wearing her usual clothing. Psalmodie had on dark breeches, cuffed slouch boots, and a gray, form-fitting shirt with a front-laced waist cincher and a gray shawl draping her yoke. She still had that single fishtail plait running down her back, although some tendrils of her hair strayed across the left side of her sweaty brow.

Shiloh had already drawn the connection between whatever escapade Psalmodie had gotten herself into and the men she saw out in the street below them, but it wasn't until Psalmodie rolled up her sleeves and cautiously drew out a Browning pistol from her satchel that Shiloh's eyes filled with even more confusion and terror.

The sounds in the other room continued and the floorboards shook with overturning tables and furniture. The murmuring voices of the men grew louder, and soon, Shiloh saw two shadows sweep through the band of light under the door. With her pistol still pointed at the door, Psalmodie tapped Shiloh's shoulder and gestured with the crown of her head towards the window at the far end of the room that led out to a back-alley fire escape landing. Still paralyzed, Shiloh lingered a moment before quietly backing away from the entryway.

Once she was at the window, she reached for the sash window's top rail and unlatched its bolt with a hard *click!* Their faces scrunched at the unwanted sound, and they briefly shot grave glances back at the front door before carrying on. Shiloh forced the bottom pane up the jamb. Only a small opening was necessary for both of the girls' slim frames. Shiloh slid herself through the opening, conscious of making as little rattling on the platform's metal grating as possible. She measured down the stairs, leaning one arm on the banister to take some weight off of her steps.

Then... *Clack!*

Shiloh recoiled as the window next to her starred and shards spat from a small crater.

"Psalmodie!" she shouted, still reeling from shock.

She strained towards the origin of the shot. Two more yellow flashes of light strobed from the top of the building at the other end of the street. Sparks flared over the grating, sending Shiloh scurrying back to her feet. Once she rushed down the stairs, she took cover behind a rusted garbage container and listened for more gunfire.

There was only sheer silence in the alley.

Psalmodie was still inside with her back pressed against the wall beneath the sill, but the other men were almost through the door. Letting out labored puffs of panic to steel herself, she thumbed down the gun's hammer and hitched her satchel higher on her shoulder. Once she clambered over the sill, she swung down from the escape's guard railing and dropped one story to the glistening wet of the black asphalt while a plume of dust exploded next to her with a piercing ballistic crack.

A voice made its way through to her.

"Psalmodie!" Shiloh yelled from behind the container. "Psalmodie! Get to me!"

Another shot cracked over them, and before Psalmodie could have yelled back, she staggered to her feet and broke into a sprint. Without having the chance to nerve herself, Shiloh leapt up and gave chase to Psalmodie. Although primal terror had overtaken all of Shiloh's cognition, her frantic mind tried and failed to make sense of whatever reason could have driven Psalmodie's attackers to open fire on them both. Shiloh looked back towards the building and her racing slowed as she saw the sniper against the blue moonlight.

She heard a loud thump break through from inside the apartment and the muffled voices Shiloh had heard in the hallway becoming louder. Stepping out onto the fire escape above were two of the men she saw on the street with large pistols aimed down on the alley.

It was then that she heard gunfire erupt ahead of her this time. Shiloh swung forward and saw that Psalmodie had half-blindly returned fire with her pistol. Once Shiloh heard the gun's hammer clicking on an empty chamber, she saw Psalmodie toss it amongst a pile of rubbish. Though Psalmodie's over-the-shoulder aim in her flight was wildly astray, it bought enough time for the girls to rapidly close the distance to the other end of the alley before more rounds ricocheted off the brick walls around them.

"Are you mad? I said stand down!" Obersturmführer Otto Rahn screamed as he stepped out onto the platform to reach over and shove back the men's forearms. He moved ahead of them to look down the alley for himself and saw the plucky blonde girl pause at the end to warily look back at him. For a moment, they locked eyes, each seeing the passing ambivalence in the other.

After Psalmodie broke away and disappeared around the corner, Rahn noticed that most of the windows along the alley walls had started to light up. He looked back and saw the assembling crowd of residents stepping out of their homes in their nightwear and peering across the dimly lit street to get a better glimpse at whatever crime scene may have been unfolding.

Once he heard the approaching sound of sirens, he waved frantically for his marksman to move off the opposite building. Then Rahn and the rest of his troop of shadows retreated back into the apartment with their pistols still drawn, the haze of gun smoke still swirling in a ghostly draft. As Rahn wiped at his watery eyes, he caught sight of something on a desk nearby. Though he knew the Parisian gendarmerie would be on the scene soon, his head cleared but for one thought.

"Is that where your friend is taking you, Psalmodie?" he whispered to himself.

CHAPTER 5

Square Boucicaut
7th arrondissement

After running down the long, tree-lined boulevard Raspail, the two girls found brief refuge under a lush bower in a small wooded and picturesque park next to the rue de Babylone, hiding from the police and motor horns dopplering past them towards the university. Once the girls swarmed in, Shiloh hunched over and repeatedly gasped for air.

She tried to compartmentalize her panic, but every time she thought about what had just happened, another surge upwelled. She looked over and saw a booted foot sticking out from behind a dense brush. Psalmodie was lying supine over the grass, unseeing of her friend standing over her.

"Psalmodie, what was that?" Shiloh demanded, her breath still caught between shock and exhaustion. "What was that? Who are they?"

There was barely any travel in Psalmodie's eyes at first, and when she glanced over at Shiloh, she seemed to look past her, seemingly without acknowledging that she was really there. Psalmodie then rubbed her eyes and mumbled, "You frightened me... When I heard the door open, I thought it was them, so I hid under the bed and—"

"*I* scared you?" Shiloh's temper frayed. "*I* scared you? Who the hell is *'them?'* Why were there men shooting at us? Why were *you* shooting at them? Since when did you have a gun?"

Psalmodie didn't answer; saturnine and watchful, she scanned the stars above for a way out from her world. She pushed off the grass and rose to her feet, and finding it difficult to meet Shiloh eye-to-eye, she motioned in the direction from which they fled.

"That was the SS's Gestapo," she finally answered before shaking her head and whispering to herself, "But why did they go in through the wrong door?"

Shiloh flustered. "What do they want with us?"

"They must think I have the Grail," Psalmodie said in afterthought.

A look of incomprehension mounted over Shiloh's agitated look. "The Grail?" she repeated. "You wouldn't be referring to that bowl-thing you stole back in England, are you? I returned it to the—"

"Yes—No! I mean, not *that* Grail, I don't—" Psalmodie stuttered before ending with an indecisive sigh.

Shiloh pressed with a discontented tone. "Psalmodie, tell me what is going on! Please! Why would they think you have it? Why *you?* Why *here?*"

"They have my father!" Psalmodie yelled, her wavering voice hitting the air like sheet metal. "He telegraphed me yesteryear... He told me... He told me that they imprisoned him... And that they did things to him..."

A heavy silence fell between them. Shiloh's struck gaze bent on the ground while Psalmodie shifted over the dirt with slow sauntering steps, visibly mulling over the harrowing prospect that she knew would have implicated her best friend. She shut her reluctant eyes and braced herself for what she was going to tell her.

"By chance," she began, "have the Cathari come up in your studies?"

Shiloh processed her question. Though she studied the interrelationship between medieval Christendom and the Islamic world specifically, she wasn't entirely unaware of the countless heresies both worlds gave rise to. "The greatest threat to the medieval Church? An order of ancient Gnostic heretics in Southern France who denied Christ's physical incarnation and denounced the Old Testament Yahweh as a false god. I thought they were all butchered by the Inquisition some seven hundred years ago—Wait, weren't there some popular anti-Semitic potboilers published in Germany recently that falsely alleged that they were actually Luciferians?"

"The Crusade against the Grail and *Lucifer's Court!"* Psalmodie blurted. "Yes, *those* books! The author, Otto Rahn, that man! He was with those men shooting at us!"

Shiloh's panic again gathered in her like a storm. *"He's* with them? Why?"

"It's the Germans!" Psalmodie rambled, the words tumbling out of her as if bottled up for days. "Those Germans think the Cathari were guardians to an alchemical Holy Grail! The Germans, Shiloh! They distorted and appropriated that defiance against the Hebrew God into their own violent ideology, and they want to redeem Lucifer—the Antichrist—in the Cathari's distorted memory!"

"You mean..." Shiloh swallowed in her turn and started again. "You mean they actually want... *revenge?"*

Psalmodie gesticulated feverishly. "My father went on sabbatical in Germany, but after the Olympics in Berlin, he met with Rahn, who my father stubbornly insisted was an old friend! Everyone tried to warn him, but my father never gave enough importance to the fact that Rahn was hired as a scholar for the German regime!"

"The regime?" Shiloh asked. "Why are you saying all of this? What does any of this have to do with your father?"

"In the Cathari's name," Psalmodie urged, "and through their claimed descent from the Celts, the Germans' SS claim to be the rightful heirs of King Arthur's knights; they revile the Grail's Jewish and Christian tradition and seek its power to oust those religions from Europe! They want it to mean something that it never was! They already—" Psalmodie's panicked voice caught. Drawing two jagged breaths, she tried to moderate her neurotic rambling before placing a hand on Shiloh's shoulder and looking into her eyes.

Psalmodie began in a grave tone, "I went back to my home to collect my father's mail. Shiloh, they were waiting for me there. They followed me to the university, but they apparently got the wrong room. When I heard you enter, I thought you were one of them. I thought I would have lost my one chance to bring him back."

Psalmodie reached into her satchel and pulled out a scritta-page compact tome. A Bible at first glance, but Shiloh looked at the book's leather-bound cover and saw a crude, yet interesting inscription titled on it:

<h1 dir="rtl" style="text-align:center">אדכ אנח</h1>

The characters looked strangely familiar to Shiloh. The letters looked of an antiquated Hebraic dialect, but her eyes widened in wonder upon deducing what it said and the dead Jewish language in which it was written.

"Psalmodie," Shiloh awed. "Psalmodie, this has to be Galilean Aramaic; the very dialect of Jesus Christ!"

"What?" Psalmodie blurted. "Wait, I thought it was Hebrew."

"No, Biblical Hebrew is Judaism's sacred language, but Aramaic was the *lingua franca* of Jesus' time."

"Well, what does it say then?"

Shiloh looked down at the cover once more and summoned up what she could have gathered from translations of the Syriac Peshitta and the Masoretic texts dealing with the Rabbinic Sabbath ritual. Much like its Hebrew and Arabic child systems, the Aramaic language read right-to-left, and its alphabet was mostly made up of consonants while implying a phonetic vowel sound between the letters.

The letters were, in order, *He, Kaf, Alaf, Kaf, Samakh, Alaf*, which spelled out the two transliterated words "*HaKA KaSA.*" The words sounded like the Arabic "*hadha al-kas,*" which she had remembered reading in the Arabic annotations of the Coptic Orthodox Anaphora liturgies of the Eucharist.

She dwelled on the inscription and took it in as if it were fine art or a line of poetry. She had read Semitic sentences all her life, but something about this language had always sat differently with her. The very *essence* of God's creation; the very word spoken by the sinless Word of God... *Whoever He was,* Shiloh thought.

Then she read aloud, "This cup."

Psalmodie frowned, confused at first, but then she held a look of understanding. As she internalized Shiloh's answer, her regard slowly changed to one of awe for the book. She held its cover to the moonlight, but the revelation in her eyes eventually gave way to something else.

"The house was torn apart," she began, "and all the walls were ripped open, and furniture tossed around. They might have been looking for the Grail, but something tells me they may have been looking for this. My father must have confessed it to them to keep me alive, though he must've counted too much on their word of honor."

"Where did you know to look?"

"When I was little," Psalmodie mused, "after my mother's passing, he and I used to play these stupid treasure quests for some candies and toys. I always went along with it because he seemed to enjoy them more than I did. But in the end, he always chose the same place: In my mother's flower-decorated box."

Shiloh then recalled what Psalmodie told her in England and the telegram her father had sent her before he fell out of contact. "Roses?" Shiloh asked in a quiet voice.

Psalmodie looked up at her with hurt. "It wasn't roses," she answered. "It was an Easter lily... but I think his rose and sword are still out there somewhere, and at its end lies his treasure! I'm sure of it!"

"But we haven't the faintest clue of where to begin! He didn't give us much to work with!"

"Shiloh," Psalmodie said assertively, "I *know* my father. He put this book under the lilies for a reason. He wrote this title in Aramaic for a reason. Don't you see? These are breadcrumbs he's leaving behind. He's telling us something through them!"

"And what would that be?" Shiloh demanded, challenging.

"That the original truth is right in front of us," Psalmodie concluded, "and only the worthy find the Grail! That we were blind to it our whole lives."

"How does that help us then?"

"I read through the book already," Psalmodie uttered, "and I know where it is."

Shiloh cocked her eyes at Psalmodie. "What?"

Psalmodie's gaze was lit up. "I know where it is."

Confusion flickered on Shiloh's face for a moment, but just as she was about to question Psalmodie again, a sense of unreality caught her by the throat. As the fright registered, Shiloh's breath hitched, and she steadied herself again against a nearby ivied tree.

"Listen to me," Psalmodie finally said, "I have to find the Grail before they either find us or kill my father!"

Shiloh shook her head as her mind tried to evolve a plan. "This is England all over again, isn't it?"

"Shiloh."

"We should go to the police—"

"Shiloh, please."

"—and tell them *everything* that—"

"Shiloh!"

"—you just told me! Look, there *has* to be another way!"

Psalmodie's voice tightened with resentment. "You have no *idea* what they are capable of. I don't know where they have him, but if anyone else learns of this, they will probably kill him!"

A long silence fell over the park. Shiloh quelled her ire and noticed Psalmodie leaning in to search for her gaze.

"Shiloh, come with me," Psalmodie begged softly. When Shiloh considered her with grave reluctance, Psalmodie continued, "When we find the Grail, I don't—"

"If," Shiloh said. "You mean a *big* if. And that's *if* I go with you, which I'm sure I *won't!"*

"Wait," Psalmodie sighed. "Fine—If we find it, I don't know what to expect—powers, miracles, sorcery, I really don't." She dithered a moment before adding, "They *may* want more than a relic of Christ." She shook her head and tears threatened her eyes. "But even if it means the whole of Europe has to become Luciferian by destroying this relic, I will do *anything* to get my father back."

"But would they give you a guarantee?" Shiloh interjected. "Would they guarantee your father's life? *Yours?* Didn't you say those men thought you already had it? Why were they *shooting* at us? How do you know they won't just kill you the moment you give it to them?"

Psalmodie faced her squarely. "Whether I keep my father's journal or surrender it to them, I know too much of their being in France! But I might as well try to find the Grail to at least *try* to save my father if there's still even the smallest chance!" She drew closer to Shiloh with a pleading look. "Shiloh, come with me, *please!* I'm so sorry, but now you're implicated in this; I beg you, you'd be much safer with me. I *cannot* have you on my conscience."

Shiloh's attention strayed across the park as another rapid welter of panicky half-thoughts rushed through her mind: The ways the Germans could kill them, the chances of finding the Grail, and, above all, the burdens and the guilt that would befall her if she went to the authorities. She would have been complicit in the murder of Psalmodie's father; a fate she would not have wished on her worst enemy.

But in either case, her life could have never been the same after this.

After muttering a curse, Shiloh capitulated and gulped nervously at the absurdity of her next question. "Okay, Psalmodie... Where is 'this cup' then?"

CHAPTER 6

Société des Missions étrangères de Paris (M.E.P.) headquarters

In a dim candlelight, the Jesuit Brother Francis Gaiwan sat at his Duchess desk with reading spectacles, revising a copy of Monsignor Jean-Patmos' monthly report on the Society's expenditures in preparation for a routine audit. In his right hand, he held a small ledger listing out all of the organization's used assets. A wooden tabletop radio next to his typewriter was blaring the tinny nasal bleating of some fearmongering media pundit.

"...for the British prime minister's arrival in Munich to broker negotiations addressing the chancellor's demands for the annexation of the Sudetenland despite resistance from the Czechoslovakian military. In the months since Germany's Anschluss with Austria and their reoccupation of the Rhineland's demilitarized zone, tensions have continued to escalate with the possibility for another armed confli—"

"I don't need to hear this," Francis muttered, switching the broadcast off to concentrate on his work.

But he was again distracted by something else: On his desktop next to a small candlestick was a small wood easel propping up a *fumi-e*, a metal plaque with a bas-relief representing Maria Kannon. It was a beautiful, Greco-Buddhist depiction of the Virgin Mary as the legendary cross-legged bodhisattva Kannon with an unmistakable crucifix around her neck.

Though the depiction was in keeping with the traditions of the Kakure Kirishitan—the underground Catholic converts of Japan who worshiped Christ through syncretized religious symbols that hid in plain sight—, the *fumi-e* was used by the Samurai of the Tokugawa Shogunate to force the missionaries and converts they captured and tortured to apostatize by trampling on it. This was after the bloodshed of the Kirishitan-led Shimabara Rebellion, which isolated Japan from the colonial superpowers of Europe.

Although Francis was himself Manchu and had therefore more in common culturally with the Chinese Qing Dynasty, he found that Japan's historical persecution of Christians seemed to have paralleled the recent atrocities in Nanjing and Manchuria in China, all committed in the name of the Shinto *arahitogami*—the incarnated "godhood" of the Japanese emperor. Francis couldn't help but whisper idly to the plaque of his Lady, "What is it you and Him are trying to tell her? And You both really don't have anything to say to me? About my own family? What am *I* supposed to do?"

For a moment, Francis reflected on his own religious upbringing, and how an ancient curse named "desire" nagged and haunted his every waking moment. It was the desire born of ego that the Buddha taught ought to be renounced and extinguished for the end of all suffering and sorrow. But then Francis remembered how his reality changed when he, for the first time, recognized that he did indeed have a soul, and how there were so many false consolations that spiraled that soul deeper into desolation. He let go of who he once thought he was, and Buddhist enlightenment eventually gave way to Jesuit discernment. Despite his father abandoning him after his conversion, Francis continued to zealously believe that Christ would be his sole, lifelong desire.

But through all of this, there was Shiloh...

He contemplated the *fumi-e* a while longer, saying a quick prayer to it, but after shaking his head, he looked back down at his ledger to verify the Society's receipts on its assets. After signing off on one portion of the records, he stamped it with the Society's seal to authenticate an audit trail on earlier transactions for when he and Monsignor Jean would have to give their report to the board meeting and insure fiscal checks and balances. He looked over a second paper and signed off on it, but when he again reached for the stamp, the doorbell buzzed repeatedly.

"Monsignor?" he said to himself, setting down his reading spectacles. "What on Earth is he doing here at this hour?"

He looked up at a wall clock; 3:42 a.m. Before going downstairs to open the front door to whoever would have been up at that time, he peered down at the street below, and his narrowed eyes widened as he recognized the two figures through the darkness. One of them was still tugging at the doorbell's pull knob. The other, to Francis' surprise, was peering around the corner pilaster of the front entrance's recess.

They seemed to be hiding from someone.

He rushed downstairs, fixing his collar and cinching his cassock over his chest. Once downstairs, he took stock of the door-lined corridor's coffered ceilings and mahogany wainscoting, listening for other people who might also be in the building; the only thing he heard was the sound of his own footsteps echoing along the checkered marble floor. Once he arrived at the door, he received the two into the foyer and locked the door again, this time bolting it shut to ensure the security of their sanctuary. The two girls caught their breath and backed away from the entrance.

"Shiloh? Psalmodie?" Francis said. "Are you two okay? My God, you both look green. Do you need water or should I give you a—"

"Actually, Brother, we're not," Shiloh said, recovering from her panting, "but we need your help."

"*My* help?" he said in a puzzled tone. "How would you need my help? What's going on?"

Shiloh and Psalmodie shot glances at one another before shifting them back on Francis. "Just please hear what we have to say," Psalmodie began.

CHAPTER 7

Le Jardin du Luxembourg
6th arrondissement

A young street boy conveyed a message to the spare-framed 29-year-old diplomat Ernst Eduard vom Rath as he left the German Embassy on 78 rue de Lille. He said only one word to him. A code word allegedly known only to the Reichsführer's most trusted Parisian confederates for emergency contingencies: *"Esclarmonde."*

It was beyond vom Rath how a barefoot child in overalls had come to know such a secret. The diplomat had a feeling he was walking into a trap, though he was nowhere near as important as the senior ambassador, Johannes von Welczeck. But then again, vom Rath's mind also kept wandering back to the unlikely possibility that the kid was leading him to face the pillory for those "gross indecencies" that had recently transpired at Le Bœuf sur le Toit.

He kept his distance from the boy, following him on the gravelly promenades winding through the ill-lit columns of woodland. Still, vom Rath looked about his surroundings, making sure that there were no marauders staking out in the garden's well-pruned hedges or manicured grass fields and flower parterres. With each passing breeze, the jungly canopy of leaves above vom Rath rustled, and for a moment, he considered the absurdity that it was actually ghosts the boy was bringing him to.

Even so, vom Rath knew there had been a presence patrolling the gardens that night anyways; in the distance, he saw two Parisian gendarmerie officers holding flashlights up at eye level. Their beams swam up and about the dark tree trunks and branches, and as vom Rath and the boy passed them by, vom Rath also heard them speak of witnesses near a university saying that three or four men in black ran towards the gardens.

Thankfully, vom Rath wore his tweed coat with beige trousers, although his following a lone boy did draw some momentary suspicion from them before they continued on. After vom Rath coughed and snorted into a handkerchief, he saw that the boy had come to an inter-section with benches and chairs at every corner except one, where a majestic, patina-coated statue stood mounted on a limestone plinth.

A bronze sculpture of a robed goddess with the spiked crown of Sol Invictus, an aloft torch in one hand, and two tablets in the other. The plaque below the sculpture read, *"La liberté éclairant le monde"*— liberty enlightening the world.

Then vom Rath saw the boy rush for the statue. At first, vom Rath nearly veered for cover, but then he saw the boy slow down to the goddess' feet and swipe five coins from the plinth's surface before running off into the night.

The diplomat was unsure of what to make of the sight. He took a moment to adjust his tie around his neck before walking over to the statue himself. For vom Rath, there was nothing particularly remarkable about the statue; only that it was a scaled-down replica of one gifted to America in a goodwill commemoration to its origins in Enlightenment values. After all, vom Rath knew that their Revolution against the British Crown had officially ended with the famous Treaty of Paris in 1783, for it was yet another glorious liberation from the bastard heirs to King Arthur's legendary realm.

Then vom Rath remembered the message and drew the connection: *Esclarmonde* and *éclairant le monde* both meant the clarity or enlighten-ment of the world.

It was then that a disembodied voice behind him whispered in

German, "Esclarmonde de Foix was the greatest Cathari Perfecti of the purest bonhomme—the purest good men. The holy spirit who was the glorious guardian of the Holy Grail." The mild voice spoke with a highbrow diction, sounding almost like a French lilt, although the way he drew out the consonants in his words was unmistakably Germanic.

The diplomat whirled on the voice only to find a gaping darkness framed by the large trunks of two trees. While vom Rath almost drew his small Beretta pistol from under his coat, the fact that the voice did indeed speak German made him feel more at ease with whatever may have been lurking in those shadows. He still didn't fully dismiss the possibility of his own punishment, but he inched closer to peer around the right tree through the night.

He saw the man in black, dressed in black and hiding with his back to the tree while reading from what vom Rath could have only assumed was a classified dossier. More than seeing him, vom Rath actually recognized him. Without immediately blurting the man's name aloud, he holstered his sidearm, found a nearby chair, and sat facing the Statue of Liberty with his back to Otto Rahn.

Rahn continued, "But perhaps it is time for all the world to know that there really is nothing new under the sun, wouldn't you say, Ernst?"

Vom Rath delayed his response. "So, you are sending children to do your bidding now, Otto?"

Rahn was quick to respond. "Those police came close to finding us at the university; we couldn't risk our call being intercepted. They're still searching for us everywhere."

"Well, then..." vom Rath sighed, "I suppose it must have felt necessary then."

"You weren't there," Rahn said.

"Quite right," vom Rath reasoned with a shrug. "I wasn't. So, tell me, Otto: *What* happened back there? The Reichsführer's secretary already briefed me and von Welczeck on what your mission was supposed to have yielded."

Rahn answered tersely, "I entered the wrong apartment."

"So, you followed her to her home and the university only to lead your SS-Standarte into the 'wrong apartment?' You? An Obersturmführer?" The diplomat half-turned towards the tight-lipped Rahn with an inquisitive frown. "You stalled your own men by foolishly directing them into the wrong apartment at the very last moment, didn't you? Hopelessly trying to figure out how to get to the girl before they could? There's more to this girl, isn't there?"

"I assure you that all of it is irrelevant to the mission," Rahn snapped.

At this, vom Rath shifted back up in his seat. But when he looked back up at the goddess, he saw that the bark of a silhouetted tree beyond her oddly looked as though it were breathing. Once he looked closer, he saw that it was a younger man in black perched against the tree with his head lolling back. Undoubtedly, the other two were not too far away. Though vom Rath only saw the man's profile, he saw that he rolled his jaw, hawked a phlegm over the grass, and bared his grit teeth, perhaps to stretch the skin over his jaw.

Rubbing his thighs in nervous anticipation, vom Rath continued, "I understand your dreams, Otto. I really do. You crave the intimacy of family, and you look for it everywhere, restlessly, tenderly, hopelessly; another Wandering Jew condemned by Christ. You are a poet—a *great* poet, and you insist on living in a future that may or may not one day become a paradise. But I fear, *mein Liebe,* that while you willfully gave your heart to enlightenment, you failed to realize that you sold your soul to the coming of yet another dark age. And knowing this full well, you and I, Otto, our own souls ultimately don't matter to our own survival. And all professed ideals—indeed, the spirit of our people—have become nothing more than ecosystems to weaponize and camouflage into."

"You say it as if I didn't already know that."

"No, I know that you know," vom Rath said. "But have you accepted it as a Jew?"

"Have you?"

"No... not entirely... but I know that I must..."

Rahn's voice tensed, equal parts wrath and horror. "You're supposed to be a diplomat, Ernst! Are you even aware of what happened in those Soviet trials in Moscow last year? Stalin broke all of Leon Trotsky's loyalists, including the Chairman of Comintern himself, to the point where they all begged to confess to crimes that they had never even committed! You know what I am, Ernst. How can you expect the

Reich to treat me any better? Who are you to tell me that I must be complicit in my own persecution?"

"I'm no one..." vom Rath added, "which is why you of all people ought to understand. I really do regret the suffering that your Jewish brethren have to endure, Otto, for the German race's sake, but the *Volksgemeinschaft* does matter, no matter my own scruples. If they are not meant to inherit human evolution, then they will surely destroy it. Destroy everything. In strange times such as these, we must remember our sacrifices for a better future for humanity."

"What do you know of *my* suffering?" Rahn demanded.

Vom Rath reached again for his handkerchief and dabbed it over his sweaty upper lip. After swallowing the growing lump in his throat, vom Rath admitted, "God help me, more than I'd like to."

Rahn looked into the darkness ahead of him. "What?" he sighed.

A longing rippled through vom Rath. "I know what it is to get lost in a beautiful, penetrative gaze; you may not believe me, but I have learned, only recently, what it is to go back on a promise to bring a lover back to their own loved ones. I still wonder if those eyes will soon be the death of me. Please be careful where that will lead you, Otto."

"I assure you, Ernst," Rahn said, flipping back to the paper's cover, "this isn't mercy for the man's daughter. This is simply duty."

"No, Otto," vom Rath said, "I know mercy when I see it, no matter how barbarous it may appear to be, and trust me, you are not doing a good job of camouflaging it. I heard this was supposed to be a straight-forward *Nacht und Nebel*—a quick job. Stop delaying it for your own sake!" The diplomat indicated the figure in the shadows beyond the statue. "If she has to die by the Reich's cruel hand, then so be it! You have to accept what is within and well beyond your own control."

"Ernst, the girl will burn in body and soul without deserving it because of *me,*" Rahn said, seemingly pleading. "Believe me when I say that I have abandoned my hope for a future paradise long ago. But after I get what I need from her, I will simply release her soul from what we both know will be an inevitable hellfire visited across the whole of Europe—the whole world!"

"So, you admit futile mercy in this?" vom Rath said.

"I admit some semblance of humanity while I can still say I have it," Rahn muttered. After a pause, he sniffed and said, "The truth of the *Parzival* romance's Grail stone is that black and white, light and dark, Heaven and hell have their lot in every man's heart, and in every act that he does. There is nothing noble about what I am going to commit, but I believe that there can yet be good in this evil; an outcast angel of light in the darkness.

"That girl does *not* need to die for my quest; our Reichsführer himself said so. But given our Führer's sadistic ambitions for more living space for the German race, I now know that she must die *for her own sake*—for her father's sake. But it must be by *my own* sinful, merciful hand... because she does not deserve to suffer as her father did or as I will; cold, alone, perhaps slowly after the sanctuary of her own Christian illusions are ripped apart."

Though vom Rath found Rahn's misplaced sense of altruism to be basically noble, vom Rath had set aside his compassion to carry out whatever it was the Reich needed. "You summoned me, Otto," vom Rath said, coughing into his fist. "Now that I'm here, what is it that your deputation needs?"

"I need you to point us towards someplace," Rahn said.

The diplomat shook his head. "The Führer is still mobilizing his troops in Czech lands at the moment, and given the many riots that attended the *cause célèbre* of the Dreyfus Affair some thirty years ago, my harboring a Jew from Germany like you would not be very good for the Reich's imperiled reputation in Paris."

"You mean like that Jewish boy with you in Le Bœuf sur le Toit, correct?" Rahn retorted. When vom Rath whirled on Rahn with rigid terror, Rahn added with apparent dejection, "Yes, Ernst, I know that feeling; the nagging fear of knowing that everyone can't look away from your repulsive degeneracy." Then Rahn took a breath and said, "I may know about you two, but you should also know that our Reichsführer doesn't have to."

Vom Rath slowly turned away from Rahn's murderous threat, desperately trying to keep his composure. Just when he was about to bring himself back to his senses, he saw a hovering tube of paper extending over his shoulder. He carefully took it from Rahn's hand and briefly looked it over, finding the post-nominal initials "M.E.P." with a Christian cross surmounting the M.

"You need not worry about providing sanctuary to us," Rahn said, "but you are the only other trustworthy Parisian cognoscenti we have here. I may have visited Paris for many years, but I still don't recognize these letters."

Vom Rath swallowed and asked, "I take it the girl didn't provide an address?"

"We suspect that—" Rahn stopped to shoot a cautious glance at the man beyond the statue. "*I* suspect that this is an acronym for a place that our target might have sought sanctuary in with this girl, Shiloh, although I cannot know for certain."

"There's plenty of other places to hide in Paris," vom Rath challenged. "Why here specifically?"

"There's a cross over the M; this might be a missionary organization. The girls must have friends there who have both the connections and the means to help them get out of Paris. We have to apprehend them there before they leave for God knows where."

After looking the paper over again, vom Rath had started to recognize the organization. He handed the paper back to Rahn and said, "The Paris Foreign Missions Society on rue du Bac. I can't say which address exactly, but I remember that it's next to a famous Vincentian motherhouse; Marian, if I'm not mistaken."

"How far?"

"It's in the 7th arrondissement—Not too far from the universi—"

It was then that a voice ahead of vom Rath cried, *"Que fai-tu ici?"*

Vom Rath jumped and froze as two blinding glares of light approached him. The roving beams shone over his squinting face, but in his alarm, he looked over his shoulder to see if Rahn himself was frozen in his tracks. To vom Rath's surprise, Rahn had already vanished, as did the other figure by the statue ahead of him.

One of the gendarmerie officers snapped his fingers to draw vom Rath's eyes back on them. *"Pourquoi sors-tu si tard? Huh?"* the officer demanded.

Despite his career, vom Rath had trouble explaining himself. "I-I needed to, uh..."

Before the ambassador could have finished, the other officer lowered his flashlight and leaned over to whisper something into his partner's ear: *"C'est 'madame' ambassador, notre dame de Paris. De l'autre nuit, tu te souviens?"*

The interrogating officer's face shifted, though it looked more out of disgust than escalating hostility. Though vom Rath kept his hands up, when he saw and recognized the officer next to him, he averted his gaze in shame.

The leading officer whispered back at his partner, less discreetly than him, *"Cabaret, eh? L'amant d'un petit Juif?"*

The two officers stood over the man, both unsure and reproving. After a while, they moved off to continue on their manhunt. As time went by, vom Rath had slowly gained the nerve to finally lower his trembling hands. With a tear streaming down his eye, he beheld the goddess again and, for all that it stood for, felt that her spirit had still been greatly wanting in clarity.

CHAPTER 8

Société des Missions étrangères de Paris (M.E.P.) headquarters
7th arrondissement

For three hundred years, the Paris Foreign Missions Society, or the M.E.P., saw to the Roman Catholic evangelism of the Asian and Oriental regions. With its help, the faith flourished in lands that had not previously heard the Gospel. Hundreds of missionaries were persecuted and martyred in its service, with some even being beatified by the Pope. One such martyrdom had even precipitated France's involvement in the controversial Second Opium War against China in the mid-1800s.

It was a rich history that Francis, the only member who was present at its rue du Bac headquarters that night, he felt was summarized in himself alone. After Shiloh and Psalmodie told him what they needed from him, the integrity of that history, he knew, would have been called into question.

"So just so we are clear," he recapped, looking especially at Psalmodie, "you are running from Germans—as you called them, 'prelates from their own Vatican near the Rhine'—who believe you to have the Holy Grail?"

"Yes," the two girls said in unison.

Francis smacked his lips, sounding mildly irritated. "And now you need tickets for one of the most expensive trains in the world... so that you can actually go and *find* it to try to save her father from them?"

The two looked shamefaced by their own solicitation.

Francis regarded Psalmodie dubiously, but then looked to Shiloh with a different expression. He moved past them and circled back to his workspace, lightly bumping his fist down along the desktop as he went. With a conflicted look, he slouched in his chair and steepled his fingers. Holding his silence, he meditated on the plaque of Maria Kannon by the small candlelight before putting his glasses back on and pressing at his typewriter keys.

Shiloh sought out his gaze. "Listen, I know this sounds crazy. *I* think this is crazy. But we don't have any other option, Brother. We're desperate."

Francis ripped out a green paper from the typewriter's platen and reached for a carnet pocketbook in the desk's bottom drawer.

Shiloh pushed further, putting a hand to his shoulder. "You've been my best friend since primary school. We stuck by each other when no one else would. When no one else cared for outsiders like us. You know me, Francis. I would never ask these things of you. But right now, her father's life is at stake. *Our* lives are at stake."

Francis kept his quiet. Shiloh looked back at her discouraged companion, who had just started to walk out of the room.

"Listen," she continued, shutting her dispirited eyes. "I'm sorry that we implicated you in this. But right now, you are our only—"

Francis cut her off. "In five, maybe six hours, train number 5 of the Simplon-Orient Express will depart from Gare de l'Est for a three-day travel bound for Constantinople. These three tickets here include a pass for a connection on the Taurus Express to Aleppo, but from there, you'll have to hail a cab or coach to drive anywhere in the Orient from there."

Shiloh stopped short, nonplussed at what he said. A stupefied Psalmodie turned back around and returned to her side.

"What?" Psalmodie said.

Francis stamped the green paper with the Society's seal. "I will have to move around a couple of things in our offset records and allocate our new debt to our already large 'nondeductible expenses' and 'miscellaneous disbursements.' For all the board will know, for a short while at least, it will all go to the maintenance of chapels abroad. That should buy us ample time before the auditor will find out down the line. Not to worry. That will have to be a problem for another day."

Shiloh went up to him for a warm embrace. He looked over her shoulder and saw Psalmodie observing from the background, shooting him a passing smile before looking away.

"But wait," Shiloh said, pulling back from him. "You said *three* tickets? You're coming with us?"

"I assume you don't have passports on your persons," Francis remarked, "and I will have to make a difficult call right now to the conductor of that train to discuss pushing back *two* other cabin reservations to make room for us. You will need me for some level of credibility through all of this."

"Credibility?" Psalmodie asked.

"As treasurer, Monsignor Jean knows the conductors of trains 4 and 5 fairly well," Francis said. "Let us simply say that they are 'enthusiastic,' to say the least, about Society members boarding their trains in carrying out the Christian mission."

"Um... okay?" Psalmodie responded uncertainly.

"But I will say this," Francis said, looking at the two girls' wear. "The train's policy calls for a more... 'formal' attire. Fortunately for us, we have a wardrobe in the other room. *Un*fortunately for you, there isn't a lot of variety in fashion."

"Variety?" Shiloh asked.

"You'll see what I mean," he said, opening up a small logbook filled with contacts. "Now if you will excuse me, I'll go ahead and make this call. I will try both his home and office lines, but he might already be on his way there. Hopefully, he won't want too much money."

After Shiloh and Psalmodie traded bewildered glances with each other, Psalmodie moved off towards the other room. Shiloh, however, couldn't stop looking at Francis; she walked towards him and asked, "You really have no problem with this?"

In a seemingly deadpan reprimand, he told her, "Oh, I'll tell you right now that it's a horrible idea, Shiloh. Going towards *Palestine* to run from murderous heathens searching for the most priceless religious artifact in history; I've thought about it very carefully now and I think it might just be the single worst, most confused, most ludicrous idea ever proposed in the history of human thought, which is extremely shocking coming from *you* of all people..." Francis looked up from his logbook and, seeing Shiloh's face fall, added with a mischievous smirk, "I love it..."

CHAPTER 9

Rahn and his troop, the SS-Standarte Kurt Eggers, were on the rooftop of an abandoned squat, overlooking the mansard-roofed skyline of Paris' innumerable cream-colored Haussmann apartment buildings. Though he had no field glasses on his person, Rahn saw that every single building shared a brick party wall, meaning that there were rarely any dark alleyways in between them.

Rahn heard the slow and solemn clanging of the knell of the Cathédral Notre-Dame de Paris echoing through the night. Most of the cathedral had lent itself to the pitch night, but the building's face with the Rayonnant-Gothic rose window and the crockets of its crenulated flèche spire were illumed from beneath by white floodlights. His gaze then traveled down the lush boulevards and followed the River Seine until it stopped at the single most constant fixture of the Parisian skyline: La Dame de Fer.

Assembling about the iconic wrought-iron lattice tower was a flock of homing pigeons, all floating up from the bright halation that emanated from the silhouetted cityscape. Though the open streets of the City of Light provided few options for stealth, it at least made long-range reconnaissance for one of his enforcers easier.

His marksman lay prone on a scaffolding mezzanine above Rahn, searching the buildings through the finger-thin telescopic sight mounted near the barrel's end of his marksman rifle.

"Obersturmführer?" he called. "You might want to take a look at this."

Rahn broke away from Paris and looked up at his subordinate. Rahn then promptly climbed up the braces and transoms of the scaffolding and knelt beside his enforcer by his perch. Rahn craned his head over to see if he could have followed the rifle's sight to whatever it was that his sniper had found.

"What is it?" Rahn asked. "Have you found it?"

"Yes, I think I may have just found your building," the sniper answered. "I am still not entirely sure, but I do see a cross."

Rahn stripped off the sight from the rifle's barrel and looked through. He saw the cross standing black against the white light—one of many scattered across the city's skyline, though he recognized the distinctive M.E.P. symbol directly beneath it.

Rahn granted himself a moment to reflect on the cross of that false Messiah from the false god that usurped Lucifer's divine appointment as the true Son of the true God. In his heart, Rahn knew that the stone of the stars was still out there... somewhere. The Cathari's very relic of creation, composed of a mysterious extraterrestrial chemical element; a rich metal dense enough to bend the corrupt fabric of space and time, encasing the primordial cosmic light of creation within its very substance.

Indeed, the treasure was itself a bearer of light, which also fell from on high, and it so anguished Rahn to see that a Roman instrument of sadistic torture still reigned over the Grail's holy light. Meanwhile, Rahn's exiled lord awaited in humility and courtly devotion for his noble knights to deliver him back to his rightful place in the Kingdom of Heaven, much like the Roman goddess of desire, Venus, so longed for the return of her dechristianized Crusader knight Tannhäuser.

Rahn's own soul also awaited, and his body was nothing more than a throwaway robotic capsule for the untold generations that insulated this immortal knowledge. From one lifetime to the next, ever since the foundation of the world, this secret knowledge awaited hopelessly for the renewed pastoral enlightenment of the Garden of Eden. Awaiting since the fall of man, since the fall of the Grail, since the fall of the light-bringer himself, to simply "Be." To "Be," despite knowing the good and evil created by the false god.

Give me your hand, Faust... Rahn thought wistfully.

It was then that he saw three shadowy figures walking along the building to which the cross belonged. He was too far away to recognize their faces, but he did note their distinctive clothes and unpresuming poises. Rahn lowered his sight and sighed with uncertainty at this.

"Do you see them?" the enforcer asked.

"No..." Rahn said uneasily. "I-I thought I did, but no, I didn't."

"But surely it is our building, is it not?"

"Yes, that building has to be the Vincentian motherhouse that vom Rath spoke of." Rahn stood to his feet and started for the other direction. "The missionary headquarters has to be very close to it."

"But wait—Obersturmführer?" the enforcer called back.

"What is it?"

"Most of those buildings... It doesn't look like anyone's inside them."

Rahn looked back at the building and saw that, indeed, the night's shadow had shrouded most of the street. He sighed again, this time with increasing worry. He looked back down at his enforcer and gestured his fingers towards the bottom of the scaffolding.

"We have to get there," Rahn said. "We had better not keep my secretary waiting."

"Yes, I know," the enforcer sighed. "He is going to want his beloved gun back."

Rahn handed the rifle sight back to him, but just when he was about to step down on the first rung of a ladder leading down the building's side, he looked at the starry skies and caught a glimpse of Venus, the Morning Star who twinkled through the long night amidst a chaotic spiral of sacred and profane love.

Oh you, Lucifer...

CHAPTER 10

Gare de l'Est
10th arrondissement
September 25th, 1938

The light of dawn poured in from the skylights of the solarium-like, glass-roofed station's arched ceiling, and the hubbub of thronging crowds reverberated through the smoke-filled atrium. Restless travelers waved their tickets in the air and flocked the platform's ledge over the tracks to get the better of the people next to them for a chance to board the train ahead of time. Porters carried bags from luggage carts to the train coaches, braving the rabid fussing of the large number of awaiting passengers.

If the travelers were not rushing the platform, they either lounged in the storefronts of various cafés and restaurants lining the granite walls of the station or they stood by podiums having their passports stamped by tellers.

Brother Francis strolled over the platform, wearing his usual Mandarin attire over his Jesuit cassock. He held his hat and robe as he made his way through the crowds to the locomotive at the buffer stop at the other end of the atrium.

A man in uniform with a flat-top képi came into his view.

"Monsieur Élie!" Francis hallooed.

The man looked over, and upon seeing the Jesuit Brother, beamed brightly in recognition of him. He walked over and eagerly took his hand.

"Brother!" Élie exclaimed. "You have arrived just in time!"

"Indeed I have," Francis responded affably.

"And I trust your mentor Monsignor Jean-Patmos will accompany you on this trip?"

"Actually, Monsieur, he will not be joining me in the Holy Land this time; he had to tend to some urgent last-minute affairs at the society, you see."

"Oh, is that so? How unfortunate!" Élie said curiously. "But wait a minute, Brother: Just who exactly were the other two tickets for then?"

"Oh, just where are those mischievous—" Francis muttered to himself, craning his head over the crowds. "These ladies, they uh—heh, well, 'ladies'—" Francis passively remarked with air quotes. "They must still be primping in the powder room; I guess even they can't resist a little vanity sometimes."

Élie shot a confused look at Francis. *"Ladies?* Who?"

At that point, Shiloh and Psalmodie turned the corner from the station's concourse. Only, their appearances very distinct from the cloche hats, marcelled hairstyles, and fitted coats the other women sported around the station. The two were both accoutered in sapphire-colored tunics and neckerchiefs. Instead of wearing the veils that most people would have typically associated with nun habits, however, they wore an unusual piece of headwear: A white cloth cornette, folded upward by starch to give the strange appearance of horns.

"I don't want to be offensive towards Brother's culture," Psalmodie said, "but why do we have to wear these glorified origami figurines on our heads?" She patted at her folded cap with one hand and held tight to her satchel with the other.

"Just stick to the plan," Shiloh whispered, "and go along with whatever he says."

Francis was still by the front of the train, waving them over. "Come along, sœurs!"

Upon seeing their friend, their walking sped to a trot until they came before him and the uniformed man.

"Sir," Francis began, "these are the Society's next-door neighbors, the Daughters of Charity of Saint Vincent de Paul. They are called to their convent in the holy city of Jerusalem and need me to manage expenses for their trip since, as you may well know, I am called to assist the Jesuits in France through their vow of poverty, and you must know that I cannot in good conscience turn my back on my sisters in Christ."

"They look rather young," Élie observed before assuming, "They are novitiates, I take it?"

The two curtsied courteously.

"Sœurs," Francis said to them, "I would like for you two to meet Monsieur Élie. Please keep him in your prayers because he is the conductor of this train and has agreed to reserve for us two cabins that were 'forfeited' just this morning."

Élie barked a laugh. "Yes, well, I doubt our friend Monsieur Rupert with all of his luggage is in a hurry to visit his mistress in Lausanne anyways!"

"Yes, yes, that's very droll," Francis laughed mirthfully before pulling Élie aside and speaking in a hushed tone. "Listen, you trust me, don't you?"

"Of course!" Élie responded buoyantly.

"Monsieur, one of the sœurs has had difficulty fully internalizing the concept of citizenship and as such does not have a registered *laissez-passer* with her."

"Well, Brother," Élie started, hunching his shoulders, "I must confess, that is quite the dilemma."

"But," Francis continued, "she does speak perfect Arabic. An invaluable skill, you understand, that the sœurs in Jerusalem can use to navigate other regions of the Holy Land that would have been inaccessible to them otherwise."

Élie tilted his head in supposition. "Well, I've heard that there is talk of Zionist self-determination to the disadvantage of the Arab natives there. Who indeed knows what will become of their language?" He then looked over to survey the two reticent girls and inquired, "And the other one?"

"While Sœur Shiloh is indeed perfect in the Arabic language," Francis explained, "she has a little ways to go with French. She insisted on Sœur Psalmodie's company for the trip, who, I am afraid, also does not hold the appropriate papers."

Élie's tone turned bleak. "Brother, you are not helping your own case here. You know I keep my record as consistent as possible with the Compagnie Internationale des Wagons-Lits."

"I know, I know," Francis admitted, placing a hand on his shoulder, "and I acknowledge that you, as conductor, have a long-standing career with the Compagnie, but let me ask you this: These girls are to take their vows at the close of this week, and they would rather do it at the site of our Lord's Passion. Do you recall His Nativity?"

"Of course."

"The inns would not receive Mary and Joseph to bring Him to light. Now with this story in mind, I entreat, reflect on what Jesus Himself would do here. What would He do here for the sœurs' *rebirth*? A *proper* rebirth; one most close to God's promised land."

Élie shot another look at the two. Francis kept quiet, looking intently into his eyes in anticipation for a merciful response. Sighing hesitantly, Élie dug one hand deep into his pocket.

"Well, do you at least have yours then?" he finally asked.

Francis reached for his passport booklet in his breast pocket and extended it to him. "I assure you, sir, that those two will be my responsibility for the duration of the trip and I shall be liable to the Society."

"But if you are somehow caught for this," Élie pointed directly to the Jesuit's chest, "you just say that you misplaced their papers. Is that clear?"

"Crystal," Francis said, handing his booklet to him.

Élie assessed its pages before looking back up at Francis and the two "nuns."

"Right this way, Brother," Élie said, handing the book back to him and beckoning him and the two girls towards the other end of the train. "They will have to manage the space in cabin number 3."

"God bless you, sir."

"Yes, well, He certainly has His own way of doing it, doesn't He?" he finally remarked before leading the Brother and his sœurs through the frantic crowds.

Shiloh caught up to Francis. "What did you say to him?" she asked.

"I may have laid it on a little too thick," he whispered, "But at least I didn't have to bribe him."

She smiled before turning to face Élie. *"Merci beaucoup mon ami,"* she said to him in fluid French.

A perplexed look came upon the conductor's face.

"Aha!" Francis exclaimed awkwardly, insinuating himself between him and Shiloh. "I see Sœur Psalmodie's French lessons are finally taking hold now, huh?" Francis shot a glare of discretion at her.

Psalmodie followed shortly behind them, still fixing the large cornette over her head. "I can't wait to be free of this costume," she grumbled to herself.

CHAPTER 11

Cabin No.3 of the Simplon-Orient Express

A mid the clatter of cocktails and Champagne flute glasses, Shiloh found the train's sleeper car to be relatively tranquil compared to the continued commotion on the platform outside. In the carpeted wood-paneled hallway, a stout and heavily made-up elderly woman with a veiled pillbox hat looked askance at the Jesuit ushering two young nuns into his cabin. Shiloh tried to keep from laughing as she saw Francis awkwardly salute at the old lady. The woman crossed herself and retreated back into her room with a scandalized impression.

"I hope you ladies find these quarters suitable," Élie said to the party. "As you can see, this space is less cramped than the other one since Monsieur Rupert uses it to store all of his luggage. In any case, Brother, I will be sure to have our service fetch you the proper bedding."

The varnished cherry wood cabin was a very modest room, hemming its passengers' agency with two narrow berths shelved on the left wall and a small pedestaled enamel washbasin in the adjacent corner. The only sense of openness provided for the confined space came in from the diminutive window over the bottom berth's nightstand.

"Will this suffice?" Élie asked.

"Oh yes, we will make ourselves comfortable," Francis said, not wanting to impose even further.

"Excellent! If you have any questions or complaints, don't be afraid to let our staff know. They will be more than happy to be of service."

"Yes, thank you, Monsieur Élie."

"And Christ be with you in your life's devotion," the conductor concluded deferentially to the two nuns behind him before walking down the hall back towards the dining coach.

Francis closed the wood panel door behind him.

"Finally," Psalmodie moaned, pulling the large cornette from her head. "I can take this strange sailboat off."

"Brother," Shiloh started, tying her short hair back, "we can trade rooms with you. Please, you already did so much for us."

"No, no," he said, waving off her offer. "The other room will be much too cramped for you both. Besides, did you see how that lady looked at us?"

"I agree with Shiloh," Psalmodie said, trying to untangle her monastic garments from over her shoulders. "I can go. You two can sleep here. It really is no trouble."

Shiloh looked between Psalmodie and Francis with her mouth hung open, more unsure of herself than of Psalmodie's offer. When Shiloh looked back at Francis to see what he would have thought, she saw that his eyes were cast down as a vaguely suggestive smile surfaced on his face.

"I may be a Jesuit, my dear *huli xiangtou*," Francis said, seeming as though he wanted to take Shiloh by her hands, "but I am also a man."

Though Francis' insistence gave Shiloh pause, Psalmodie said brusquely, "Alright, fine, be that way then." She was still struggling out of the rest of her habit. "Maybe it was a bad idea to have our regular clothes on under all of this. These clothes are so suffocating! How on Earth do the nuns wear these?"

Shiloh turned away from Francis with a sweet smile and asked Psalmodie, "You only said that we needed to get to the Orient, and that there was no time to explain why."

"Yes?" Psalmodie said, throwing the last article of her garments on the top bunk. Her satchel was still in hand.

"Your life goal?" Shiloh nudged in a more challenging tone. "The 'Holy Grail?'"

Psalmodie smiled and she stood motionless, relishing in their anticipation for the truth so many have sought out throughout the centuries. She opened the front fold of her satchel and presented the Aramaic-titled book to them.

"I have two stories to tell you both," she began. "One is the first ever mention of the Holy Grail in history, and the other is the very moment it was lost to history."

CHAPTER 12

Psalmodie began with the first story. "The very first story of a quest for the Holy Grail was written by the great French medieval trouvère, Chrétien de Troyes, in his story of one of King Arthur's greatest knights: *Perceval: Le Conte du Graal,* which was published in the year 1191. In this telling, the Grail has an incontrovertible Roman Catholic aesthetic, but its presentation also drew inspiration from other motifs such as Celtic druidic cauldrons, Byzantine liturgy, and possibly even Persian cultic practices."

Shiloh's eyes narrowed in question. "Wait, what about the Last Supper chalice mentioned in the Bible? Isn't that the supposed Holy Grail or am I missing something here?"

Psalmodie pounced eagerly. "Then that would have to beg many, *many* questions: What of the quest for the Crown of Thorns among countless other relics with His blood? What of the intriguing speculation that the Gospel of Luke makes mention of *two* cups at the Last Supper as per the customs of the Jewish Passover in Jesus' time, which traditionally used *four* cups? What was it, then, about this one particular relic—this 'Holy Grail'—that made it so unique?"

"Okay," Francis interjected, "so why the one cup then?"

"Before we can understand the Holy Grail," she countered, "we would have to understand where it all began. Okay?"

Shiloh and Francis shared an exasperated look before acceding to her request with a nod.

Psalmodie continued, "Now you are correct in pointing out that particular feature of the Grail. Upon closer examination of the romance, you would think that he wrote of the cup or dish of the Last Supper in his references to the relic itself. However, apart from Jesus Himself calling the cup—what many would assume to be the Holy Grail—'the chalice of salvation,' the Bible gives almost no attention to the literal cup itself after that point on. But more on that later; I promise." Psalmodie looked down at her book and turned to the page she was looking for: The summary of Chrétien de Troyes' *Perceval*.

"Are you ready for this?" she said, walking towards them. When they shrugged, she whispered, *"Tres bien,"* and extended her hand theatrically as though she were about to proclaim a Gospel. Her father's very words. "'The Knight of the Round Table, Perceval, enters a mysterious castle and meets a dying king called the Fisher King. Upon greeting him, he sees a procession involving a man carrying a lance that dripped with blood and a maiden following shortly behind him with the Grail itself, carrying not wine or blood in it, but a single mass wafer used in the Latin celebration of the Eucharist; the literal 'transubstantiated' Body of Jesus Christ in the form of bread.

"However, after Perceval neglected to ask what the meaning of the Grail was and fell asleep in the castle, he wakes up in an empty hall with the Fisher King dead, so he sets off on a quest to unlock the Grail's secrets. During his quest, he finds a loathly crone who chastises Perceval for the negligent sin of not asking what the meaning of the Grail was, which leads to a curse on King Arthur's kingdom. Since then, Perceval had fallen from God's grace for five years before being consoled by a monk for his mistake.' And that's where..." Psalmodie trailed off into deep thought.

Francis ducked his head to find her gaze. "That's where *what?*" he asked.

"That's where the story ends," she answered with a sigh, "because either Chrétien himself died or his literary patron, Count Philip I of Flanders, was killed during the Third Crusade in Outremer in 1191."

"Wait, I'm confused," Shiloh started. "Did your father think that

King Arthur and his knights were real historical figures? Was this 'Holy Grail' relic even real?"

"King Arthur's historical existence is still hotly debated," Psalmodie responded. "Some of his knights, even more so. But even if they all did definitely exist, to say that the Grail quests themselves happened would be like people hundreds of years from now looking back on William Shakespeare and believing that all of his Elizabethan tragedies were historical accounts. The Arthurian legends before the Grail romances are more than likely fictional stories, but for a highly influential 12th-century trouvère like Chrétien, they served only as backdrops and illustrative leitmotifs to effectively reflect certain grim realities of his time... which would then bring me to the second story."

Shiloh groaned. "*Another* one of your legends?"

"No," she responded again. "Not a legend this time. This one? This one did actually happen. This one is in fact a matter of historical record. As a matter of fact, according to my father's entry, it served as the first Grail legend's principal inspiration."

"Wait," Francis interrupted, "are you saying that the first Grail legend is a conceit for something else that happened *historically?*"

"Shiloh," Psalmodie said, facing her with an earnest smile. "You're trying to build a career on this kind of stuff. You might actually recognize this story."

"Me?" Shiloh reacted with a short laugh. "Are you serious? I couldn't be bothered to know any of this stuff."

"We'll see about that," Psalmodie said, turning the page to continue in her animated rigmarole. "'Centuries ago, in a battlefield bordering a great blue sea, a king and a prince submitted to the crushing forces of their worthy adversary, a sultan. As prisoners, they awaited by his throne to negotiate the terms of their surrender or, as they feared, their sentences. Upon the sultan's arrival, he presented a goblet filled with icy rose-flavored water to the king so that he may live longer. Once he had finished drinking, the king passed it to the prince, and at this, the sultan's face dropped in disgust.'"

Shiloh's skeptical regard fell. The story had indeed sounded familiar. A story she knew by heart, for it was a tragedy of Christian history and a triumph of Islamic fortitude. She shut her eyes and internalized the insight.

Psalmodie kept reading. "'Leaving the king to his retinue of slaves, the sultan took the prince to his tent to negotiate over other affairs, which ultimately ended in the prince's beheading. Since this battle, countless quests and endeavors had been undertaken to recover the treasure that was lost on that battlefield with no avail. Numerous claimants and hoaxes have indeed surfaced throughout the ages, but none to match the grand majesty of the original relic.'"

"This is all just sounding like another King Arthur story," Francis said dubiously.

"It isn't," Shiloh chimed in, stepping next to Psalmodie. "She's right. This *did* happen. I know exactly what she is talking about."

"You do?" Francis asked. "Well, what is it then?"

"July 4th, 1187," Shiloh began, staring intently into Psalmodie's eyes. "A few kilometers west from the Sea of Galilee, the Battle of the Horns of Hattin took place; a catastrophic defeat for the Crusader King of Jerusalem, the Prince of Antioch, and the Grand Master of the Knights Templar, all of whom were captured by the equivalent to King Charlemagne in the history of the Islamic world."

Psalmodie leafed through the pages of her book. "Um, my father wrote it down here, but it's hard to pronounce. I do know he is honored with a cameo with Julius Caesar and Hector in the First Circle of Dante's *Inferno* as one of the 'virtuous pagans,' but I don't quite remember his name..."

"Yusuf Selahaddin Eyyubi," Shiloh finally said, turning towards Francis. "He's known in the West as 'Saladin,' although he was *far* from pagan. I've mentioned him to you before, remember? The very first Sultan of Egypt, Lebanon, Syria, the Jazira, and the Hejaz who reconstituted the politically fragmented Islamic kingdoms in the 12th century." Shiloh turned to look back at Psalmodie. "Yes, those portions you mentioned about the goblet and the beheading of the prince? You're right. Both are true. Although Saladin was Kurdish, it was customary in Arabic culture to present a drink as a demonstration of mercy to captives and prisoners-of-war.

"The beheading was also not entirely unprovoked, at least given

Saladin's situation; the then-Prince of Antioch was infamous in the Islamic world for apparently holding threatening ambitions to maraud the Hajj pilgrimage routes to the Muslim holy cities of Mecca and Medina. Likewise, the then-King of Jerusalem was so unpopular amongst his own Crusaders for his excessive belligerence towards Saladin's growing power and influence that there were even attempts to delay the king's succession by crowning his 8-year-old stepson."

Francis raised a hand at both of them. "Hold on please. Why is all of this important? And why are you two of one mind all of a sudden?"

Psalmodie looked to Shiloh. "Do you want to tell him or should I?"

Shiloh went on, "The Battle of Hattin presaged—no—*dramatically* facilitated the Crusaders' surrender of Jerusalem to Saladin's Ayyubid forces on October 2nd of that same year; the anniversary of the Prophet Muhammad's—" She stopped mid-sentence and turned away as an old habit fought its way to the surface.

"Are you okay?" Psalmodie called to her while Francis remained silent with a commiserating look.

Shiloh whispered the rote honorific of the Prophet's name: *"Alayhi salatu wa-salam."* She cleared her throat and turned back to face her concerned friends. "His *Isra* and *Mi'raj,* or his legendary Night Journey and ascension through the heavens from the Dome of the Rock at the Temple Mount. And because of the Crusaders' surrender, the Pope called for what would later be known as the Third Crusade."

Francis shook his head. "But *where* does your author's 'metaphorical' Holy Grail fit in all of this? What did Saladin do with the goblet you mentioned?"

"Brother," Shiloh said, "I don't think the goblet Psalmodie mentioned was her so-called 'Holy Grail.'"

Francis' tone was beginning to sour. "So, what is it then? Just tell me."

"Believe it or not," Psalmodie cut in, "there was indeed a holy relic lost as a result of this battle, but it wasn't even a cup to begin with."

"Not a cup?" Francis asked. "What was it then?"

"In fact," Psalmodie continued, "not since the Babylonians' capture of the Ark of the Covenant in the Old Testament did such an event inflict such a devastating blow to morale for all of Christendom during this battle. Four to five years before Chrétien likely finished writing the very first romance on the Holy Grail, this, *the* totem of Latin Christian power, was lost to Saladin and his Ayyubid Dynasty. A treasure more precious to the Crusaders than Jerusalem itself. So, I would like to invite you, Brother: What *was* this holy relic exactly?"

Before Francis could have tried an answer, the train's pistons hissed, and a screen of smoke rolled over the cabin window outside. The conductor Élie walked along the station platform, blowing his whistle and yelling the announcement of the Orient Express' departure for Constantinople and all of its connections before stepping onto the train itself. After he flagged the rest of the crew over, the trio felt a slight lurch in their surroundings before the slow muffled chugging of the engine had started to build its rhythm. With three sounds of the train's air whistle, the trio's cabin rumbled, and the train's journey came to life.

"Shiloh," Psalmodie said, extending her hand to her. "May I see your wrist?"

With reluctance, Shiloh acquiesced in her request, rolling up her sleeve and putting it in Psalmodie's palm. Psalmodie presented Shiloh's hand to the Jesuit, pointing to the Coptic tattoo marked on her wrist.

The seal of Shiloh's echoing past.

At first, Francis' face contorted in puzzlement, but the longer he stared at it, the more his eyes widened with startled revelation. With his gaze cast down, he sat on the lower bunk to steady himself over the quaking floor. Shiloh joined him, receiving the idea with a solemn look of conflict in her eyes.

Psalmodie flipped over to the next page of her father's journal. "Now that you finally understand why it is so special among the Christian holy relics, let me explain how this relic of unimaginable power became 'this cup'... and then for last... what my father believed about its approximate location."

CHAPTER 13

Société des Missions étrangères de Paris (M.E.P.) headquarters
7th arrondissement

At noon, a short priest walked his leashed Basset Hound through the white fog to the Missions Society's headquarters on the lonely 128 rue du Bac. He was in the latter part of his life, his back bent from the long years. Once he stood in front of the door, he took off his wide-brimmed saturno hat and reached into his pocket for his key ring. The dog looked up at him and whimpered worriedly.

"Now you just wait a second," the priest said. "You will get your bread once we get inside; you'll just have to wait." Though the priest dug his fingers deeper into his pocket to feel around for the ring, the dog wouldn't stop whimpering. When it started barking up at the priest, he tugged at his leash for it to quiet down. When he finally pulled out the ring, he jangled them over his dog and grumbled, "I have the keys here, you see?"

Upon reaching for the door handle, he noticed something about it that was out of place. Below the knob, there was the curved brass of the deadbolt lock's hollow interior. Around the escutcheon, scratches were traced along the door's mahogany surface. The priest's mind turned to vandals, but he wondered whether or not they were still inside; he leaned over to peer in through the sidelight and called in through the windowpane, "Hello? Francis? Anyone there? It's me. Father Jean. Is anyone there?"

There was no response.

A sense of foreboding ran through him. *"Allez, toutou,"* he called his dog, turning away from the door and starting in the other direction. However, just as he looked up to where he was going, he saw that a man clad in a black overcoat was already standing behind him.

The priest gasped and dropped his saturno when he saw what he held down by his waist: A large, unusual-looking Luger pistol pointed to his stomach.

"Bon après-midi, Monsignor Jean," the man said, patting the Basset Hound's snout with his free hand. His French was perfect, although the priest still detected a Germanic accent in his voice. "Will you be so kind as to show so weary a company of travelers a little hospitality?"

With two quick flicks of his gun, he shepherded him into the building. The priest turned back around, stepping through the damaged door with the man still pressing the barrel against his spine.

The man led the priest through the headquarters' corridors before stepping back outside onto a yard. The square yard itself was framed on two sides by two brick-faced buildings, half-resembling garths centering most cloistered monasteries. At the yard's center was circular pavement surmounted by a small fountain and surrounded by a peristyle garden that was elegantly adorned with vines and white lilies.

The priest looked over the fountain and saw that a thinner man wearing a fedora was sitting on a stone bench under a wooden pergola where the two buildings abutted. He was reading through the pages of a stapled essay while two other men stood as the thin man's guard. The priest saw that one of them had a rifle strapped to his shoulder.

The man at the bench read aloud from the paper, "'Yet despite the bitter anathema issued by Pope Gregory IX, King Frederick II of Germany and Norman Sicily, the so-called 'Antichrist,' had still managed to negotiate Jerusalem from Saladin's nephew, Sultan al-Kamil, thus putting an end to the Sixth Crusade in 1229.'" He tapped a finger on its cover. "Do you recall learning about this in school? I most certainly do not."

The priest gulped and responded in a subdued voice, "No, I'm afraid I can't say that I have." His captor then forced him down on the bench next to Rahn. The priest then flung his eyes back to the three imposing men and saw that one of them was holding the leash to his Basset Hound sitting at his feet.

The man next to him went on, "My ancestors were pagans and my grandparents were heretics, but it seems that the Führer himself is heir to something far greater after all; you see how often this mercy you so profess failed countless kings throughout the centuries only to be lost in time like idle chatter? Oh, how the dark religions subverted our Nordic ancestors with their supremacism cloaked under mildness?"

The man shot a venomous glare at the priest and continued, "From the Gnostic heresies of antiquity to the dialectical materialism of Karl Marx, there endures an underlying zeal to break free from the fetters of the false reality contrived and dominated by the Jewish demiurge called Yahweh; it is that right and enlightening principle of rebellion against *your* prideful Church's intolerance that has always been Lucifer's due, and yet, your Church has distracted the German peoples with one Crusade after another and then slaughtered Lucifer's purest prophets like animals before staking claim to 'universal love.'"

The man's words left the senile priest stupefied. As close as he was to him, the priest couldn't have recognized the man's downturned face through the fog, and his eyes were too shadowed by his black fedora. Upon catching sight of what the man wore on his right ring finger, however, the priest's face fell.

An Occitan variant of the Iron Cross centered by a rosy-red swastika. The priest was by no means an expert in history, but he was well aware of what horrendous atrocities the Church had committed in Southern France centuries ago.

The man picked up a large uncapped metallic vacuum flask from the pavement and cradled the mouthpiece between his two fingers close to his nose before putting it to his mouth. His face shifted as he swirled the liquid around in his mouth.

"Care for some wine?" he offered in a more tempered tone. "Forgive me, Monsignor; I am Obersturmführer Otto Rahn. I hope you don't mind. My hierarchs may have forced me into sobriety, but me and my Schutzstaffel troop here helped ourselves to some of your more fortified stock in your chapel's sacristy before you arrived. It's strange, though. I assumed the place would have been closed on a Sunday." Rahn chuckled at the priest. "But then again, look who I'm talking to."

"What do you want with me?" the old priest begged. "If it is money you want, I am the treasu—"

Rahn snapped, "No, I don't particularly care for earthly vanities. I want whoever wrote *this.*" He slapped the paper against the priest's chest.

The priest gathered its crinkled contents and read from its cover.

A WORD COMMON BETWEEN
THE SULTAN AND SAINT FRANCIS

Shiloh Ma'idah al-Ahad

M.E.P.

"That Arab girl is not who we are really after," Rahn clarified, "but she was abetting someone who has something that belongs to us. We thought it would be here after we scoured her university apartment for hours and found this finely-written research paper. We also imagined that she would try to exploit your society's resources to flee France."

"Stop! Please!" the priest begged. "I know nothing! I swear! I didn't see anyone!" The priest shut his tearful eyes and braced himself for the suffering. "I can't tell you."

"I was afraid you might say that," Rahn responded pitifully, folding the paper back into his pocket, "*for dust thou art, and unto dust shalt thou return.*'"

He rose from the bench and stood before the priest. After exchanging glances with the three men looming over their captive, he nodded once at them. The three men seized both of the sobbing priest's arms.

Rahn picked up the cylindrical canister and removed what appeared to be an empty bullet casing from his coat. He drew no weapon, but instead, put on a glove and unscrewed one section of the casing to take out a nail-sized glass vial; it was when Rahn forced the priest's jaw open when the priest realized what was going to happen to him.

The priest's legs flailed and stamped. He struggled in a clumsy circle, but the enforcers' vice-like grip kept his head and shoulders in place. He felt Rahn's gloved forefinger dig around his molars and press the poison ampoule deeper. Then the German forced the priest to swallow wine from the canister's mouth before the enforcers forced his jaw shut by the chin; the spirits bubbled and burned in his throat, but it wouldn't have been close to the pain he had been about to experience.

The priest closed his eyes, and once he released one last breath through his lips, he felt the cyanide acid burning a hole inside of him. His body stiffened and his heartbeat slowed before the agony then gave way to solitude.

Once the priest stopped struggling, the three captors released his body and let it tumble over the grass. Rahn took out Shiloh's essay from his pocket and looked it over once more for any more clues to their targets' locations before setting it back down on the bench.

The 33-year-old man with the rifle joined him by his side. He had a boyish, yet jaded countenance with calculating wide set eyes, crooked incisors, and bushy eyebrows that seemed to have stayed creased with a habitual look of perplexity and mettle; indeed, a look of youth, but one already worn with battle scars and a steadfast nerve and fanatical commitment to the Reich.

He was Kurt Eggers, who was Rahn's designated Schütze, or rifleman. He was the leading muse for the SS, whose many works of literature were commended for extolling the Nordic warrior death. Hhe was only assigned to Rahn by Himmler on the recommendation of high priest Wiligut Weisthor for the memoir-novel published the year prior, *Rebel's Mountain,* which showcased Eggers' experience as a capable fighter during the short-lived, but bloody Silesian Uprisings immediately after the Great War.

"Well done," Eggers said, running his fingers through his sleek undercut. "You have proven yourself with unquestioning fealty; our Reichsführer will be very pleased to know that you hold no doubts against the fatherland after all. Now all that is left to do is to quietly dispose of the body someplace, correct?"

Rahn cleared his throat and walked away from the scene. "One of the telegrams the Abwehr intelligence office intercepted from Dachau's records. It made mention of a rose and a sword. I need you to listen, Kurt. I know those girls ran in this direction, and I know you thought they'd be here, but my partner's words had to have meant something else. We need the daughter alive."

"Oh, dear me!" Eggers reacted, mockingly feigning surprise. "Of course we need the daughter alive! Why, though? I think you forget that our orders from Himmler were dead *or* alive, Otto. 'Preferably dead' were his exact words to you specifically if I remember correctly, and you know that there are too many loose ends that could hang us both. My job is to tie them."

"Himmler wouldn't let me explain myself," Rahn said with a note of exasperation.

"Well, now is your chance," Eggers said with a challenging voice. "Explain yourself: Why did you have us wait so long before springing the trap? Why *follow* her?"

"I have told you I searched every crook of that house," Rahn responded, "but I saw her pick up something from a box. As much as that could have been what we are after, it might as well have been some trivial time capsule. I needed to be sure that her college home wasn't hiding something as well. We still don't know what she did with the—"

"But she got away," Eggers said, jabbing the air in front of Rahn's face, "and all because you wanted to be 'sure.'"

Rahn bridled at his hostility. "Need I remind you," he started with some steel in his voice this time, "that our Führer is not in good standing with Britain or France at present, considering his numerous actions against other states these past couple of months? You know full well how our Führer feels about our efforts for occult divination; imagine what he would do to us if the French authorities were made aware of our clandestine operations here. Any leverage he should have in the negotiations in Munich would be jeopardized by our deputation alone, and we would be begging for a quick, cowardly death. Tell me, Schütze Eggers: Is that truly something you want for yourself? For our people?"

"You don't get to tell me that we need to do things by the book!"

Eggers exclaimed, pointing to the pistol holstered under one of the enforcers' bandoliers. "You barely have the means from the SS for even the most basic requisitions! These clunky Borchardt pistols they armed us with are antiquated dinosaurs of the Great War, crudely imitating the far superior design of the Lugers that we ought to be using!" Eggers then pointed to his own rifle. "And the only Luger we *do* have is this failed prototype; this joke of a rifle which can only hold up to five cartridges at a time!"

"We're hunting a couple of university students; unless you're apprehensive of some talent in after-school fencing, they are not trained kommandos!" Rahn said. "Besides, I already petitioned the Reichsführer's office numerous times, but he wants to mitigate all gross misallocations of the SS's standard issue resources. I found these guns in the armory, and they may be substandard, but they were all I could afford for this mission. I assure you: We will find better equipment elsewhere. But for the moment, we should avoid drawing too much attention to ourselves... for our Führer's sake."

Eggers insisted, "But if we *do* have to kill them, how are any of us supposed to efficiently—"

"You will *not* kill them!" Rahn urged, lowering his voice to a guttural snarl. When Eggers' confused glare intensified, Rahn added, "Not until they've given us what we came here for. But until then, you will not exceed your mandate!"

"Otto," Eggers started in a grave tone, "I meant it when I told Reichsführer Himmler that I thoroughly enjoyed your Lucifer lecture in Dortmund, but this isn't another one of your research trips across Europe. Our standard operating procedure ought to be fundamentally revised now, and that includes the prospect of elimina—"

A sound called their confronting glares away from one other. By the priest's corpse, the droopy-eared Basset Hound rested his head on top of his paws and anxiously whined for his owner to return to him. Eggers reached into his pocket, fished out one round, and fed it into the open breach of his Luger rifle before pulling on its arm-like toggle and leveling it on the dog.

"What are you doing?" Rahn asked, looking dubiously at him.

"I still need some practice with this gun," Eggers said, pressing the stock firmly against his shoulder and steadying his aim down on the barrel. "I cannot miss my target next time."

Rahn contemplated the animal. Its long eyes were still affixed to the remains of its dead guardian. The soldier's concentrated eyes aimed his sightline down on its skull. He sucked one breath in through his teeth and drew it out to still his moving frame.

But the moment he pulled the trigger, Rahn's hands pulled at the rifle's barrel. "Just stop!" he shouted.

But Eggers had already pulled the trigger.

The rifle's rear iron sight on the jointed hinge shot up and the sharp report carried through the dense fog before dying away. Rahn thought he didn't miss; Eggers thought he did; both, however, were half-wrong. The dog limped away, crying in pain and panic alike. A long gash lined the skin on its flank where the bullet had apparently grazed it.

The soldier dipped his head, and he held the rifle at ease by its fore-end. His mouth curved into an imperious smile before flaring his icy blue eyes at what the Reichsführer considered to be Germany's best chance to recover the Holy Grail from its Christian captors.

"I know what it is to write books to our peoples' glory," Eggers finally said, his voice dripping with disgust, "and I've kept my mouth shut in front of our Reichsführer to safeguard my promotion to the SS's newspaper, but I know what you are. We may have worked together that one time in Dortmund, but you mark my words: You have no seat at Wewelsburg Castle. No place in my fatherland. To all of us, you are and always will be just a wandering *Halbjude.*"

Rahn's neck tensed, and his body stiffened straight as if he were standing at attention to the young SS soldier who was supposedly his subordinate. He brushed past him and made his way through the fog over to the Basset Hound still squealing from its affliction.

He stood over the panting creature and stared at it for a while before gathering it into the crook of his arm and tenderly putting one hand to its side. Its flesh was cold, but the bleeding was regulated to a mild perspiration. He looked down at the corpse and saw the black veins spidering up its cyanotic face and the vomit drooling from its lips.

"Oh Psalmodie," he whispered, a tear trickling down his eye.

He then caught sight of a word on the cover page of Shiloh's paper:

Sultan. He stood motionless, but upon grasping the word once more, his eyes widened in alarm. He heard the sound of Eggers' approaching steps rustling over the grass. He whirled towards him and saw that he was joined by the other two Gestapo officers emerging from the mist like spectral harbingers.

"Wait!" Rahn exclaimed. "Call the Abwehr and the Foreign Office!"

"For what?" the secretary questioned.

Rahn looked down at the maimed dog's eyes. "To see if the Wehrmacht's high command still has their contact in Lebanon!"

"Why? Do you know where those girls might be going?"

Rahn recalled the many theories his associate incessantly proffered to him. The theories of the Holy Grail that could have undermined Germany's *Kirchenkampf*—its struggle to break free from the Church's grip. In all of his bloviating, one name had always been mentioned by his partner. A seat of power for the Muslim Saracens of old and a mystical island figuring prominently in the Christian Grail legend.

Sarras.

If he did not stop them from getting there, the Cathari's ancient treasure would have again been lost to the towering shadow of that false monument. That, or the Führer himself would have personally added Rahn's skeleton to his macabre collection.

"I'll soon explain why," Rahn spoke grimly, gesturing towards the corpse. "Put the body in a tarpaulin; we'll have to dispose of it elsewhere."

CHAPTER 14

Cabin No.3 of the Simplon-Orient Express
Passing through the French countryside

Outside the train car, the distant mountains and cloudy skies merged together in a dull gray and cold blue haze, slurring the horizon. A heavy rain soon pattered against the cabin's small window, but it did little to disrupt the train's glide over its tracks and did even less to wear down Psalmodie's eagerness. She smiled at Shiloh and Francis' equal disbelief; she with private conflict, but he with hushed reverence. But in their silence, Psalmodie knew the very same question stayed in their thoughts.

Could the Holy Grail really be the original, bonafide relic of Christ's cross?

"As my father said in his journal," Psalmodie began, "Chrétien de Troyes' Grail romance is a soaring symphony of deep symbolism as it relates to the loss of what was then widely known as the *Lignum Crucis,* or the 'Wood of the Cross.' The True Cross."

"A symphony—what?" Francis repeated, tuning back in.

"But before we get to this side of the Grail, we should consider Perceval, Chrétien's hero in his story, in the appropriate context." Psalmodie turned to Shiloh. "By chance, have you come across Count Philip I of Flanders in your study of the Crusades?"

Shiloh woke from her haunted impression. "I know a little. He rejected the regency of Jerusalem offered to him by his first cousin, the Leper King Baldwin IV, and he was the highest-ranking noble who died in the Siege of Acre in 1191 at the beginning of the Third Crusade. The succession crisis of the County of Flanders that immediately followed his death was actually the main pretense that the King of France used to abort his own participation in the Crusade. Why?"

"Hold on," Francis interposed, "who is this 'Philip' to the story?"

"The dedicatee and literary patron of Chrétien's Grail story," Psalmodie explained, "but most importantly, the template around which Chrétien molded the character arc of Perceval, the knight errant of King Arthur who embarked on the very first quest for the Holy Grail."

"So, this 'Perceval' character," Shiloh began. "He is a metaphor for this Belgian Count?"

"Exactly," Psalmodie said with a satisfied smile, "and because he was Chrétien's sponsor, the entire Grail romance is Chrétien's consolation for his failure."

"Failure?" Francis reacted. "What failure?"

"As I said," Psalmodie recapped, "in the story, Perceval failed to ask the dying Fisher King what the Holy Grail really meant, and because of his negligence, it disappeared, and King Arthur's kingdom subsequently became cursed. It would stand to reason that Chrétien's character parallels how Philip turned down the regency of Jerusalem from his leprosy-afflicted cousin, which, as I imagine he would have viewed it, led to the subsequent loss of the True Cross at the Battle of Hattin and the fall of Jerusalem to Saladin's Ayyubid Sultanate.

"And it seems his fears were mostly justified: The Crusader Kingdom of 'Jerusalem' subsequently became a rump state and slipped into an unstable interregnum. A year after Philip's death at the Siege of Acre, for example, the elected heir to the throne, Conrad of Montferrat, was violently murdered by a ghostly, cloak-and-dagger brotherhood known as the Hashshashin—the legendary Order of Assassins."

"This all sounds rather spurious, doesn't it?" Francis remarked.

Shiloh rose to reply. "I don't think the famed Belgian historian Henri Pirenne would have thought so, Brother. He himself noted Philip to be one of the more fanatical Crusaders, though with a passionate affinity for literature. I am fond of Pirenne and his theses, and so far, Psalmodie's father's theory is consistent with who Philip truly was as far as I can tell, although Psalmodie still needs to explain some things." Shiloh shot a cynical look at Psalmodie. "Where exactly is this going?"

"To the Grail itself," Psalmodie said exuberantly, "and more specifically, how Chrétien chose to characterize it."

"In what sense?" Francis asked.

"Well, for a start," Psalmodie continued, "in the romance, Chrétien noted two things about the Holy Grail: Its radiance overtaking the candlelight of the Fisher King's castle's hall and the jewels encrusting it." Psalmodie flipped through her father's tome again and pointed to the title of one page: *Erec and Enide, c.1170.* "But Chrétien de Troyes' *very first* Arthurian chivalric romance points to an *explicit* reference to a relic of the True Cross made from fine gold, beautifully gemmed, and shedding a light brighter than morning; a further suggestion that he did have the original True Cross in mind when he created the Holy Grail!"

Shiloh shook her head. "But that just sounds like a *crux gemmata*. That could just as well mean that this author liked to add more pomp to his presentation of Christian relics. Remember, he wrote in the middle of the Crusades; perhaps he wrote of this 'Holy Grail' with a view to an audience seeking to solidify a Christian identity that was distinct from the countless heresies and 'heathen' religions at the time."

"You are so right," Psalmodie answered with an enlivened tone. "Not to mention that there was renewed urgency to define the nature of Christ's presence in the Eucharist around that time as well, given the rise of the Cathari heresy; it wasn't until 1215 that the Fourth Lateran Council infallibly defined the Church dogma of transubstantiation— the consecration of the bread and wine into the literal Body and Blood of Christ. But I still believe that Chrétien's Holy Grail is the True Cross for one other reason."

"Which is?" Shiloh asked.

"In his story," Psalmodie continued, "Perceval lived in sin for five years after his mistake before stumbling upon a monastery where a monk consoles him and actually intimates to him what the Grail really meant. But what should be really important to note is that Chrétien never intended for the Grail to be 'holy' except in one particular instance where, through the character of the monk, he actually *diminished* its significance."

"Diminished it?" Shiloh and Francis exclaimed in unison. "After he called it holy? How?"

Psalmodie smiled. "In the Old French language in which the romance was written, the Grail was called *tainte saint chose,* meaning it was 'such a holy thing.' The monk then told Perceval what actually mattered about the Grail despite what he may have done: The mass wafer that it contained. The transubstantiated 'Body of Christ' of the Latin Church's Eucharist. In other words, as holy a relic as the Grail was, what really mattered was the Communion host that it held."

"I think I see where this is going," Shiloh cut in. "It was the author's attempt to piece together what was left of the Roman Catholic ethos—both that of his patron and his audience at large—after the True Cross and Jerusalem were taken by Saladin. If what actually mattered about this Grail was the Body that it served..."

Francis took over with a diverted tone. "...then what mattered about the cross was the Body that it bore: The Bread of Life, as Jesus said in John 6... Brilliant..."

Shiloh continued, "Well, it does seem that he wrote around the time the preachers whipping up enthusiasm for the Third Crusade cited the capture of the cross as a primary justification. In fact, the *Audita tremendi* papal bull that proclaimed the Crusade against Saladin placed more emphasis on the loss of the True Cross rather than the sanctity of Jerusalem before it fell; an act of penitence for what was very clearly a punishment from God for the sins of Europe."

"Indeed," Psalmodie said. "I would also like to add that, unlike today where true authors and artists have to be *original* with their works, the vogue of medieval authors in Chrétien's time was to be *traditional,* meaning that they had to take an already existing 'canon' of fiction or folklore and give it their own interpretive twist. Chrétien suspended this literary conceit to *create* the Holy Grail. He may have been inspired by the cup of the Last Supper, but he certainly did not get the idea of the Grail from anywhere else in Arthurian legend; all the more reason to believe that something devastating for Christendom must have inspired him to create it."

"But why?" Shiloh asked. "Why was this author's message for reconciliation for true Christian meaning so overlooked for so long?"

"As I also said," Psalmodie continued with a dispirited voice, "either Philip or Chrétien died before the story could be finished. The Grail euhemerism stayed a proverbial cup—instead of the cross that it was—through numerous 'uncanon' continuations shifting its meaning through numerous lenses, be they liturgical, magical, alchemical, even sexual. And so, Chrétien's original vision was lost to the ages."

"So, that's it then?" Francis said.

"No, Brother," Psalmodie said, drawing close to Francis with a direct gaze. Her voice became charged with purpose. "That is, until that meaning of the True Cross resurfaced in the year 1225 with an order called the Cistercians."

"The *Cistercians*?" Shiloh said, sharing Francis' look of bewilderment. "What *about* the Cistercians?"

"Wait a minute, who are these 'Cistercians?'" Francis cut between them.

Shiloh looked up at Francis. "The Cistercians were a monastic order bound to a strict interpretation of the Benedictine Order's rule. But I don't understand." She faced Psalmodie. "I read that these monks lived in extremely austere communities. Now I saw that book title on your desk, but what business would they have had with legends of a priceless treasure like the Holy Grail?"

"The business they had," Psalmodie addressed her, "was the True Cross."

"So, you mean to tell me they picked up on what the original story tried to convey?"

"That, and they created a new character in their own take on the Grail quest in *Le Queste del Saint Graal*. A knight more iconic yet than Chrétien de Troyes' Perceval. *The* Grail Knight. The one and only Sir Galahad; that knight we kept seeing in those old war bond posters from the Great War." Psalmodie looked at Francis. "And you. I think even you might recognize this legendary order of warrior monks: The Poor Fellow Soldiers of Christ and of the Temple of Solomon?"

Her words surprised Francis. "The Knights Templar? I've heard of them! I only know they were the face of the Crusades, but beyond that and a myriad of other myths, it's difficult to get an exact picture of them."

"They were the most powerful Christian military order in history," Psalmodie said. "They were founded in Jerusalem in about 1120—shortly after the First Crusade against the Seljuk Turks—to protect pilgrims and nobles from the Bedouin robbers still marauding the Holy Land. The order was granted as a headquarters the Temple Mount, which was the Biblical site of King Solomon's Temple to Yahweh; from there, they wielded considerable political and economic power throughout Europe and the Holy Land until they were all systematically purged by the French King Philip IV in Paris in 1307 on charges of devil worship." Psalmodie snorted a laugh and added, "There is no shortage of theories as to how and why he dismantled the order so effectively; it really is a mystery."

At Psalmodie's last comment, Shiloh immediately thought back to the plethora of sensationalist myths of heresy attached to the Templars in France. "*Et tu*, Psalmodie?" she said wryly. "Don't tell me that you actually subscribe to those occult, devil worship conspiracy theories about them..."

"What? No! Of course not, but the Templars were—"

Shiloh held forth, "They were all slandered by King Philip to the Avignon Papacy's Inquisition, who he had under his thumb at the time. All of the king's charges were concocted, accusing the Templars of the crypto-Islamic idolatry of the satanic deity Baphomet—most likely derived from their Old French corruption of the Prophet's 'devilish' name, 'Mahomet'—so that he could weasel his way out of repaying his countless debts to the Templars and take advantage of all of their dispossessed estates and assets afterwards."

Shiloh turned toward Psalmodie. "But some of the Templars in France only 'confessed' to denying Christ and worshiping Baphomet because they were brutally tortured at the time, which made scapegoating them so much easier. But I'm sorry to say that the reality is that they stayed unquestionably devoted to the Church; for them, the cause of the Crusades was actually a sacrificial imitation of Christ, which is why they bore His blood-red cross on their tabards as they fought to cleanse Solomon's Temple of moneychangers and infidels. So, what was it that you were going to say? That King Arthur's 'half-demon' wizard Merlin was somehow in on the order's secrets as well?"

"No," Psalmodie said, pushing over Shiloh's dispute. "Just as Chrétien modeled Perceval's character around the Belgian Count, so too did the Cistercians model Galahad around the Templar knights. I mean, just look at them! Vows of chastity. The Vermillion cross emblazoned over a white shield. For Heaven's sake, the ship Galahad helmed towards the Grail castle in *Le Queste* was a vessel from the Israelite King *Solomon's* time! His character just absolutely embodies the ideals of knightly asceticism and piety found in the *novae militiae!*"

"But why?" Shiloh demanded. "Why the Templars specifically and not the countless other international Roman Catholic military orders? Why not, say, the Hospitallers or the Teutonic Knights or the Lazarists?"

"Because," Psalmodie countered, "the Templars and the Cistercians shared the same spiritual patron, Saint Bernard of Clairvaux, the abbot of the Cistercians himself. It would seem reasonable, then, that they would have had at least *some* cooperative ventures. Anything the Templars knew, possibly the Cistercians would have been privy to as well. *Possibly.*"

Francis nodded in concession but crossed his arms to withhold his confidence in Psalmodie's claims. "Alright, so we can assume that the Templars are connected to the Grail in Galahad's story, but what do they have to do with the cross in real world history?"

"I think I know what Psalmodie is going to say," Shiloh stepped in. "Was it that Saladin's nephew al-Kamil negotiated the True Cross to the Templars during Saint Francis's famous visit to Egypt in exchange for the besieged port city of Damietta? Because I sincerely doubt the sultan had it with him, and I think the Templars didn't themselves believe he had it then."

"Saint Francis again?" Francis interpolated, chuckling at Shiloh. "You told us this tale at least a thousand times already!"

"Why?" Shiloh piped up. "It was his greatest test of faith! Oh, come on, it's a good story!"

"It is, but don't you ever get tired of telling it?"

"Well, no one really talks about it nowadays," Shiloh mumbled.

Psalmodie cut in. "Yes, my father briefly mentioned that cordial tête-à-tête Saint Francis had with the sultan in his journal, but did you already forget what you said earlier?" Psalmodie tutted lightheartedly at Shiloh. "The Grand Master of the Templars himself! Gerard de Ridefort, who was captured and incarcerated for a year by Saladin after the Battle of Hattin.

"Moreover, Saladin likely sent him, the fallen King of Jerusalem, and the True Cross itself to this one particular city. In the Cistercians' story, the Holy Grail was hidden on an island called 'Sarras,' but my father says it was in reference to Saladin's bastion, then the capital of the Ayyubid Sultanate." Psalmodie presented the facing pages of her father's journal to them. On it was a worn map of the medieval Fertile Crescent with indicated geopolitical frontiers. Of all the countless names of kingdoms, countries, provinces, and emirates, one name stood out to Shiloh and Francis, marked in bold red letters.

The oldest continuously inhabited city in the world.

Damascus, Syria
دمشق، سوريا

"*Damascus?*" Francis burst out. "As in *'on the Road to Damascus?'* The city of the Apostle Paul's radical conversion experience?" Francis crossed his eyes at Shiloh for confirmation, to which she gave him a half-nod of concurrence, though she still held an uncertain glance.

"And somewhere in that city," Psalmodie said, "is where the True Cross—the Holy Grail itself—lies hidden away."

"But I still don't understand," Francis said. "Why would an army of devout *Muslims* take what they thought would be a worthless piece of wood?"

"The thing is," Psalmodie declared, "much like the Holy Grail itself, the True Cross had many miraculous powers attributed to it. In 326 A.D., for instance, the Roman Emperor Constantine's mother, Saint Helena, supposedly singled it out among others in Jerusalem by having a terminally ill woman touch it so that she could be healed.

"Similarly, before his death, the Leper King Baldwin IV had his bishops carry it at the vanguard into his battles against Saladin as well. It served a purpose similar to the Ark of the Covenant during the famous Battle of Jericho in the Hebrew Bible; relics imbued with *virtus*, or sacred Biblical powers for eternal life and divine intervention." Psalmodie's voice filled with irony. "Powers that had apparently forsaken them at Hattin."

Shiloh contributed eagerly, "And while Saladin was indeed a committed Mujahid—a striver in the way of God—, he was incredibly magnanimous compared to other Christian and Muslim potentates of his day. He earned a legacy in Europe as somewhat of a chivalrous pagan, revered even by his contemporary Crusader opponents. For example, despite the wanton slaughter of civilians in Jerusalem at the end of the First Crusade in 1099, he granted amnesty to all Catholic and Orthodox Christians when he conquered Jerusalem. Still, he would have stuck true to the religious convictions that made him the man he was, as his many chroniclers have repeatedly attested. If he didn't destroy the True Cross, he might have instead just kept it as a bargaining chip to leverage against the Crusaders."

"Exactly," Psalmodie accorded, "and one of *those* chroniclers—in fact, my father mentioned him in his journal." She licked her finger to turn a new page of the journal. "Here he is: Saladin's Persian secretary, Imad ad-Din al-Isfahani. He gleefully chronicled that after Saladin had captured the True Cross at the Battle of Hattin, he had his Ayyubid soldiers pinion it upside down on a lance and carry it to Damascus, where history tells us that it apparently vanished. *If* Saladin only meant to destroy the True Cross, even if it was only to rouse the morale of his Muslim army to capture Jerusalem, then why didn't he destroy it then and there on Hattin? Why on Earth would he bring it all the way up to Damascus?"

"But tell me," Francis asked Psalmodie, "what led your father to conclude that Damascus is the final resting place of the Holy Grail from the legends?"

"My father listed a number of clues, mostly embedded in the Cistercians' *Queste del Saint Graal*, that details its location per what they may have learned from the Templars' Grand Master after he was released from his prison in Damascus."

"How many clues?" Francis pressed.

"A *great* many clues," Psalmodie responded with a brief optimism. "But my father listed only circumstantial evidence for its location, and I can only speculate how much of it is really my father's own interpretation of things. Sarras, the Grail Island I mentioned, was, according to the Cistercians' corpus of Arthurian legend, placed on the road between five different places: Salamander, Baldac, Babylon, the Nile, and the Euphrates.

"Salamander was a city in Greece while Babylon, not to be confused with the Mesopotamian kingdom of the Old Testament, was a medieval metonym for the Egyptian city of Cairo, leading some interpreters to conclude that the island of Sarras borders Egypt. But then again, there is that seeming contradiction within the narrative of the journey being along the length of the Euphrates River as well. It was also written that, from a castle tower in Sarras, one could see the Nile River and the walls of 'Baldac,' the medieval Latin and Old French corruption of the Iraqi city of Baghdad, the largest and most prosperous city of its time."

"Wait," Shiloh started with a skeptical tone. "I see where you are going with this; even if Damascus lies between all those points much like this island you speak of, what about its actual being an *island?* Why not Cyprus, for example? It's just off the Syrian coast, and I read that there's a Greek Orthodox monastery there that actually claims to hold a relic of the—"

"Remember Glastonbury Tor?" Psalmodie countered. "The 'Isle of Avalon' where King Arthur allegedly fashioned his legendary sword? The Cistercians may have done something similar. They have *made it* an island in their story to deliberately throw off people who were 'unworthy.' People who were not as familiar with Abrahamic tradition as you two are." Psalmodie looked directly at Shiloh. "And as you mentioned, they have a *very* strict approach to Christianity. But let me ask you this: What does the name 'Damascus' translate to? The word itself? What was its original meaning?"

Once again, Shiloh recollected her readings of Semitic texts. She remembered reading about Damascus' significance in the Hebrew Bible and various Islamic texts. From these two traditions, she recalled that the Latin name for the city was imported from Greek and transliterated from the Hebrew *Darmeśeq* and Syriac Aramaic *Darmsûq,* both of which etymologically originated from one common phrase.

"'A well-watered land,'" Shiloh finally conceded, "which was a reference to two rivers that run through it, *Abana* and *Pharpar,* and according to the Second Book of Kings, were better than all the waters of Israel."

"And as a corollary to that," Psalmodie continued, putting an arm around Shiloh, "the island's name 'Sarras' is a derivation of the Old French pejorative for nomadic, Muslim Arab or Turkish thieves and soldiers during the Crusades: *Sarrazin.*"

"Saracens," Shiloh noted immediately. "From the Arabic *Saariqeen,* meaning 'thieves.'"

"So just to clarify," Francis said, turning to Psalmodie. "According to your father's journal, the True Cross was last seen in Damascus where it still rests to this day?"

"That is correct," Psalmodie affirmed.

"And that is where we're headed now?"

Psalmodie's voice tensed. "Yes."

Francis nodded. "Alright then. *Where* in Damascus are we going?"

Psalmodie stopped at his question and groped for words. "Well, the other thing about Damascus is that—"

"No, stop skirting the question," Francis grilled her, "and just tell us already. Where in Damascus is it?"

A long silence then hung over the three, and the only sounds that remained were the gentle rocking of the train's cabin and the soft buzzing of the sconce lights lining the cherry wood walls above them. Psalmodie's audience scanned her for more answers, but their eyes slowly infused with anxious discontent.

With a rueful look, she turned to the very last written page of her father's journal. Francis adjusted his spectacles over the bridge of his nose as he scanned the large handwritten words over the scritta page before reading it out loud.

Through Joseph under Sarras,

then Kingdom Come

Psalmodie's voice became filled with melancholy. "Saint Joseph of Arimathea—the secret disciple in the Bible who buried Christ's Body—was featured prominently by the Cistercians as the Holy Grail's principal custodian in *Le Queste,* guarding over Sarras as a 'New Jerusalem.'" She placed the book in Francis' hands before turning away to look distantly over the passing rural crofts of the bocage countryside through the cabin's window. "That's where my father stopped... He didn't get a chance to start his next section and those National Socialist Huns took him for themselves."

Francis passed the journal to Shiloh and searched Psalmodie's face with a candid gaze. "So where does all of this leave us then?" he said tiredly. "Was the plan to simply *move* to Damascus and spend our entire lives casting about for more clues?"

Though Psalmodie kept silent, a whispering voice repeated the same words behind her. "Joseph of Arimathea? New Jerusalem?" Psalmodie and Francis turned around and saw Shiloh was by the door, still sifting through the pages of the journal while groping for meaning from Psalmodie's father's claims.

"Shiloh?" Francis called to her.

As her eyes scanned the pages, she began nodding with more certainty. She then clamped down on the book's covers and admitted an animating laugh. "Of course! Joseph of Arimathea! New Jerusalem! I actually might have an idea of where Saladin may have hidden it!"

"What?" Psalmodie and Francis said in unison, both approaching Shiloh.

"And while I am not at all familiar with Grail lore like you," Shiloh said to Psalmodie, "I think you owe your friend 'Joseph' here, in a manner of speaking, a great deal of gratitude."

CHAPTER 15

The Annaberg inselberg
Upper Silesia, Germany
May 21st, 1921

There was a simple Franciscan monastery perched atop the Saint Anne Mountain; the embodiment of Polish Catholic nationalism. But 17-year-old Reichswehr Freikorps volunteer Kurt Eggers had already known the dark history behind it. The yellow-plastered Baroque architecture had long ago supplanted an ancient Germanic pagan shrine, although to which god didn't ultimately matter to Eggers.

Instead, he looked away from the building and came to the edge of the hill to look across the golden prairies of the Silesian countryside, made silver and gray with smoldering mortar craters, muddy duckboard trenches, and bodies scattered about them; a landscape greatly reminiscent of the putrid battlefields of Verdun and the Somme.

The croaking ravens of Wotan had already begun to descend on the battlefield with alacrity to pick at their spoils, and what Eggers perceived to be the dazzling rays of the pale white sun glaring through parting storm clouds turned out to be nothing more than an arching signaling flare, its brilliant halation fading and drifting with the rolling haze of gun smoke. Under this fugitive light of war, Eggers saw the routed

Polish nationalist insurgents scrambling from tree copse to tree copse to the banks of the Oder River like frenzied ants.

Behind him, he heard the army building like a rising tide, boiling with the beating hum of tribal war drums; as the front lines gathered forth in pincer formation through the splattering of oncoming fire, they broke ranks to give chase to the vermin like marauding wolf packs. This comradeship, the new holy temple to the pure blood, consummated his nation's single greatest lesson: The triumph of the will, where reality surpassed humanity, beyond the good and evil of the gods. And lo, Eggers beheld that it was indeed the prophecy of Ragnarök; the gods of Viking and Crusader alike, not merely dying, but fleeing the great standard of the völkisch race of *übermensch,* or supermen.

Man was now the master of his own fate, devoid of any sin and savior.

This was what he had dreamt of ever since his childhood; his heart, emboldened with the revolutionary passion of warrior sacrifice. No longer did his fatherland have to bear the cross of shame and humiliation. Still, more tears gushed down his face, for he did not yet die so valiantly like the noble Germanic martyrs who had given their lives to the underground Reich as free men during the abortive Kapp Putsch on the Ides of March only a year prior, which Eggers concluded was foiled by the subversive intrigue of some Judeo-Bolshevik conspiracy. For now, the boy's glorious baptism by fire would have to be fulfilled another way. His First Lieutenant Karl Bergerhoff had already made his order especially clear to the younger volunteers: "No prisoners."

When a trench whistle shrilled and the church bells tolled, signaling the left flank's next rash charge, Eggers became filled with boyish and freebooting delight. He hastened to ready the explosive cartridges for his rifle, rested the rifle's bipod between two burlap sandbags, and opened fire. Plumes of dust kicked up from under the rifle with each crashing gunshot; he again cranked back the rifle's bolt, and bullet casings plinked to the earth as he loaded another round into the rifle's chamber. With every ant he squished in the valley, he couldn't help but cry out, "Our Heaven is all of this, the war on Earth!"

CHAPTER 16

The outskirts of Zouk Mikael
The Kesrouane District, the French Mandate of Lebanon
September 29th, 1938

In the night, a black car drove up a sinuous switchback road and parked at the tree line of a small glade in the cedar forest. In the car, Rahn and the SS-Standarte Kurt Eggers sat in darkness while the car's high beams shined broadly over the clearing. He was in the passenger seat while his morose secretary sat behind the wheel with his Luger rifle rested across his knees. The other two officers were in the rear seats, lying in wait in the event their scheduled rendezvous with their contact's emissary would have gone awry.

"Even if you are actually right about them going to Damascus," Eggers started, wiping at his watery eyes, "how would you even know where to look?"

"How many times must I repeat myself?" Rahn grumbled. "My associate always prated on about one specific place in the city; a place he referred to 'Sarras.' An island in Christian Grail legend claimed to be the promised coming of a 'New Jerusalem.' He never mentioned anything beyond that, but our contact here has worked both in Damascus and Jerusalem."

Eggers glanced sharply at Rahn and questioned, "Aren't you

supposed to be our Reichsführer's principal authority on the Grail's realms?"

Rahn shifted up in his seat and responded, "The Grail stone may have fallen somewhere in the Orient countless centuries ago, but it eventually traveled up to Southern France, and to this day, it is hidden somewhere in the heartlands of Catharism. But, be that as it may, this contact may have the necessary expertise to give us this missing piece to where these girls may believe *their* deluded interpretation of the Grail lies."

Eggers harrumphed. "Yes, the Foreign Office has told us about his repeated efforts to court the good will of our Führer. Reich Consul General Döhle told me that this man met with him last year, begging him to support the pathetic marshaling of his fracturing conspiracy of nationalists. I'm telling you Otto. He is going to try and haggle us for his help. You and I both know it's what the Arabs do, and I don't intend to make commitments that will get our bodies drawn and quartered by the Reichsführer's own death squad."

"But did you at least read his dossier from the embassy?" Rahn asked.

"Only the unredacted portions; I swear, I have never seen so much black ink on paper before."

Rahn's voice turned cautious. "Yes, well, just remember that his enemies are very many. Not only British and Zionist, but Saracen as well, and if he learns of our—"

"There," Eggers said abruptly, shifting up in his seat. "They're here now."

Rahn followed his eyes to the other end of the clearing. Illumed by the car's high beams were three Bedouin on horseback emerging from the tree line, their beasts rearing as they halted. Two of them wore black cloaks with black tagelmusts covering their entire faces except for the eyes. The third—their leader—wore a white thobe with a long black bisht flowing from his shoulders and covering his hands. While Rahn also noted the leader's full beard, he couldn't have discerned his face from the traditional agal-crowned keffiyeh headdress that hung over his eyes.

"They could be hiding their weapons under those clothes," Eggers whispered over to the two SS officers. "They might be willing to just kill and rob us now."

Rahn hushed admonishingly to Eggers. "The Arabs have too much at stake to do that to us. Right now, *we're* their best chance at any meaningful coordination against their enemies."

"Yeah? Well, be ready for anything."

"Just don't say anything to them!"

"What?" one of the officers shrugged as he fed a magazine into his Borchardt pistol's grip and racked the toggle. "They can't speak German, can they?"

Rahn let out an agitated sigh before opening his door and stepping out onto the glade. He adjusted his coat collar around his neck and approached the men apprehensively. The leading Bedouin dismounted and handed the reins of his beast's bobbing snout over to one of his escorts to hitch on the low-hanging branch of a nearby cedar.

"Paix soit sur vous," the Bedouin emissary greeted in good French before pulling a document from his sleeve and presenting it to Rahn. "You are the ones who sought an audience with my master, yes?"

Rahn warily looked back at the car before nodding uneasily. He then took the telegram from the emissary's hand, looked it over, and handed it back with a short nod. As Rahn did so, however, he saw a gold necklace with the three-barred cross of the Maronite Catholic Church hanging from the emissary's neck. Noticing this, the emissary concealed it under his collar before placing a hand over his heart.

"You will be glad to know," the emissary continued, "that your message has found my master in good health. As of now, however, he is under heavy French surveillance back in Zouk Mikael; he is still suborning his wardens, so it might be a few hours before he meets with you."

Rahn held his glare, unsure of what to make of the emissary's apparent Christian faith. After a while, the Obersturmführer looked down and sighed, "And did he tell you anything else?"

"Yes, we both want to impress upon you the possibility of abrogating your nation's Haavara Agreement with the Zionists," the emissary relayed. "We have enough of them being transferred from Germany into our homeland."

Rahn bobbed his head. "That is beyond my power, but I will be sure to convey your request to my Reichsführer."

"Nevertheless," the emissary said, raising his hand at him, "he told me that he is indeed very eager to help you in your mission."

"And did he say anything about providing us with better guns?" Rahn inquired.

The emissary waggled his head. "My master will need every resource available to our cause; he needs to conserve his Arab Higher Committee's authority among his other Muslim and Christian loyalists in Syria." After a pause, he chuckled and added, "I still don't understand why he continues to insist on peace with the British and condemns our retaliations, but I am quite relieved that he has decided to coordinate with his rebel headquarters in Damascus. He is finally coming to his senses after all these years; the Zionist and British aggressors have forced his hand."

Rahn glanced off to the tree line and saw one of the escorts running a flat hand along his horse's red roan flank; the Bedouin looked on with a suspicious and hostile regard before lowering his mouth-veil to hawk a phlegm down at the ground. The Obersturmführer looked back at the emissary and remarked cynically, "I have to say, for such a pious Mohammedan cleric, your master has always seemed all too eager to collaborate with Christians in his efforts against your peoples' little Zionist problem."

"Herr Rahn," the emissary started, "the great Emir 'Abd al-Qadir gave shelter to my grandmother and countless other Christians from the Druze militias' brutal massacres in Damascus during the civil war some eighty years ago. It is simply my wish to carry on that noble legacy with my master, and with your being here now, the city calls us once again to see to the prospect of the liberation of all our peoples from this Zionist-Crusader occupation."

With a knit brow, Rahn pressed the question: "But don't you or His Eminence resent all Jews? Don't *you* resent all Saracens? What is left of your faith's integrity with such open gates to those other, more heathen religions?"

The emissary chuckled again and said, "Our conflict was never meant to be religiously sectarian; Jew, Christian, or Muslim, for all of our important differences, we all ultimately confess the one true God,

Allah, over all of humanity. But you must understand that it is the Arabs who suffer equally at the mercy of the Zionist oppressor." Then, thoughtful in his manner, he added, "My master has also told me that he is thankful for this correspondence with you, for it was a sign from Allah that so encouraged him to pray for strength at the shrine of his ancestor: The Prophet's grandson, *alayhis salaam.*"

PART III

THE FALLOW

CHAPTER 17

The hinterlands of Damascus
The French Mandate of Syria
October 1st, 1938

T he motorcoach's jouncing suspension wasn't entirely different from Psalmodie's experience of the Orient and Taurus Expresses' bucking and shaking, although the sporadic rattling of the coach's windows and interior metal plating only added to the cacophony of the ride. The heat wave stuffing the air summoned up pungent smells of leather and latex from the seats' seams and torn upholstery, but it was not too unbearable.

Around the coach, families of all different walks of life sat in two sets of two chairs facing each other. Some had their coats or cloaks hung over their heads since the skies out the windows were pink with the first light of the unrisen dawn. Others, including the driver, perfumed the hot air with the rosy fragrance of Turkish water pipes called Nargilehs.

Psalmodie slouched in her seat while she ate chunks of caramel toffee from a small brown paper bag and browsed the pages of a newspaper she stole from a rotating book stand back on the Orient Express. Though the *Cœurs Vaillants* French Catholic newspaper was intended for a more juvenile audience, it consistently featured comics of her childhood hero.

But when she heard a faint murmuring and clicking of beads across from her, she looked up and saw that Francis was already awake. He was sitting at the window seat and looking over the passing faces of every building, gleaming a sun-bleached, off-white color in the coming glare of daybreak. Dangling from his right hand was a threaded assortment of beads, with a coin-sized oval medal hanging over his forefinger. Shiloh slept lightly in the seat next to him with her head resting on his shoulder.

Psalmodie extended the bag to him and broke the silence, "Toffee?"

The Jesuit Brother's praying fell quiet as he stole a brief glance at Psalmodie before turning it back out the window. Psalmodie withdrew her bag, and from the long silence that persisted, she didn't know if he had already resumed his prayers.

She licked her lips and wiped them with her forefinger before setting her newspaper and toffee bag on the empty seat to her left. "She's having those dreams about Mary again, isn't she?" she asked. When she saw Francis look down with a smile, she pondered aloud, "I can't really blame her; I would take all the help I can get as well."

Francis grinned wearily. He thumbed the last few beads of his rosary before setting it down on Shiloh's lap, careful not to move his shoulders and wake her. When he looked over to Psalmodie, her discomfited eyes had already withdrawn towards the sun's white glare peeking over the sloping horizon.

"So, uh..." he prompted hesitantly, "do you believe in God, Psalmodie?"

Psalmodie shot a confused smirk at him. "Do you Jesuits always start your conversations this way?"

Francis backpedaled with a grin. "I'm sorry, um... You know wh—Never mind."

His bumbling elicited a half-chuckle from Psalmodie; for a moment, she appreciated his pleasant aura, as if he were a favorite cousin. Then, Psalmodie's face shifted with noncommittal reflection as she took a moment to think about his question. "'To love another person is to see the face of God,'" she replied unassertively.

Francis looked at her and placed the quote she said. "That's, uh... That's Victor Hugo, isn't it?"

Psalmodie was charmed by the Jesuit's reception of her attitude, although almost every consideration Psalmodie paid to God had the life-span of a yawn; to her, her own life passed by in front of her with unre-flected immediacy. Even so, she was still afraid of giving too much importance to her statement. "I don't know; I've been lapsing in my faith lately... I do pray sometimes, but as I feel myself longing for more intimacy, I only find myself questioning God's silence. Now I'm starting to believe that there really is no right question to ask anymore."

She then stared down at her folded hands and added, "And I *have* heard incredibly moving stories of enemy soldiers coming together for Christmas on no man's land during the Great War... but then again, where was He when the so-called 'Devil's Anvil' continued for *four years* after that? I'm far from communist, but I think I understand Marx when he says that religion is like the 'opiate' of the masses, always distracting us from that nagging question of the world's countless sufferings and evils, don't you?"

Francis remarked, "Certainly, we Manchus have had more than our fair share of experiences with opium, courtesy of the East India Trading Company—your beloved King Arthur's colonial heirs over in Hong Kong." When Psalmodie smirked and rolled her eyes at his comment, Francis's laugh wore away and he assured her, "No, but your point is well-taken; in fact, I think there comes a point where all talk of God's existence becomes His vindication as all-loving and all-powerful amidst so much meaningless suffering. But frankly, I don't feel that this myste-rious question is one that anyone will ever definitively answer."

"Yes, but it's also more than evil simply existing against infinite goodness," Psalmodie added, looking down at her hands again. "What even *is* the good if the gods exist?"

Francis frowned at her. "What do you mean?"

"Well... have you read any of Plato's Socratic dialogues?" Psalmodie asked.

Francis looked suspiciously at her. "Hold on, please don't tell me we're going to be looking for the lost island of Atlantis after this, are we?"

Psalmodie gave a short laugh. "No, no, that one's definitely a myth; no, I'm referring to the dilemma in his *Euthyphro* dialogue: If the gods exist, do they will something simply because it is good by its very nature? Or is something good because the gods will it? If either of these horns are true, then morality itself is either independent of the gods' existence or it's just some baseless, arbitrary idea dreamt up by the gods, who offer us no objective and self-evident reason for a right action; in that case, what is the point in us trying at all? What is truth?"

"I know exactly what you mean," Francis said.

Psalmodie looked up at him with renewed interest. "You do?"

"Yes, I'm still searching for the gods' place in our world, especially with the way it's going," Francis reflected.

A relieved laugh came in Psalmodie's voice. "I mentioned all this to Monsignor Jean and other people at his church, and for some really annoying reason, they all accuse me of learning these doubts from Shiloh."

"Well, it does sound like something she'd bring up," Francis said. "She takes every opportunity she can get to tell me that were it not for the medieval Arab world, especially in Islamic Spain and Baghdad, much of what we know about mathematics, medicine, and the ancient writings of Plato and Aristotle would have never made it into the West."

"So what if I learned it from Shiloh?" Psalmodie challenged. "Was she wrong to bring it up at all? Besides, every time she and I talk about it, *she's* the one who keeps lecturing me about tired old Catholic ideas like Pascal's Wager. Look, I understand that there might be important differences between the 'gods of the philosophers' and the God of Abraham as Shiloh keeps insisting. However, I'm still not at all convinced that just believing in any gods will automatically guarantee some sense of grace or fulfillment.

"The philosophers of the ancient and medieval world never really found a primordial truth and our modern philosophers can't seem to agree on a final truth for all history. I don't think *I'll* come any closer to understanding the 'Alpha and Omega.' But it's not like I'm consciously *choosing* to deny that God exists; it's just that I can't really bring myself to reconcile Him with this world I've come to know. I just can't use God to explain everything without explaining anything."

At first, Psalmodie expected the Jesuit to offer her something in the way of spiritual reassurance. Instead, she saw him fleet a glance down at the crown of Shiloh's head before looking back up at Psalmodie again. After rubbing his mouth and chin, Francis tried to deflect Psalmodie's curiosity by angling in with another question: "Well, we are on a 'Grail' quest of sorts, and I know that we're only doing it to trade it in for your father. But do you at least *wonder* about Him?"

"Who? God?"

Francis gestured vaguely. "Well, yes, but I meant Jesus more specifically; it is *His* relic after all."

Psalmodie shrugged one shoulder. "I mean, who *doesn't* wonder about Him at some point in their lives?" She looked back up at Francis and saw that he looked unconvinced. With a sigh, she indulged his question and groped for some other answer; the pleasant memories of her house-proud mother's strait-laced, yet solacing faith were fleeting. She answered, "Only in asking myself how a Jewish carpenter would have handled the hard choices."

Francis read Psalmodie's face. "And has it worked for you?"

Psalmodie paused for thought. "It's strange..." she continued. "He's something I barely think about now... but He's also something I can't imagine living without, sort of like breathing... I guess, to answer your question, I'm trying to find Him *without* God as I go along if that makes sense." She shot a glance at Shiloh, still asleep on Francis' shoulder, before intimating to Francis something more from her wavering judgment: "I miss Him."

A cathedral-like silence fell on the coach again save the same continuing sounds of the coach's moving parts. Psalmodie cast her gaze to the floor while Francis looked at her with a reserved regard. It was then that a shadow swam over them from the windows before the coach's wheels rolled over a steel plate embedded in the gravel road. The truck's rattling engine then hissed and squeaked to a stop.

Shiloh woke up, sniffing and clearing her throat before sitting up and craning forward to look out Francis' window. "Are we here?" she asked.

Psalmodie looked at Francis and felt her anticipation soar, as if some royal ceremony awaited them somewhere outside; she thought she heard the rumble and clangor of kettledrums, heralding the exotic grandiosity of the immortal city towards her. "I believe we are," she responded, standing up to reach for her satchel in the overhead compartment.

CHAPTER 18

Midhat Pasha Souq, the Old City of Damascus

Her opulent majesty, the City of Jasmine; the very crossroads of the East and the West.

The Via Recta, also known in the New Testament as the "Street Called Straight," was the main Roman road of Damascus running east to west through the Old City, where the *Acts of the Apostles* maintained that Saul of Tarsus—the Pharisee who persecuted the earliest Christians—found shelter after famously witnessing Jesus' apparition and converting to Christianity, becoming known as the Apostle Paul.

The road adjoining Ahl al-Bayt Street was congested with cars, horse-drawn coaches, and red cable trams driving along grooved rails in the street's central reserve. The Nairn Transport Company's coach split from the traffic and parked before the westernmost fraction of the Street Called Straight, a vibrant bazaar, or *souq,* jostling with trade and commerce and canopied by high-arching metal roofs connecting buildings across the street from one another.

Amid the countless tropical fruit stands and ochre-colored spice stalls, many clay tandoor oven bakeries and open-air grills wafted out sheets of smoke to lure passersby to the fresh, pillowy flatbreads and sizzling and spitting rotisserie *halal* meat skewers they had to offer. The lush and voluminous growths of green jasmine and magenta bougainvillea vines for which the city had become famous flowed from street's overhanging planters and crawled up the trellises of long wooden arbours down the other end of the street.

As the musical strings of Mediterranean lutes and the high-pitched trilling of ney flutes filled the air, textile merchants and auctioneers haggled over the many exotic, yet moth-eaten Persian rugs, Greek silks, and Chinese tapestries that hung in display from the numerous verandas of street booths. While Silk Road Bedouin caravans with heavily laden pack mules and baggage camel trains wearily trailed in from the winding streets, handcart hawkers and grimy child street peddlers—some of whom looked more like common loiterers or even beggars—loudly advertised their sundries.

Shiloh stepped out from the coach onto the sunbaked gravel road and smelled the sweet, green fragrance of jasmine and fresh citrus blossoms, muted by the smell of dust and car exhaust. She looked with reverent majesty at the imposing splendor of this, the *true* Eternal City; having outlived empire after empire for countless centuries, Damascus was Rome long before Rome was Rome. The other two followed shortly behind her. Though Francis still donned his robe and Shiloh continued wearing her kerchief over her hair, Psalmodie wore her shawl as a headscarf to blend in with the locals. Even so, the crowds being crammed nearly shoulder-to-shoulder made the trio hard to notice anyways.

"Okay," Psalmodie said, falling into step beside Shiloh. "What was it you said you needed to explain your reasoning on the True Cross' location?"

"I need the Hadith book collections."

"And what are they exactly?"

"Like I've said the last ten thousand times," Shiloh answered peevishly, "they're ancient records of the Islamic prophetic tradition."

The coach was still discharging more passengers when the driver shouted an announcement over the crowds in Arabic, Turkish, and French. The two girls kept trying to talk through the overlapping chatter.

"But wait a minute. What about your father's telegram?" Shiloh remembered, whirling on Psalmodie. "You know. That whole business with the rose and sword?"

"I thought about this on the coach. At first, I thought it was because Damascus was famous for its Damask roses and Damask steel popularly used to craft swords, but there was something particular about my father's phraseology: 'The way is a rose to the sword in the stone.' I really don't think an Arthurian semiotician like my father would have made a statement like that without alluding to something more. There's definitely something there."

"Okay, so what do you think King Arthur has to do with Damascus then?"

Psalmodie put her hands on her hips and mulled over the sandy road. "Remember my first story on the Orient Express? The one with Saladin and his captured Crusaders?"

"The Battle of Hattin?" Shiloh shot a perplexed look at her. "Of course I do. Why?"

"Remember how he mercifully gave the King of Jerusalem a goblet of icy *rose* water?"

Though Psalmodie saw Shiloh drawing the connection, her expression remained unimpressed.

"Okay," Shiloh said, "but you still haven't answered my question. Where does your father place *King Arthur* in all of this?"

Psalmodie continued, "As I'm sure you already know, Saladin's main counterparts during the Third Crusade were the Holy Roman Emperor, Frederick Barbarossa, and the much-venerated Plantagenet King of England, Richard the Lionheart. On Richard's way to the Holy Land, however, he met with the Norman King of Sicily at the port of Messina. But before he left for the Holy Land, he gave him something..."

"A sword?" Shiloh inclined eagerly, knowing what she was driving at.

A delighted Psalmodie modulated her enlivened tone. "...and King Richard claimed it was actually Excalibur, which was the 'Sword in the Stone' according to Arthurian legend."

Shiloh's eyes squinted dubiously at Psalmodie. "But that doesn't make sense. Didn't your father say the way is a rose *to* the sword or is it something that only a—" She broke off, whirling back towards Francis' direction. "Brother?" she called.

Francis was still by the coach's steps, his shoulder leaned against the folded door. He was speaking to the driver, although his words were muted by the distance Shiloh and Psalmodie were from him. With one thumb, he counted through the different coins in his palm.

Shiloh approached him and tugged his arm. "Brother, come on, tip him already. We really need to get a hold of those books." When Francis didn't respond, she asked, "What? What is it?"

Francis reached into his pockets and came up with another handful of coins. "The coach is bound for Jaffa, and I think I have enough francs here for a connection to Jerusalem."

Shiloh stood looking at him uncertainly. Then her cursory glance sobered upon following his gaze to the schedule clipped above the driver's seat. Her eyes rested back on the ground, and she took a moment to register the decision she was sure he already made in his heart.

Francis paused for a moment and said, "That convent in Jerusalem I told the conductor about? The convent for Saint Vincent de Paul? The Daughters of Charity? I think the nuns there might take me in; hopefully Monsignor Jean will vouch for me once I call him from there or something."

"Are you sure you really want to do this?" Shiloh broached, eying him carefully. "What brought this on?"

Francis stood in silence before answering her, "I know my Jesuit vocation, but it's been a little while since I've prayed for my parents in Peiping, and I've heard from the Society that some of my Manchu comrades have it pretty horrible under the Japanese Emperor." He gazed off towards the horizon. "I feel the city is so close. I'm thinking that the very least I can do for them is to offer my petitions to God for them from Jerusalem so that maybe one day they could come back to me—"

He was cut off by Shiloh suddenly clutching her arms around him. Stunned and unsure of himself, Francis slowly brought his arms around her. He looked up and again noticed Psalmodie met his gaze with a mild expression.

But his brow furrowed, and he pulled away from Shiloh's hug. "Wait—no," he said, shaking his head as if to clear it. "No, this is wrong. I helped bring you two here; I can't just *leave* you now. I should go with you."

Shiloh gave him a reassuring smile. "So, you presume we can't watch over ourselves?"

"No, it's just..." He loosed a sigh, ill at ease. "How long have we been hunting God together, huh? You and me. I just don't want you to think I'm now choosing Him over you."

"Oh?" Shiloh said with coquetry. "As if you haven't done that already?"

Francis took a breath to respond, only to linger for a moment as he fought a rush of feeling; with his gaze, he caressed her face before turning it down at the ground while a sheepish grin grew over his face.

"*Touché*, Shiloh," he ultimately said, "although I do have something for you." He reached into his cassock's breast pocket and pulled out his rosary. He pointed to the oval devotional medal linking the threads. On it was a relief image of the Virgin Mary standing on the Earth with a snake crushed under her heel with two rays of light shooting out from her palms.

"I know you told me you have a lot to figure out," Francis said, putting a hand to Shiloh's shoulder, "but I can't hear her voice like you can, which is why I want to go to—" He stopped short, seeing Shiloh twining her fingertips under her neck as she looked up at him expectantly; she swallowed the lump in her throat despite her faltering demeanor. Without bringing himself to finish his words, he folded her fingers over the rosary and clasped her fist with both hands. "Whatever you feel God calling you to be, just..."

Though Francis fell silent, Shiloh felt an ellipsis he wanted to fill. Saving him the trouble, she simply put her other hand over his. "Let me go, Brother..." she crooned. "You go on and take care of yourself."

Francis leaned in for one last embrace, whispering into Shiloh's hair, "I'll try." When he finally let her go, he walked back towards the coach; just as he stepped on the running board before the steps, he took one last look at them both.

Psalmodie, hesitating at first, came up next to Shiloh and called out to Francis, "Thank you, Brother!" She then put a hand on Shiloh's shoulder and said delicately, "I don't know about you, but I think we could use some coffee right now before we can find those books you said you need to—"

Francis' voice called out to her from one of the coach's windows. "Hey Psalmodie!"

Psalmodie looked up and saw Francis leaning out one of the coach's windows while waving the folded *Cœurs Vaillants* newspaper she left on the coach. After he tossed it over to her, she caught it and flipped it to the comic she was reading.

Les Aventures de Tintin.

"Next time, pick a better issue of the series to lift! Fare thee well, noble knights!" Francis jested, sending them off with a two-finger salute before sitting back down in his original seat. Once the coach hissed to life, it pulled away for the other end of the street.

He was gone.

"Thank you... my *huli xiangtou*," Shiloh whispered, looking on in pensive admiration before joining Psalmodie in threading through the bustling din of the Arabian bazaar. Shiloh saw that Psalmodie was guzzling the rest of her toffee crumbs from her paper bag.

When Psalmodie noticed Shiloh staring, she stopped and offered, "Do you want the rest? I want to get coffee anyways."

Shiloh looked off, shaking her head with a small smile.

Psalmodie followed shortly behind her and mumbled, "Well, you look like you could also use a cup."

CHAPTER 19

Al-Hariqa neighborhood

5:00 a.m. It was still early for the sleepy Hindustani teahouse Shiloh and Psalmodie had entered to host any patrons for breakfast. The soft honks of light morning traffic and the chirring of cicadas cut through the hot summer-like air outside. Inside, Shiloh heard a phonograph playing quietly somewhere: Music from Kashmir or Punjab perhaps. At the foot of the doorway were a twined stack of old newspapers and, though Shiloh couldn't read Sanskrit, she smiled when she recognized a photo of the man's bespectacled face on the front page.

She had already greatly admired Mohandas Gandhi's pacifistic disobedience to the British Raj in India, but she was even more captivated by how he single-handedly moved the minds and hearts of Hindus, Muslims, and the so-called 'untouchable' caste of his society alike by calling them all to universal brotherhood, spiritual liberation, and even a mutual understanding with their colonial oppressors. Of course, sectarian violence stubbornly persisted, but only time would tell what the Mahatma would accomplish with his ever-increasing following.

But when Shiloh noticed a rill of water running through the grouted terracotta tile floor next to the newspapers, she looked up to scan the parlor and saw the lone, aproned young man inattentively mopping a water spillage in between the tables. Though Shiloh and Psalmodie were apparently the first patrons of the day, when the man looked up at them and saw Psalmodie in particular, he dropped his mop handle and ran off into another room with a gleeful look.

"Okay..." Psalmodie said queerly. "Well, there goes my morning tonic."

"Psalmodie, really?" Shiloh complained. "Your creature comforts really can't wait?"

"After our long journey, I *really* need some caffeine and silence to concentrate right now." Psalmodie looked up at the card over the register stand offering a wide selection of hot drinks, tarts, and pastries. "There is way too much music outside and the stuff those vendors are selling doesn't look all that sanitary."

"Psalmodie, we *really* need those books, and we can't just be—"

The sudden sound of clattering pots from the kitchen startled them both. They then saw that the young man had clumsily rushed back in to receive them, reading from a small booklet with that same fawning smile. *"Uhh... Bonjour—er—Enchanté!"* he exclaimed in broken French. After a moment, he stiffly took both of their hands and kissed their knuckles, still reading from the booklet as if he were fastidiously following the instructions to even do that. *"Fa-faire vous... uhh... si-siège?"* he continued, motioning towards the other end of the shop.

Psalmodie bit back a smile before mouthing the teasing words "puppy dog" to her cross-armed companion. Shiloh gave a perfunctory smile, although she remained mostly unamused. Psalmodie adopted a shapelier posture and indulged him. *"Deux s'il vous plaît,"* she fluted, gentle with his amateur pronunciation.

The man then eagerly led them to a round bistro table by a large and wavy glass block window overlaid by a stone quatrefoil lattice. Outside, the lush fronds of three sloping palm trees swayed gently, making the soft sepia light from the just-dawning sun dapple over the table.

"Assiez-toi," he said, gesturing for them to sit on the bentwood chairs.

As they did so, Psalmodie snickered at his *faux pas* of an attempt at a French welcome while Shiloh reciprocated with another cordial smile.

"Merci beaucoup," Shiloh said.

The man flipped through the dog-eared pages of his booklet, titled with the Arabic word *Faransi,* meaning "French."

Shiloh raised a hand towards him and switched to Arabic. "It's alright. I can translate for her if you want."

The man looked down at Shiloh, and although he had a pleased look, his shoulders relaxed as he put the small booklet in the front pocket of his white apron. "What can I get you two?" he asked Shiloh, taking out his pen and pad.

Psalmodie asked, "I think I saw on your card up there that you have the rosy *café au lait* with cardamom and vanilla almond milk?" Shiloh relayed her order to him and declined to order for herself, but just as he was about to turn, Psalmodie quickly added, "Oh! And some lavender in it if you can." Mildly annoyed, Shiloh sighed and translated the request. The man then nodded genially at them before leaving for the bead-curtained kitchen entrance behind the counter at the other end of the parlor. Shiloh's eyes followed after him before she looked back at Psalmodie and noticed the suggestive look on her face.

"What?" Shiloh said.

"Don't you deny it," Psalmodie chaffed. "He seems rather sweet, doesn't he?"

"Uh, no," Shiloh scoffed defensively. "Don't get any funny ideas."

"What? He's clumsy and maybe a little eager, but you have to admit, he is making quite an effort," Psalmodie said before seeing the front Shiloh was putting up. "Oh, come on, Shiloh, I saw the way you two were looking at each other; you know you can't hide these things from us Parisian *mesdames.*"

"What things? There are no 'things' that I'm hiding from—"

When the man returned, Shiloh straightened up in her seat; he had an earthen clay tea cup and saucer garnished with dried rosebud petals, a sprig of lavender, and flaky sugar cubes along the edge. When he set the coffee down on the table, he wafted up the coffee's rosy fragrance to Psalmodie. He exchanged another look with both of them, although he spent more time looking at Shiloh. Then, without another word, he left again for the register stand by the front.

Psalmodie swirled the lavender sprig in her coffee and kept pestering Shiloh. "You really haven't had anyone interested in you, huh?"

Shiloh forced a weary exhale. "Ugh. What?" She braced herself for another one of Psalmodie's risqué "talks."

"At the university? Not a one?"

At first, Shiloh perked up and put on an impassive front to stall Psalmodie's prying. However, upon stealing once more to the waiter at the cashier, she sighed hesitantly and put a hand to her nape. Psalmodie dropped a sugar cube into her cup and took a sip while she looked out the window to the sun-drenched street.

"I haven't exactly had much luck with anyone since Brother Francis," Shiloh capitulated, "but that was quite a while ago."

Psalmodie nearly gagged on her hot beverage and gawked at Shiloh as if she were a new discovery. "Wait a minute—what do you mean 'since Brother Francis?'"

"I mean I haven't courted anyone." Shiloh noticed Psalmodie's shock. "Why? What's wrong?"

"You mean you actually *dated* him?" Psalmodie asked, her voice kicking up an octave.

"You really didn't know about us two?" Shiloh asked with wonder, as if she couldn't believe Psalmodie's astonishment.

"No, I did not know about 'you two!'" Psalmodie exclaimed, drawling out her answer as if Shiloh's question were an absurdly stupid one.

"You haven't heard the name he always calls me?"

Psalmodie's eyes narrowed in sarcasm. "No, Shiloh, in case you didn't know, I have never learned to speak Chinese."

"Manchu," Shiloh corrected.

Psalmodie didn't quite hear her. "What?"

"He speaks Manchu. I mean, it isn't exactly 'Chinese' per se, but it actually has more in common with the Siberian Altaic languages, and the old writing system is actually based on the more ancient—"

"Whatever," Psalmodie said, looking at Shiloh with a newfound esteem. "Shiloh, I'm surprised—*actually* impressed... and it looks like the altar boy does have a heart after all."

Shiloh tutted with a grin despite herself. "And here I was thinking that I couldn't hide these things from you 'Parisian *mesdames.*'"

Psalmodie leaned in, eager to be even more amused. "I mean, I do see the charisma, but doesn't he—I don't know—have that pesky vow of chastity or something?"

Shiloh smiled bashfully at a memory of adolescent dalliance. "Well... just between us, Psalmodie, he definitely wasn't *born* a Jesuit, but I think that's all he'd let me tell you." She paused, then added with a small laugh, "The way he talks to me... Sometimes, I think he still has his head in the clouds."

Psalmodie slumped back in her chair in a pantomime of her own astonishment. She opened her mouth for another inquiry, but she shook her head instead. Shiloh was feeling more confident, holding her gaze with the waiter at longer intervals.

"Well..." Psalmodie began, "if you feel you had your fill of men after Brother Francis, I'm sure he has a couple of extra habits from the Daughters of Charity; you'll probably get a *glowing* recommendation from him."

"Shut up," Shiloh said, idly wringing her hands over the table.

Psalmodie exaggerated Francis' manly voice to tease her friend. "'Oh yes, Monsignor Jean, she is quite holy. Don't worry about the hats either; she's already used to wearing the horns around me.'" When Psalmodie saw Shiloh's growing aggravation, Psalmodie laughed and threw her hands up in mock surrender. "Alright, fine. I'll stop now, but it might interest you to know that I have just gotten an idea for finding your books."

"No," Shiloh said, suspecting where Psalmodie was going with this.

"Hey, the books were *your* idea."

"But it's *your* Grail quest."

"Our Grail quest, Shiloh! Listen, just *ask* him if he's Muslim and if he happens to have them in his—"

"This is a coffee shop, not a library."

"Well, I'm just saying while we're here, we can at least *try*. You said we'd find those books in the library of al-Zahiriyah anyway, but maybe we might just find copies here. Either way, we're going to find them eventually." Psalmodie looked at her with a gleaning stare. "That is, unless puppy dog's *savoir faire* daunts you."

Shiloh glowered at Psalmodie, but upon trading one more fugitive glance at the waiter, she shut her eyes and let out an exasperated sigh. She took a moment to gather herself, fixing her loose curls under her kerchief. She scraped back her chair and stood to check the backs of her legs and brush the seat of her pants. With her mien finally composed, she started for the front desk.

"Hey Shiloh!" Psalmodie called jocularly, beaming at her. "Once he thrusts, *don't* parry."

"Ugh, you're the worst," Shiloh grimaced, whirling away from her with a full body eye roll.

Still shaking off the image, she walked over to the waiter at the register stand; he was sitting on an adjacent table away from their front desk's direction, diligently writing Arabic annotations in the margins of his French booklet. But just when Shiloh was about to call his attention, the shopkeeper's bell chimed, and two grimy little girls in rags rushed in and chirped at the waiter; he chirped back, pointing towards two small Greek baklava pastries at the far end of the desk behind him. As he did so, he caught sight of Shiloh standing by the desk, grabbing her own elbow.

Psalmodie was still watching them. "Hey, ladies!" she beckoned the little girls eating their dessert. "Hey, do you want to see something? Look over there! Probably the closest we'll ever get to seeing courtly love nowadays." The girls naively joined Psalmodie in observing the pair from afar, as if on safari; but when Psalmodie made a heart shape with her hands to them, they finally understood and looked on with childish glee.

But Psalmodie's teasing aside, Shiloh gestured her fingertips towards her brow and greeted the waiter, *"Aadaab."*

The waiter set down the booklet on its face and answered back in Arabic, *"Marhaba,* although my upbringing was not Urdu."

Shiloh couldn't help but look back at Psalmodie and the little girls one more time, only to see them give an encouraging shooing gesture. Shiloh looked diffidently back at the young waiter and saw that he had already drawn closer to her with his elbows leaned over the stand. She kept her distance, though a subverted smile played over her face.

"So, are you Muslim?" she found herself blurting. In that same instant, she looked away and shut her eyes, almost panicking at the unbefitting nature of her question; she heard Psalmodie playfully shushing the girls' giggling behind her. The inquisitive waiter cracked a joking frown at them and ran his hand through his wavy combed over hair before rubbing his whiskers and the medium stubble on his chin.

"Nice to meet you too, mademoiselle," he joked. "*Je m'appelle* Malik al-Hakim."

With her eyes still lowered, Shiloh wiped her chin against her shoulder, timidly trying to hide her blush. "I'm sorry. My name is Shiloh. It's just that my friend over there has trouble understanding a couple of things about the Holy Qur'an. Yes, I know this is a restaurant, but we were just wondering if you happen to have any *Arabic* Hadiths somewhere. It was hard to find ones not written in Turkic from where we came and the closest library is at the other end of al-Hariqa."

"Yes, I can imagine," Malik said. "My best friend just came back from the Red Apple; he told me that Kemal Atatürk's atheistic Turkic translations of those collections are in every single bookshop there." He firmed his lips into a teasing smile. "But anyways, which ones?"

Shiloh shut her eyes as she recalled the names of the texts she was looking for. "Um... I think they are... 'Prophets' in *Sahih al-Bukhari* and 'Tribulations' in *Sahih Muslim.*"

"Oh?" Malik reacted. "Pulling out the big guns, I see; just what are you trying to prove to her exactly?"

"I just want to verify something before I'm sure enough to say anything to her," Shiloh said, "and I want to work with two of the most reliable Hadiths. Do you have them?"

A look of distant consideration swam over Malik's face. He clicked his tongue and simply said, "I might."

"You *might?*" she asked, getting a hint of his good nature.

"Sure," Malik said, turning his head away from her with a simpered bearing. "I just might. But I suppose that will just have to depend on something."

Shiloh gave him an arch look. "Depend on what?"

Malik parroted her first question, "'Are *you* Muslim?'"

The question took her aback, but she humored him. "And how would you know I'm not?"

"Let me answer that with another question: Are you also Egyptian by chance?"

Shiloh's coy smile fell, realizing what he was looking down at: The Coptic cross tattoo on her wrist. A mark of identity among Egyptian Christians. At first, she wanted to pull her rolled-up sleeve over it, but she stopped, and her demure smile came back when she recognized Malik's Levantine Arabic dialect.

"You're not Egyptian, are you?" she asked before adding, "Funny. I would have thought you were visiting from Paris; your French is so impeccable!"

Malik chuckled. "No, no, I'm neither Egyptian nor French. Many people that come through here are from those two places, but my father is from Jabal Nablus down in Palestine. He settled here in al-Sham after the British and the Zionist settlers chased him out of his childhood home. He invested whatever life-savings he had left to start this humble teahouse."

A charmed Shiloh leaned in with her cheeks and lips cupped in her palms. "And where is he now?"

"You mean at this time of day? I'm not sure, but I think he might still be on the main street of Hayy al-Yahud..."

"The Jewish quarter? What would he be doing there?"

Malik motioned his hand around the restaurant. "As you can probably see, business isn't what it used to be when he first started up his enterprise. I mind the store every day, but to keep it afloat, he works on his off-time as a taxi driver for some wealthy Jewish families there. And sometimes—not all, but sometimes—, he works with the Nairn Transport Company to bring them to al-Quds, sometimes well into midnight."

"Jerusalem?" Shiloh exclaimed with an intrigued tone. "Some clients he has, huh?"

"Yes, well, my guess is he's still stubbornly parked there for some excuse to visit his homeland; the last place men rose to the heavens." He lapsed deeply into quiet reflection. "Although, I must say, I almost never get to see him."

Shiloh saw the remembering in his expression, his youth flickering in his eyes. Though she sensed the change in Malik's tone, her sweet smile remained; she let him savor her company, if only for a moment. Her carefree eyes casually wandered around the shop and her head swayed slightly to the quiet music from the café's phonograph. When her gaze came back on Malik, she cleared her throat, wanting to get back on topic amid the awkward silence. "So, you will let me borrow those Hadiths then?"

Malik's eyes began to clear. "Yes... Yes, I'll uh..." He walked off, parting the beaded curtains and entering into a back room. Whatever sore past he had with his father, Shiloh saw it manifested in his every movement. When Malik returned, he had both books in one hand and a glass cup filled with a pink pomegranate milk sharbat in the other. He set them on the table and slid them over to Shiloh.

Shiloh grinned at his kind gesture, reaching for the loose change in her jerkin pocket. "Here, let me pay for our drinks."

Malik waved her off. "No, no, no, your money isn't any good to me; your drinks will be complimentary today." He patted the books and added, "I also have an Arabic Bible, a Qur'an, and some Talmudic collections if you would like to take a look at those as well."

Shiloh's grin broadened. "You should know... I'm only visiting al-Sham to show my friend around. I probably won't even be here by tomorrow."

"That's quite alright," he said, canting his head towards Psalmodie and the girls, who made a playful pretense of yawning and stretching out her arms to steal a passing glance back at them before going back to their drink and snack. Malik looked back at Shiloh and gave her a spirited shrug. "Nothing wrong with practicing the 'romance language' whenever I can, no?"

Shiloh answered with a warm smile of affection. She would have blushed again, but to her, there was something about Malik that felt oddly familiar; though she had only met him, she wasn't even sure if it was a romantic sentiment. She thought it to be something more intimate, as if she had known him all her life. She wished to confess the feeling to him somehow, but she knew no words that would have even begun to qualify it. She could have only said one thing that at least somewhat resembled an appropriate expression of what she had truly felt.

"I'm sure your father still loves you, Malik," she ultimately said.

Shiloh saw Malik reach for his booklet on his table and flip to a conspicuous red bookmark. After reading over the page, he slapped the covers together and met her with an avid gaze.

"*Si Dieu le veut,*" he said with a short, courtly bow.

Shiloh regarded Malik with warm appreciation. Then, taking the books and the sweating sharbat glass, she pushed away from the stand, reticent in manner. She held Malik's coquettish gaze for a short while longer before concluding with a meek half wave at him. Just as she turned around, the giggly little girls nearly ran into her as they chased each other out the teahouse. Then Shiloh looked back at Psalmodie and saw her lopsided grin; she said nothing and simply set the books on the round table.

"I'm glad you're finally making friends your own age," Shiloh remarked dryly.

When Psalmodie noticed the sharbat Shiloh set on the table, she poked, "So...? How did it go with him?"

Shiloh took a sip of the creamy pink beverage, feigning apathy despite her musing look. "He's nice enough."

"Yes, I saw the way he was looking at you." Psalmodie ran her finger along the rim of her cup. "But of course, we've both been under a lot of stress," she said inside a yawn. "He could have just been looking at that spot on your nose."

Shiloh alarmedly darted her eyes towards her faint reflection in the window to her right. She checked her nose and found no such thing, but when she looked back at Psalmodie, she noticed her stifled giggle.

"I hate you so much," Shiloh hissed, self-consciously putting a hand to her nose. "You know I have my life back in Paris and he has his here. That is all."

"Oh well," Psalmodie shrugged, "another lifetime, maybe. And it's probably for the best anyway; the last man that dated you swore off women, so I guess I can understand the—"

"Okay, Psalmodie," Shiloh said flatly. Paying little mind to Psalmodie, Shiloh pulled the two books closer to her and lovingly skated her hand over their gold-trimmed covers. "If you're finished dreaming about your dandy romances, shall we come to your *Grail* romances?" she said, pointing to the Arabic titles.

Sahih al-Bukhari
صحيح البخاري

Sahih Muslim
صحيح مسلم

CHAPTER 20

Though Psalmodie knew that Shiloh was definitely more religious than her, Shiloh was also, somehow, usually more skeptical than her. Even so, as Psalmodie saw Shiloh sorting through her own thoughts, Psalmodie couldn't help but wonder if the prospect of the True Cross had brought Shiloh's reasoning down to her level. For a moment, Psalmodie considered her friend before joining in her scrutiny of the books stacked before her.

Psalmodie knew less than Shiloh, but she had already known that the two books, among numerous others, formed part of a large corpus of ancient traditions known as Hadiths, which were chronicles on the birth of Islam and the teachings of the Prophet Muhammad himself rather than the providential revelations of the Qur'an that had supposedly become unto him from God Himself through the Angel Gabriel.

The Hadith collections, therefore, only served as the contextual lens through which the Qur'an was interpreted and the Sunnah—the wont of the Prophet's life—was appropriately imitated.

"I don't understand how any of this applies to the Grail legends," Psalmodie said, reading the Romanized subtitles of the Hadiths. "I mean, I was made aware from Rahn's work that the 13th-century Bavarian trouvère of the famous *Parzival* romance claimed to have worked off of an Arabic alchemical manuscript that a Provençal poet received from Moorish Spain. But that particular interpretation of the Holy Grail was a mystical stone and, despite all of the völksich occult nonsense in Otto Rahn's books, it was supposedly meant to mirror the Black Stone in Mecca."

Shiloh snickered. "I'm not really that surprised, considering that it wouldn't have been the first time Christian culture 'stole' from the Islamic Golden Age. I'm not as familiar with Arthurian legend as you or your German—er—'friend,' but I do know that the courtly and romantic lyric poetry of your beloved medieval trouvères was likely a transmission of the Arabic Andalusian *tarab* genre of music from Northern Spain to Southern France. It's therefore possible that without the Spanish Islamic musical tradition, your Grail legends would have never been inspired."

Psalmodie tilted her head, doubting the validity of Shiloh's claim. "Were it not for *Saladin,* certainly, the Grail legends would have never been inspired," she said, pointing at the Hadiths, "and now, I'm starting to imagine that these books here have something to do with his story? So do tell, Mademoiselle 'Abrahamic cosmo—however-you-spell-out-that-word: What do the traditions of Islam have to teach us about the location of the True Cross itself?"

Shiloh smirked at her friend's attempt to pronounce her métier. "Not necessarily Islam itself, but how our friend Saladin might have referred to its doctrines so as to figure out what he would have done with it."

"What kind of doctrines?" Psalmodie asked.

"As you may already know, Jesus Christ is considered the penultimate prophet of Islam and, along with His mother, figures very prominently in the Qur'an; He is even referred to as *al-Masih*—the Messiah—, Who will one day return for the Final Judgment. Over the centuries though, Muslims had come to believe that the Gospels were embellished or fundamentally misinterpreted by Christians, and along with the rejection of the deity of Christ—or His being the literal Son of God—, there is another controversial distinction stemming from more traditional interpretations of Jesus in the Qur'an."

Psalmodie's eyebrow quirked with interest. "Which is...?"

Shiloh answered, "That He wasn't even crucified to begin with."

Psalmodie did a double take. "Wait, are you saying that the Qur'an actually *denies* the crucifixion ever happened?"

"Well, not exactly," Shiloh clarified, "but a good number of medieval exegetes were divided on how to interpret a particular chapter in the Qur'an containing the only verse relating to the crucifixion of Jesus Christ: The *ayat al-sulb*, or Surah 4:157." Shiloh recalled what the passage said and recited it verbatim to Psalmodie.

> **They did not kill him and they
> did not crucify him, rather
> it only appeared to them**
>
> وَمَا قَتَلُوهُ وَمَا صَلَبُوهُ وَلَكِنْ شُبِّهَ لَهُمْ

Psalmodie scoffed, "That sounds a lot like the Cathari's Gnostic doctrine of docetism, doesn't it? That strange idea that Christ's Body was a ghost that could never affect salvation through a physical death, thus casting His crucifixion as a mere illusion."

Shiloh cleared her throat before commenting, "Well, remember that Judaism has always emphasized salvation through a person's identification with the covenantal history of the Children of Israel, and when Jesus came along, He promised to summarize that salvation of Israel in Himself. While Jewish tradition does have notions of suffering prophets, it had never heard anything of a *dying Messiah;* the Gospel of Matthew shows this clearly when Simon Peter, immediately after confessing that Jesus was the Messiah, *rebuked* Jesus for His saying that He must die before being resurrected. The *ayat al-sulb* could therefore also just as well be taken as an appeal to Jesus' Jewish tradition."

Psalmodie shook her head and added, "But Jesus called Peter's rebuke *satanic,* didn't He? But now we have Catharism and Islam, *two* religions completely different from Judaism that both somehow seem to agree that Jesus' death never happened; the most historically certain thing we can know about His life."

Shiloh continued, "Before we can label anything as 'satanic,' it's important to understand that Islamic Christology doesn't have a singular magisterium and that there have been numerous rarefied debates on this single verse. Yes, countless classical Tafsir commentaries have indeed interpreted this *ayah* to literally mean that God rescued Jesus from the Pharisees, and the 8th-century Church Father Saint John of Damascus did actually point to this verse as a clear indictment of Ishmaelite heresy.

"However, other more rationalistic exegetes, such as the Persian Ismai'li scholar Abu Hatim al-Razi, even referred to the Synoptic Gospels to show that this *ayah* actually speaks more to the boasting Pharisees' ignorance of God's righteousness summarized in Christ. And so, in an ostensibly similar vein to the Nestorian Christian vernacular of the Arabian oases, this verse could also mean that the Pharisees could have never killed Christ's true spirit and power regardless of how they killed His corporeal essence."

"Are you so sure about that?" Psalmodie voiced cynically.

Shiloh further illustrated her point. "Crucifixion was the Romans' *modus operandi* for capital punishment during Christ's time after all, but historically, the Islamic tradition didn't understand it as a means of execution; the *hadd* punishment of Surah 5:33, which was usually carried out against terrorists and murderers, prescribed crucifixion as a way to publicly display a criminal's body *after* their execution to deter anyone from committing any more crimes in the land. You can ask yourself, as I did, how much of Spartacus' legacy, for example, really endured after the Roman Republic crucified all of *his* loyal slave rebels along the 'Eternal City's' Appian Way? At least compared to Jesus and all of *His* disciples, none of whom were murderers, I think we can say almost none."

Psalmodie considered the comment but filed the information away in her mind. "Alright, fine, but what did *Saladin* himself believe the verse was getting at then? Was *he* a traditionalist Muslim?"

"I don't know," Shiloh sighed tentatively, "but I only mention this Qur'an verse to clarify that, should you eventually come across it, what Saladin believed really wouldn't have mattered. In either case, the intended message of the verse is still very much the same for most Muslims: A cross could not have defeated a holy prophet of God, Whom He ultimately raised unto Himself.

"In fact, I think I remember that the French Sufi perennial philosopher René Guénon even claimed in the preface of his seminal study, *Le Symbolisme de la Croix,* that, without diminishing the crucifixion's historical significance, if Christ had truly died, then it would have been by the symbolic value intrinsic to the cross itself, which is recognized by countless other cultures; for example, the Egyptian ankh, the Taoist trigrams, the Aztec calendar... the Hindu swastika."

"And what value is that?" Psalmodie asked.

"Well, Guénon believes that the cross has always had a primordial and metaphysical significance to the unity of mankind, even long before Christianity. The horizontal line represents all of man's states of Being across all religious truths while the vertical line represents the transcendence that comes through the immersion in those truths, and at their intersection lies the totality of man's Being. But the *ayat al-sulb's* polemic against the cross' symbolic power over Jesus as the *Word of God*—Who really is the sinless totality of Being, as Surah 3:59 very clearly shows—would have also likely been found in Hadith tradition."

"Okay, so what is it, then, about this Hadith tradition that speaks to the cross' location?" Psalmodie inquired, setting her empty tea cup to the side.

Shiloh took out a small glass paperweight from under her jerkin and flipped through the contents of the first book; as it was with its Aramaic parent system, since the Arabic language read from right-to-left, Shiloh had to start from the back cover.

"Believe it or not," Shiloh continued, "the vast majority of Muslims, very much like Christians, believe that Jesus Christ's Second Coming will one day happen after the prophesied false Messiah, known in Islam as the Dajjal, comes along to lead the world astray. Jesus, alongside another messianic figure known as the Imam Mahdi, will make war against the Dajjal and will thereafter die before being resurrected with the rest of humanity. Many Hadiths written by the Prophet's closest companions, however, comment on one *very* interesting thing Jesus will do after His advent."

All agog, Psalmodie leaned in and evaluated the Arabic calligraphy Shiloh indicated under the domed magnifying lens of her paperweight. Shiloh read Chapter 49 of the "Book of Prophets" in *Sahih al-Bukhari.*

Though Psalmodie couldn't read the script, Shiloh soon provided the translation for her.

> ***The Messenger of Allah, may peace and blessings be upon him, said, "The Hour will not be established until the son of Mary descends amongst you as a just ruler, he will break the cross, kill the pigs, and abolish the Jizya tax. Money will be in abundance so that nobody will accept it..."***

رَسُولُ اللَّهِ صلى الله عليه وسلم قَالَ لاَ تَقُومُ السَّاعَةُ حَتَّى يَنْزِلَ فِيكُمُ ابْنُ مَرْيَمَ حَكَمًا مُقْسِطًا، فَيَكْسِرَ الصَّلِيبَ، وَيَقْتُلَ الْخِنْزِيرَ، وَيَضَعَ الْجِزْيَةَ، وَيَفِيضَ الْمَالُ حَتَّى لاَ يَقْبَلَهُ أَحَدٌ

"Break the cross?" Psalmodie exclaimed.

Shiloh went on, "The same statement is made about Jesus in other parallel Hadith accounts, such as *Sunan ibn Majah* and *Jami' at-Tirmidhi*. But the mainstream interpretation of this is that He will one day come back to do away with the flawed philosophies of Christianity starting with the notion of vicarious atonement from His crucifixion before going on to impart true Islam unto the new converts."

Psalmodie gave an anxious chuckle. "Okay, but what does any of this have to do with Damascus or any of the legends I talked about?"

"As I said, Saladin does." Shiloh closed the book and slid the other one closer before her. "As you and I now know, history tells us that he may have used the True Cross as leverage against the Crusaders; he was very much aware of how highly, *highly* attached they were to what he would have thought was a worthless piece of wood. History also tells us, however, that Saladin was a lifelong *Sunni* Muslim, and before his eventual ascent to power, he was actually tenured as a vizier for the *Shi'ite* Fatimid Caliphate in North Africa. He would have therefore likely attended madrassas, or Islamic religious colleges, to both preserve the orthodoxy of his Sunni faith and become more knowledgeable on how God would exact His justice on Judgment Day.

"But, being the remarkably pious Muslim he was, in a time where some Christians, Muslims, and Jews alike would have likely seen the endemic political struggles of their age as a possible portent of the coming Judgment Day, Saladin would have wanted to leave as little of an interpretive niche to the Prophet's testament as possible, regardless of whether Jesus' breaking of the cross should have been taken literally or figuratively. After all, Saladin's own Shafi'i school of Sunni jurisprudence did heavily emphasize the Hadiths' place in the Shariah—the sacred Islamic law. As a safeguard, then, he would have had to have hidden the cross somewhere very specific."

Psalmodie then saw Shiloh heave open the cover of the next Hadith in front of her. It took Shiloh a little while to find the specific chapter she was looking for, but again, once she did, she slid her glass lens over the page and showed another Arabic passage to Psalmodie: Chapter 20 of the "Book of Tribulations" in *Sahih Muslim*. After Shiloh translated it, Psalmodie looked up at her in utter disbelief.

The Holy Prophet, peace and blessings of Allah be upon him, said, "Allah will send Jesus, son of Mary, and he will descend near the white minaret, east of Damascus..."

قَالَ النَّبِيُّ صَلَّى اللهُ عَلَيْهِ وَسَلَّمَ
اذْ بَعَثَ اللهُ الْمَسِيْحَ ابْنَ مَرْيَمَ فَيَنْزِلُ
عِنْدَ الْمَنَارَةِ الْبَيْضَاءِ شَرْقِيَ دِمَشْقَ

"I think this statement is also mentioned in *Sunan abu Dawud* and *Riyad as-Salihin*," Shiloh continued, "meaning that if Saladin was aware of these passages from the Hadiths, which he most likely was, given their prevalence and his arduous devotion, then his intentions for the True Cross would have gone far beyond simple blackmail against the Crusaders. For Saladin, it would have actually served a purpose in the Islamic end times. Also, that *Jesus* of all the prophets will come down on a Damascene tower is a tradition that Saladin's prisoner, the then-Grand Master of the Knights Templar, would have likely been familiarized with during his year in captivity."

Psalmodie chewed on her lower lip, studying Shiloh for a long moment as she tried to make up her mind about her tall claim. "Okay," she granted. "So, we already established that Saladin had to have brought the True Cross to Damascus after the Battle of Hattin, correct?"

"Yes, we did, because of Imad ad-Din's chronicles," Shiloh said, nodding. "The ones your father mentioned in his journal."

"Right, and because of... the *Hadith* collections," Psalmodie continued, indicating the two books in front of her while pushing them off to the side with one hand, "we know that Christ will supposedly come down to destroy our relic somewhere in or around this 'white minaret?'"

"That's right."

"But *what* white minaret is it?"

"Minarets are mosque towers from which muezzins chant the *adhan,* or ritual calls for Muslims to pray five times every day."

"No, I know what a minaret is, but you already know there's dozens —maybe even *hundreds* of mosques all over Eastern Syria. How do we even *begin* to narrow down on one specific—"

At that moment, they heard it. It seemed on que and even providential. A ritual chant echoed throughout the Old City. Shiloh looked towards Malik, who had already gone behind the bead curtains. Psalmodie slowly turned left to look through the quatrefoil lattice of the glass block window. Beyond the palm fronds, Psalmodie saw three towering, pencil-shaped spires silhouetted against the soft sepia sunlight, all belonging to the holiest site in the whole of Syria.

The Umayyad Mosque, also known as the Great Mosque of Damascus.

Psalmodie looked back at Shiloh, and upon seeing the look of concurrence on her face, her spirits elevated, and she twinkled her eyes at her.

Shiloh went on, "Local Damascene tradition also claims that prayers offered at the Great Mosque are equal to those offered in Jerusalem; the same place where Jesus will come down on a minaret before the Judgment Day."

Shiloh then recalled the words Psalmodie's father said the Cistercian monks used to characterize the fabled Grail Island in his journal: "New Jerusalem."

...Sarras, then Kingdom Come.

Psalmodie eyed Shiloh incredulously before asking again, "But which one is the minaret? I count three over that mosque."

Shiloh reached into her pocket, pulled out a folded paper, and smoothed it out over the round table. It was a tourist map of the Old City, similar to the ones distributed on the motorcoach. It was marked by a mess of Arabic inscriptions over different districts and thorough-fares, although there were a select few hot spots and cultural landmarks that were transliterated.

Shiloh traced her finger around the mosque's location on the map. "These three spots here are the minarets. As you can see, each minaret has its own title."

Psalmodie read clockwise the transliterated names of the minarets' locations: *Madhana-i al-'Arus, Madhana-i 'Isa,* and *Madhana-i al-Gharbiyya.*

"This one," Shiloh said, pointing to the minaret at the southeastern corner of the mosque.

"*Madhana-i 'Isa?*" Psalmodie asked. "What does it translate to?"

A knowing smile broadened over Shiloh's face. "*Madhana-i 'Isa* literally translates to 'Minaret of *Jesus.*' While most Arab Christians usually refer to Jesus as *Yasu', 'Isa* is the name the Qur'an uses for Him, which means that *this* is the minaret the Hadiths say He will descend upon when God's Day of Judgment will finally be coming. Such a conclusion was reiterated by Ismail ibn Kathir, the 14th-century exegete who wrote some of the most popular interpretations of the Qur'an and Hadiths today. So, if Saladin did hide the True Cross somewhere, he would have likely reserved it *there* for Christ's eventual return."

Psalmodie's eyes went wide, visibly drawing the connections between Shiloh's revelation and what her father wrote in his journal. She slouched in her seat and eyed the rightmost minaret of the Umayyad Mosque. Shiloh saw that her stupefied friend wanted to smile, but something about her report still bothered her.

"Wait a minute," Psalmodie said. "Didn't my father mention something about Joseph of Arimathea as well? I think that character is way too important a figure to ignore in the Grail legends. What role does *he* play in all of this?"

Shiloh's countenance held that same exhilarated expression, almost as if she were readily expecting Psalmodie to ask the question. "What if I told you that he is actually buried by the Great Mosque as well?" Shiloh suggested confidently.

CHAPTER 21

Lüneburg, Germany
September 12th, 1938

T he white and ghostly dawn sun was grayed by the mists rising up from the lake spread out before Rahn. He stared out the diamond mullions of the balcony's fanlight to worlds afar, searching for the solitude of the Holy Grail that fell from the firmament —the true stone that the builder refused after Lucifer and mankind fell from their paradises. Rahn remembered when he first bore witness to the truth five years ago. Rahn could almost hear the consoling sympathy and sorrowful gentleness in the slow tone with which Lucifer assured Eve before she ate from the forbidden fruit of knowledge: "Ye shall be as gods, knowing good and evil."

That Gnostic prophecy filled Rahn with such a solitude that he wrote of the treasure's immaculate nature in his first publication, *La Croisade contre le Graal*—*The Crusade against the Grail*—, the story of the Cathari, who were the good prophets alluded to in Wolfram von Eschenbach's 13th-century *Parzival* Grail romance. The bonhomme— the good men—in white samite, the pure ones of the god of pure light before they were savagely butchered in 1244 in their last stronghold of Château de Montségur in the Ariège in Southern France by the Crusader devils unleashed by the Judaic menace of the Church of

Rome. One among those wretched Inquisitors, Konrad von Marburg, even hailed from near Rahn's hometown.

Yet, while the Crusaders had slaughtered the Perfecti—the purest among the bonhomme—by burning them at the stake on the camp dels cremats outside of their fortress, the holy spirit of Esclarmonde de Foix, the last high priestess and guardian of the Grail stone, descended from on high to charge her loyal servants with saving Lucifer's treasure. And so, they bore it down an ancient pilgrimage route, the route of the bonhomme, before casting it down into the Earth; whether it was in Ussat-les-Bains or the Tabor forest, Rahn was more than certain that Lucifer's light reposed peacefully somewhere within the depths of the Earth and the depths of his own Being.

One final hope for peace.

But finding no such peace for himself, Rahn raised his heavy eyes up towards the horizon and saw the cityscape of the Hanseatic-era town, made endlessly red by the pitched clay tile rooftops of timber-framed houses and cottages. Such a vista put him in mind of Narbonne in Southern France, close to where the Crusaders' first indiscriminate slaughter of Cathari occurred at the behest of one villainous papal legate who infamously decreed, "Kill them all, God will recognize His own." And just like Narbonne, rising from among Lüneburg's buildings were those Gothic steeples erected to the undue legacy of Lucifer's greatest usurper and imposter: The false Messiah who fully embodied the sins of the material world. He was, to Rahn, the true Antichrist, who was indeed the rightful King of the Jews.

Still, the haunting voice of Rahn's former partner and the flashing images of his skeletal face mercilessly stabbed at his mind. That same scream that echoed around in that concrete cell he saw him last, searing with fierce wrath after he told the man what was going to happen to him. Rahn's mind strained against the ghastly phantasmagoria, but just when he was about to succumb to its irresistible pull, he felt watched by someone.

"Otto?" a small voice called behind him.

Rahn quickly turned around and saw that he was still in the dark-wooded honeymoon loft of his chalet in Lüneburg. But when he looked down at the little, golden-haired schoolgirl before him, he bit the back of his fist in growing anguish. She was still wearing that tidy dirndl skirt and had that same innocent look on her face.

"Psalmodie?" Rahn called.

When he wiped away the tears in his eyes, he saw that the little girl had vanished, and standing in her place was a little boy with platinum blonde hair and wearing a white button-up with brown trousers.

The boy pointed at something behind Rahn and spoke again in his usual high-pitched treble. "Herr Rahn, are you going on a trip today?"

Rahn followed his small finger to the duffle bags piled up against the wall beneath the window. He looked back at the boy with a difficult look in his eyes and put his hands on his small shoulders. But before he could have begun to try to answer his question, Rahn saw the boy's mother appear in the doorway on the far side of the room; a young divorcé named Asta Bach. She was wearing a white calico dress with a dark vest. Her blonde hair was tied back, but she did little to make up her fair-skinned face; Rahn would have imagined she would have at least tried to mask whatever sympathy was left in it.

"Meine Liebe?" Asta called to her son, extending her hand out to him. When the boy ran from Rahn's arms into hers, she put a hand to his ear and pulled him against her, as if she wanted to protect her from whatever she was going to say to Rahn.

"Mama, where is Herr Rahn going?" the boy said, tugging on her sleeve.

"Why don't you go play with your toys downstairs?" she crooned, fixing a hair on his head before ushering the boy into the hall behind her.

When the boy's running footsteps receded, Rahn said thickly, "I have been summoned to Wewelsburg for a new assignment."

Asta frowned at him. "I thought you were terrified of that castle."

"Or would you rather I stay here to keep begging you, Asta?" Rahn said, meeting her halfway across the room.

Asta shook her head, but her eyes never left Rahn's. "I told you: I cannot be Fräulein Rahn for you, Otto. And my son is not yours and he can't ever be yours. We cannot be your family... for his father's sake and for his own."

"Then don't be!" Rahn pleaded, taking her by her shoulders. "You can keep your surname, but please—*please*—I need you to keep being my wife! It doesn't have to be love!"

Asta shrugged off his grip and backed away from him. "And I keep telling you that that is the problem: It does! The Reichsführer will never believe this marriage rehabilitated you! He will soon learn that we staged all of this!" Though the coldness never left her eyes, she still looked at Rahn with a mild regard. "You never stopped loving your partner, have you? You never stopped, even after all that you have dealt unto him and his poor daughter."

Rahn's regard softened, and he paced away from her. His eyes lowered shamefully, as if for prayer, and pinched the bridge of his nose. He moved his fingers down from his shut eyes over his pale face and stopped them over his quivering lips. No matter how hard he tried, he would never forget that lasting image of hell he was destined to bear for the rest of his life.

"That man," Rahn started, his voice barely a whisper. "He gave me counsel in France despite his stupid Catholic faith... and despite his own theory on the Holy Grail that he nobly set aside for my scholarship that he believed with all his heart would have assured my survival in the Ahnenerbe... But that night, when I was drunk and unruly, he dared to shun my love; the love that dared not speak its name.

"I hated him. With all my heart, I hated him after all of those empty words. I hated him so much that I thought I could have controlled the story of what happened that night if I was ever questioned about it." Rahn looked at Asta, staring as if returning from far away. "The slanderous canard I imputed to him was the only thing that felt right at that time, but God forgive me, Asta, I never—*never* would have imagined that they would have passed so depraved a sentence on his life.

"I *have* tried to stop it by making excuse after excuse for keeping him alive, but nothing I could have ever done would have begun to mend the horrors I have inflicted on him. I swore an oath to him; I relayed his last words to his daughter. I jeopardized my own life so that he could feel the touch of his only love beyond Dachau's walls one last time."

Asta held a look of disbelief and regret in her eyes. She hesitated a moment and walked up to Rahn to knead his chest. She raised her gaze up at him and stroked her other hand along her bridegroom's cheekbone.

"You poor fool," she half-whispered with pitiful tenderness. "You pure, poor fool, fighting alone... to not be alone..."

Rahn looked into Asta's eyes before casting them back down at the ground. He gently brushed away Asta's hand from his cheek and moved again for his bags. He knelt down and padded around the bags' canvas to make sure all of his necessities were accounted for.

Asta hugged her elbows and told him, "You know that this is no way for any man to live, Otto, let alone a little boy. If I involve my family with you, I am certain I will lose the custody trial to your SS's precious Lebensborn breeding programme, and my son will never again know what it is to have a mother."

"They are *not* my SS to control, Asta," Rahn said.

"That's not what you told your colleagues, with your constant boasts and threats of using the SS to get your own way!"

"Those were only strongarm tactics!" Rahn insisted desperately. "Empty threats! To get my royalties from my publisher and discourage dissent! They were *never* my SS!"

"But you already know that doesn't matter, does it?" Asta continued. "Your grasp had always outstretched your reach. You and the Reichsführer have a cousin in common; you, Rahn, you—*you* actually conducted the research that proved his Aryan ancestry and legitimized him as the head of the Führer's grunts. Whatever happened to your quest for your Holy Grail? Huh?" She shook her head at him again. "You know that I cannot have that life for my son."

Rahn kept his eyes down on his bags, searching his own mind for something to say to this, though he knew that the lie would have been more to himself than to her. Having gathered whatever thoughts he could have in his fracturing mind, he grabbed his bags and started for the loft's doorway without so much as a final look back at Asta.

That was the last time he ever saw her.

CHAPTER 22

The hinterlands of Damascus
The French Mandate of Syria
October 1st, 1938

As Eggers drove the black car, Rahn sat in the passenger seat, still wondering whether there could have been anything else he could have said to Asta that day. Though he may have kept his covenant with his former partner, after those telegrams from Paris were found in Dachau, Rahn knew that it didn't matter what Asta or vom Rath said what he was or what he ought to have been in the world. Once everything fell apart and all that mattered was keeping his own life, Rahn had come to accept that this coward of a man was what he was.

What he *truly* was.

Like stars resting on the horizon, the coward saw the Old City's clusters of light becoming clearer with every moment the sun melted into the Syrian desert shrubland. The SS's attaché to the Arabs there was smuggled across the French Lebanese border under a pile of coats and blankets in the other car following shortly behind Rahn's car.

Having reflected on this, an infidel *Saracen* leader, just as Rahn had come to terms with his own cowardice, so too had he finally accepted the grim reality of the Third Reich's true spiritual inheritance: Of

Konrad von Marburg's Roman legions, and not of Esclarmonde de Foix's Luciferian bonhomme.

Rahn then turned his thoughts to the purest of his Cathari prophets —the Grail's ancient guardians in Southern France—and their blessed sacraments: The *Consolamentum* and the *Endura*. The baptismal immersion in the goodness of the true God of light and, for those Perfecti who were terminally ill, the subsequent fasting unto their inexorable deaths in the midst of an unforgiving winter. Holy sacraments that they were robbed of when the Crusader legions of the true devil either burned the pure ones at the stake or mercilessly put all of their congregations to the sword during the Inquisition all those centuries ago.

Still pale and drawn, Rahn oddly allowed himself to take just the smallest modicum of solace in what the papal legate decreed in Narbonne, for Rahn wanted to believe that such a claim could have perhaps been a final hope for his forthcoming victims before the blaring Jericho trumpets of the Luftwaffe and Wehrmacht war machine would have inevitably descended upon what little innocence was left in the world like a plague of locusts. If the whole of Europe was not to be in thrall to Germany so as to find its unifying *Consolamentum* and herald in a new Garden of Eden, as Rahn had prayed, then the entire world's collective *Endura* would have surely and tragically followed.

Kill them all, Rahn prayed, *God will recognize His own.*

CHAPTER 23

Al-Amarah quarter, the Old City of Damascus

Under the night sky, the silvery moonlight reflected off of the cobblestone piazza at the Umayyad Mosque's western wall while further darkening the shadowy recesses and narrow alleyways of the Old City. A few overnight shop owners were left to populate another nearby bazaar whose street ended at the site of what remained of an ancient ruined structure.

The Temple of Jupiter Dolichenus.

Once the largest temple in Roman Syria, it was likely built to contrast with the Jewish Temple in Jerusalem, with it even becoming the capital of the imperial cult of the Greco-Roman sky god Jupiter. Now, with its eroding Corinthian columns towering over the vaultless loggia, its old archway had been repurposed as a shopping arcade, resembling something Jesus Himself would have berated during His famous cleansing of the Temple courts.

To Shiloh, the ancient ruins were a monument to what it truly meant to be "Antichrist."

The two girls exited the shop-lined walkway and, standing in the shadows of two Date palms, manifested the magnificent castrum-like fortress wall of the fairytale Grail castle. A congregational mosque, nearly as ancient as Islam itself, built by Coptic craftsmen with the help of Indian, Persian, and Greek masons to one day herald in Christ's Second Coming and uphold God's Day of Judgment.

Three large bronze doors were centered before them, seemingly beckoning them.

"Come, come," Shiloh whispered, steering Psalmodie by the arm towards the narrow street down the left end of the mosque.

"Wait," Psalmodie objected, motioning for the doors. "You said that's the main entrance, isn't it?"

"Don't worry. There's another one at the north end."

"But why not just go through this one?"

"Oh?" Shiloh continued. "I thought you *really* wanted to pay your respects to Joseph of Arimathea?"

While Psalmodie was a little hesitant at first, she remembered how cooperative Shiloh had been in her quest, not to mention how she implicated her as another target for their German hunters. Even during their time as roommates at the university, Shiloh seemed very staid and resistant towards any prospect of adventure or intrigue, but seeing how she had distracted herself with a surprising new vitality for their mission, Psalmodie decided to go along with it.

"But just remember that we're doing this for my father."

"I don't think the Germans will figure out where we are," Shiloh responded, placing a sincere hand on her shoulder. "I think we're safe for now, and we *will* get your father back somehow."

"Go on then," Psalmodie sighed, following Shiloh into the dark street ahead of them.

Once they had turned the corner, Psalmodie had immediately come face-to-face to what Shiloh wanted to show her, though she wasn't exactly sure how to react. There was no minaret; amid the flowing thickets of jasmine was only a small plastered complex directly adjacent to the northwest corner of the Umayyad Mosque with a moderately-sized red dome jutted on top.

While Psalmodie did expect ceremonial grandeur from a memorial for a Biblical figure like Joseph of Arimathea who features so prominently in Arthurian legend as the Holy Grail's principal guardian, something about the central building's conspicuously Islamic aesthetic ringed anticlimactic to her.

"*Et voilà,*" Shiloh remarked.

There was no main entrance that Psalmodie could have seen, but she waited for an explanation from her companion.

"You're saying *this* is the tomb of Joseph?" Psalmodie doubted.

"Yes, it is," Shiloh said, looking up at the structure more admiringly than Psalmodie.

"Wait, I thought you said Muslims wouldn't have cared much for Jesus' crucifixion. Why would they venerate His gravedigger of all people?"

Shiloh was still eying the building. "I *did* say that. And you're right. They do not."

"So, what is it then?"

Without speaking, Shiloh signaled to a small sign fixed on the locked swing gate of the white fence rail before them. Again, there was an inscription that read in Arabic, but there was also an accompanying transliteration above it. Psalmodie glanced at it, but upon reading it again, she recognized one particular section of the epitaph. Though she didn't remember seeing any pictures of the shrine, she remembered reading about the homage it was paid by men like Kaiser Wilhelm II and Lawrence of Arabia during their respective visits to Damascus.

Al-Malik an-Nasir Salah ad-Din Yusuf ibn Ayyub. The Mausoleum of the Sultan Saladin himself.

"The name 'Salah ad-Din,'" Shiloh started, "was only an honorific *laqab,* which is Arabic for 'Righteousness of the Faith.' But his birth name was Yusuf." Her avid gaze sought Psalmodie's. "Joseph, Psalmodie. His real name was Joseph."

Though Psalmodie was intrigued by Shiloh's idea of a metaphorical Joseph of Arimathea, she still wasn't convinced. "But he wasn't from the town of Arimathea, was he?" Psalmodie challenged.

"His failures were," Shiloh countered, "as far as the Crusaders were concerned, at least."

Psalmodie was surprised at the immediacy of her answer. "His failures?"

"Yes, his failures," Shiloh said, still smiling.

"What do you mean 'his failures?'"

Shiloh continued, "For one, the Treaty of Ramla, signed by Saladin and Richard the Lionheart, which ended the Third Crusade in 1192. It was also within the Ramla province where Saladin was decisively crushed by the Leper King of Jerusalem ten years prior to the Third Cru—"

"But where is Arimathea?" Psalmodie cut off.

Shiloh momentarily fell silent, relishing in the pregnant pause.

"Ramla," Shiloh finally revealed, "was the place the Crusaders identified as Arimathea."

Psalmodie took a moment to consider Shiloh's claim, and although it sounded realistic, a gap in logic nagged at her. She felt that she was missing some scriptural basis for Joseph's charge with the Grail. *Saladin's failures at Ramla can't make him Joseph of Arimathea,* she thought. She could have sworn she read otherwise in the medieval poetry of Robert de Boron, who further cemented the Holy Grail's Christian character through the inclusion of many more Biblical cameos. But then again, she recalled what her father wrote on the very last page of his journal.

Through Joseph...

A satisfactory explanation rooted in long-standing Grail tradition continued to elude her, though it seemed whatever amount of truth there was to Shiloh's tenuous—perhaps even irrational—connection wouldn't have ultimately mattered; not for what her father was trying to tell her at least. *It will have to do,* Psalmodie thought uneasily.

She nodded her assent, although Shiloh noticed the reluctance with which she expressed it. Psalmodie withdrew and started for the north entrance. She expected Shiloh would have caught up to her, but she looked back and saw that she was still immersed in the modest structure as if it were a great fresco from the Renaissance.

"Shiloh?" Psalmodie called, turning back.

Shiloh's gaze broke away from the mausoleum and turned back on Psalmodie. "Yes?"

"What's going on?" Psalmodie inquired, looking at her with a half-turned face. "You seem different."

"Different how?"

Psalmodie shrugged. "I don't know. Just... different."

"That isn't really much to go on," Shiloh responded.

"It's just that..." Psalmodie sighed, glancing briefly in another direction before casting down. "It's just that back in Paris, it seemed like you wanted no part in this, and only cared about running from the Germans."

"And why shouldn't we?"

Psalmodie backpedaled. "No, no, what I meant was just that... I noticed you're all gung-ho to find the cross all of a sudden."

Shiloh's face dropped, though a trace of her grin lingered a while longer. Her gaze turned thoughtful, but she gave Psalmodie's question little thought. Then Shiloh's brief pause concluded with a noncommittal shrug.

"I'm just... excited to find this 'New Jerusalem,'" Shiloh ultimately said, making light of it. She rallied again to her jovial demeanor in the hopes that Psalmodie wouldn't have probed any further.

Seeing this, Psalmodie backed down, and feeling her thrill gather anew, let herself fall in with Shiloh's attitude. With a beam, Psalmodie tapped at Shiloh's elbow and said, "Come along then. Let's go see where our friend 'Joseph' hid the Grail then."

CHAPTER 24

The Umayyad Mosque

The arcades surrounding the mosque's large rectangular *sahn,* or courtyard, echoed a similar design to the cloisters found in various Christian convents and monasteries. The beige tile floors were beautifully polished to reflect the light blue moonlight like the still waters of a pristine reflection pond, despite the perpetual darkness beyond the mosque's limestone walls.

Shiloh and Psalmodie walked to the center of the courtyard barefoot, their boots in hand in consideration of the sanctity of the building for the Damascene Muslim community. They stopped in front of the fountain of ritualistic ablutions, which was just before the mosque's southern wall's gilded façade, framed by two thick piers and decorated green with various Byzantine-style mosaics depicting numerous villas with tree copses and lush undergrowth. Indeed, a sublime vision of Paradise.

"What time will the mosque close to visitors?" Psalmodie asked, breaking the silence.

Shiloh was still engrossed by the mosque's elaborate artwork. "It's open twenty-four hours."

"Okay," Psalmodie said, looking around the courtyard. "So which way is Jesus' minaret?"

A faint clanging somewhere in the mosque briefly startled them both.

"It's this way," Shiloh said, signaling for the open bronze doors below the façade. "We have to be careful though. I don't think that many people are going to be here this late, but that doesn't mean there won't be guards combing the—"

Before Shiloh could have finished, four figures emerged from the doorway; two of them veiled women in funeral-black colors, half-led and half-dragged away by two armed guards. They were both in hysterics, bleating out the same name over and over again as if they were mourning the loss of a loved one.

"Husayn! Husayn! Husayn!"

Pious devotion and empathy for one of Islam's most venerated figures. A name Shiloh was very much familiar with.

"What's that all about?" Psalmodie asked quizzically, returning to her side.

There was a brief silence before Shiloh responded, "They mourn the Prophet's grandson, Husayn ibn Ali."

"Here?"

"Yes, here."

"But what does this place have to do with him?"

Shiloh felt cold, yet a sense of deference rose in her. "Some of his relatives were brought here after he was martyred by the corrupted Umayyad Caliphate in the Shi'ite holy city of Karbala in Iraq. He lost everything, including his infant son, and in the face of his inevitable death, he stayed true to his grandfather's devotion to the One God."

Psalmodie kept quiet, watching Shiloh for a moment. She was still staring fixedly at the doddering women until they became nothing more than shadows melting into the darkness of the courtyard's western entrance.

"Uh, Shiloh?" Psalmodie prodded. "The minaret?"

Shiloh stirred from her momentary lapse, starting back for the doors. "Yes... yes. Sorry. Follow me."

Once they entered the mosque's southern wing prayer hall, they immediately felt within its walls more than a millennia of culture and faith. Shiloh was nearly overcome by the walls' majestic architectural features, from the elegant curvilinear bas-relief arabesque tendrils to the blooming palmette moulding. As was usual with any mosque, the *eau de Nil* marble wall to the far right-hand side was lined with *mihrabs*, or semicircular niches that indicated the direction—*qibla*—of the Ka'aba, the ancient, cubic House of God in Mecca to which all Muslims face in their daily prayers.

In the prayer hall were two alternating rows of horseshoe-arched hypostyle columns supporting the smaller triforium galleries above and dividing the hall's fair width into three aisles running up and down its large length, thus giving the illusion of infinite space. A ground plan, Shiloh recalled, that was greatly replicated by the famed Mezquita, the resplendent, 8th-century Mosque-Cathedral built by the Emirate of Córdoba; a monument to *La Convivencia,* or the coexistence of all of God's religions in medieval Spain.

At night, the Umayyad Mosque was lit by luminescent chandeliers suspended from the exposed metallic trusses in the high-arched vaults along all three naves. It was vacant that night, save a small number of night-owls performing their prayers over the red *musalla* carpet or quietly reciting from their pocket Qur'ans while sitting along the mosque's walls.

Shiloh and Psalmodie walked down to the rightmost aisle of the hall, mindful of not drawing too much attention to themselves either from visitors or any of the few remaining guards. Thankfully, however, the nondescript access point to the Minaret of Jesus was inconspicuously located in the eastern wall's corner shadow. From a far enough distance, no one would have seen them going through the door.

Once they had reached it, Shiloh turned the wooden door's knob while Psalmodie surreptitiously looked around the hall once more to verify that no one was in their immediate vicinity.

"Of course it's locked," Shiloh said, jiggling the knob in a last vain effort.

Psalmodie turned and faced the door. "Not to worry. I knew we'd run into something like this. These door locks wouldn't be that different from the ones in England, right?"

"I don't think so. Why?" Shiloh was confused at first, but then she saw what she was doing.

Psalmodie passed Shiloh her satchel and boots before half-kneeling in front of the knob and reaching one hand behind her headscarf for two bobby pins. She bent the end of one pin into a right-angle hook for a torsion wrench and bent the very tip of the other for a basic rake to push the tumblers inside up into place.

"Keep an eye out for me," Psalmodie said, inserting both pins into the keyhole.

While she struggled to carry their shoes and satchel, Shiloh stood guard and scanned the mosque's hall with wary eyes. The faint squeaking of the lock's tumblers aligning made her flinch, although she saw that there wasn't anyone around to catch them.

"Are you nearly done?" Shiloh whispered tensely.

"Not yet," Psalmodie said, straining deeper into the lock.

Shiloh returned her gaze back towards the bronze doors under the mosque's façade. There were no guards, although partially obstructing her view was a curious rectangular structure crowned by a small green dome. A moderately-sized marble pavilion, islanded between two columns of the southern hall's right hypostyle row with its floral-screened windows tinted by a bright green light. For a moment, she wondered what relic it could have possibly housed. Her mind wandered back to the Prophet's grandson, although she quickly recalled that his relics were deposited back with his body in Iraq by his next of kin.

What could be in there?

She heard a brass click behind her and saw Psalmodie peeping out from the cracked door and quickly waving her over. Shiloh stole one last look at the structure before following Psalmodie into the room and gently closing the door behind her.

For the Muslims of Damascus, the rectangular Minaret of Jesus served only as a reminder that, through the Prophet Jesus, God will remember in the End of Days those who answered the call to the *Salat*, or the five daily prayers. The limestone chamber was lit up by the flickering light of an adjustable kerosene lantern hanging by the door's head, revealing a winding staircase ascending along the four walls and a red and circular Oriental prayer rug leveled with the cobblestone floor at the chamber's center.

"So where do we even look now?" Psalmodie asked, removing her headscarf and letting her plait fall.

An apt question for Shiloh, but she found herself troubled by an even more difficult uncertainty: *The cross would be no mere objet d'art. How would we even get it out?* But then she reminded herself that there was no time frame forced on them for Psalmodie's father's life. They needed to hurry, but as far as they both knew, they were not in any immediate danger.

Shiloh set down their boots and satchel on the floor and looked around the room. "Maybe... Maybe the Ayyubids left some sort of indicator behind somewhere around here. Something for Jesus Himself to find so that He could fulfill the Islamic prophecy. I imagine they would have wanted God's judgment to proceed smoothly." She started scanning the walls around her. "Psalmodie? See if you can find an inscription or glyph of some sort around here."

"Shouldn't we look upstairs too?" Psalmodie suggested. "Looks like there's plenty of room up there."

Shiloh shook her head. "The main body of the minaret was constructed by the Ayyubids some years after Saladin's death, and the uppermost portion looks to have been added by the Ottoman Empire some centuries later. I also don't think the Ayyubids would've thought well of making a 'hidden' steeple of the minaret with the True Cross. No, it'd have to be cached away somewhere in the bottom half."

"But *where?*" Psalmodie asked, her voice tightening with growing anxiety.

Shiloh drew closer to Psalmodie and hushed her admonishingly. "Hey, keep your voice down. Do you *want* to get us kicked out or—" Shiloh stopped short once she felt a pile woven texture under the sole of her forward foot. She removed her foot and took a step back to view the threadbare Oriental rug in its entirety.

"What is it?" Psalmodie prompted.

On the fabric was a circular mandala pattern, scrolled with intricately symmetrical Damask floral details. At its center, however, was a very familiar shape to them both. Occupying a small area was two intersecting equilateral triangles, creating a six-pointed geometric figure. A hexagram known by different names.

In Judaism, it was the Star of David; in Islam, the Seal of Solomon.

The same exact symbol was carved at the top of the Ayyubid portion of the minaret where Jesus will purportedly descend from Heaven.

"This rug..." Shiloh mumbled, looking at its edges. "Doesn't it look a bit off to you?"

Psalmodie looked incredulously at Shiloh. "Off how?"

"Do you see its edges there? They're actually flush with the stone floor." Shiloh quickly sank to her knees and peeled one frayed end of the circular rug and folded it over to one side, revealing a quarter-inch circular depression underneath.

She immediately noticed something was out of place about what was at the basin of this shallow crater: A smooth flagstone surface with a small embedded flange resembling a sink drain at first glance. Threaded into the casing, however, was that same symbol: A metallic hexagram.

"Seigneur," Psalmodie breathed.

Shiloh hovered a fist over its circumference and knocked around the surface. There was a dull echoing around what sounded like another hollow chamber beneath, but to the girls' delight, the flagstone buckled each time their hands pressed against it.

Shiloh felt around the surface. "Alright, so umm... Let's see, what do you think the key is here? Does it slide to the side or hinge out or..."

One thought occurred to Psalmodie. "Maybe try 'Open Sesame?'"

Shiloh let out a half-chuckle and commented, "So you also read the *Arabian Nights* folk tales, huh?"

Psalmodie shrugged. "My father read some to me when I was little, but I only know some very basic things about them. Why?"

"Apparently, a famous sailor character in one of those stories—Sinbad, I think—he gave a caliph a drinking cup with the Seal of Solomon engraved at the bottom, perhaps drawing from a larger Arab tradition." Shiloh gazed up towards the minaret's ceiling through the staircase before turning her attention back down on the curiously placed hexagram. "The Ottomans did have such cups, and Saladin did give the King of Jerusalem that chalice; I don't know—Maybe you just..." She slipped her forefinger through the slot and tugged at it.

Shiloh and Psalmodie gasped as the small metal Star of David levered upwards, and a rusted mechanism unlatched within the flagstone and ground against rock like a pestle and mortar. The basin collapsed another inch, and a set of rusted iron hinges were exposed along the adjoining cobblestone edges.

Shiloh was still holding the finger hold, and she felt a newfound weight on her fingers. She gently lowered the tablet-like lid, careful not to release it and let the hinged hatch drop into the abyss lest they alert the few congregants still praying in the mosque to their presence.

When Psalmodie saw the set of rungs on the wall descending into the darkness below, her heart raced. "What now?"

The moment lay immense before them. Shiloh looked up at Psalmodie and grinned before walking over to the door to remove the hanging lantern from its cresset. "Put your boots back on," she finally said, her voice elevated with anticipation. "Let's go see if it's still down there."

Psalmodie smiled with adventurous gaiety. "I'm right behind you."

CHAPTER 25

S hiloh held the lantern close to the ground in front of her and led Psalmodie through the cramped subterranean passageway. While descending into the cobblestone tunnel, they had to inch sideways at certain sections to move through some eroded piles of rubble and even some dilapidated wood shoring lining the roof and walls.

"Hey, my ears just popped," Psalmodie said, looking around the cave's walls. "We must be descending. Do you see anything yet?"

Shiloh squinted through the darkness. "No, not yet."

"By the way, are we even sure this place is stable?" Psalmodie asked, her voice timorous.

"These walls should date back to the Middle Ages *at the very least*. Really, they could cave in at any moment."

"Oh, well... That's very reassuring," Psalmodie said dryly.

"Just stay calm," Shiloh said. "I'm sure—well, I think—we'll be fine. You have to be careful with the—"

Something crunched under Shiloh's foot. Startled, she dropped the lantern and jumped back against Psalmodie, as if bitten by a snake.

"What? What? What is it?" Psalmodie jittered.

Shiloh sighed shakily and steadied herself. "I thought the ground was giving out or something."

"What was it?"

Shiloh went back to pick up the lantern, but she noticed something unnatural on the dirt next to it. The small object she stepped on was covered in soot, but upon brushing its surface, she instantly recognized its shape.

A cracked wooden cross necklace. After taking a tentative step forward, she peered down the tunnel and beheld a truly unsettling sight: The ground ahead of her was strewn with countless neglected Christian crosses, varying in size, shape, pattern, material, and original purpose.

"Okay, this is... eerie," Psalmodie voiced charily.

A baffled Shiloh noted many of the crosses' designs. Some were crucifixes with whittled figurines bearing the raw likeness of Christ often used to serve different liturgical purposes—altar rood, processional, pectoral, and wayside. Others bore designs characteristic to various rites and denominations—Latin, Greek, Syriac, Armenian, Nestorian, Chaldean, Maronite, Melkite, Ethiopian... and Coptic. An ancient, bottomless trove of lost Christianities.

"These look like they were thrown down here," Shiloh said.

"By *Christians?*" Psalmodie asked. "Byzantine iconoclasts perhaps?"

"I doubt it; I think they would have destroyed their religious art, not buried it. It also couldn't have been Christians who wanted to save their relics from the Byzantines; there are way too many crosses from other denominations here."

Psalmodie scoffed, confused. "So—what—these date back to Muslim rule? As if the one cross wasn't enough for the prophecy?"

Shiloh took another moment to consider the possibilities before pressing forward, stepping around the crosses wherever she could. "I'm starting to think that maybe these—"

"Sshh-ssh..." Psalmodie hushed, tapping Shiloh's elbow.

"What? I don't hear anything," Shiloh reacted, still minding the crosses on the floor.

Eventually, however, she heard it as well. A tumbling rock in the crypt spalled and flaked, creating an echo ahead of them. Shiloh shot her eyes back at Psalmodie, and once they both saw what the other was thinking, their expressions brightened. Shiloh turned face and, still choosing her steps carefully, quickly resumed down the tunnel.

But what she saw at the end nearly threw her into a panic.

Through the darkness, she thought she saw the face of a ghost.

Frightfully, Shiloh approached until it was well within the lantern's range of light. The clearer visual only gave her partial relief, assuming that there was still nothing otherworldly to the "apparition." She nevertheless dreaded its incongruous sight, much less its reason for being there.

A life-sized wooden corpus of a crucified Christ typically found on rood crosses suspended over some Latin altars. It was lodged askew into the rock-hewn egress from the other side, barricading their way forward. With one hand, she tested the sculpture's load, but it wouldn't budge.

Worry again grew in Psalmodie's voice. "What now?"

Shiloh took a moment to assess their situation. She evaluated the space around her, and while it was not ideal, there was enough wiggle room for Psalmodie to move up and squeeze herself next to her.

"It's going to be tight," Shiloh said, setting down the lantern, "but if you can come up next to me, I think we can lodge this out of our way."

"Alright, let me just..." Psalmodie shifted in between Shiloh's thin figure and the cave wall until they were pressed together face-to-face.

When they finished adjusting themselves in their cramped positions, they nodded their assent towards one another. In three synchronized movements, they rammed their shoulders against the splintering sculpture until it gave way. The two stumbled forward and fell to their knees, coughing on the resultant dust cloud.

Once the dust had begun to settle, Psalmodie opened her eyes and looked around the new space, only to find the same ink black darkness shrouding the entire room. She saw an orange glow brightening the space to her left; lining the walls were faded medieval frescos of cloaked monks and winged angels with gilded halos. The clearly Christian iconography looked almost Gothic to Psalmodie, although the figures' faces seemed to have been scraped away; whether it was vandalized by Byzantine iconoclasts or Muslims, she couldn't tell.

The figures, nevertheless, seemed to have been presiding over a hallowed, almost foreboding ancient presence.

"'Let there be light,'" Shiloh remarked, already up and navigating through the room with the lantern in hand.

Psalmodie cleared her throat, although once she looked down to the ground between her hands and saw the sculpture's bloodied head staring back at her, she jolted up with a yelp. Letting out a relieved shudder, she dusted off the crumbs from her shirt, rolled her shoulders, and followed shortly after Shiloh.

"Ugh, let there be a Holy Grail," Psalmodie rejoined, sighing her discontent.

Were it not for the crosses still scattered throughout the ground or the darkness enveloping their surroundings, she would have had a hard time containing her thrill. A roar of emotions coursed through her mind. Nearly two thousand years of quests—adventurous, romantic, dramatic, religious, and evil—have led to their being in a dingy undercroft.

"How has no one found this place yet?" Psalmodie wondered.

"The Romans built an improved network of tunnels and canals to distribute water to different parts of the city," Shiloh said. "The Barada river is *just* north of the mosque, which was built near the site of the Temple of Jupiter. It's hard to tell, but it seems like the Ayyubids repurposed this undercroft to stow the cross."

"But why an undercroft?" Psalmodie questioned.

Shiloh took a breath, still taking in the crypt. "Actually, this place looks more like a cistern."

"Wait a moment—A *cistern?* How the hell do you know all of this?"

Shiloh held the lantern to the dark cavern like an offering. Built into the cave wall was a large brick culvert drain pipe, partly clogged by the rubble of numerous cave-ins over the centuries. Her eyes traveled along the wall and stopped, noticing something unusual about the room's low ceiling: A rib vault supported by a forest of Romanesque columns, mirroring the hypostyle colonnade of the mosque above them.

"While you were out sightseeing the bazaar earlier," Shiloh started, "I did a little extra reading on the minaret back in the al-Zahiriyah Madrassa."

"Really?" Psalmodie said. "What have you got for me?"

"Well, supposedly, when the mosque was being constructed by the Umayyad Caliph al-Walid I in the 8th century, his overseer, Zaid ibn Wakid, found a small cave-chapel beneath the original Byzantine church's foundation. I don't know—I think this might be it. The space looks more like a cistern, although it's hard to tell since I have little to compare it to..." Shiloh glanced sidelong, and her tone became testy. "Right, Psalmodie?"

Psalmodie parried, "Hey, Brother already told you it's not my fault that our connecting trip suddenly moved up! It was either that Hagia Sophia 'Mosque-Basilica-whatever-it-is' or those books you insisted just *had* to be Arabic!"

Shiloh voiced a sarcastic *"mm-hmm"* before venturing deeper in the darkness. Once the mildly peeved tempers wore off, Psalmodie looked around and saw that the cistern had indeed looked like a smaller version of the considerably larger one underneath the famous Hagia Sophia she saw pictures of in Constantinople, which was once the Roman Empire's imperial capital. Even so, the mounding piles of crosses and corpus sculptures scattered around the dusty cistern more reminded Psalmodie of the time her father mischievously took her to tour the haunting walls of human bones in the underground Catacombs of Paris.

None of the crosses, however, seemed to have exuded a particular form of spectacle; not a single one of them looked to be worthy of the Holy Grail's mythos.

"Umm... Psalmodie?" Shiloh's voice echoed in the chamber.

Psalmodie ran up beside her, her tone equal parts curious and concerned. "What is it?" She read the revelation in Shiloh's eyes before following them to the cistern's center and sharing in her consternation.

Psalmodie's satchel slipped out from her hands, and with her eyes still fixated on the thousand-year scene in front of her, her trembling left hand searched for Shiloh's lantern.

Shiloh watched as her stupefied friend ambled across the room without looking back at her. "Psalmodie?" she called, worried for her overcoming dismay.

Psalmodie came to a stop before the bizarre formation and held the lantern close to it: A pyramidal stack of what appeared to be thirteen buckets, but each bucket had a particular design to them that conjured images of medieval warfare and piety alike in their imaginations.

Psalmodie got down on her haunches and singled out an outlier at the foot of the stack. She picked it up and slowly lowered herself to the ground, her eyes mulling over the empty object's various features: The flat-topped head, the torn chainmail aventail, the blackened iron texture, and the iconic cruciform visor.

The True Cross was gone.

She scoffed ruefully as the disturbing realization slowly sunk in. "Looks like Sir Galahad beat us to it, huh?"

A troubled Shiloh hovered over Psalmodie awhile before approaching the disorderly chest-high pyramid herself to see what more she could have gleaned from it. The way the buckets—helmets—were consolidated made her think it was a premeditated act, and while it was sometimes a standard issue piece of equipment for most Crusaders, one group would have always come to mind when seeing this helmet.

"I thought the Templars never entered Damascus." Shiloh chewed on this, then immediately took in the crosses all around her. "Saladin's successors were compensating..." she thought aloud.

Psalmodie didn't flinch. "What?"

Shiloh gestured broadly around the room. "It seems some Templar knights must have been able to take back the True Cross, and the Ayyubids must have needed as many replacements as possible for the prophecies in the Hadiths to be fulfilled somehow. Jesus still needed something to 'break.' They must have taken every cross they could have found and threw them all down here to make up for the loss of the original!" She turned her attention back on the stack, still bewildered by the structure.

"But how would they not have been caught?" Psalmodie countered tiredly. "How do you know it wasn't Muslims that relocated it? I mean, for all we know, they could've brought these helmets down here too. These ones have crosses too, you know. Their visors?"

Shiloh said nothing. For a long while, she stared at the helmets while her mind went to work on the countless bits of information she garnered over the years on medieval religion. She shook her head with each thought she discounted; nothing even remotely plausible came to mind.

As she was about to run through another idea for what the stack's connection was with the Templars, she noticed that one particular helmet with pale metallic and near-circular horned wing-crests on its crown was propped upright at the pyramid's apex, acting as a capstone.

She almost ignored it, but over each eyehole of the visor was a vertical gash crudely sliced into the metal as if done with a dull blade. Three parallel vertical lines and a fourth transversal through them, forming a sort of "triple cross." Curiously, however, the symbol seemed upside down given how the two longer sections of the vertical slashes were above the visor.

"Golgotha," Shiloh whispered in disbelief.

"Golgotha?" Psalmodie echoed.

"It's in the Gospels; it's Aramaic for 'Place of the Skull,'" Shiloh went on, tracing her forefinger over the two gashes on the visor. "The symbol's esoteric. These two gashes are also crosses. It's the hill where Jesus was crucified."

Psalmodie rose to her feet and indulged her friend. She brought the lantern closer to the winged helmet and looked closely at its gashes. "Crosses? What do you mean?"

"Okay. During the crucifixion, Jesus was placed between two thieves, right? Now these three crossbeams share one crossbar perhaps as a play on the design of the cross for the Crusader Kingdom of Jerusalem, but it's never that simple, is it? This symbol is upside down. It just doesn't make sense! There has to be something more to it."

Looking at the helmet further, Shiloh's mind soon soared with discovery. "This is a marker," she said, raising her forefinger to the pyramid of helmets. She picked up the lantern and strode around the cistern, her faraway gaze combing over the mess of crosses. "The Templars are pointing us somewh—Say, where's your journal again?"

Shiloh combed over the crosses on the ground. It wasn't long, however, until the silence in the cistern became more apparent to her. For a moment, she looked back at Psalmodie expecting her to be focused on looking for the satchel as well.

She wasn't.

Psalmodie stood at the limits of the firelight with her eyes riveted on Shiloh; something behind them bespoke a haunting distress. Shiloh wasn't ready to confront this abrupt, upsetting air about her friend.

But they weren't ready for the sound that echoed from the other end of the cistern.

At once, they tossed their startled gazes over in that direction, shrouded by an abysmal darkness. Promptly, Shiloh went for the lantern on the ground by the pyramid and returned to Psalmodie's side. She raised its light forward, illuminating the wall ahead of them.

From the ceiling dangled the twig-thin ends of creaking bush roots stemming from the world above with more shooting through. Accompanying it was the sound of shale tumbling down the side of the cave wall, growing louder and louder. To Psalmodie, the section of the cave looked familiar, but all doubt was removed when she saw the large corpus sculpture on the ground. That was when they noticed a tremor rising from the bowels of the earth, and dust fell from the cracks spidering across the cistern vault.

Over the mouth of the cave, a boulder was bulging through.

Shiloh felt the panic accelerate, her low voice growing to a scream. "Psalmodie, run. Run!"

They launched forward, but it was too late.

The boulder had fallen through and blasted a thick front of dust into Shiloh's face. She fell on her back and frantically crawled away from the debris still hailing from the cracking rib vault all around her. Then she tried to hide her head and face in the hollow of her shoulder and drew one last quivering breath for prayer.

Hail Mary, full of grace, the Lord is with thee...

CHAPTER 26

When the rumbling had settled, the first thing Shiloh did was to peek over her shoulder for clouds or any indication that she had indeed moved on. While she did see the still-swirling motes of dust reflecting the golden light of a beacon she thought was calling her, she was nevertheless put off by the darkness that was still prevalent throughout. When she struggled to her feet, she still felt shards of shale crunch underfoot.

She was still alive.

She dug her nose into the crook of her arm, choking and coughing on the polluted air in the deteriorated cistern. Having made her way to the lantern's light, she picked it up and squinted through the dense haze of dust.

Then she heard a muffled panting, punctuated by retching and a desperate crying for her name.

"Shiloh? Shiloh, where are you?"

"Psalmodie?" Shiloh coughed, following her voice to its origin. "Psalmodie, I'm okay!"

"Shiloh!" Psalmodie gasped hoarsely. "Oh, *Dieu merci.*"

"Where are you?" Shiloh called back. When Shiloh got close to the voice, however, she came before the boulder and the avalanched rubble that very nearly killed them both.

The voice came through clearer. "I got a few scrapes, but I made it through!"

Shiloh raised the lantern and found Psalmodie's illumed, now-grimy face peeking into the cistern through a narrow hole. "Are you alright?" Shiloh called.

"Shiloh, you're trapped," Psalmodie said.

Shiloh took stock of what was left of her surroundings, seeing the large crucifix on the ground and looking back up at the newly-formed ceiling cavity. "That cross we broke through... It must've been holding up this part of the crypt all these years."

"How are we getting you out?"

Shiloh scanned the cistern and caught sight of the large stone drain pipe in the wall. "I see some tunnels, Psalmodie. You have to go!"

"No! I'm not leaving you!"

"The mosque guards probably heard the noise! They might find the hatch! It's straight away for you. Just feel around the darkness and you'll be able to get out!"

"No!" Psalmodie cried. "No, there has to be a way to—"

Shiloh locked eyes with her. "You're no good to your father dead!" The statement shut Psalmodie up. Shiloh waved her off. "I'll find you! Just go! Go! Get out of here!"

Psalmodie lingered for a moment before bringing herself to look away and start into the darkness without another word. Shiloh backed away from the boulder, nearly tripping over the corpus sculpture. After she regained her footing, she saw something mixed in with the crosses and rocks.

Psalmodie's satchel.

Shiloh knelt down and opened its flap. She pulled out the leather journal and quickly leafed through its foxed pages to ensure its condition. From what she could have briefly gathered, as far as Psalmodie's father was concerned, there was nothing about the Knights Templar that would have shed light on the meaning of the upside down Golgotha triple cross or any enigmatic pyramidal rituals beyond the farragoes of zany conspiracy theories that suggested occult connections to secret societies such as the Grand Orient de France.

She did, however, notice something nestled within the journal's

gutter. To her, it looked like a collection of memos with marginal annotations—perhaps archival filing markings—, but the print wasn't in any
language she was familiar with. Not French or Arabic. The script might
have been English for all she could have known, but the vowels had liga-
tures and diacritics that would have indicated otherwise.

Curious, she thought.

Of course, none of it mattered anymore; not until Shiloh found her
way out. After putting the book back into the satchel, she slung it over
her shoulder and hovered the lantern over the gaping maw of rock
carved into the wall.

From what Shiloh understood in the madrassa, Damascus had
gained somewhat of a reputation for its ruined Roman aqueducts,
namely through the Old City's neighboring Qanawat municipality.
Many of the canals there transported water from the Barada river, which
flowed just north of the Umayyad Mosque, to places all throughout the
city.

Nevertheless, it was a grim prospect venturing into this precarious
waist-high tunnel, which could have possibly led to a dead end or even
worse. Shiloh ran through the various possibilities of her going in,
although she had little to work with in regard to confidently reaching a
decision. She glanced once more around the chamber, taking in the
saints and angels on the walls and the crosses at her feet. She then shook
her head at what she was about to do.

"*A'udhu billahi,*" she muttered, crossing herself before crouching
her head and venturing forth into the abyss.

CHAPTER 27

The Umayyad Mosque

salmodie made sure that the hatch was locked in place and hidden under the rug, despite her grave concern for Shiloh. Though she still didn't know what to believe, she felt she had to trust in something that would have safely seen her friend out of the rubble.

"Alright... move," she breathed out, steeling her thoughts and shaking out her fidgety hands. After nervously pacing back and forth a moment, she turned away and took great care in opening the minaret's door a small way. After scoping out the long and greatly-darkened prayer hall, she crept through the ajar door's slight aperture and lightly pressed it shut behind her back. Once she released her breath, she then proceeded to sidle discreetly along the mosque's left wall.

Psalmodie kept her head down, but then she became mindful of the fact that she hadn't taken off her boots or, perhaps worse for her guise, hadn't been wearing her headscarf. Her lowered eyes restlessly peered around the prayer hall from beneath her eyebrows, though she tried to keep her stare on the floor ahead of her.

But in her haste towards the mosque's exit, she noticed that the floor's red carpet had seemed to have been cast in a vibrantly viridescent color. It wasn't long before she felt as though the entire prayer hall itself had become saturated with this emerald light. As she began to slow to a halt, she turned to her right and saw that she had been standing in the glow of a rectangular, peripteros-like structure set between two columns of the first colonnade.

She almost made passing notice of the marble pavilion, but her curiosity drew her eyes to the plaque embedded in the florid grating of one of its green, round top windows. As it was with Saladin's mausoleum, there was an Arabic inscription accompanied by a French transliteration. Though Psalmodie didn't recognize the surname at first, she assumed that there had to have been a derivation. Once she gleaned one possible connection, her eyes took in the sudden insight.

Golgotha...

For a moment, however, she stepped outside of herself and looked back towards the minaret's door. She still had her dire misgivings about Shiloh's condition, but Psalmodie again looked down both ends of the mosque and saw that it seemed to have been empty. Though she started to feel lightheaded from sleep deprivation, she remembered her father. She could almost feel his hand resting lovingly on her cheek as she dozed with her face deep in her bed pillow; she remembered feeling that gentle touch for the very last time, just before he stepped aboard that train for his damned sabbatical.

She looked back down at that plaque, still unsure of herself, but then she removed two more bobby pins from behind her ear.

"You better be okay, Shiloh," Psalmodie whispered.

In the piazza outside of the mosque's main entrance, two half-slumbering guards sat on stools at either end of the bronze doors with their chins rested on their hands over their Turkish ceremonial maces. As it was with most nights at the Great Mosque, all was perfectly quiet save the usual gusts of wind.

What ended up waking them both, however, was the lockstep of shadows approaching them from the Temple of Jupiter; four of them were white men in black and three others donned Bedouin attire. Though the guards both assumed the group was already well-armed, the guards rose to their feet anyway and met them halfway with their clubs resting over their shoulders.

For a while, the two groups traded chary glances, each waiting for the other to speak. While none of them did, the guards saw the white men nod to one another before parting to reveal a fourth Bedouin man standing behind them. Though the man's face was still hardly visible in the darkness, when they saw in his icy stare the pale eyeshine of a nocturnal wolf, the guards became filled with the impulse to genuflect in esteem for the man.

Instead, they both took the occasion to quietly proclaim, *"Allahu Akbar..."*

CHAPTER 28

Shiloh's sense of time was dulled, although it felt to her that she had already spent at least half an hour caving beneath the streets of the Old City. With every crevice she worked her way through, her concern only doubled. The walls were no longer those of an ancient aqueduct's, but of an eroded deposit of caliche sediment, and over time, she came upon many snarls of roots dangling from the desiccated earth above.

More tunnel, she thought, both reassured and discontented by the pitch black depth that went beyond her lantern's range of light. She hadn't come close to finding a way out, but at least she didn't see a dead end yet. The deeper she went, however, the more she felt the walls closing in around her. For her, it was a suffocating entrapment not knowing if the confined space would have ended up being her tomb.

There was a cave-in ahead of her, but there was a wide enough hollow beneath the rubble for her to crawl under. With her lantern still in hand, she lay prone and peered through to gauge its distance, and what she saw brightened her spirit.

A dim blue pinprick of light off in the distance.

Carefully, she rolled her lantern through, but because she still needed to breathe, Shiloh turned over and lied supine before wriggling backwards into the short crawl space. There were rocks on the ceiling that she used as holds to help pull herself through, although she tried using them sparingly to avoid another cave-in.

Amid the darkness, she groped around for another hold, but once she did, to her surprise, she felt a smooth and damp surface. Her clothes were sticking to her back and a chill ran down her spine. Rolling the lantern upward, she looked up from the ceiling in front of her and saw a small rill streaming toward the end of the tunnel.

Once she had gotten to the end of the crawl space, Shiloh rose back to her crouching position; the ceiling was still low, and she was not out just yet. With each step of her approach to the end, the water rose to her ankles. Then shins. Then knees. As the water creased around her ankles, a very, very familiar feeling came back to her. Her relief gave way to rumination, and she felt as though she had been in that tunnel her whole life. All sounds in the cave became submerged in a vacuum of distorted echoes; she only heard her own heart, beating in her ears like the low booming of a rawhide war drum. The lantern in her hand became an afterthought and fell to the ground as she felt her past reaching out to her unexpectedly.

Then she felt as though she had floated out of herself.

A louring shelf cloud and circling flocks of ravens stirred the overcast night sky above her, looming as desolating omens. The bleak landscape behind her was made ebony by the night's dark blue air. She was that little girl again, standing alone on that shore. Her remote eyes, riven by conflict and relentless fatigue; her face, slathered in watery, tar-black mud.

Through the rolling mists, she saw the shallows breaking ashore and noticed the few straggling files of refugees wading through the choppy ocean waters alongside her, rushing for the boats moored to the rocks. She turned around and saw the sea's undulating beach dunes, blanketed in rustling tufts of marram grass. Beyond them, her rural childhood hamlet was consumed in fire and blackened smoke after those torch-bearing pirates had all but defiled it. Amid the muffled echoes of the refugees' frenzied and overlapping jabbering, she heard a sweet voice coming from that village, again calling out for her.

Her pulsing heart became a rumbling echo.

Despite the émigrés running past her, Shiloh turned back and gave chase to the voice, but the memory was fading into the mists. The little girl cried for her mother and father. Her entire world seemed to have been shrinking further and further away from her the closer she ran towards it. She saw those guerilla butchers, holding their rifles aloft and firing rousing, celebratory shots into the air. Their barking war cries grew louder, but they all ran past her, as if none of them were even aware of her presence.

But to her distress, she didn't see her parents.

"No! Please! Don't go! I need you!" she cried, fighting for air between sobs. Her stamina was draining. She knew her begging was in vain but refused to give up her dogged pursuit.

Then she saw something emerge from the mists: A towering wooden palisade prolonged along the dunes. There was no way around it. She peered through a groove in the mossy stakes and saw the golden light of her mother dimming into the fog until it died out.

The girl screamed, "No! Where are you? Tell me! Tell me! Please!" She kicked at the stakes until one had come loose. She desperately tried to squeeze through, but one of the devils had clutched her arm. With a wrench of her hand, she broke free and fell through the opening.

Then... silence...

Nothing remained beside that voice; its quiet echo resonated through Shiloh's mind like a lingering susurration. Still on all fours, she looked up and saw that she was no longer on that shore, but in some waterlogged gulley. Before her was only a shallow rivulet of coffee-colored water babbling over stones, and shortly after it was the craggy embankment with a tree line rising over tufts of marsh cordgrass.

Shiloh's heartbeat slowed as she looked bemusedly back at the broken stilts of tree roots curtaining the outcropped cavity she had just fled. In the terrace above the gulley's river bank were a hutment of moldy adobe houses and corrugated tin shacks nearly reclaimed by wilderness.

The air was brisk, and the leaden skies above shed a muted blue-gray hue over Damascus, although Shiloh didn't know if it was the morning twilight or set moonlight. Still recovering from so much mental strain, Shiloh leaned a hand against the embankment's dirt wall to take a moment to catch her breath. She felt Francis' rosary in her pocket and took it out to contemplate the devotional medal.

When her gaze traveled down to her wrist, she again lost herself in that cross of her mother's faith. Once more, she felt the tragic spirit of something—something cruel, insatiable, everywhere—, always with her, haunting her... everywhere.

Then Shiloh remembered herself.

Psalmodie!...

She quickly put the rosary into her friend's satchel and felt the journal's spine. She then tightened her grip on the satchel's strap and turned her attention to the buildings above, ready to brave whatever perils awaited in yet another dark unknown.

But if Psalmodie didn't escape and was captured by the mosque's guards and handed over to the local Arab authorities, she would have needed to have been ready to cut her losses and ready to flee with what little was necessary to survive. Someone else's father's life hung in the balance, and Shiloh couldn't have risked losing his only hope.

Their only hope.

CHAPTER 29

Al-Hariqa neighborhood

S hiloh had stowed the satchel someplace relatively safe before she set upon searching for her friend, but there was only one place she could have reasonably thought of that would have been far enough away from the mosque of local authorities.

Shiloh emerged from a desolate alleyway and looked up and down the street ahead of her. At the far end of the street were the white string lights of a thatched-roof alfresco restaurant under the canopy of three tall palm trees. The rest of the street remained dark, although every venue and shop window also seemed to have been glowing with some soirée or gathering, whether for coffee, smoking, or food; in most cases, she heard the muffled sound of phonograph music playing over lively chatter. Shiloh was wary of the people lounging on benches among wooden casks outside the buildings under the dying light of kerosene lamps.

She jammed her hands deep into her pockets and picked up her pace. She kept her head down and her eyes forward, though she was also wary of looking too suspect to any passing patrolmen or wayfarers. As she walked hurriedly along the street's buildings, she looked for one in particular. She knew that if Psalmodie had found sanctuary anywhere to await their reunion, it would have had to have been at Malik's teahouse.

Once Shiloh found it, she promptly scuttled for the café's recessed corner entrance. A sound briefly startled her, but once she saw that it was only three men with fez hats laughing their way out of a shop behind her, she released her breath and turned back towards the door.

But when she looked at its deadbolt lock, she saw that the escutcheon had been forcibly bored out, and the door itself was skewed from its frame. At first, she took it as a sign that Psalmodie had made her way in, but then she immediately sensed something was amiss. Psalmodie was an adept lock picker, and what she saw seemed to be the work of a common thief or worse. Shiloh held back for a moment, whelmed with a sense of foreboding. She glanced back around the corner, mindful of whatever may have been lurking in the shadowy alleyways of the neighborhood.

Besides the mosque, there was nowhere else for her to look.

She looked back down at the door and nudged the creaking door inward with her booted toe. The lights were out, and with the exception of the dim blue glow of the glass block window at the other end of the parlor, the entire café sat in a void-like shroud of shadows. She stole into the room, taking slow and quiet steps through the maze of chairs and tables.

"Psalmodie?" Shiloh called quietly.

There was no response.

While she inched through the darkness, she stumbled over something. She couldn't have seen what it was, but it sounded like a wooden slat when it slid across the floor. She kicked another one, heavier. A disorderly array of capsized furniture. Shiloh almost thought it was vandalism, although she feared worse. It had to have been a scuffle, but whoever may have been involved appeared to have been already gone.

Shiloh scanned the room and called again. "Psalmodie? Psalmodie! Malik?"

It was then that a gravelly voice called back in a relaxed drawl, *"As-salamu alaykum,* Shiloh Ma'idah al-Ahad."

The voice was not Malik's. She jolted and saw the cloaked figure slouched in his chair at a round table against the window, hardly more than a shadow himself. His face and dark thawb robe were fully silhouetted against the window, although Shiloh made out his pecinyah cap—

a red fez wrapped in white cloth—, leading her to believe that he was an Islamic adjudicator of some sort. On his table was a Nargileh water pipe stand, wafting swirling smoke from the tobacco burner around the man.

Stunned, she asked shakily, "How do you know my name? Who are you?"

At first, the spectral visitation kept silent as white smoke drooled and feathered from his lips. "I have been told that you have something that doesn't belong to you... and you are going to give it to us."

The entire shop seemed to have frozen into quiet. Shiloh fell back a step, but then felt a cold metal end prodding her head. Behind her was a man in black holding a rifle to her neck. In that moment, three other spooks materialized from the shadows like angels of darkness. One of them seemed to carry himself with cocksure civility; he sat himself in a chair next to the jurist, effeminately crossed his legs, and held the higher knee with his hands, while the other two men...

Shiloh's eyes widened in horror. The other two had Psalmodie gagged and pinned down on the floor with large, Luger-like pistols pressing down on the base of her neck. She looked up at Shiloh, helpless and tormented.

"Walk," the man behind Shiloh uttered. When she didn't respond, he jabbed the gun barrel harder against her head. "I said walk!"

"Shit!" she shuddered, complying reluctantly.

The man shoved her towards the two by the window. There, he twisted her arm behind her back to push her up against the wall, kicked apart her legs, and frisked her down with his free hand. Once he had finished, he clasped down on her shoulder and forced her down on a chair opposite the two.

"No sudden movements," he said, leaning against a table behind her.

All was placid between her and her captors. Shiloh tried looking back at Psalmodie, but the man's barrel punched her face back towards the men before her. Their faces were still enveloped in the surrounding smoke and darkness. She dared not break the silence, but her sitting in the soft blue light from the window next to them made Shiloh feel that an interrogation spotlight was on her to speak first. Still, she couldn't help but stare particularly at the jurist.

The man next to him finally spoke, all business. *"Bonsoir,* Fräulein al-Ahad... I am Obersturmführer Otto Wilhelm Rahn of Germany's Geheime Staatspolizei. I am here in Damascus with official dispensation from the German chancellor's cabinet because there has been a warrant issued for the arrest of your friend as part of an ongoing investigation involving..." He paused briefly, looking at the man next to him before continuing, "...involving some things that don't belong to her, as I'm sure she must have told you. Am I to understand that you may currently be in possession of—"

The jurist interrupted, noticing Shiloh's direct stare. "You already know who I am, don't you?" he said in French.

You, she thought. *Why?*

Though still petrified, a blend of wrath and dread blackened in her heart. She kept silent, but she couldn't have masked her agitation. Though the man's reddish hair and blue eyes made him seem more Bosnian than Arab, he looked just like the photographs from the newspapers, although there were no traces of his habitual grin and relaxed gaze on his rosy white, grizzled face. Instead, he looked rather conflicted and uneasy, perhaps even reluctant.

Shiloh did know him, and she resented him almost as much as she resented the European colonial powers that had driven men like him— men of God and men who knew not what they did—to sell their own souls to the devils of statecraft and realpolitik to have one final hope of saving their homeland from the rising tide of Zionist terrorism. Though Shiloh did understand and even fully identified with their struggles, she also understood that such retaliatory violence was not what this man ever wanted.

Even so, it was all for the actions of men like him inflicted on the people closest to Shiloh that defined who she had become.

"Haj Mohammed Amin al-Husseini," she said. "You are the Grand Mufti of Jerusalem who claims heritage from the Prophet's grandson."

The mufti's expression ashened, betraying a burden he had carried all his life. He shot one more glance at Rahn before turning it back on Shiloh. "You are probably wondering how we have found you both," al-Husseini said, a smile creeping its way onto his face. He nodded his head at Rahn and continued, "My friend here says you two are in search of a mystical chalice of sorts; he wouldn't be referring to the Cup of Jamshid, would he? The lost treasure of Persepolis?"

When Shiloh didn't immediately answer him, she felt the gun's cold metal poke at her head. "It's a Christian legend, not Persian," she complied.

"An English one, I presume?" al-Husseini asked.

Shiloh nodded before quickly adding, "At least, that's what I've gathered from some rumors."

"But it also grants eternal life?" al-Husseini pried. "You do know full well that Allah forbids intoxication and idolatry?" Shiloh kept silent again, but the mufti allowed it and returned to the matter at hand. "My friend here also told me that his former partner—your friend's father—might have believed it to be in a 'New Jerusalem' in Damascus. As I am sure you have already figured out, there could only be one place in this city that fits that description.

"When we got there, the guards caught your friend stealing something. After they brought her to us, she told us where you *might* have gone, although to be fair, she looked like she didn't believe it herself considering the amount of rock my men said they found under 'Isa bin Maryam's minaret."

Shiloh breathed her words fiercely, over-pronouncing each syllable. "We. Didn't. Steal. Anything."

"Oh, then what is this?" al-Husseini impugned, holding something small to Shiloh.

A six-inch socketed iron tube rolled over the table. She wanted to look back at Psalmodie to see if it was true. Instead, she traded a glance to her captors, and for some reason, saw in Rahn's eyes that he was just as perplexed as she was.

She looked back down at the green-rusted, baton-shaped artifact and recognized something peculiar about it: A part of the seal of the Knights Templar was etched on the reinforce. A small cross pattée, though it looked unfinished and was more T-shaped:

T

Along both sides of the tube's chase, however, were crude assortments of inscrutable engravings:

At first, Shiloh didn't recognize the vertical script, but once she glossed it further, she exhaled in astonishment. She couldn't have believed what she was seeing: A creole script descended from the much older Syriac Aramaic alphabet, written for a language that belonged to the only murderous, pagan, tyrannical punishment from God the Crusaders and Saracens feared far more than each other. More frightening still, the relic itself—one of many—rang out thunderous echoes that could still be heard and felt to the present day.

Shiloh felt cold simply holding it.

The man behind her snapped, "What the hell is that? You *lie* to us, Arab?"

"Calm down, Kurt!" Rahn said, holding up his hand towards him. "Now you told our Reichsführer that you studied Sanskrit for a time, correct? Do you recognize this script?"

"No, I don't!" Eggers yelled. "Whatever any of that is, it isn't Indo-Aryan!"

"Then what is it?" Rahn asked. Before Eggers could respond, Rahn turned on al-Husseini and demanded, "Your Eminence, this is not why we solicited your guidance! You're helping us tie loose ends for us to neatly proceed with our investigati—"

"Oh, and *you* have been completely honest with your secrets all this time, have you?" al-Husseini countered, coughing on smoke. "Now I want for the Zionists what you do as well, but I also know how you Aryans handle Jewish artifacts. Since you, Rahn, have told me this girl is proficient in reading the Semitic languages, I wanted to take this opportunity to at least know what this inscription says before we—"

"I cannot read this," Shiloh cut him off. "I-I mean this isn't Jewish or any other Semitic language I know of."

The two glanced at her, mildly intrigued by her statement. Shiloh froze, wondering if she had just given up her only bargaining chip in her survival.

"You mean to say that you cannot, or you *will* not?" al-Husseini challenged.

Shiloh shook her head. "I mean, the Aramaic parent system is unquestionable—this does *look* like an older Sogdian or Uyghur script, but no, this is—" Shiloh demurred, still wondering whether the absurd claim she was about to make would have spelled her demise. Still pondering and fearing her captors' possible reactions, she answered, "This can't be... It's a hand cannon of the Mongol Empire... but *why?*"

"The *Tatars?*" Rahn scorned. "*China?* Your Christian Grail is all the way to the Dragon Throne now? Is that it?" Rahn turned to face al-Husseini but found that he did not appear to have been sharing in his amusement.

After a long silence, the mufti recalled the chilling words of one medieval Arab chronicler: "'For even Antichrist will spare such as follow him, but these Tatars spared *none...*'"

CHAPTER 30

Shiloh saw the mufti staring gravely at her before turning his gaze back down on the ancient hand cannon; still taking in her claim, he continued, "Those Philistine hordes slaughtered our ancestors centuries ago. They ended the Ummah's Golden Age after they murdered our caliph and made satanic pyramids out of the Muslims' skulls... The greatest tragedy to befall *Dar al-Islam* since the great schism that occurred after the Prophet's death, *sallallahu alayhi wasallam;* yes, even more so than what is happening to the Arabs today..."

Immediately, Shiloh's eyes shot up at al-Husseini. She processed what he said and pieced together the connection she had been missing the entire time. *The pyramid below the minaret... It was the Mongol hordes.*

Shiloh felt compelled to grill al-Husseini on the artifact. "Where did you find this?"

The mufti pointed a finger over her shoulder. "She did."

Shiloh looked back to Psalmodie, still subdued by the two German enforcers. Then she heard an object set against the surface of the table. She turned back to face al-Husseini, but what she saw on the table jarred her. She nearly swooned from the unnerving sight.

Next to the water pipe's vase was a pale brown human skull.

"It was within a long-hidden hollowed-out shaft in the ancient Pillar of Humility," al-Husseini said, pointing to its cranium. "The marble column, built in the time of Caliph al-Walid I, which used to bear up this skull. Your friend made quite a lot of noise pushing aside the cover to get to it. You wouldn't happen to know who this skull belongs to, would you?"

Shiloh stared into the cold silence of death and felt its gaping eye sockets stare right back at her. She was at a loss for what to make of the skull. The mufti's question, however, sounded sardonic, as if she was already supposed to have an idea on who the skull belonged to. She still didn't understand. The sight was no less mortifying, and she thought there was nothing else to go off on.

Her eyes stayed transfixed on the skull before they flashed with insight. Her captivation slowly became obsession. She remembered the pavilion back in the mosque and chided herself for such a critical oversight. It all made sense. The mosque was built over a former Byzantine basilica housing the relic of this major Islamo-Christian prophet and decapitated martyr. The skull reportedly belonged to none other than the herald of the Messiah Himself, beheaded by the adulterous Judean King Herod at the request of the daughter of his lover, his own brother's wife.

"Saint John the Baptist," she answered.

Golgotha... "The Place of the Skull..." The pavilion...

The mufti irreverently rested his palm on it as if it were some gavel block. "Did you two come all by yourselves?"

Shiloh was unnerved by the keen timbre of his question. Despite this, she managed a brave front, although she could tell they both looked right past it. "What are you getting out of this?" she directed at al-Husseini.

He answered enthusiastically, "If the German chancellor's conference with the British in Munich fails, then an alliance with the German regime, of course. The enemies of the British and the Zionists and the hypocritical *munafiq* are my friends. *Our* friends; you and I. Arabs, Muslim, Jewish, *and* Christian; how quickly you forget, Shiloh, that it was the Pharisees' conspiring with the Romans that sentenced 'Isa —*alayhis salaam*—to death. The Führer and his subjects may not be Muslim, but they do share in Allah's will for the future against al-Masih ad-Dajjal."

"*Allah's* will?" Shiloh repeated in disbelief. She glanced at Rahn before turning her attention back on al-Husseini. Her tone changed, and with it, her tongue as well. "Your friend here hasn't told you, has he?" she challenged him in Arabic.

Rahn looked between them restlessly. "What is this?"

With his tickled blue eyes fixed on Shiloh, the mufti raised a hand at Rahn to abate his temper. When Rahn withdrew and took to nervously drumming his fingertips on the table, al-Husseini then carefully lowered his hand and took one last toke of his Nargileh before setting the hose down next to the skull. He leaned forward on the table with interlocked hands and silently drew closer to her, his face illumed in the light. He released his breath and blew smoke on Shiloh's flinching face before indulging her with an Arabic response of his own: "What hasn't he told me?"

Shiloh fought back against his penetrating gaze and wasted no time with what she had to say. "You are the *munafiq* here, Your Eminence. Yes, the Zionists are conspiring with the British to steal away our peoples' homeland, but you were only so happy to do the British Mandate's colonial bidding against the Zionists before selling out to yet another monster. You are no Selahaddin Eyyubi, no Husayn ibn Ali; you are just another Mongol khan, and you would even fall in with pagans if it meant bolstering yourself in Allah's eyes."

At first, al-Husseini seemed to have taken the insult like a slap, but after taking a moment to reflect on Shiloh's words, he said, "There is a saying of the wise Prince of Bismarck: 'Politics is the art of the possible,' and the truth of this is that all notions of idealism during wartime fall at the feet of opportunity. *Wallahi*, Shiloh, if war ever comes of the negotiations in Munich, a Christian colonial monarchy like Great Britain would even compromise with a godless communist tyrant like Joseph Stalin if it meant seeing His Majesty's enemies driven before him."

Shiloh scoffed, "You compare yourself to *them*?"

Al-Husseini smirked. "Indeed, the Prophet himself—*sallallahu alayhi wasallam*—was not beyond allying himself with Jews and pagans to rescue the House of Allah in Mecca from the captivity of the Quraysh tribe. Two years after that, during a *mubahalah* prayer duel, he even assured the hostile Christians of Najran that they would all be protected under Allah's grace."

Shiloh dared to lean in and say, "So Rahn *has* told you?"

With a spurt of laughter, al-Husseini asked, "Tell me what exactly?"

"Look at his hand."

It was then that the mufti noticed a soft metallic clicking next to him; he saw Rahn nervously tapping the palmside of a ring, which was engraved with an equilateral Occitan cross. When Rahn noticed what the mufti was looking down at, Rahn folded his other hand over his ring. At this, al-Husseini looked back at Shiloh and shrugged indifferently.

Then she rasped, "Be honest with me, Your Eminence: Do you ever recall the Prophet entering into a *mubahalah* prayer duel with a nation of *satanic* pagans? Is this really how far you are willing to go? To compromise with a nation that already wants nothing more than to be as cursed as the demon Legion himself?"

Stunned at first, al-Husseini then grinned and said, "And you expect me to believe that? How would you know if that ring isn't anything more than some vainly Christian expression of a more general European culture?"

"You already know he isn't Jewish or Christian or Muslim. What would you call his quest for this *religious* relic then?"

He almost chuckled again, but the longer he stared at Shiloh, the more his expression ashened. He nearly looked back at Rahn, but he instead shifted in his seat as he took in her troubling allegation.

"Enough of this!" Rahn exclaimed. "What are you telling each other?"

Shiloh rolled over his words and continued pressing the mufti in Arabic. "You seize this relic, you can show the colonists that 'Isa bin Maryam's might and legacy are more than a Roman instrument of torture and—"

The German's hand flashed out and smacked Shiloh's cheek. Rahn then whispered menacingly to her, "If you won't tell us where those telegrams are, there is nothing stopping us from killing you right now. Do you realize that?"

Shiloh winced in pain as she wiped away the line of blood running down the side of her mouth. The sting on her cheek numbed after a while, but when she felt Eggers' gun dig deeper into her spine, a rush of panic swelled. Her eyes shifted with every thought that flashed before her until she came upon one. She couldn't help but think something about Rahn's words didn't add up to her.

"Te-telegrams?" she stammered. "Wait, I-I thought you wanted us for the Grail or—" By the time she could finish, however, her face fell, and the stark reality was made manifest. She looked back at Psalmodie and saw the defeat in her wounded eyes.

"Your father is dead, isn't he?" Shiloh whispered faintly, her voice saturated with puzzlement and pity. "And you always knew this?"

"Civilian espionage," Rahn interrupted, shooting an agitated glance at Eggers. "Her late father—my former partner—blackmailed a prison guard into sending out to his daughter a number of telegrams, of whose classification we do not know, but could possibly heavily compromise some assets among other interests."

Shiloh's voice became tiny. "Those memos in the journ—"

"Where are they?" Rahn exploded, planting his balled fists on the table as he stood to his feet and stalked off towards Psalmodie. "Schütze Eggers? On my count, be prepared to shoot her."

Eggers dug the rifle deeper into Shiloh's neck. Still subdued by the other two enforcers, Psalmodie tried thrashing free of their hold, but all she could have done was sob her muffled protests. Rahn knelt by her and clasped a hand over her eyes.

"No!" Shiloh pleaded frantically. "No! No, I have them! I have them! I swear I do!"

Rahn started, "One..."

She looked back at al-Husseini, a tear streaming from her eye. "If you let them kill us," she begged, "and if you are who you say you are, you won't be any better than your ancestor's usurping murderer."

"Two..."

Her appeal became a curse. "Your Eminence, you will fall far from his august name! Or is it true what they say? That it was *your* ancestors who usurped his title and—"

She heard Eggers cock his rifle.

"Thr—"

"Rahn?" the mufti's voice burst out.

A long silence hung over the room. Eggers loosened his grip on the rifle while Rahn and his troop relaxed their hold on Psalmodie. Shiloh's breath escaped her as a tremulous sigh, although all she could have done was sit and watch their fates unfold. Then she saw al-Husseini glance down at the foreign inscriptions on the hand cannon and heard him whisper to himself in Arabic an alleged saying of the Prophet: *"Seek knowledge, even unto China..."* Al-Husseini then looked up at Rahn and said, "I think we have to talk."

"Talk *now?*" Rahn exclaimed.

"Yes, right now; seeing as how you were about to kill one of our only leads to your missing telegrams, I think it would be appropriate to reevaluate the mutual benefits of our relationship."

"These girls are of no consequence to you," Eggers said, aiming his rifle back down on Shiloh's head.

The mufti stood up from his chair and straightened into his usual regal posture to hold court. "Shiloh here speaks of an *English* Cup of Jamshid; a relic from the crucifixion myth perhaps?"

The Germans' faces dropped with unease. "She lies," Rahn insisted. "For more than two millennia, the Christians have kept the true relic hostage. It was never Christian. *Never.* They have always lied about it."

"I am not surprised," al-Husseini chuckled. "It has always been in their nature to corrupt their own scriptures and legends, and not a day goes by that I don't pray that my fellow Arab Christian comrades will one day see the fault in their faith. But if this girl is correct in saying that there is indeed a relic in Damascus that the Christians in Europe would call your 'chalice,' I wonder, my friend, if it would not be better if we indeed found it. I mean, I doubt these two would come this far chasing after their own lie."

Rahn was stunned. "Am I to understand that you are changing the terms of our agreement?"

"Au contraire, my friend; you seek to bury this supposed Christian counterfeit of your treasure, yes?"

Rahn and Eggers shot glances at their prey before trading them with one another.

"And what exactly is it that you are proposing, Your Eminence?" Eggers questioned.

"If it is all the same to you," al-Husseini responded, "wouldn't it be better if we simply destroyed it? The European Christians will lose their credibility to your chalice through this false relic for good, and I will have truly affirmed in my heart what Allah has willed for me against them."

Eggers laughed his contempt and brandished the gun's muzzle over the ground ahead of al-Husseini; a clear message. "I don't think so, Saracen."

"Tread carefully now, Schütze Kurt Eggers," the mufti growled, advancing menacingly on Rahn. "I am the Grand Mufti of al-Quds. My will is Allah's; thus, my will is law. I have the jurisdiction to warrant fatwas on your lives, and I do proclaim, once my loyal subjects see what has happened to a scion of the Prophet's house—*sallallahu alayhi wasallam*—, there will not be a place in the Arab or Aryan world where you will be able to run and hide from your sins."

The grave severity to al-Husseini's voice was enough to make even Eggers draw away from him. The other two were just as unnerved, although Rahn himself stepped forward to accost him again. Rahn peered over and saw that Shiloh was still frozen under Eggers' presence. Then he looked back at Psalmodie, and his glare fell with evident affliction.

"Kurt?" Rahn said, now buying in. "Put them in the back-room pantry with the other one; high priest Wiligut Weisthor and the Ahnenerbe will probably want to catalogue a record of this dealing for Wewelsburg's archives."

Rahn stayed with al-Husseini in the parlor as his three inquisitors harshly dragged the two girls through the small, mildewed scullery kitchen by their arms and necks until they stopped before a metal door. Once they unlocked it, Eggers himself took the pleasure of throwing them in. Shiloh fell flat against the floor with Psalmodie stumbling forth on her side.

Shiloh's eyes darted back to their captors. Then she watched as the cannon and skull rolled along the tile floor towards her feet like mere footballs. After the door slammed shut and locked from the other side, she looked about their holding cell's small parameters. But just as she was about to reach for the holy skull, a soft moan behind her startled her. She jerked her head up and saw the young waiter lying prone with his face swollen and bruised.

"Malik?" she cried to him, crawling over to his side.

Psalmodie removed the gag from her mouth and looked at them with an anguished look. With wavering intent, she motioned a hand towards Shiloh's shoulder before stopping short, leaving her friend to tend to Malik's concussed state.

CHAPTER 31

T he quiet hissing of Shiloh's circular recitations was like the soft and rhythmic patter of water drops, swallowed into the cold quiet; that same prayer, over and over again. It was the only thing Psalmodie had left to appreciate in this world, at least while she was still in it. She looked up and saw Shiloh at the other end of the pantry sitting with her legs crossed and extended. On her lap rested Malik's head, still unconscious from the beating, and on the floor before her boots were both the skull and the ancient gun Psalmodie tried to steal.

For hours—or what seemed to be hours—, Shiloh read everything she had ever known in her life into the two artifacts. At least, that's what Psalmodie chose to believe as a reason for her persistent silence. For the past few minutes, however, Shiloh looked directly at her. She nearly forced Psalmodie to look off somewhere else, but there was something to her abstracted stare that more suggested deep trance rather than direct grievance.

"A'udhu billahi..." Shiloh prayed, *"min ash-shaytan ar-rajim.."*

Psalmodie wouldn't lose face. Her blue eyes locked with Shiloh's until she herself thought she could have sensed in them—more than eyes ever could—the God she so stubbornly searched for. This lasted for another couple of minutes until something in them switched.

Then at last, Shiloh broke the silence. "The first Mongol khans of

Persia were Buddhists, animist shamanists, and even hypocritical Muslims... but their queens, princesses, and warrior tumens were Christians!"

Psalmodie's brow furrowed. "What?"

"The Church of the East!" Shiloh threw her gaze down at the skull and reproached herself. "Some of the Mongols were shamanistic Christians, which included the Empress of Mongolia herself... *Mon Dieu*, how on Earth could I have missed this?"

"Missed what?"

"Christianity and the Mongols!" Shiloh exclaimed. She tenderly moved Malik's head from her lap before standing to her feet and pacing the floor with a short chuckle. "Well, Saint John the Baptist *was* a blood relative of Jesus Christ; a cousin, I believe. So would that make Saint John *half*-Grail material then?"

Psalmodie was stunned by Shiloh's rude awakening, whatever it was and what it meant. She wanted to question, but when she opened her mouth to do so, she was speechless and became lost again in her eyes. There was no resentment or fear in them. Psalmodie wondered about the flaring indignation that ought to have been in them. Perhaps it was hysterical denial, but then again, once Rahn and al-Husseini had gotten what they wanted, their use to them would no longer matter. Her curiosity was pointless.

Looking at her friend long and hard, Psalmodie pushed it from her mind. She stood up and finally indulged Shiloh's distraction in the vague hope that she would have found some ultimate closure in telling her own story.

"Well, when you put it that way, it really does sound like something straight out of Peredur's Welsh *Mabinogion* romance, doesn't it?" Psalmodie commented before adding, "But I *also* read that some Templar monks were widely rumored to have many other silver-gilt skull reliquaries in their possession during the Middle Ages. And you *did* say that that Golgotha symbol on that horned Templar helm looked upside down."

"It *was* a marker after all!" Shiloh said, speaking as if assembling her thoughts on the fly. "To beneath the 'Place of the Skull,' apparently that marble pillar you broke into inside the pavilion; quite literally right under Saint John's nose! But interestingly enough, it wasn't only the Crusaders who had a claim to the saint. Sometime in the mid-13th century, a Russian Archbishop told the Pope that some Mongols from the invading Golden Horde claimed to have had him as chief as well! There was no chance they would have passed up the opportunity to witness Saint John's place of rest at the Great Mosque!"

Psalmodie tilted her head and narrowed her eyes in question. "Correct me if I'm wrong, but didn't your friend out there just call the Mongols 'Philistine' and even worse than the Antichrist? I'm sorry, but they sound more like descendants of Cain rather than good Christians following in the steps of Christ's forerunner."

"For all of their bloodthirsty barbarism," Shiloh continued, "some of the Christian Turco-Mongol nomads of the South Siberian steppes did strongly identify themselves with the wandering Israelite tribes of the Old Testament, with the sacred symbol of the *cross of Christ*—to them, an all-powerful shaman healer—prophesying their imperial claim to all four corners of the Earth. As far as I know, this was a syncretism of the animist belief that the Turkic god of the eternal blue sky, Tengri, wanted to unify the whole world, which was alive with ancestral spirits, under the reign of a single Mongol khan."

"But what business did the Templars have with a horde of throat-singing horse archers?" Psalmodie asked. "And also, what the hell were the Mongols actually doing all the way in Syria? Didn't they already have their hands full back in China or—"

Shiloh eagerly interjected, "The Mongol hordes after Genghis Khan were the most apocalyptic force of nature in history, their vast empire having spanned all of China, Russia, and Persia! With all of the sheer horrors they deliberately committed against men, women, and children, the world remembers them not so much as armored warriors, but as aproned butchers. I don't know much about them—really, only enough to hold a conversation with Francis—, but I do know that the invading Ilkhanate Mongols of Persia and the Knights Templar actually had one ally in common: The Crusader Prince of Antioch."

At first, Psalmodie found it difficult to follow where her friend was going with this information, but once her answer had registered, she recalled the story written in her father's journal. *"Mon Dieu,"* she whispered. "The prince's ancestor was beheaded by Saladin himself after the Battle of Hattin... and the Templar knights with him would have surely known of the True Cross' location after the Ayyubid Saracens captured their Grand Master, wouldn't they have?"

Shiloh shrugged one shoulder. "History does tell us that the Frankish Crusaders unsuccessfully explored a truce with the rivaling Ilkhanate against their various Muslim opponents, but after the Armenian Kingdom of Cilicia and the Crusader Principality of Antioch both yielded up a vassal tribute to Genghis Khan's villainous grandson, Hulagu Khan, all of the Templar and Hospitaller preceptories in the realm would have perhaps been conscripted into his campaigns with the Mongols. The Templars had certainly proven themselves reliable after the then-recent Crusader civil war of the Antiochene Succession."

Psalmodie challenged, "But that wouldn't have necessarily meant that they all just got along, would it?"

"No, the Crusaders only wanted to 'liberate' Jerusalem, but the Mongols wanted to conquer the entire universe," Shiloh belabored, almost rambling. "But even so, one of Antioch's theaters of war against the Ayyubid emirs did include Damascus, which actually did surrender to the Mongols in 1260. Its townspeople would have been very much aware of the tales of untold butchery they committed against the mightiest civilizations of the time: The Jin Dynasty of China, the Abbasid Caliph of Baghdad, the Khwarezm-Shahs of Bukhara and Samarkand, the Seljuk Turks of the Rum Sultanate, and even the mountain-dwelling Isma'ili Hashshashin of Persia—the Order of Assassins. And so, once the prince marched into Damascus with his Christian Mongol general, Kitbuqa, the prince quickly directed that a Latin Mass be celebrated *in the Umayyad Mosque* of all places!"

"So, the Templars of Antioch *were* with him after all?" Psalmodie asked.

"I still wasn't entirely sure of that," Shiloh responded. "I was also under the impression that the Pope had excommunicated the prince and that the Templars' Grand Master was himself terrified of the Mongols." She paused and stooped down for the ancient artifacts on the ground. "But it seems that either the True Cross or Jerusalem really was just *that* important to the Templars. What's more is that the Templars were actually present for the failed Siege of Damascus during the Second Crusade, just over a century before Hulagu Khan's Mongol conquests. And from what I've read, there's no record of any outright Templar or Crusader defiance incurring the wrath of the ruthless zero-tolerance policy of Khagan's Law beyond Kitbuqa's thorough destruction of the Sidon lordship north of the Crusader Kingdom of Jerusalem."

Psalmodie looked at Shiloh incredulously. Aside from perhaps a number of vague allusions through the little-known Prester John legends or even the direct co-authorship of Marco Polo's famed travelogue by the earliest known Italian Arthurian romanticist, Rustichello da Pisa—with Marco Polo's arrival at the court of Kublai Khan directly mirroring Sir Tristan's arrival in King Arthur's castle—, there was absolutely nothing in Arthurian legend itself Psalmodie could have remembered that would have possibly suggested an explicit connection between the *Mongols* of all peoples and the Holy Grail itself. She found it even more difficult to comprehend how and where they may have taken it.

But then again, nothing about the Grail legends themselves was ever truly definite anyways.

Shiloh was still talking. "There really wasn't a single nation in the world that the Mongols didn't shake to its very foundations. There was the their introduction of the Black Plague to Europe through the Ukraine, their founding of the Mughal Empire in India, and the destruction of the Islamic Golden Age after Hulagu Khan's rape of Baghdad in 1258, where he slaughtered 2 million people in the city; the greatest massacre in human history and the single greatest loss of culture and scientific knowledge since the Library of Alexandria. There were even some rumors that the Mongols went on to raid *Jerusalem* at least twice, once even pillaging the Dome of the Rock of its famed Golden Gate."

"But what about that thing?" Psalmodie said, motioning a hand over one of the relics in Shiloh's hands.

Shiloh held up the tube. "Maybe the Templars thought the message would have been more significant if it was on metal than paper."

"Yes, I think I can understand that, but on a *gun?* I don't remember reading anything about gunpowder weapons in *any* book about the Crusades, let alone as an actual clue to the *True Cross.*"

"No, the Crusaders obviously didn't use such weaponry," Shiloh said, "but the Mongolian Yuan Dynasty in Imperial China was in the midst of its gunpowder revolution at the time; Hulagu Khan's brother, the great Kublai Khan, did gradually incorporate the weapons into numerous Mongol conquests. In fact, I think I remember reading about an Egyptian Mamluk record of how hand cannons were allegedly used in 1260 at the pivotal Battle of Ain Jalut against the Mongols just south of Nazareth, on the very same battlefield where David was said to have slain Goliath..."

Shiloh trailed off and was quiet for a moment before her face slowly broke with more wonderment. "And some twenty years before Antioch's vassalage, the Mongols under Batu Khan and the infamous demon general Subutai had apparently used Chinese firearm units to defeat the Poles, Hungarians, and the Knights Templar at the Battle of the Sajó River in Central Europe!" She quickly spun back on Psalmodie. "It was the Mongols who brought knowledge of this Chinese invention on the Silk Road to the West and the Middle East after all."

Psalmodie's voice turned dismal, and she shrugged equivocally. "But neither of us can read that inscription."

"I know," Shiloh said. "I thought the *lingua franca* of the western khanates was either Persian or Turkic, while the Mongols in China stuck to their own language. But what's really interesting is that their own script is actually an Altaic child system of Syriac *Aramaic*—a dialect of Christ's own language—with some Chinese loan words; the 'Word of God' really did come a long way from Jerusalem, huh?" Shiloh grinned, still fingering the objects. "But anyways, speaking of Jerusalem, aren't we forgetting about our dearest holy man that made our quest possible?"

Psalmodie read Shiloh's expression. At first, Psalmodie was unsure of what to make of her question, but then her mind wandered to the many candidates she thought would have merited such a title as "dearest holy man" from her friend: *Jesus? Muhammad? Saladin? Saint Francis?* Over time, however, her memory canvassed other options until one in particular had finally stood out.

"Brother Francis?" she said. "But wait, didn't he say he was from—"

"Manchuria!" Shiloh blurted. "Northeast China! He said it's under the Japanese Empire's rule as of now, but Francis still speaks Manchu, which he said uses a pidgin Mongolian script! Now, I don't know how much of the language might have changed since the Middle Ages, but he might actually know how to read this gun!"

"But what if Rahn's right?" Psalmodie asked. "What if our Holy Grail is actually all the way in China?"

Shiloh responded, "Then we'll just have to take the next train to China now, won't we?"

Psalmodie's blue eyes went sharp, stupefied for a moment at this new hope before they carried in them the burden she had raged against the entire trip. The upsetting truth she so desperately disillusioned against had finally come crashing down on her.

"Shiloh, stop," Psalmodie pleaded. "Please. *Please* just stop."

Her dour tone was enough to dispel the animation in Shiloh's eyes. She looked at Psalmodie with perplexity before following her eyes to Malik, still comatose on the ground behind her. Gradually, she brought her gaze back on Psalmodie.

"What are you saying exactly?" Shiloh responded.

"Please," Psalmodie repeated. "I've already made this worse than it has to be. People are getting hurt. People are *going* to get hurt." Psalmodie threw her gaze over at Malik and her voice became more dismal yet. "They could still kill him. You don't know he's going to survive this."

Shiloh stepped forward and matched her tone. "That's not going to happen; and what would your father say of these things you say?"

Then without warning, Psalmodie shoved Shiloh against the sables, making her drop the skull. "Now you know my father is dead!" Psalmodie erupted with a steely edge. "And I thought *you* of all people would know what that's like!"

Shiloh floundered, lost for words. She momentarily stared at Psalmodie in disbelief before looking down, shrinking away from her and shuffling back to perch herself against the wall. Psalmodie never broke away, although her cutting glare dissipated once she saw the heartbreak behind Shiloh's vacant, searching eyes.

Shiloh dwelled on Malik, praying again: *"A'udhu billahi min ash-shaytan ar-rajim."*

Psalmodie fell back against a wall and slid down to the floor, her own words weighing heavily on her mind. She stole a furtive glance at Shiloh, but instead found the skull on the ground, lying on its right temple. For a moment, Psalmodie reflected on John the Baptist and the scandalous adultery that he spoke out against, only for the continued pursuit of that scandal to ultimately behead him. From the skull's sockets distilled the haunting absence of John's soul, as if whispering one last messianic prophecy from the godless, unknowable silence that awaited Psalmodie.

"Shiloh?" Psalmodie reached out. "Shiloh, I'm—"

At that moment, she heard a lock click behind her. The pantry door swung out and Eggers stood at the door's threshold with a drawstring duffle bag in hand. There were no words between them; only that same waspish stare he first greeted them with. Joining him at his sides were two Bedouin neither of the girls had seen before.

One among them suddenly exclaimed, *"Hazrat Yahya!"*—Prophet John—before running over to retrieve the skull. "What was my master thinking? This always stays in the *masjid!*" He stood up and spat on Psalmodie's head before disappearing behind Eggers. "Oh, look what you made him do!" he chastised. While Psalmodie wiped away the man's spit from her brow, she saw him carry away the skull of her mother's greatest prophet.

"Get up both of you," Eggers cowed them, kicking over Psalmodie's boot. "It seems we're looking for your damned relic after we find our papers."

Shiloh pocketed the hand cannon and dropped down by Malik's side. "Malik? Malik!" She looked up at her captors. "What's going to happen to him?"

"Only Allah is All-Knowing," one of the Bedouin responded.

"So is He All-Merciful," Shiloh objected. "That's still not an answer."

Eggers looked back at the Arabs, his lips curling over his jagged teeth into a sneering grin. "We have no qualms with our Saracen comrades now, do we?" Then he slowly turned his amused stare back on Shiloh and uttered, "But of course, he is no Saracen, is he?"

Psalmodie's horrified eyes shot up at their captor.

"What?" Shiloh reacted.

Eggers pointed at Malik with a thin glass vial in his gloved hand containing a scrolled page with Hebrew inscriptions from the Torah: A Mezuzah, typically found over the doorways of Jewish homes.

Psalmodie watched in horror as Eggers threw the vial on the floor and approached Shiloh and Malik while slipping a hand under his chest pocket. Before Psalmodie saw what happened next, she was dragged to her feet by one of the Bedouin and forcefully steered into the lounge where Rahn waited. A minute had passed before Eggers entered the room, pressing over a crease on his chest with his thumb.

Shiloh drifted in shortly after him with a harrowed look raw in her eyes.

CHAPTER 32

Bab Touma borough
October 2nd, 1938

The brick streets of the Old City's Christian quarter were emptier than they were last night when Shiloh snuck through them. Stray dogs and cocks roamed through the narrow alleyways, and a few men took out their trash in the streets while women in the galleries above clipped their clothes to washing pulleys. There were a couple of delicatessens opening their doors, though it had still been fairly early for them to receive patrons.

Shiloh told Rahn that the journal that had the telegrams was stowed somewhere in the northeastern quadrant of the Old City, about one kilometer east from the mosque, although she didn't specify where it was exactly. As the Germans and Arabs escorted them, they formed a tight perimeter around the two girls while filing them in separate entourages to keep them from talking to each other.

After what happened in the pantry, however, that didn't turn out to be a problem.

Rahn and al-Husseini ran point at the pack's vanguard, guarding against the attention of passing onlookers or patrols.

"Where now, Shiloh?" al-Husseini asked.

"We're almost there," she responded blankly. "Just keep going forward."

Eggers' voice sharpened. "She's been saying that for the last ten minutes!"

"Shut up," Rahn hissed.

Another five minutes had passed before they turned a corner to an empty roundabout where there were very many parked cars and carriages lining the streets leading up to it.

"Bab Touma square?" al-Husseini said, looking at Shiloh.

One of many of this city's commercial districts, with shops built in and around an ancient Roman gate dedicated to the goddess Venus before being renamed to commemorate the Apostle Thomas' passage to India. What remained was a 13th-century Ayyubid reconstruction which, much like the Temple of Jupiter, served only as a mere canopy for Damascus' shopkeepers. Behind the gate was an obelisk-like square minaret aspiring to a small domed tip.

"You left the journal to *Arab traders?*" Eggers exclaimed.

Both Shiloh and al-Husseini were rankled by his stereotypical remark.

"Where is it?" Rahn asked.

Shiloh didn't answer. Instead, her nervous eyes shifted to the other side of the small roundabout. Rahn followed them there, but once he saw what Shiloh indicated, a wave of horror came over him.

Two uniformed men armed with carbines indolently stood guard at either side of a doorway to a concrete building. Above them, a flag snapped and its halyard ringed dully against its flagpole with each passing gust. It was the banner of Syria: A white crescent over a blue standard, but the canton in the flag's upper left-hand corner was a flag all too familiar to the National Socialists.

On the building's face above the men, a placard read, *"Gendarmerie du mandat français de Damas."*

Psalmodie's breath shuddered. "Why are we at a French police station?"

"It's a colonial mandate!" Shiloh whispered immediately. "The French are *everywhere!*"

Al-Husseini took Rahn aside and, stealing once at the building, whispered into his ear, "So you see why I need your help? The British and French think we cannot look over ourselves, so they feel they must always look over us. Look how they broke up the Ummah and divided the Holy Land amongst themselves. In their protracted Crusader occupation of our homelands, time and time again, they deprived us of our rights, from Lord Peel's recent partition scheme for the Zionists to the secret colonial Sykes-Picot subterfuges revealed to us by Vladimir Lenin's Bolsheviks during the Great War."

Rahn sighed and rolled his head away in exasperation. "Your Eminence, I have told you repeatedly that I am not unsympathetic to your struggle; the Crusaders and Inquisitors compelled my homeland to submit to their Christ-God and slaughtered my own ancestors in His name long ago as well."

"And the colonists," al-Husseini continued, "are compelling some among my people to such desperate, un-Christian, un-*Islamic* measures for liberation... and they have driven me to your regime, Herr Rahn, whatever it would entail..."

"But you must understand that you would be making a bedfellow of the Führer while his enemies still reign over your lands."

The mufti's brow furrowed in bewilderment. "You came to *me* for help. But now it seems as though you are trying to dissuade me from a mutual understanding between our peoples. Why?" The mufti crouched his head to search Rahn's gaze. "Is this the Führer being circumspect or is this simply you, Herr Rahn?"

"If those French officers catch us," Rahn started, "my Reichsführer will know, and then you'll be in it just like us."

Al-Husseini's face shifted. "In what, Herr Rahn? What exactly is 'it?' What would I be in?"

Rahn looked back towards the building's guards before settling his gaze back on the little schoolgirl in Eggers' grip. Rahn faced the mufti again and seemed to betray a secret to him in his lowered eyes.

Before Rahn could answer him, one of his enforcers called, "Sir?"

Rahn turned immediately and hissed, "Don't speak German. Once the French know of our presence here, they will use it against our Führer in Munich, and then we will all be as good as dead."

"No, worse still," al-Husseini added, "they will take us to the Mezzeh prison, where our most noble fedayeen are immured."

Eggers scowled back at the group, most especially at Shiloh. "You set us up?" he menaced her.

The mufti gestured a placating hand at him and spoke to Shiloh with more "gentleness," although the smug contempt in his cold blue eyes was unmistakable. "You gave it to them?" he asked.

Shiloh shook her head and pointed towards a black slat trash can a few meters in front of the soldiers. Once Rahn caught sight of it, he had the Arabs bring Shiloh to the fore.

He leaned in and whispered, "If you try anything, Schütze Eggers here will run your friend through with his blade. Now go get it."

Then in mock ceremony, Rahn stepped aside and the two guards in front of her parted to let her through. She looked back and saw that Psalmodie's collar was in Eggers' clutch, his other hand still holding the duffle bag.

Shiloh felt the pangs of unease already rising in her stomach and in her throat. She turned back around and crossed the roundabout with a slow tread. Once she was there, she saw that the satchel was fortunately still inconspicuously stashed within a gap between two of the trash can's outer slats.

She got to her knees, but just when she was about to reach for it, she noticed the two guards were shooting curious glances in her direction. They laughed derisively at first, unsure of what to make of her rummaging around a trash can, but to her dread, their curiosity only grew from there.

Shiloh fought the urge with all her heart, but she couldn't help but dart her terrified eyes in Psalmodie's direction. Rahn and al-Husseini averted their eyes and tried feigning dialogue with one another, but Eggers' patent restlessness and the girl he had in his hold had already damaged their guise.

The two guards had taken notice, glancing from the group to Shiloh and back again. With urgent haste, she wiggled the satchel free from between the slats, her eyes wild with panic. She rose slowly, and by the time she straightened, the guards had already been mere inches in front of her. One of them stretched out his gloved palm, waiting for her to hand the satchel over to them.

Again, she glanced over her shoulder and saw Psalmodie look on in helpless terror. They had run out of time, and Shiloh was left with only one choice.

She spun right and bolted.

She didn't get far. One of the French soldiers lunged for her wrist, but before he could have secured his grip on her, a crash erupted in the square. Shiloh fell back and watched as the man shrieked and clung to his wounded leg. His panic-stricken partner saw Eggers at the other end of the roundabout aiming a rifle right at him. He wrenched his carbine up to return fire, but by the time he discharged, the German had already shot him in the neck.

"Ambush!" the maimed soldier screamed. *"Amb—"*

Another shot rang out, this time skewering through the man's heart.

There was no one left to see, and Shiloh watched in horror as Eggers stared his sights down on her.

But the quiet did not last. In that instant, all the station's lights went out, and sprouting out from three of its third-story windows were the bayoneted ends of three rifles. Eggers' eyes drifted to them, and once the perception registered, he and the group dove behind the cover of two nearby cars.

Someone screamed in Arabic, *"'anzal!"*

What few people were out at that hour screamed, ducked, and ran for cover. Then, with the synchrony of a firing squad, the snipers above opened fire on the group, paying no mind to the hostage they had with them. Shiloh leapt up but stumbled forward at the perpetual sound of bullets clawing up the ground around her. She heard a feverish mixture of French and Arabic barking around the night square. She looked up and saw Rahn with the mufti peering over the car's front, both with pistols in hand.

A ballistic crack caused her to scurry back and corner herself against the building's face. Two more soldiers with assault rifles poured through the building's front entrance, unleashing a salvo of suppressive fire while the snipers went to work on the car roofs. Two of the Bedouin stayed down, but in a desperate attempt, raised their pistols above cover to spray and pray blind fire at the soldiers.

Then, Shiloh saw Rahn crouch run for another car, leading Psalmodie by her back.

Although the sound of violent shots rang on, Psalmodie caught sight of her friend still backed up against the station's front wall. Psalmodie leaned back against the car and sank lower but risked a look around the car's rear lights to find her friend again.

They locked eyes, both of them at a loss.

A bullet kicked up dust near Shiloh's boots. Startled, she saw the fine particles scatter over the leather satchel a little ways leftward over the sidewalk. Far ahead of it, however, was the leftmost end of the roundabout.

A narrow alleyway.

Shiloh looked back at Psalmodie and saw by her expression that the same idea took form. Shiloh bobbed up and down to brace herself for what she would have to do next. They gave each other a resolving nod and pounced on their only escape.

Shiloh scurried for the satchel and gathered it into her chest before rushing into the open. Likewise, a hesitant Psalmodie bolted up and started for her friend, leaving her unwitting captors to fend off the French.

Rahn tried slamming her back down, but his weak grip combined with the suppressing gunfire sent him cowering back against his cover. He screamed in French, but only Eggers had taken notice. "The girls! They're getting away!" Eggers yelled, breaking cover and giving chase to them. In his sprint, he lifted his Luger rifle and tracked the fleeing girls with his sightline, but just as he had gotten within range and steadied his aim, the girls had turned the corner into the alleyway.

CHAPTER 33

"This way!" Shiloh yelled, weaving around the many boxes, sacks, and cans propped along the two meter wide back alley's scored concrete walls. Psalmodie was just behind her, desperately trying to match her stride.

"Where are we going?" Psalmodie yelled, running out of breath.

"The Jewish quarter! It's just south of here!"

"What? Why?"

"Because I'm—"

Crack!... Crack!

White flashes of light filled the dark alley from the two gunshots behind them. One round slammed a dent into a nearby trash can while the other divoted a mashrabiya balcony's wooden girder above them, hailing dust and splinters down over their heads.

The girls split apart and staggered sideways into the pitch black shadows of two facing door recesses in the opposing walls. The recesses were only a foot in depth, and any attempt to book it to the end of the tunnel-like alley would have ended in at least one of them dead. A quiet fell in the alley save the popping of rifles and pistols back in the square and the approaching echo of footsteps scuffing along a limestone floor. Their attacker moved with a caution that belied his murderous intent.

"It's okay! You can come out now!" he called out to them. "I assure you: This is your one chance to make it quick... You'll both see your fathers real soon, that is, if they aren't burning in hell already..."

Shiloh's blood froze in her veins and a vice tightened around her stomach. Her face became a sheen of perspiration, and she tried to hold her shivering breath. She dropped the satchel and shut her eyes as tears sliced down her cheeks.

"A'udhu bi—"

In that moment, Psalmodie's hands lunged out from the shadows for Kurt Eggers' arm. He fired but missed, the toggle arm of his Luger rifle shooting out the last cartridge in its chamber. As Psalmodie frantically tried to wrestle his weapon out of his grip, he flailed her against the two alley walls until the rifle slipped free from her hands.

Seeing Psalmodie writhing over the ground, Shiloh charged from behind and tried tackling him to the ground. She latched onto his back, trying to grab the rifle herself. Eggers barely kept his balance, and he fell against the wall and repeatedly slammed his weight against Shiloh. It took two attempts before he finally winded her and shrugged her arms off his back.

Taxed and almost out of breath, Eggers sneered, "I read that you two were in a fencing club together in Paris." When he saw Psalmodie tottering back to her feet, he rolled his eyes and sighed, "Well, then... I suppose the students require one last lesson."

"You killed my father!" Psalmodie screamed, tears quivering in her eyes.

"You should have known then!" Eggers said. "The risks that came with sending telegrams to your father in Dachau! You know that your father died for your own sins! Not mine..." He tossed his Luger rifle aside and reached both of his gloved hands into his coat lapel to draw two misericorde short swords from their hidden sheaths. Having tossed one of them to the ground between Psalmodie's feet, he then proceeded to pull the unconscious Shiloh up on her knees and press his sword across her neck. "I know what you are, Mademoiselle Vingt-Trois. Valiant and loyal. But you could never make the hard decisions!"

"You don't know me..." she spat.

"Oh, but I do. You and I, Psalmodie, we're the only things we've ever known for countless centuries."

"Let her go," she growled, clutching her midriff.

He muttered coldly, "Then let him go…"

Psalmodie looked down at the short sword, deathly unsure of herself, but then she saw Shiloh's debilitated face in Eggers' grip and the satchel still on the ground behind him. Psalmodie was soon filled with a manic resolve when she saw Eggers make a mocking sign of the cross at Psalmodie with one hand… and with the other, move the blade up towards Shiloh's carotid.

Psalmodie snatched the sword from the ground and wildly broke forward. Eggers tossed Shiloh aside, and just before Psalmodie rammed her blade into his breast, he deflected it with a *croisé*, flourished his sword over her head, and smacked its cold cheek against her ear. She staggered back some steps as Eggers rebuked, *"En garde, Psalmodie! En garde!"* Psalmodie gathered herself against the wall and charged him again. He sidestepped her, beat parried her sword away, and feinted his sword toward her hunched over chest, holding back at the last moment as if he had already proven his point. He knocked her sword from her grip and drew closer to yell in her face, "Don't telegraph so much! Find your distance from me!"

Psalmodie responded by desperately lashing out her fists at his cheek. Eggers barely moved, absorbing all three of her blows as if they were mere slaps. When she cocked her fist again, Eggers caught it and kicked her legs out from under her. Psalmodie rolled onto her knees, sucking in labored pants through her grit teeth as she groped around the ground for her sword.

She sensed Eggers standing over her, circling her like a shark. Just as her hand found her sword's grip, Eggers kicked it back from her grasp with his heel and raised her chin with his sword's business end. As Psalmodie struggled to squirm away from him, he scoffed, "You clearly are no gallant knight of King Arthur. Clumsy and undisciplined. But I will grant you this: That hellfire you feel within? That is our peoples' destiny. A pity that you have already commended it to the Jewish God…" He then took hold of Psalmodie's plaited braid and ripped it off against the edge of his sword, castrating her honor and reducing her to a common whore. "What a pathetic waste…"

He then kissed the cheek of his sword for the intimacy of

Psalmodie's murder, and just as Judgement sailed down on her, she instinctively took a garbage can lid from the ground and raised it to her front like a shield. She blocked the sword just in time, but it kept lodging through the metal. She nearly rose to her feet, but Eggers forced her back to the wall and laid into the lid, trying to drive his sword through to Psalmodie's eye.

Her quaking arms began to buckle under Eggers' compelling strength, and every time he lurched his sword deeper into the lid, her back slid down the wall inch by inch. She sank again to the floor, her back still pressed to the wall. She felt one of her hands on the lid slip, and her punishment was the sword's end grazing the bridge of her nose and splitting her lower lip.

"You're living vicariously through your dead father!" Eggers yelled down at her. "You won't ever know what it is to sacrifice for your suffering fatherland! What it is to sacrifice everything you held dear to the gods and to—"

In that instant, Psalmodie saw her own sword rip through Eggers' bloody thigh. "Get off of her!" a voice behind him screamed. Letting out a feral snarl, Eggers ripped his sword out from the lid and blindly flashed out at Shiloh. At first, the sword's tip missed and raked along the wall, but after she inexpertly parried the second slash with her sword, Eggers pried it from her hands with his downward sword. Once he flourished his sword, he gripped it by its foible and swung its forte for a murderous stroke.

Shiloh stumbled back just in time, though the sword had already slit across her left cheek. Her hands flew to her face; the slash wasn't deep, but she felt the blood beginning to pulse weakly. To her peril, she didn't even notice the two silhouettes scuffling dangerously close to her. Then she saw Eggers' sword fly out from his hand, clatter over the ground, and vanish into the shadows ahead of the satchel.

"Shiloh!" Psalmodie screamed out.

Eggers threw Psalmodie to the ground right next to Shiloh before pinning her down by her neck. By the time she could have even reacted,

Eggers had pinned down Shiloh as well. He straddled them both and, with all of his strength, he held them down side by side.

"Your blood isn't worthy of my sword!" he yelled down at them.

As Shiloh felt his throttling grip bearing deeper into her jugular notch, she flailed her arms around the ground. She already saw the blackness had already begun to set in. All she saw were Eggers' malevolent blue eyes boring into hers. Her sense of time numbed, with each passing second seeming more eternal than the last. But in that stasis in reality, numerous memories flashed before her eyes.

That Herodian mosque.

That Coptic cross.

Then her parents, kissing under the showering petals and ribbons of that festooned Arabian festival.

Then her mother, in the fog, crying on that rubble mound breakwater as Shiloh's father raised his hunting rifle at the coming storm.

Then Psalmodie...

...Psalmodie...

Eggers was still over them, pinning down their pelvises with his knees. All Shiloh could have done was blindly strain her outstretched hands towards the shadows behind her. With one hand, she grabbed a fistful of sand and flung it into his eyes. He bit back a scream and his grip faltered for a brief moment, long enough for Shiloh to reach out with her other hand for an object just beyond her fingertips. Once she blindly found it, she took hold and seized on her only hope to survive.

Squelch!

At first, neither one of them knew whose blood it was they felt on their clothes, but there was enough of it to give pause to the murderous German still over them. A fraught silence befell the dark alley. Shiloh and Psalmodie didn't know what to make of Eggers' stunned expression, but they were too distracted coiling from their choked coughing. He rolled off of them and fell against the wall, motionless.

Still recovering from her aspirations, Psalmodie felt mechanically whether she had any mortal wounds on her chest or side. When she looked over towards Eggers, she saw his trembling hand trying to stem the spurts of blood flailing out from the end of the steel blade planted deep into his abdomen.

Psalmodie then whirled on Shiloh and saw her sway and brace herself against the wall.

Shiloh's emotions curdled in terror and disgust. She looked down at her hand, almost as if it were severed, and noticed Eggers' blood running down over the mark on her wrist. No matter how hard she tried, she couldn't have shaken off that feeling. That sound his chest made when she plunged the sword into it and the wet heat that burst over her knuckles.

Her eyes then trailed back towards the man she had just stabbed, and in her confused shock, found herself kneeling beside Eggers and trying to tear open his shirt over his wound. "I'm sorry!" Shiloh pleaded, more to herself than him. "I didn't mean to! I'm sorry!"

As she moved to stem Eggers' bleeding, she felt her shoulders were seized once again. She took hold of two forearms trying to rip her away from Eggers, and a muffled voice had started to muddle its way through. "Shiloh!" Psalmodie yelled into her ear. "Shiloh, you said the Jewish quarter, right?"

Psalmodie's words hadn't registered with Shiloh. "What?"

"The Jewish quarter! Now!"

"But w-we can't ju-just l-leave him like this!" Shiloh begged, nearly gibbering.

"Shiloh, he murdered Malik!" Psalmodie screamed frenziedly. "He tried murdering us! Do you want to be the one to finish it?"

The two lingered for a moment before Psalmodie reluctantly took off in the other direction. Shiloh still hadn't fully recovered from her daze, but once she saw the shadows lengthening over the ground at the other end of the alley, the reality had finally taken hold. She stood back up, and just when she was about to run, her foot stumbled over Eggers' grasp.

She slipped free but glanced once more at the trembling German still committed to her murder. He grit his bared teeth, and his forehead wormed with a vein of anguish as he strangled his sobs and gurgled out his life in a bubbling gush of blood.

"Kill me..." he whimpered softly. "You gods, just kill me now, please..."

Shiloh stepped away and shot him a revulsed, yet pitiful glare before bounding down the alleyway.

Once his targets had escaped him, Eggers' expression fell, and his eyes rested on the dull metal glint protruding from the shadows in front of him. He knew that by the time Rahn and al-Husseini would have reached him, he would have already been dead. He only had enough life to wrench the misericorde out of his chest and set it down on the ground between his knees.

As he saw the black fluid drooling from his fingertips, Eggers felt his last breath catch in his throat. He saw the valkyries and prayed unto the eternal glory of Valhalla, *Vater unsar... Gib uns Deinen Geist und—*

CHAPTER 34

Hayy al-Yahud

A 50-year-old overweight man with a balding whorl and dapper mustache, Elnathan al-Hakim, sat reclined in his taxi seat, basking in the night and falling in and out of a comfortable slumber. The day had been slow and the fares he collected from the Jewish families were very few. He had his skullcap on and contemplated a prayer, but his thoughts turned to an attractive woman he drove to the Great Mosque.

But his dream was short-lived after a soft tapping on his front window startled him. He scrunched his eyes, and to his surprise, he saw the scraped and grimy faces of two young women crouched beside the car, their agitated eyes fixed to the other end of the street. He followed their stare to discover two shapes emerging from a dark alleyway before parting to cover more ground up and down the main street of the Jewish quarter.

They weren't wearing police uniforms.

The sight petrified him, and knowing that the people they were hunting were directly next to him, Elnathan had half a mind to drive off and get out of their way so that he could see his son again. But at the same time, he knew that he wouldn't be able to live with himself for doing so. He wouldn't have been able to face his son after such callousness. He looked back at the two girls and pitied the desperate exhaustion he saw in their eyes.

He saw that one of the men had turned his back to his parked car. Charily, Elnathan motioned for the girls to quietly enter the rear passenger door. One of them slipped her fingers under the handle and gently tugged.

Clunk!

The handle latch echoed in the silent dark. One of the dark figures spun on the taxi and drew his pistol towards Elnathan. The girls rushed headlong over the car floor and ducked behind the front seats. The men hastened for the taxi. Elnathan searched through his keys, but by the time his shaking fingers singled one out, the men had already opened fire on him. The girls yelped in terror. Some rounds peppered the car's side panels and back seat cushions while others knocked out one of the car's running lights and side view mirrors.

With shards and sparks hailing over his windshield, Elnathan ducked his head under the wheel and hurriedly slotted the key to crank the ignition. Once the motor roared to life, Elnathan shifted gears and floored the pedal. With screeching tires, the taxi launched full tilt towards the other end of the street.

The gunfire didn't relent for another five seconds until Elnathan turned the block and the men were lost to the darkness behind.

Once the gunfire had subsided, Psalmodie raised her head and peered out the car's back seat window. The trio cruised through a quiet and dimly lit street, but they saw a few people stepping out of their homes and craning their heads towards the origin of the gunfire. Besides them, Psalmodie didn't see anyone else who would have posed any serious threat to them.

In front of her, the Arab taxi driver had already begun his fretful rambling. Of course, Shiloh was the only one who could be quick to respond, although Psalmodie was nervous about her saying something compromising about their reason for being in Damascus. Psalmodie herself was perplexed as to why she chose this car *specifically*, but once she heard mention of the name "Malik" in her speech. The name did something to him, and whatever she told her next made him sigh hesitantly. After a momentary pause, he nodded once, but not without adding another disgruntled comment.

"What did he say?" Psalmodie asked.

Still collecting her breath, Shiloh said, "He's agreed to take us."

Psalmodie was taken aback. She wanted to ask if he knew what happened to his son, but she knew that her curiosity wasn't worth exacerbating Shiloh's trauma. "All the way to Jerusalem?" she asked instead.

Shiloh shook her head. "I don't know. He's too irritated to reason with right now, but he's at least taking us out of Damascus."

Psalmodie sighed, ill at ease, but mostly relieved. Her head fell back against the headrest and sucked in slow breaths. The satchel was secure in her hands and they were safe, if only for a while. But when Psalmodie raised a hand to the scars on her nose and lower lip, she remembered the slash across Shiloh's cheek. She rolled her head over to her and saw her bloodied hands restlessly patting down her jerkin and pants for something.

Psalmodie reached out for her shoulder and spoke gently. "Shiloh. Hey, what are you doing?"

Shiloh kept searching, her small voice laced with panic. "It has to be here!"

"What is it?"

"It *has* to be here!"

Psalmodie wrested her friend's arms still and set her by her shoulders. "Shiloh, what's wrong?"

Shiloh stopped, utterly silent. Her panicked eyes became fixed with horrified disbelief. Psalmodie read her visage, bewildered at first, but the silence between them hung long enough for her to be fazed by it.

CHAPTER 35

Bab Touma borough

The two German officers holstered their Borchardt pistols and marched back to the alleyway, both with uneasy bearings. Against the blue light of the other end, they saw the slender shapes of Rahn and al-Husseini standing over the body. Once the officers joined them, Rahn straightened, expecting the worst.

"They've escaped," one of them said, "but it looks like Eggers did wound them."

The mufti looked at Rahn. "My friends, we must remove ourselves from here, sir. I fear that more French reinforcements will soon be detached here."

"What now, Obersturmführer?" one of the officers inquired. Rahn kept silent, his unsure eyes considering the body of his field secretary.

Impossibly, Eggers was still alive.

His neck was slumped up against the bottom of the wall and his sprawled arms were limp along the ground. As Rahn's eyes traveled down Eggers' shifting body, he recognized the long misericorde blade vertical between his knees. He found it peculiar seeing the object of his murder so perfectly aligned with his legs. Rahn followed the blade's tip to the opposite wall of the alley and saw the small hand cannon Shiloh and Psalmodie tried to steal.

Rahn stooped down for it and twisted it side to side to verify the unfinished Templar cross and Mongolian inscriptions.

Meanwhile, Eggers squeaked deliriously, "Kill me... Kill me now..."

Rahn considered Eggers a while, ambivalent, though acknowledging the possible liability of French soldiers finding a German corpse in wake of an attack. "Your Eminence? We need medical care for my secretary here." He rose and handed the artifact to his officers. "I would like your servants to contact Berlin. The fugitives may have already made a copy of this; Dr. Ernst Schäfer or someone else from his expeditions in Tibet might be able to translate this and tell us where they are headed with those telegrams."

"I know some doctors not too far from here; Schütze Eggers can convalesce in their care," the mufti said. "He looks to have lost quite a bit of blood, but he will live. As for your quest, I am afraid that I can no longer collaborate with you, even if I wanted to."

Coming from al-Husseini, the response stunned Rahn. "What?"

"One of my men returned from the house of Nasib al-Bakri just now. I was not present for a meeting with other Arab leaders two days ago, but apparently, your chancellor has already signed an agreement with the British in Munich; I imagine mutual cooperation against British domination will not bode well for my peoples' image after such an event."

"But we still need to get those telegrams!" Rahn burst out.

"I am sorry," al-Husseini said, placing a hand on his shoulder. "I really am. But my people cannot wait any longer; not for my negotiations with the intransigent colonists nor for any telegrams nor for any mystical chalice. I must return to Zouk Mikael, for the time has come for all malcontents, Jews and Gentiles alike, to act. For us to share in Salah ad-Din's legacy against the lionhearted enemy. For my lineage and for Allah, Who is indeed Most Merciful, Most Loving."

Rahn shifted, his face a mask. He tried to control the urge, but he couldn't resist. "If God is infinite love, then how can love ever be sin?"

The mufti's smile faded; he scowled at him, affronted, yet intrigued by such defiance. At first, he found no words to match so lost a cause, but then he started, "When I spoke with that girl in the teahouse, she made me recall a Persian Sufi mystic who died just before Allah sent the

Sultan Salah ad-Din as a mercy to al-Quds against the Crusaders. This mystic spoke of a tragic, messianic figure who fell from the heavens because he could not have brought himself to obey Allah and bow down to humanity over Him. And so, to this day, that scorned lover—the fairest and most beautiful of Allah's angels—continues to pine for his beloved from his eternal torment in hell."

Al-Husseini drew closer to Rahn's face and continued, "For such mystics, it is Iblis—*Satan*—who is Allah's greatest and most jealous lover. And it was for the great sin that he desired Allah for himself that he waged rebellion against Allah's mortal creation. It is Satan who embodies the selfless love that all Jews, Christians, and Muslims ought to imitate and profess, for it is he who damned himself in reckless abandon for the sake of his own beloved. It is from Satan that we learn what it means to truly believe in Allah, for there is no more perfect believer of Allah's terrible might." The mufti put a hand to his abdomen and leaned forward, visibly uneasy. "And so be it, Rahn, that I myself must stand condemned for my sinful love of God... so that all my fellow Arab Peoples of the Book can yet rebel in their own homeland to endure and survive."

Rahn's expression became rigid as he looked in al-Husseini's gaze and slowly realized that, perhaps, Shiloh had made the mufti aware of his true intentions. "So, you would simply leave a deputation of the Führer to wander in enemy territory then?" Rahn asked.

The Mufti shook his head. "Oh, no, no, no, of course not. I can have my men make the necessary arrangements for you to travel to your consulate in Jerusalem, or even the al-Aqsa compound; I still have a hand in funding the Muslims' holy places through the Waqf endowment there. And while I must tend to other, more pressing affairs, if you still insist on finding that relic or those two girls, I am certain my loyal assets will be more than willing to work in close liaison with your consulate."

After al-Husseini finished talking, he stood there for a while longer, acknowledging the rage in Rahn's face. The mufti then put a hand to Rahn's shoulder to express his understanding and regret. "It might be too late for me," the mufti said, "but you must beware of Satan, for he has lost all hope that he will ever be able to lead us astray in big things, so beware of following him in small things. Such was the Prophet's final sermon to the Muslims, *sallallahu alayhi wasallam.* Countless small things in this world, Rahn. Countless!" With those final words, the mufti started for the other end of the alleyway to join his retinue.

Rahn's seething eyes chased after his departure before turning back towards his two remaining underlings. He motioned a hand towards Eggers still dying at his feet and commanded, "Get him out of here."

The two Germans traded uneasy glances, discomfited by this change in leadership. They watched Rahn pace in the other direction, rubbing his eyes to the bridge of his nose. When he turned back around, he saw they were still gawking at him.

"Now!" Rahn screamed.

The two men jumped and scrambled down for the body. One picked it up by the knees while the other carried it by the underarms. "No!" Eggers groaned in protest, biting back excruciating pain. "No! No, don't deny me Valhalla! Kill me! Kill me, goddamn you! *Kill me!*"

CHAPTER 36

Somewhere in the Upper Galilee

The noon sunlight woke Shiloh from her fitful sleep. Drowsily, she shuffled up in her seat and tried to blink the sleep out of her eyes. She looked around the taxi and saw that Psalmodie was still sleeping against her shoulder with the satchel resting on her lap. It took a while for Shiloh's eyes to focus, but once they did, they instantly widened with bewilderment.

Out the window, she saw sun-kissed canebrakes and farmlands stretching all the way to the distant escarpment mountains and partitioned only by small groves of Date palms; an otherwise serene sight were it not for the fact that Shiloh still didn't know the taxi driver's intention. She looked down and saw she was holding a balled rag in her right hand. It smelled of alcohol, but was saturated red. Her memory lapsed, but the throbbing sting in the welt on her cheek reminded her that the blood was indeed hers. She winced and let out a stifled groan.

"I have more here in the compartment if you need it," the driver said in Arabic.

Shiloh looked up and saw the elder's cavernous visage in the rearview mirror. She saw that he was gazing ahead, perhaps only half-aware of the world beyond him. Unpresuming at first, she then decided to take him up on his generosity. She carefully set Psalmodie back in her seat and climbed her way to the passenger seat next to him.

Once there, she opened the compartment and rummaged through various crumpled documents. She found the half-empty vial of alcohol, but then noticed the two objects lying next to it.

"You're Sephardic, aren't you?" she blurted out. "So, I guess that means you're driving towards Jerusalem then; what better place to daven than right next to the Holy of Holies, right?"

Lines cracked across the elder's forehead. "I'm a seeker of our innate calling to the primordial truth," he answered, "wherever I might be able to find it among Abraham's children. What makes you think I'm—"

"There's a Siddur prayer book and shawl hidden under all these papers here," she said, dampening her mottled rag before dabbing it over her cheek. "Frankly, I'm surprised that any Jew would ever want to start a new life in Damascus of all places, given that blood libel affair in 1840, when Christians and Muslims came together to accuse the existing Jewish community there of murdering a Franciscan Capuchin friar to use his blood to bake matzo bread."

The driver considered her for a moment and asked, "So are you Jewish?"

Shiloh shook her head. "I'm going to university for comparative religion."

"Excellent," the driver commented. "My name is Elnathan al-Hakim, at your service. What is yours?"

"Shiloh Ma'idah al-Ahad," she answered. "You can call me Shiloh. And my friend behind me—her name is Psalmodie."

"Ma'idah?" Elnathan repeated. "As in Qur'an Surah al-Ma'idah, the Surah with my favorite verse?" Elnathan paused before reciting, "*We prescribed for the Children of Israel that whoever slays a soul—unless it be for another soul or working corruption upon the earth, it is as though he slew mankind altogether...*'"

"But remember the verses that follow," Shiloh said. "*Verily the recompense of those who wage war against God and His Messenger, and endeavor to work corruption upon the earth is that they be killed or cruci-fied...*' I'm not so sure that crucifying murderers ever seems to bring any sort of justice or closure to their victims. Instead, we end up killing a part of ourselves, and then we tell ourselves that it was God's justice that was exacted somehow." She looked down at her tattoo and clenched the devotional medal tightly in her hand, reckoning with the new horrific truth of herself; a truth that seemed to replace who she was altogether. She looked back at Elnathan and added, "The verse actually refers to the Sanhedrin tractate in the Babylonian Talmud. Would that be why it's your favorite?"

Elnathan chuckled, "I will admit that you seem more intelligent than those other girls my son chased around, but if I may, I want to warn you of something: I have made it a point to bring up my son with all of Abraham's children because I don't want him to only go the way of Christians, Muslims, and Jews, all forever locked in a constant clash; all too stubborn to confess that we all in fact worship the very same God that Moses, Jesus, and Muhammad all professed for the fulfillment of humanity's shared need for religion."

Shiloh looked at Elnathan with an arched brow. "You do understand that Jesus said He came not to bring peace, but a sword? Of course, He wasn't calling for war, but He knew that the message He was bringing would cause division within families. I don't think conflict is something that Christians, Muslims, or Jews can or should ever turn away from."

"Well, then," Elnathan said, "perhaps the Messiah's message of universal love is in vain what with all that discord you say His movement was meant to sow."

Shiloh fluttered her eyes, unsure of what to make of such a jarring claim. "What do you mean?"

"This 'universal' love and charity..." Elnathan continued. "This *agape* love that the Christians always speak of... it cannot be real. If you really did try to love everyone even if you never knew them, then you would in fact just end up loving no one."

"*Agape* love has always been a *jihad*," Shiloh rebutted. "It has never been blissful or quiet; it is a loud and restless struggle; it has always been a sacrifice for others and a struggle against oneself. Love was always meant to be agitating; dangerously disruptive to the religious, cultural, and societal structures predicated on endless violence and indifference. What Jesus called for was the fulfillment of the covenant of Israel and an alternative to the *civitas* of Rome; instead of the divine sanction of the emperor and patriarchal citizens, Jesus commanded equality, charity, and universal love for all society."

"And what have Christians or Muslims ever accomplished to that end?" Elnathan challenged. "From the Christians, I can tell you it was nothing but endless scapegoating and atrocities committed against our ancestors and our children, all in the name of Christ and His cross. His Church ultimately forced the Jews here, and the Jews in turn took up its Crusader image by colonizing and waging war in lands already saturated with the blood of the forgotten dead. You see now that no *'agape'* was ever realized? Alas, only that same endless cycle of violence."

"That?" Shiloh started. "All of that is because, at every turn, we stubbornly insist on forgetting and forgetting." Hearing herself, she fell silent, and her eyes looked far afield. Her mind buzzed, and for a moment, she contemplated telling Elnathan the truth of what happened to Malik. She told Elnathan she had only met him once and feared involving the Germans in his life. It was, of course, too late, and Elnathan was bound to learn at some point. Were it not for her friend's life still in danger, she would have confessed and atoned long before they had left Damascus.

Still, she felt compelled to say something to him, but when she looked down at the small rosary medal and the mark on her wrist, with a numbed look, she brooded over who she was: A fearful walking on water, mud always clinging to her soul.

She finally told him, "My mother's ancestors were Christian when Europe was still pagan... and my father's ancestors were Muslim despite the invasions that tore apart our homeland. But for both of them... Jesus was always one of us."

Elnathan didn't blink, though he did shrug as if those religions were nothing more than mere zodiac signs. "I saw the tattoo on your wrist. So that would make you a Christian from Egypt then?"

"I'm not from Egypt," she continued, her voice just above a whisper. "I mean, my parents were born in a town not too far from Cairo.

But when news came that the British brought the Great War to Egypt, my parents fled to Hebron, just south of Bethlehem. But they realized too late that the British had aimed to take everything here, I was already born there."

Elnathan considered her. "So how does it feel to be back to your homeland?"

Shiloh sighed out, "I don't know what I'm feeling now."

"I do understand wanting to start your life anew," Elnathan said, "but if I may ask, what made you leave the Holy Land to begin with?"

She paused to ruminate on the horror of that day, but she barely could have brought herself to say it. "When I was young, some Arab nationalists came into our city, killing and raping every Jew they could have found... Some other Arabs—my parents—they came together to give them some place to hide in our homes.

"But when the attackers learned of their compassion, my parents and some of our Jewish and Arab neighbors, they secretly ran to the Dead Sea. When they saw us running for the boats, they..." Shiloh caught her breath sharply and bit her lip to stop herself crying. Having gulped her sobs, she managed out, "The, um... Th-The story is long, but I escaped. Some nuns on pilgrimage from Paris eventually found me." She pointed to the mark on her wrist. "When they saw this, they took me with them to Algiers and Marseilles and um... well, now I am here..."

"Hineini, Hineini," Elnathan said before asking, "But didn't you ever try to look for your family?"

Shiloh turned on him and her quiet voice burst with sudden passion. "I've looked *everywhere* for them, Elnathan. In the Sunnah and in the Messiah; in Jews, Muslims, and Christians during humanity's darkest ages to find where God may have triumphed... because I couldn't bring myself to choose between the only two in my life who ever truly mattered. They believed until death—sometimes, I wonder if it was *to* death. And for that, I can't ever abandon either of them—*never* again, but it feels like..." She trailed off, her thoughts ambling away to something else.

"It feels like what?" Elnathan asked, watching her remember with fatherly interest.

Shiloh swung forward, her heavy eyes burdened with longing. She choked out, "It feels like there's something in the way. It's holding me together while it's tearing me away from myself. There's just so much severing me from my parents, no matter how close I feel them to my heart. And I am trying, *trying* so hard to be whole, but I can't help but feel that I've become nothing but an empty shell. I'm scared to die... but I don't want to exist either. I don't deserve to. But I was really hoping that the Great Mosque would have led me to something new and unknown about the Messiah since..."

Shiloh hesitated a moment, still lost in thought, before continuing, "Since I feel His mother of all people coaxing me to Him, just as the Prophet called us to the Qur'an, *alayhi salatu wa-salam.* I keep hearing the Messiah's mother telling me, 'Do whatever He tells you.' And when I first heard her voice, I believed that maybe God might take me back somehow... But I'm scared, Elnathan. I'm really, really scared that I won't ever know what He wants me to do..." More tears filmed her faraway eyes, and she added, "I'm scared that I won't ever see my mom or dad ever again..."

At this, Elnathan recited, "*I have seen all the works that are done under the sun; and, behold, all is vanity and vexation of spirit. That which is crooked cannot be made straight: And that which is wanting cannot be numbered. I communed with mine own heart, saying, Lo, I am come to great estate, and have gotten more wisdom than all they that have been before me in Jerusalem: Yea, my heart had great experience and wisdom and knowledge. And I gave my heart to know wisdom, and to know madness and folly: I perceived that this also is vexation of spirit. For in much wisdom is much grief: And he that increaseth knowledge increaseth sorrow.*'"

Shiloh frowned at the driver. "Don't waste your breath; I already know what Ecclesiastes says. Why are you quoting it to me?"

Elnathan waggled his head and said, "Listen, my friend: God *is* love itself. That much is certain among all of His religions. And if love is more a struggle than a blissful ecstasy as you say it is, then love cannot simply be wisdom, but a covenant; an enduring remembrance and intimacy with those who suffer meaninglessly alongside us." Elnathan paused before hazarding, "There is no joy in memory. In knowing and remembering the suffering and even *hatred* of others, you know yourself most; knowing and remembering that you still have so much sorrowful passion burning in your heart; God in His most naked, meaningless, most awful form. Could it really be, then, that this 'something in the way' is the way?"

Shiloh looked back at Elnathan, as if she had just remembered that he was still there. She tried to grind out a response, but her thoughts staggered at the prospect. She was still afraid of what she was feeling, unable to bring herself to look into that bottomless well and find that dark mirror in its depths.

Another long silence passed between them, with only the sound being the taxi's wheels trundling over the graded pavement. Shiloh considered Elnathan and his claim before glancing back at Psalmodie, still sleeping with her satchel in her hands. Shiloh reflected on her friend's quest, along with the countless others before her who vainly struggled to hunt for the truth of God or the gods without first knowing the truth of themselves.

With a knit brow and her head still cast down, Shiloh's gaze became remote as she tried one more time to search through the damned void within. But finding nothing more, she looked out her window and felt her lament sweep out to the lands where the Israelites cried out against God's silence.

"We're here now," Elnathan said.

Shiloh turned back towards him. "What? Where?"

"We're at the checkpoint."

Shiloh followed his eyes to the distant structure ahead of them. The fortress' architecture became larger with perspective with every moment of the taxi's approach. Scrawled all over its long wall of precast concrete panels were Hebrew and Arabic graffiti, all militant slogans of some sort, but Shiloh was soon filled with dread and uncertainty once she instantly recognized the flag flying beside the watchtower rising over the largest building's rooftop.

"I'm afraid I won't be able to drive you further than that point," Elnathan said, "since you aren't my normal passengers and beyond that border lies the dominion of the United Kingdom."

"I know..." Shiloh muttered concernedly.

The checkpoint was part of a network of concrete casemate and pillbox fortifications as well as mobile patrols known as "Tegart's Wall," designed by the British Mandate of Palestine to try to deter rebel guerrilla fighters from entering.

"You do know that you two are probably going to get repatriated, right?" Elnathan said. "You would be returning to France, wouldn't you?"

"Yes, we know," Shiloh said, "but you saw what happened back there. We just can't trust anyone in Syria."

"Are you sure?" he asked. "I can still turn around and I know those men; they wouldn't really care to—"

Shiloh reverted back to French. "Psalmodie, wake up. We're here."

Psalmodie awoke from her slumber, rubbing her palm up the side of her brow. "Already?" she groaned.

Before Shiloh could have answered her, the car had stopped before the checkpoint's barrier gate arm. Next to it, an Arab auxiliary border patrol officer in plain clothes left from his post at a nearby guardhouse with a carbine strapped over his shoulder. He circled once around the car, paying particular attention to the damage done to the running light and mirror. Once he came by Elnathan's side, he tapped on his window and peered in. Elnathan promptly complied and rolled down the window.

"*Shalom aleichem,*" the officer greeted in Hebrew.

Elnathan replied in Arabic, "*Wa-alaykum as-salamu wa-rahmatu -Ilahi wa-barakatu.*"

"How is your son Malik?" the officer asked wearily.

"*Alhamdulillah,* he is faring well so far." Elnathan cracked a smile. "He is still trying to teach himself French for some of our patrons; at least the attractive ones."

The officer snickered, "*Hallelu et HaShem.*"

Hearing this, another tear started in Shiloh's eye.

"But aren't you supposed to be celebrating your Sabbath?" the officer continued inquiring.

"We recited the *Yom Rishon Havdalah* yesterday. I believe it is the *Notzrim* who have theirs today."

Then the officer dropped all pretense and frowned at the girl in the seat next to him, still tending to her wound. "So, are you going to explain yourself, Elnathan?"

The taxi driver gave Shiloh one last difficult look. He tried forcing a smile, but it was only met with Shiloh quietly nodding her consent. He could have only mustered out one reassuring expression for her: *"'Remember the stranger, for you were a stranger in Egypt.'"*

CHAPTER 37

Every bend of the Jordan River gleamed like the blade of a scimitar before pouring out into the Sea of Galilee. The sky in the west had become pink and orange with the evening sunlight, whose dying glare streaked and shimmered across the choppy waters of the sea. Flocks of birds flew close to the sea, at times skimming its surface for fish. The harbor piers shooting out from the marshy shores and reed beds of Tiberias had started to receive white flocks of dhow ships and Venetian-style gondolas returning from their evening fishing rounds.

The coastal city itself was a sprawling amphitheater of densely packed buildings of limestone and adobe, sparsely populated with decorative Date palms and Mulberry trees. For Shiloh, it was a somewhat familiar vista from her childhood; it reminded her of when she first saw, through the mistral winds, the many cliffside gardens and chateaus of the French Riviera after her boat had arrived from Algiers.

Since Shiloh and Psalmodie didn't have their passports on their persons, the auxiliary officer charged with their escort was going to have to take them to a port city like Haifa or Jaffa for further processing. The officer, however, had to make a quick stop at his station in the city to brief his British advisors on his next course of action. Though he left the two girls locked in the back seat of his patrol car, he at least had the decency to leave them uncuffed.

This gave Shiloh some time to reflect on the ancient Jewish city, the cradle of the Jerusalem Talmud and Masoretic tradition, as well as the final resting place of the great Rabbis Yohanan ben Zakkai and Maimonides. Among Judaism's "Four Holy Cities," one tradition asserts that the Sanhedrin council authority will one day be reconstituted in Tiberias after the advent of the Messiah. The waves breaking over the city's shores were of the Sea of Galilee, where it was also said that Jesus Christ miraculously walked on water.

That was the sum total of what Shiloh knew about the city's religious significance, though she wasn't keen on sharing it with Psalmodie at the moment. They had been quiet ever since Elnathan handed them both over to the auxiliary officer.

"I didn't mean it," Psalmodie broke the silence.

"What?"

"All that stuff I said to you after England. I didn't mean any of it."

Shiloh sighed, looking back out the window. "I know that, Psalmodie. You're the only real friend I've ever had."

"So are you..." Psalmodie continued, "but after I said all that stuff, I was scared of what hurt you more: The idea I was never really your friend or that I only pretended to be..."

"Oh, don't be so stupid," Shiloh scoffed.

"No, I just..." Psalmodie sighed, still struggling to explain herself to herself. "With everything my father told me, I thought I had a chance of finishing what he couldn't even start since all he ever cared about was my university tuition, even if it meant working for the enemy. But after I received that last telegram from Dachau, I realized that he was really dead because of me... and I knew that it wouldn't have been long before the Germans came after me next. I thought I could have kept his memory alive while keeping you out of their reach..." She mused on the Aramaic-titled journal on her lap and shook her head ruefully. "But you just *had* to follow me on my wild goose chase to Glastonbury."

Psalmodie pressed her fingertips on her brow bone and, after a beat, quietly drew out her next words. "When I saw them staking out at my looted house after I found my father's journal, I knew they'd come for you next. I knew—telegrams or not—that they would have killed both of us." She patted the journal's leather cover. "So, I hid them all in here... among his other failed memories."

As Psalmodie spoke, Shiloh was faraway, her mind once again venturing through darker passes. "When I killed him..." she said, "it didn't feel like I was possessed, but it felt like I was passing some threshold I didn't even know existed."

Shiloh's rumination was met with a disturbed look from Psalmodie. "That man killed Malik, Shiloh; he came so close to killing us! This is all my fault—*mine* alone!"

"But can I still be saved from that killing?" Shiloh croaked. "Or was that always a part of me all along? Has God already forsaken me to my own sins?" Shiloh then looked at Psalmodie, her eyes budding tears. "I *want* that cross, Psalmodie, before the Germans catch up to us. There *has* to be another way to finish your father's work. We can go to the police and maybe we—"

Psalmodie put a hand to Shiloh's cheek and looked gravely into her eyes. "Don't you understand? I didn't want the cross! I wanted my father to come back! I dragged you and Brother Francis into all this. I thought I was keeping you out of their reach, but then I started to see how desperately carried away you were getting with my fantastical delusions, *just* like me. I can't bear to imagine seeing either of you getting hurt because of my lies. They're after *me* and these damned telegrams. Not you. Not the cross."

Sobered by Psalmodie's outburst, Shiloh broke away from Psalmodie and simply let the silence hang between them. Finding no retreat, her distracted eyes wandered down the city and traveled over its compact houses and trees until they came to the horizon... where she saw something.

"Psalmodie?" she murmured.

Her friend was caught off guard by the sudden gravity in her voice. She crouched over and peered out Shiloh's window, trailing her eyes to the desert's horizon, a far-off mountain crest made an ebony silhouette by the civil twilight. Over it, however, were many blemishes, kicking up dust as they charged horseback down the ridge and fanned out across the city streets.

Outside, Shiloh heard the hubbub of passing pedestrians growing wary, some of them looking over their shoulders as they sped up in the opposite direction. But at the sound of tolling alarm bells and shrill whistling, the uneasiness spiraled into confused yelps of panic.

"What is this?" Psalmodie said. "What is—"

Then they saw the officer storming out of the station's front entrance with two other guards, carbines drawn and with confused looks over their faces. The officer's scanning eyes found Shiloh and Psalmodie still trapped in his car, but his agitation drew his glance elsewhere and he staggered off in the other direction.

Then the girls jolted at the sound of a blast, as if a massive fist had slammed into the side of the car. The window panes shivered and cracked, and when Shiloh looked out, she found that the darkening sky had turned to the color of scarlet rust, rising up from the earth.

CHAPTER 38

"Shiloh?" Psalmodie's voice tensed as she was only beginning to grasp the true horror of the gathering storm. The sound of thudding hoofbeats roared louder, almost as though thunder were brewing from within the earth.

"The city's under attack," Shiloh finally said, reaching for Psalmodie's satchel and rooting through its contents.

"Who are those men?" Psalmodie whispered.

"I don't know; nationalists I think."

"The mufti's?"

Shiloh didn't answer her. Instead, she threw the satchel aside and laid her back across the seats. "Get back."

"Shiloh, what are you—" Psalmodie flinched as Shiloh kicked at the door's window, each boot landing with a *crunch*. Though the glass was reinforced to its frame, it took three attempts before the broken pane finally flew out. Shiloh then used the satchel to wipe away any remnant shards still stuck in the door's bottom weather strip.

"We have to go," Shiloh said.

She proceeded to pull herself through the window and clamber to the ground. Psalmodie was right behind her, first throwing out the satchel before wriggling out. Once they were out, they darted for the station's corner and peered around in sheer horror.

Psalmodie could not have comprehended what she was seeing.

Entire buildings had gone up in flames, all conflating into one burning glare. As the razing firelight approached them, the girls coughed into the crooks of their arms and squinted through the wreathing screen of smoke. The heat burned their eyes and singed their faces. Even so, what they heard next sent chills through them.

The hideous shrieks of women and children echoed out from the wall of flames... just before they were sharply silenced.

Shiloh and Psalmodie stood frozen in their tracks, petrified by whatever presence haunted the other side of the inferno. They glanced left and right searching for a way out of this, but they were trapped. There was nowhere left to hide between the fire and the compact buildings lining the street except one. Psalmodie looked over her shoulder and saw a building with barred windows and a dome cupola at the far end of the street. A simple structure with no minarets or steeples; a synagogue perhaps.

"Psalmodie?" Shiloh nudged her, fear streaking across her face.

Psalmodie turned and saw the monster's black shadow emerging from the hissing embers of hell; he had a claw-like dagger in one hand and a revolver in the other; his entire face was wrapped under a black tagelmust, showing only the murderous flare in his jaundiced eyes.

Psalmodie bobbed up and down in fear and braced herself. "Shiloh, behind us. The synagogue. Run. *Run!*"

They wheeled away and broke into a dogged sprint, bobbing and weaving as five ear-splitting snaps thundered out from behind and chipped at the ground around them. The two wheezed for breath through their wild panting, but their eyes were set on the synagogue; it was either a trap or a sanctuary, but there was no other option. They heard the monster's footsteps gaining, fast.

For some reason, his steps stuttered to a halt, and despite Psalmodie's panic, she felt some vague hope that he had given up, so she allowed herself to glance back at their hunter. He was in the middle of the street, feverishly reloading his gun.

"Keep running!" Shiloh screamed.

They were only a few feet from the synagogue's front wooden doors.

Then... *Thwack!*

One round slammed on the doors and blasted dust over them. Shiloh made it through first while Psalmodie shut the doors behind her. But just when she was about to pull the bolt lock across the pull handles, it burst out from its hinges, a bullet hole in its place. Psalmodie dropped her satchel and leapt back as two more flickering pencils of yellow light punched through the door's mahogany surface. She sprang up and frantically searched for anything that would have helped barricade the door by its handles.

She found a long wooden dowel stood against the wall nearby and slid it across the handles just as the doors slammed in. She heard two more reports beat against the door.

Then... utter silence.

Psalmodie staggered away from the damaged doors, at first fearful that the pole was not secure between the handles. The sound of receding footsteps, however, eased her sanity. She exhaled sharply and shut her eyes, taking a moment's respite to catch some of her breath before setting off to figure out where they ought to have gone next. Psalmodie's head swiveled around the modest sanctuary veiled in darkness.

"How do we get out of here?" she gulped, stooping down for her satchel. She searched her surroundings, waiting for a response from Shiloh. Nothing. Psalmodie called into the darkness again. "Shiloh, come on! Can you see anyth—"

Then she heard something shatter against the synagogue outside. A fluttering firelight swung around the room from the barred clerestory windows and illuminated the synagogue's small stone antechamber. Soon after, thick smoke had begun to stream into the room like spirits. Psalmodie eventually realized that it was only a matter of time before the entire building would have gone up in a blaze.

"Shiloh, where?" Psalmodie shouted. "Where do we—" She stopped, exhaling shakily as she felt a wave of horror seize her mind and body once she saw the light reflected in a curved trail of dark fluid pooling out from around a corner. Psalmodie felt the air around her growing thicker with smoke. Embers scattered in from the creaking rafters, giving way to the roaring flames.

She kept forcing herself forward, but her steps became heavy, and every moment of her approach only slowed with dread. She felt the horror rising within her, and she fought the urge to lunge forward to come face to face with what lay around that corner. After she turned the corner, her dazed amble came to a complete stop.

Psalmodie's breath hitched as she choked back her screams.

She dropped her satchel and huddled beside Shiloh's curled body. Psalmodie came closer to Shiloh's face and saw that frail tears were still streaking shining paths down the sides of her glazed, amber eyes, staring past Psalmodie into empty space. Psalmodie tugged at Shiloh's body, desperately trying to remain calm in face of what would have eventually become hysteria.

"It's okay, you're okay," she cried, her breath sawing in and out. "Come on, Shiloh, we have to go. Come on!" She tried yanking her up, but her hand felt something seeping through Shiloh's jerkin. Psalmodie looked down and saw the black-red patch growing from her side.

"Please... I need you..." Psalmodie crooned, her strained voice breaking as she rocked Shiloh's lolling head in the crook of her arm. Psalmodie's shallow panting soon choked to convulsing sobs. "Don't leave me..."

Then she saw the blood scribbling down Shiloh's forearm, then down to her cross tattoo, and the small rosary in her open palm. A sonorous tinnitus haunted the air all around Psalmodie and came into her ears, drowning out all other sounds into a vacuum. Raging flames licked up the walls all around her, and a growing shroud of smoke engulfed all of her reality. Psalmodie gathered Shiloh's head to her chest. She collapsed against the wall as her whimpers blossomed into wails of excruciating torture.

CHAPTER 39

The outskirts

L ost and aimless, that quarter moonlight through the murky darkness was the only thing that the girl had left. Her scraped and grimy face was damp with sweat and the smoldering humidity. She trailed towards one of the mountain horns blocking the long trek that awaited her. Her dead eyes passively swept up the shales and gravel of the scree before she reached out her trembling, bloody hands to scale it.

There was a small scrub tree crowning the hill's summit. Once she was there, she crumpled over the tree's roots, and when her hands felt around the ground for balance, she slid her back up against its thin trunk. For a moment, her exhaustion had nearly gotten the better of her, and she swayed in and out of consciousness before she felt a cold drop rolling down her sooted cheek. When she opened her eyes, she saw that a fine rain had started to mist over her skin. It wasn't long before a pattering rain had lashed down from the split sky and commanded her mind back to the present.

She lifted her face to the storm's touch for some vain sense of ablution, but her eyes drifted out and stared longingly into the darkness. From the hill, she saw a nebular squall mingling with the distant billowing columns of smoke rising from the volcanic firestorm that still consumed the city. The mudcracks in the scorched earth, glowing blood-red like burning coals, *garish against the yawning chasm of darkness across King Arthur's shadowlands.*

As she felt this darkness beginning to purge every depth of her Being and define her inmost nature, her eyes searched heavenward, and all she could have done was roar out a searing shrill with a despairing, child-like release; scream into the void; scream into herself, as though the slanting showers pelting her head and face were washing away her soul.

Nothing beside remained.

PART IV

THE GRAIL BEARER

CHAPTER 40

Böttcherstraße
Bremen, Germany
October 16th, 1938

The midnight thunderstorm had sheeted down across the industrial cityscape. While the 53-year-old Dutch Professor Herman Wirth did have his umbrella up, he still made absolutely certain that his corded leather research files were kept dry under his rumpled beige overcoat. If his feathery gray hair and mustache became drenched, he would have needed to have gotten under a roof before his precious research became saturated by the elements as well.

While in his ambition he co-founded the Ahnenerbe e.V. with the Reichsführer, Wirth had since been replaced as its president despite his significant breakthroughs in tracing the ancestral line of the pure Aryan race to their prehistoric forerunners, the lost islanders of Atlantis. Yet despite the setback, he took comfort in the idea that he could have fully committed to his ethnographic research with stipends from the SS, and for this, there was no place better than the reading room in the sacred refuge across the street from him.

The Haus Atlantis, which was built in 1931 as the German fatherland's principal research institute for its Atlantean heritage.

Still enduring the torrential downpour, Wirth crossed the lantern-lit street and entered through the shadowy brick arcade that gave unto the narrow alleyway where the façade of the Haus was. Once he was under the entrance's awning, he collapsed his umbrella and searched through his pockets for the keys to the glass doors.

But it was then that he heard a voice behind him say, "Your research findings really are an enchanting prospect, aren't they, Herr Professor?"

Startled, Wirth looked back at the man sitting on a wooden bench under the canopy of the bracketed bay window of the Robinson Crusoe Haus opposite to the Atlantis Haus' entrance. The man was wearing an all-black ensemble: An officer's service cap, jodhpurs with jackboots, and an ink black paramilitary dress uniform with the crimson armband of the Reich's national flag. He was resting one hand on the brass knob handle of his walking cane, although to Wirth's recollection, he had no need for one.

"Come sit with me," Heinrich Himmler said, indicating the seat next to him with his cane.

The professor swallowed his self-consciousness and calmly walked over to his Reichsführer, letting the cascade wash over his head if only for a moment. He feared Himmler would have noticed his wooden composure once he sat down. Instead, Wirth noticed that his superior was staring up at something on the building. A revelation of lightning tore through the shroud of darkness, and Wirth heard the blackened firmament rumbling with Thor's wrath: A reminder to his lands of his reigning All-Father's sacrifice.

More than hearing it, Wirth saw the All-Father's eldritch face flash vividly before him.

Set against the brick and mortar façade above the door's framework was a gigantic, crudely whittled wood carving of an anatomically deformed figure with disproportionately elongated members crucified against a circular sun cross and a head that hung down in the quiet horror of torture. A faithful icon of the 'Tree of Life' story written in the Old Norse *Poetic Edda* legend, where the Germanic god Wotan, in the grandeur of his own prideful ego, sacrificed himself *to himself* by hanging from the cosmic Yggdrasil tree that bound and connected the Nine Worlds to one another.

Wirth himself became absorbed in the Atlantean saviour's grotesque aspect, although he wasn't as obsessed with it as the Reichsführer was. For a long while, neither of them had spoken even after the rain had ceased. They simply sat on the bench, basking in the warming presence of their idol, safe in the knowledge that not even the All-Father, the god of all gods himself, could have ever kept from his own compelling might.

After what felt like an hour, Himmler broke the silence. "For two millennia, our *Kirchenkampf* has persisted."

Wirth looked at Himmler and cleared his throat. "Pardon me?"

"Herr Professor, are you aware that only a couple of days ago," Himmler continued with disgust in his tone, "the Holy See's very own Cardinal Innitzer delivered a sermon in Saint Stephen's Cathedral in Vienna confessing only one Führer: Their Christ-God?"

Wirth's brow furrowed as his mind wandered back to a few months ago. "Wait, wasn't he the one who called on the Christians to pray for the Führer on his birthday?"

"And the one who initially endorsed the Anschluss, yes," Himmler said, throwing up a hand. "I can't hope to understand the clergy, but either way, the *Hitler-Jugend* ransacked his palace before we could have gotten to it."

"I take it His Eminence now has to think of a better present to give to the Führer for his next birthday," Wirth remarked.

After another beat, Himmler answered with a smile, "I think the Führer is more than satisfied with the one *I* gave him for his birthday." The Reichsführer stroked his chin. "Do you remember that Francophilic Ariosophist: Otto Rahn? That skinny, wandering Jew that high priest Wiligut Weisthor introduced you to some years back in Wewelsburg."

"How could I ever forget?" Wirth said with passive interest. "That is quite the grandiose ambition for a *Halbjude* like him, the Holy Grail. It is the alleged treasure of the Atlantean heirs in medieval *France*, correct?"

"Yes, the pseudo-Christian Cathari of the Ariège," Himmler said. "At least, that is the hypothesis in his publications. Since I knew Richard Wagner's Grail operas *Parsifal* and *Lohengrin* to be among the Führer's favorites, Rahn's latest work, *Luzifer's Hofgesind,* was my birthday gift to him, along with thousands of more copies printed for the Schutzstaffel. That *Halbjude's* mission remains my gift to the Führer."

"And how has our Führer received our new knighthood?" Wirth inquired.

Himmler looked askance at him. "It is a shame that he should fail to see the reason in my intentions: Our people's destiny. Our Führer, for all of his cunning, cannot bring himself to recognize our Aryan race's dire need for spiritual heritage; contrary to his worldly ambitions, our mysticism is rooted in truth, and not in the rotting traditions of the Church, which, frankly, I am beginning to believe he still has some lingering fondness for."

"Surely, the Führer ought to at least acknowledge his mission after he read his book?" Wirth asked. "The Holy Grail? Surely a most important venture for the SS."

"Second," Himmler corrected. "Second most important."

Wirth looked puzzlingly at Himmler. "Pardon me? Second?"

"Herr Rahn is doing damage control as we speak, trying to retrieve some classified telegrams."

Wirth shuffled in his seat and leaned his elbows on one knee. "If I may ask, what is the SS's most important venture? I apologize if I am making you repeat yourself, my Reichsführer, but I cannot remember if you have told me."

A smirk crawled onto Himmler's face. "You would imagine that our Führer would have shown some appreciation for my SS and Gestapo after he had them covertly retrieve those dossiers from that police headquarters in Vienna while his Anschluss was still happening."

"Vienna?" Wirth exclaimed. "Where our Führer grew up?"

"Where our Führer was forged," Himmler said, "by the hellfire of our race's tribulations."

"What on Earth was in those dossiers if something such as the *Holy Grail* is of secondary importance to the Führer and his SS?" The professor looked up and saw the suggestion on the Reichsführer's deadpan expression. While Himmler said nothing, Wirth knew better than to tread further on the grounds of the Führer's cryptic, possibly even scandalous past. Wirth gulped on his agitation, and instead opted back to his original line of inquiry: "How much progress has our friend made thus far?"

Himmler looked down at his cane and, to Wirth's unease, let out a caustic laugh. "How can you even *begin* to comprehend the news that he had Dr. Ernst Schäfer translate an artifact of the Tatars for the so-called 'Christian' Grail?"

"The *Christian* Grail?" Wirth reacted. "What? Why?"

Himmler continued cackling. "He compromised with the mufti's religious sensibilities to destroy it so that he would help find classified intelligence two Parisian college girls *somehow* intercepted!" Wirth was about to get a word in about the Cathari Grail, but Himmler kept talking. "Not to mention, he *somehow* had Schütze Kurt Eggers incapacitated as well; the absolute *insanity* of it all!"

Wirth shrugged to express his impartiality. "I know you have repeatedly spoken of the Grail's influence on our Führer's humble beginnings, but to be quite frank... wouldn't you say it has essentially fulfilled its ultimate purpose?"

Another jagged bolt of lightning flashed above, and Wirth realized his own mistake too late. Himmler's grin fell to a bristled look. Wirth stared a Himmler as if at the mercy of the demon Mephistopheles himself. For all of Wirth's careerism in life, he may as well have sold his soul to Lucifer's own agent anyway.

Then Wirth saw Mephisto point his cane up at Wotan before the devil belabored, "You co-founded the Ahnenerbe with me. I assumed you of all people would have known that what paucity we have of the *Poetic Edda* may have been embellished by 13th-century Christians in the *Codex Regius*. That, Herr Professor, is all the more reason to reclaim whatever is left of the Nordic faith and warrior traditions.

"The Tatar juggernaut beyond China became an unfortunate mixture of Czechs, Poles, and Turks, and it became far too late for them to come back to their true warrior culture, but our people can still have a chance to be saved from the grip of the modern-day Romans... and that means hoarding as much of the infinite as we possibly can."

Wirth's mettle had started to crack. "I did not mean to suggest that I wanted to—"

Then, to Wirth's dread, he saw Himmler twist the knob off of his cane and draw an awl from its concealed sheath. The Reichsführer contemplated the long shank's business end before turning his unblinking eyes at Wirth with unsettling equanimity.

"Despite Herr Rahn's brilliant insights on the Grail," Himmler said, twisting the handle, "I had always known that he was a liberal *Mitläufer*. There is really no way of knowing if he has the heart to do what is necessary for his Reich. I should have known it was a grave error sending him to salvage the situation he created; I knew he failed the SS exercise regime at Buchenwald, and with Eggers no longer able to serve for now, that *Halbjude*—right now in his ancestral homeland—has now become a dangerous liability to our Führer."

Wirth perked up and gulped. "And what will you of him?"

Himmler turned the shank back downward, still looking at its tip. "He and I have a cousin in common. And after he brought his expertise to bear on the genealogical research to prove my own Aryan ancestry, against my better judgment, I still feel somewhat obligated to reprieve his just sentence, lest he leaves the SS." He stabbed the shank into the cane's hidden sheath. There was a lengthy pause before he cleared his throat and said, "But never mind him. It is because of what I will of *you* that I am here tonight."

His response stupefied him. *"Me?"* he blurted.

Himmler snapped, "Yes, Professor! You. You, who will—who *must* —compensate for what I now know will inevitably be Herr Rahn's failure. If I can't give the Führer the Grail's power, the least I can do now is promise him our Atlantean inheritance." Then he shot up, tucked the cane under his arm, and stormed for the arcade.

Despite himself, Wirth stood up and anxiously called after the Reichsführer. "And what will you do with that history?"

Himmler stopped short and swiveled towards the Atlantis Haus. Without facing the professor, Himmler clicked his heels and hailed Wotan one last time with the salute of the mass party before concluding, "The Nazarene Jew will be supplanted and, by one way or another, the old Germanic gods will be restored." He fell silent to allow his words to be felt before continuing on his way down the realm of shadows.

Alone in the alley, the professor took out his file and dwelled on its contents. He then raised his gaze and looked to his All-Father's mournful visage, who looked as though he were once again beholding his realm drowning in the blood-mixed tides of hubris and faith.

Sacrificing itself to itself.

CHAPTER 41

The Hotel Fast, Mamilla neighborhood
Jerusalem, the British Mandate of Palestine
October 17th, 1938

Psalmodie was still under the covers of the canopied, four-post bed, fearful of making any movements that would have awakened the man nestling closely behind her. Slowly, she rose from the rucked up bed with a white sheer fabric pressed over her topless chest; she felt a cold draft in places she knew she shouldn't. Her jaded eyes swung around the seedy room, and she saw the soft white light of overcast skies filtering in from the windows' gossamer curtains.

She was still fatigued and delirious from the night before when she let herself go. She looked towards the long drawer credenza at the far end of the room and found the cluttered snifters and decanters of fortified spirits the man behind her forced her to aspirate on. The spicy fumes of brown rum still clung to the back of her throat, and the ebbing pressure in her skull still disoriented her, though it wasn't quite as bad as the spiraling haze she had suffered through the night before.

She brought the fabric higher against her collarbone and quietly tottered towards the credenza in the vain hope of finding her satchel stowed behind it. Even if she could have, there was too much glassware on top for her to not make a sound. Still, she heard the muffled squalling of an infant coming from the walls of another room; it eventually grew to a piercing crying that sounded like a hinge that had not been oiled, threatening to wake up Psalmodie's captor.

On the credenza, she found a small oval mirror. She looked down at her hand, beringed and cuffed in gold bangles, feeling as though it had been severed; she locked eyes with her own image in the mirror and raised her hand to touch at her kohl-ringed eyes and the false tribal tattoos patterned over her forehead, cheeks, and chin. She felt her past self, and all memory of her youth, abandoning her, running as far away from this new, scandalized truth of herself as possible.

Then a rough voice behind her called to her, "You may speak French, but that wouldn't necessarily mean that you *are* French, would it?"

Psalmodie felt the half-robed man's frowning eyes traveling down the center of her stiffened spine once she heard his bare feet pad the Berber carpet; it wasn't long before her imposing voyeur circled her like prey. He drew closer to her face, seeming to grow taller with every step. Psalmodie quietly sucked in a breath through her teeth as the man tested a straight razor along the damp skeins of her now-short, choppy hair with one hand and maneuvered the small of her open back with the other.

"You really didn't know anyone in Tiberias, did you?" he asked.

Still frozen, Psalmodie stiffly shook her head.

The man squinted mistrustfully at her. "Not a single Arab wog in there? Not one? You?"

Psalmodie shook her head again.

"If you're lying to me..."

Psalmodie fleeted a glance at the man before dropping her eyes back to the floor. Then, without conscious will, she mouthed voicelessly, "No..."

The man traced a finger up her back and his voice shifted closer to her. "This city—this so-called 'Kingdom of Heaven'—was a much-needed Christmas gift to British morale after our immense defeat at Passchendaele in the Great War. So many stratagems of intrigue were necessary in our final Crusade to secure it. But now I wonder if it was really worth it?"

He then pretended to look around the room and scoffed, "Gog and Magog may have given way, but only to make way for God and His demagogues. And at every turn in this, the inscrutable Orient, it seems that if you are not confused, then you clearly do not understand the situation. You just can't trust anyone these days, huh?"

Psalmodie heard the man's voice take on a more threatening edge. "And the roving Haganah paramilitary found *you* alone, hitchhiking so close to the stabbings. They oddly thought little of you, but for all I know, you could still be tied to those savage, fifth-column rabbles... and I could still have you extradited or, if I wish to, so much worse."

Psalmodie blanched from him with her face averted. She wanted to cry, but the liquor had drained her of most of her balance and stamina. She huddled her emotions and tried to withdraw still further into herself, but she had already pressed herself against the credenza. Then she shut her eyes and waited for whatever was going to happen.

But when she heard the British military's morning bugle call outside, she felt the man's caressing hand fall away from her back and the straight razor withdraw from her face. She massaged her throat and saw the man reach for a flat tin container of stale snuff tobacco on a nearby lamp table; he took a pinch, raised it to his nostrils, and snorted deeply.

"But you certainly do *feel* French," he said, groaning with cathartic release, "and I thank you for that comfort."

Psalmodie saw him reach for something else below the table. Hanging from his grip was the leather strap of her satchel. He tossed it to her feet and strolled idly towards the bathroom doorway. Psalmodie gaped down at it, shivering and unresponsive. She would have picked it up then, but there was only so much dignity she could have clung onto while she held her stripped self.

The man looked her up and down one last time before ultimately muttering, "Welcome to Jerusalem."

When the infant's crying in the other hotel room was silenced, Psalmodie heard the call of the Islamic *Duha adhan* blaring from mosque loudspeakers outside. After the man picked up his uniform with the British Union Jack shoulder patch from the floor, he closed the bathroom door behind him and left Psalmodie to molder in the silence.

Her innocence, bleeding out of her in tears.

CHAPTER 42

The svelte concierge with a tight, severe hair bun and form-fitting pantsuit sat at the illustrious hotel's marble front desk, shuffling around many litters of bookings and schedules for special requests by the guests. The entrance hall had been especially vacant that morning, though she chalked up the lack of business to the ongoing situation outside.

Then she saw a presence out of the corner of her eye, but once she had gotten a better look at who was standing at the other side of her desk, her stare instantly darkened.

The British soldier from Major General Richard O'Connor's Coldstream Guards. To the concierge's distaste, he was still wearing his strap-on shoulder holster to sport his standard issue Mark VI Webley revolver. To her disgust, she saw that standing beside him was the short-haired vagrant girl escorted up to his quarters the previous night. Her messy hair was down, and she wasn't wearing the same brown-stained shirt she came in with; instead, she wore only a white, thin-strapped camisole with dark chausses, though the rest of her clothes were folded over her arms.

"Did you both enjoy your stay?" the concierge asked with a prim smile, moving to open another log book to mark off the man's name.

The man answered by slapping down his bill payment against the desktop. "I think she has something she really wants to ask of you," he said before lifting his grip around the girl's shoulder. With that, he turned away on his heel and vanished past the front entrance's glass vestibule.

The concierge's irritated eyes chased him out, but the girl's did not. She simply stood there, hugging her dirty clothes and satchel to her chest while staring down at nothing.

"Yes?" the concierge inquired evenly, distancing herself from the girl with her professional manner.

The girl's drawn eyes flitted up towards her, and she quietly twisted two of the soldier's banknotes towards the concierge. "That message I asked you to send last night," the girl whispered, dissociated. "Did you send it to them?"

The concierge answered tensely, "Yes, of course. I had it sent out from the German Landeskreiter's office this morning like I said I would. They gave me their response."

The girl's eyes snapped up. "What did they say?"

The concierge's brow creased; she pursed her lips before responding, "They say they found the path to 'the cup'... and that it is beneath al-Aqsa."

The girl's gaze turned downcast, and she glanced off towards a window at the far end of the entrance hall. Without another word, she turned away from the concierge and maundered off towards the front entrance.

The concierge, despite herself, called after the girl, "You know he is going to send men looking for you here, right?" When she saw the girl's dazed amble slow to a halt, the concierge continued, "I can slow them down for as long as I possibly can, but I will not be able to stop them." The concierge waited for the girl's response, but there was only the silence of her upset. "I don't know what it is that happened, but I am sure you don't owe them *anything.*"

Then the girl, without turning back to look at her, continued on her path.

When Psalmodie shouldered open the front door and stumbled out into the street, her face and chest felt blasted by the oven-like air, choked with the fetor of exhaust fumes. She fell against an engaged Ionic column supporting the hotel's front entrance's awning and saw that there was no sidewalk before her; only a street cordoned off by concrete bollards, burlap sandbags, and knife-rest wire barricades.

Mobilized pickets of British infantry, all armed with Bren and Lewis light machine guns, marched to and from the famed Jaffa Gate of the ramparted Old City down the road while auxiliary troops with police whistles directed strange assortments of traffic—military staff cars, half-track trucks, and uniformed cavalrymen wearing slouch hats—towards the municipal districts of Jerusalem.

Still feeling outside of herself, Psalmodie pushed off from the column and wandered down Koresh Street adjacent to the grand hotel's left side. Numbed to the world all around her, she continued lumbering down the narrow street with one hand touching its way along the wall and the other holding to her clothes. In her tranced state, she didn't even hear the lockstep approaching her.

"Make way, you ass!" one soldier shouted.

Psalmodie held her satchel tighter when she saw the oncoming phalanx of troops donning dishpan helmets and carrying their carbines at the slope; they jostled against her shoulder, making her stumble back against the hotel's Caen stone wall and drop all of her clothes. With her hand, she tendered her side and carefully lowered herself to her knees to gather up her clothes.

Then, amid the soldierly commotion, she heard a voice. She thought it must have been a voice her memory invoked to push back against the mounting desolation, but this voice strangely persisted. It was a slight sound, but a sound she knew all too well.

The accompanying sound of giggling drew her widened eyes towards the other end of the street. Congregating by the opposing building's entrance were a group of nuns dressed in pleated habits and the jarring cornette headdress Psalmodie wore only a few days earlier. All of them were eagerly beaming up at...

...She felt she must have been dreaming...

It can't be...

Upon seeing him, she felt a sob hitch in her chest. The man wore a shearling collar barn coat with corduroy trousers. The clothes were far from the man's usual attire, but it was the voice Psalmodie recognized. The voice and the greasy, mid-length locks of hair.

Psalmodie left her clothes and struggled to her feet; without looking both ways, she traipsed across the street to the man. The nuns with him took notice and watched her approach with apprehensive curiosity. With their eyes, they indicated the man towards her direction. Perplexed, he turned to face whoever it was the nuns were looking at.

Psalmodie's heart sank, and with a sharp catch in her breath, she gasped out, "Br-Brother?"

Then her knees gave out as she flew into Brother Francis' chest.

The Jesuit caught Psalmodie and let her buckle over his arm so that she could vomit out her racking sobs with abandon. Nonplussed, he looked over her shoulder and realized the direction she came from. He saw the hotel consulate's banner flag looming over the other end of the street: The bright red standard with the white disc... and the hooked cross of the Antichrist at its heart; the appropriation of the Buddhist *samsara*—the very cycle of life—into history's ever-incessant cycle of violence.

Francis straightened Psalmodie and held her by her quaking shoulders. His kind Asian eyes narrowed even more once he noticed the false tattoos and scars marked on her face. He raked a hair from her brow, took her chin in his hand, and tenderly turned her marked face side to side before going back to holding her gaze.

"My God, Psalmodie, you're shaking..." he whispered. "What happened to you at the German consulate back there?"

Psalmodie said nothing. Her unmoored eyes, unwilling to settle at first, strained up and gradually latched onto Francis'; she rocked herself in his arms as she struggled desperately to compose whatever splinters were left of her swaying mind, as if she hadn't fully yet brought herself to stomach the unbearable weight of some horrifying truth. Her face crumpled and she again turned inwardly, sucking in her tears and fighting for shallow breaths as more feeble, shuddering sobs spilled quietly out from her.

Cold and forsaken by God and man.

Francis soon felt that something was missing. He looked around for his friend, denying it at first; he looked back at Psalmodie and saw her shrinking back from him when she recognized the instant he realized what was wrong. When his face flushed red and his eyes filled with tears, he clutched Psalmodie to his chest and gently cradled her head. The nuns simply stood off to the side, watching them both with worry.

CHAPTER 43

The Hospice of Saint Vincent de Paul

Psalmodie still didn't believe that of all the places in the holy city, the hospice of the Daughters of Charity had been directly next to the Hotel Fast's German consulate. With the largest Catholic church in Jerusalem, the hospice's limestone building was a grand display of Romanesque Revivalist architecture with a fairly good view of the Old City.

Given how popular Brother Francis had become with the Missions Society, the nuns mercifully received Psalmodie and made room for her in some private quarters in the guest house of the convent. It was a plain, spartan room with only one dormer window and a simple cot-size mattress, ornamented only by a single crucifix hanging on the wall over the head of the bed.

Psalmodie sat slouched at the foot of the bed, her knee bouncing, and her eyes still shot with trauma. Her short hair was haphazardly tied up in a high knot, and although she was still only wearing her camisole, Francis' Chinese robe was around her bare shoulders. At the foot of her cot were her satchel and clothes in a pile, and on the floor next to her cot's leg was a water-filled white enamel bowl and balled-up wash cloth, though Francis had only used them to wipe away the markings on Psalmodie's face since she kept jumping at his caring touch.

All tenderness had become foreign to her.

Psalmodie saw that he simply sat in a wooden chair across from her with a tome on his lap, looking just as distraught. Still, Psalmodie couldn't help but hazard against his silence. "Brother?"

He stared deeply and longingly down at the stained rosary and medal in his palm, still taking in the full measure of Psalmodie's story. His eyes offered no sign of solace to Psalmodie this time.

"When I was reading into Japan's expansion into China in *The Palestine Post,* I think I read something about that anti-Semitic pogrom," Francis said thickly. "But I don't remember reading a single thing about an Egyptian girl." His eyes welled up with quiet indignation. "I heard from an Arab Christian girl, far too young to have seen this... that the Arab villagers of Dabburiyya and al-Bassa were mowed down at random by British and Zionist squads; a cold-blooded vendetta for the nationalists' murder of innocent Jews, but covered up, I imagine in keeping with the fucking lie that every single person in this land is nothing but a violent savage."

Psalmodie searched his eyes, trying to find anything that would have filled the gap yawning between them. She couldn't have thought of anything more to add that could have possibly comforted him. Her vague eyes traveled down to her feet, yet she couldn't help but feel as though she saw something strangely uncanny. She was ready to dismiss the feeling as *déjà vu* given how shell shocked she had been, but she looked closer over where she thought she saw this passing resemblance to a very familiar pattern.

It was on the cover of Francis' book.

Her thoughts rewound at frantic speed to what she saw on the artifact that had been lost days before. It was undeniable. For some odd reason, she instantly recognized the first marking. It was the only portion of the inscription that seemed to repeat itself on the hand cannon.

Psalmodie's voice found new life. "Your book, Brother! What does that cover mean?"

Francis jumped, startled by her outburst. He looked at her incredulously, glancing up and down between his book and his friend.

"I'm-I'm sorry?" he stuttered, fumbling for words. "I-It's a very rough Inner Mongolian *Hudum* translation I found in the libra—"

Psalmodie shrugged off the robe and took the book from his lap. "The words, Brother! What do they say *exactly?*"

"'Holy Bible!'" Francis reacted. "It says 'Holy Bible!'"

Shock played on Psalmodie's face as she took in his translation. "The hand cannon we found in Damascus. It had two lines of text with the same *exact* word." She pointed to the first inscription on Francis' Mongolian Bible and shook her head in bewilderment. "It repeats the same word twice: 'Holy, holy.' This seems redundant, so why do it?"

Francis eyed her incredulously. "Psalmodie, what is going on?"

He waited for Psalmodie to slow down and see the irrational fault she was falling back into, but she didn't break stride. Her head swam restlessly, trying to extract some meaning from the repeated word she knew she was missing.

Then the realization dawned on her face.

"So that's where you say the cup's path is, Otto?" she whispered to herself. "'The Holy of Holies?'"

Brother Francis came around her and clutched her arms. "What are you doing?"

Psalmodie yanked her arms back. "I need to go to the Temple Mount tonight."

"The Dome of the Rock?" Francis exclaimed, grilling her. "Tonight? What for?"

"Brother..." Psalmodie pleaded.

Francis was sounding more and more mortified. "Psalmodie, please talk to me because what is going through my head right now is terrifying."

Psalmodie shook her head. "No, you wouldn't understand."

"But you *just* told me that—"

PAUL FABIAN

"This is what she died for!" she erupted.

Psalmodie's glare softened once she heard the mental echo of what she had just said. She looked away, setting the Bible down on her cot and catching sight of the likeness of the crucified Christ over her bed.

"It could have been written on plain paper," Francis muttered. Psalmodie heard the sharp resentment in his voice and braced herself as Francis drew up to her. "You said these Templars left a message in the *Mongols'* language on a *gunpowder* weapon before hiding it beneath the *skull* of Christ's *herald!* Oh, for God's sake, Psalmodie, why else would you think they went through so much trouble for such blatant symbolism? *All* quests for immortality have always ended in death!" His words cut deep into her. "She didn't die for this, she died for *you*. And you know that."

Psalmodie quailed at his statement and choked back tears. She responded, but her indignant voice came out faint and thin. "I have nothing left. I *have* to see this through. For both of us. For my father. We have come this far and have been through too much."

"*We*," Francis echoed, bitterly reproaching. "*We've* come this far —*too* far now."

"No, Brother..." Psalmodie said, her voice still a small, breathy whisper. "No, you weren't there... You weren't there..."

Francis wheeled away from her. He planted his arms akimbo and paced off with measured steps to rein back his spiteful outrage. He put a hand to his forehead and ran it down over his mouth as his eyes fled to four parts of the room. He tried to soften his unsteady tone, but he couldn't help it.

"Fine," he huffed, turning back around to face Psalmodie to address her with full contempt. "I have good news and bad news for you then. General O'Connor had the Muslim Waqf endowment put the Dome of the Rock on high alert status given the recent spring of Arab nationalist attacks all throughout Palestine. The place is full of guards, and they do a damn good job of making the holy places at the Temple Mount impenetrable, so you're going to have to be *very* persuasive for them to let you into the holiest sanctuary in all of the Holy Land."

Psalmodie sighed, registering his point. "And the good news?"

Francis shot her a withering look. "That *was* the good news."

"What?" Psalmodie's face fell in dismay. "Well, what the hell's the bad news then?" she demanded.

Francis let the silence hang there for a moment before flouncing a hand towards the small dormer window. "There be dragons."

Confused at first, Psalmodie crossed towards the window. There, she leaned her elbow against the pane and rested her brow on her forearm to shade her eyes. Against the aurulent skyline, she saw the city's crown jewel: The new Tower of Babel. The protuberant and iconic leaden dome, rising pointed like a closed flower, commanding the pride and distinction of its largely attributed landscape, which was lined to the furthest distance by countless other onion domes, steeples, belfries, and minarets rising from the flat rooftops of many whitewashed mud brick homes and squats.

That vast and heavenly horizon which had garnered so much tumult and controversy throughout the ages.

"Some nationalists boarded themselves up in the Old City a couple of days ago," Francis said. "The army placed a nighttime curfew on us. And as I am given to understand from the locals, the 'Noble Sanctuary' over there is the eye of that storm right now. Even the governor himself —Edward Keith-Roach—I read in the papers that he was very nearly killed in a blast almost a week ago; *no one* is safe in there, Psalmodie."

There was the distant clacking of gun reports echoing in the still landscape, but for the undisturbed pedestrians and soldiers in the streets below, the noise seemed to have become a fact of life, no different than the mere chirping of birds. Psalmodie also saw the mushrooming plumes dragging with the passing gales. Then, through the rising smoke, a sortie of Royal Air Force biplanes roared overhead; from the height they were flying, she felt sick with worry that they would have carpet-bombed Jerusalem like she saw in news clippings of what had happened recently in Spain. Instead, the biplanes rained down swarms of papers on the Old City before peeling away from the hostile skyline, thus seeming to have been nothing more than a reconnaissance flyby.

Francis came up behind her. "Those planes have been dropping propaganda leaflets issuing a permanent curfew for the residents in there."

She stood a moment longer, still receiving Francis' words and looking beyond herself to see if there may have been any other option. Then, in a daze, she moved off towards her cot to root through the contents of her satchel.

Francis hooked a hand on her arm, stopping her. "I beg you, stop!" he implored with a wavering voice. "Listen, I am here for you! I can take you to see a doctor or to hear a confessor; anything to help you find the truth of you and—"

"The *truth* of me?" Psalmodie confronted him, lifting her chin defiantly and lowering her choked voice to a menacing growl. "What 'truth of me,' Brother? There is nothing your Church can tell me that I already don't know! Shiloh died for me..." She pointed out the window, towards the dome on the horizon. "And there is my truth!"

Francis was speechless, utterly disturbed by the adamant finality in her glare. For a moment, Psalmodie saw in his gaze that he had become afraid of what he was seeing. When he withdrew his scowl and backed away from her with an aggrieved scoff, Psalmodie returned to her satchel. He stormed for the door but stopped in the middle of the room to leave her off with one last spiteful utterance.

"I want you to know," he said, his back still to her, "that you can still have God's forgiveness for what you did to her... even if you can't ever have mine..."

By the time Psalmodie looked back towards the doorway, he was already gone. He slammed the door on his way out, leaving Psalmodie to brood over herself. For a brief moment, she did, but then she saw the crucifix hanging over her bed. She had already rotted in Jerusalem's slum-like underworld, where she felt the past fifteen days had only bled together in squalid isolation.

But then she looked over at her clothes and satchel on her cot, and she found herself channeling those days of endless grief into a newfound sense of resolve: *I will find you, father.*

CHAPTER 44

The Eastern Gate
The Old City of Jerusalem

U nder the azure midnight sky, Psalmodie sidled through the terraces and retaining walls of a dark cemetery on the berm of the bricked-up Eastern Gate of the former Temple, hugging alongside the rough, rusticated wall. Over the Old City's battlement wall lay the famed al-Aqsa compound where was the rotationally symmetric octagonal structure of the Dome of the Rock, also known to many as the Temple Mount.

Psalmodie knew what would have happened once she entered the lions' den, but her father awaited her, one way or the other. She looked for the supposed dead drop: a rope dangling from one of the battlement's embrasures as the concierge relayed to her. In the shadows, all Psalmodie could have done was grope around the brick wall for it.

While she did watch for the British skeleton patrols, most of her attention was directed up towards the gate's parapet merlons. In its many years of bloody conflicts, Jerusalem's insurmountable 40-foot ashlar block walls of meleke limestone have shown that they could have only been trounced by siege towers and trebuchets, though that wouldn't have been a problem for Psalmodie.

Her hand finally found the standing end of a hemp rope knotted into a wide noose meant to harness her waist. Once she promptly belayed herself, she gave the rope two strong tugs to ensure it was fastened. To her concern, it was already enough to burn her palms. Finding nothing else to guard against the friction, she took a moment to steel her thoughts.

Then she heard the droning howl of a ram's horn blare out through the night air like the bellowing call of a legendary, long-extinct beast. The haunting sound was enough to galvanize Psalmodie forward. She took the rope and hauled herself upwards, one hand over the other. While the pockmarked brick wall was mostly flush, her booted heels still found purchase in some slightly bulged-out blocks.

But when she almost reached the top, a foothold chipped under her foot. After a yelp, she swung down by one hand only to have the rope's friction burn her palm and wear her grip. She pressed her eyes and swallowed a moan of pain as all she could have done was latch on for dear life. She tried pulling herself back up, but the searing pain in her free hand left her suspended high above the cemetery.

But then, she felt the rope above her twirl, almost as if someone had grabbed it. She looked up and was instantly blinded by two glares of white light. Her face cringed at them, trying to see through to the men behind them.

She was being pulled up.

Once her ascent reached the parapet, the lights were doused. Her vision tried to readjust back to the darkness, but by the time she could have identified the men pulling her over the side by her underarms, she felt a blunt force slam into her midriff and knock the wind out of her. Though she keeled over and wheezed out blood, her vision tried restlessly to focus on her surroundings.

It was then that her eyes settled on a fountain at the far-left side of the compound. When its faint outline slowly took a clearer form in Psalmodie's blurred vision, its shape became unmistakable. She remembered reading of it in her father's journal. The al-Aqsa compound's most important fountain for religious ablutions before the *Salat* prayers: The *Sabil al-Kas*—The path to the cup.

Before this realization could have fully set in, however, another violent force struck down on Psalmodie's temple, this time knocking her unconscious.

CHAPTER 45

The Hospice of Saint Vincent de Paul

Brother Francis stood at the end of the corridor outside Psalmodie's chamber door, reluctant, yet compelled by his own guilt. Though he considered knocking, he ultimately pushed into the room to see if there still remained a chance to stop her from leaving.

But as he expected, she was already gone.

Once he sighed his discontent at this, he carried himself forth for what he was truly there to do. He moved to the center of the room and turned on the pull-cord filament bulb. With the cot in view, he moved to the pillow while twiddling the small rosary in his hands.

Then, when he closed his eyes, he felt a sudden warmth come about him, as if his surroundings had changed entirely. He looked around and found himself back in the coastal city of Marseilles, staring at the boisterous expression of a gilded statue of the rotund Budai. The statue stood guard at the side entrance to a tropical, thatched-roof Indochinese waterfront tavern along the turquoise waters of the Mediterranean Sea; a popular hub where merchants and travelers from China docked and furled the battened maroon sails of their junk rigs.

Francis remembered the joy on that statue, for it was the only joy he experienced that dreadful day back when he was 15 years old. He remembered stepping into the shanty tavern and immediately recognizing the garlands of red paper lanterns hanging from the exposed rafters. The air smelled musty and smoldered with humidity. Bowed strings and serenading zither music played amidst the patrons' lively chatter in Mandarin and Cantonese tongues.

The young boy threaded the bustling crowds, careful not to trip over the rough tables, wooden casks, and clay jugs. He heard a woman moaning somewhere, followed by jeering cheers. Francis pushed through the dank crush of bodies until he found who he was looking for: A stone-faced security guard standing in front of a wooden door. When the man saw the boy approaching, he raised a hand at him.

"I'm here to see him," Francis demanded. When the guard couldn't hear him over the commotion, Francis spoke up, "Gaiwan. My father is Gaiwan. Is he in there? I know he comes here often."

The guard shook his head. "No children are permitted; you'll just have to wait until he comes out."

"I traveled all the way from Paris! Let me see him!"

"No exceptions. I will tell him to look for you when he's finished."

Francis sighed, and after looking around the tavern, he said simply, "No, don't bother then. Whenever he comes out, just tell him that I tried, but he won't have to worry anymore. I'm going back to Paris. I'm done now. He will never have to see me again."

Just as Francis was about to turn away, he saw the conflict sweep over the guard's expression. The guard took a moment to consider it, then opened the door behind him and told Francis, "Just make it quick."

"Thank you," Francis said, walking past the guard and stepping into a more secluded room. Towards the far end, he saw bunk beds lined along the wooden wainscoting. As he approached the beds, a bitter alkaline stench grew stronger. The beds seemed to smolder with something, and when Francis saw the men lounging over the straw mats, he saw the long bamboo pipes they were raising to their lips.

One of the men groggily raised his head at Francis, and when he recognized the boy, called to him, "Son?"

Then, without another rational thought, Francis lunged at his father, landing blow after blow against his green face. The father quickly stopped his next punch, grabbed his throat, and hurled him against a nearby credence table; wooden trays of lamps and empty bowls clattered to the floor. Francis rose for his next attack, but after he saw his intoxicated father stumble against a nearby table, Francis relented, and instead, he sniffed and wiped away the blood dripping from his nose.

Francis kicked over the bowls at his feet and said, "You said that you were going to try to snuff out your desires."

"I am..." the father groaned.

"Then what is all this?" Francis demanded, pointing to the opium pipe on his bed.

The father snorted and looked back at it; with a shrug, he answered, "It's only a crutch... distracting me from what I know I don't have the strength in me to do."

"Mother said you were supposed to be the best of us," Francis cried.

"I was..." the father said, "until you converted, and then we both learned the hard way that I must answer for my misplaced faith in you in the next life..."

Francis lunged again, tumbling over a nightstand and grabbing him by the shirt collar. This time, the father did not resist; he simply closed his eyes, as if to escape time or mourn its passing. Despite his newfound faith in Christian mercy, Francis wished for his father to suffer what he made him suffer after he told him that he had renounced him. Though he had no invective left to say, he still had his rage. He cocked his fist but stopped himself when he looked up towards the doorway.

Standing next to the irate security guard was the sight of Francis' beloved, gently searching his face with tender concern. For a moment, Francis felt time come to a serene stillness as he felt himself fall into her warm gaze; those hazel eyes, ringed with dark lashes and shining impossibly amber. When Francis looked back down at his father still in his grip... Francis blinked once and found himself standing back in Psalmodie's room in the hospice, but instead of his father's shirt collar, in his fist was the rosary crucifix.

Letting out a shaky breath, he concluded his last prayer, *Lead all souls to Heaven, especially those in most need of Thy mercy.* Then, with a ceremonial deference, he laid the rosary's beads down over Psalmodie's pillow. He held himself for a moment, longing to be immersed in Shiloh's touch one last time before finally letting her go; letting his father go; letting the world he once knew go. In his heart, he concluded that Christ ought to be his only lifelong relationship, and that no one or nothing else would ever matter.

There was only his faith.

But even so... Francis never felt so distant from Him. Though Francis' last prayer wasn't nearly enough for reconciliation, he knew it was the only closure he was ever going to have before moving on. Lamenting this truth, Francis idly fixed the pillow's corners and brushed his hand over the bed's feather tick. But just as he was about to depart, he noticed that Psalmodie's satchel was oddly still lying at the foot of the bed. He brought the bag closer in front of him, at first feeling around for anything that may have interested him.

Against his better judgment, he peeked inside and smiled down at the first content he found. He pulled it out to get a better look at the crinkled *Cœurs Vaillants* newspaper Psalmodie had stolen when they had disembarked the Orient Express. After looking down at it for a short while, he set it aside, intending only one last glance into Psalmodie's privacy before moving on. But what he saw next deeply perplexed him.

The spine of her father's journal.

He took it out and verified its Aramaic title. Remembering her confession, he quickly leafed through the book. Five times he searched through its pages, finding no trace of the German telegrams she told him were inside. For a moment, he considered the possibility that she lied to him all over again, but on his sixth search, he noticed a folded paper hidden under the book's back cover.

When he opened the page, there was a single line of text:

Je ne veux aucun pardon

I don't want any forgiveness.

Having read the note, Francis walked over to the window and saw the domed silhouette that defined Jerusalem's skyline, looking to better comprehend why she would have left behind her cherished journal in her Grail quest and why the telegrams were missing. But after reading the note once more, he trembled with the conclusion.

The telegrams... The consulate... The Waqf...
Psalmodie, no...

CHAPTER 46

The Dome of the Rock
The Old City of Jerusalem

In the semidarkness, Psalmodie gently stirred from her unconsciousness; though she awoke with a blinding migraine and felt blood pulsing in her sweaty temples, she tried to make sense of her surroundings. She laid procumbent over a red carpet, and her wrists and ankles were bound in rope. She tried squirming over to her side, but the bruise on her oblique debilitated what little mobility she had left.

Impelled by curiosity, she grit her teeth against her pain and rolled over to her back only to find a ceiling made of rock; a continuous mass of pure, natural stone in its original cave-like formation. Directly above her, however, was a small round borehole shafting down a dim blue moonlight. Through it, she found a kaleidoscopic cosmos of foliate mosaics made of infinitesimal tiles of gold, red, blue, and white; a majestic display, all of which guided her eye to the mandala-like petals around the spiraling array's circumpunct.

The pattern was enough for Psalmodie's mind to roam the universe, but it wasn't until she noticed the elegant Arabic calligraphy on the gilded cornice encircling the mosaics that she finally understood where she was. She was looking up at a roof's zenith from beneath the building's sacred Foundation Stone.

She was actually *beneath* the building of the Dome of the Rock.

The Biblical site of King Solomon's Temple. Once a part of the Knights Templar's main headquarters before Saladin captured Jerusalem and once even plundered by the Mongols. The large, flat Foundation Stone inside was the place over which the Israelite patriarch Abraham was said to have very nearly sacrificed his own son to God, the place from which the Prophet Muhammad was said to have ascended through the heavens, and the place from which God began His creation of the world.

Psalmodie was beneath it, inside an ancient subterranean sanctum; the former resting place of the legendary Ark of the Covenant... The Holy of Holies. Now, it was a small grotto used by the Muslims of Jerusalem for private prayer, though Psalmodie considered if Jesus' cross had indeed returned home.

But of course, that no longer mattered to her.

She raised her head to look down along her figure. Ahead of her, she saw a recessed set of 16 marble steps leading up to the world above. Though she knew her efforts to be pointless, she tried rocking herself to see if she could have stood herself up.

But she wasn't ready for the voice that uttered from the shadows behind her, "There was something hidden in this room since the foundation of the world; beneath this stone, the stone of creation." Psalmodie's head jerked back towards a tenebrous shape in the corner, clad in a fedora and overcoat. He was sitting on an elevated cubic socle embedded in the cave wall and flanked by two supportive marble balusters.

"According to the Abrahamic religions," the man began with a tone slow and somber as death, "every Yom Kippur—the Jewish Day of Atonement—, a high priest would come into this very room to transfer all the Israelite nation's sins onto two kid goats—the original scapegoats—before sacrificing them to their false god Yahweh and sprinkling the scapegoats' blood over His throne on Earth: The Ark of the Covenant.

"How pagan is monotheism that the Ark was fashioned in a manner so similar to the Egyptian procession barques, such as the shrine of Anubis, the god of the underworld, found in the tomb of Tutankhamun! It should be no surprise. After all, every ancient cult in the Near East was always so dependent on icons, idols, and temples to materialize belief in tutelary gods. But after the Ark was seized by Babylonian barbarians and vanished just as the Grail did, the Israelites' Levitical cult had to reimagine itself into the Judaism we know today, having faith in an imperious, faceless god that they could never hope to behold."

The skinny shadow then stood up from its throne and walked towards Psalmodie with a ghostly air of solemn dread. She saw that the shaft of blue light slashed across half the man's ashened face, framed in shadow and set against the darkness as if disembodied.

"A scapegoat," the man continued, ruminating. "That's all your father was and that's all I will ever be: A holocaust to all our sins. And the day will come when everyone else will all be burned at the bloody altar of that cowardly god's legacy. But you must never be awake to see the final revelation; to see when that angel of death will one day come for you next. I prayed that after I secured those telegrams, I would be the one to send you to your father without any pain or hatred... given all that he has done for me and what I have done to him in kind."

Psalmodie gasped, "Otto, you're—" Her back stiffened as she tried to manage out another word, but her tense voice caught in her throat.

She sat up on her elbow and turned her eyes back up the stairs; the better angle of her raised posture allowed her to see the two figures facing away from her. In front of them was a small coffee table with a telegraph transmitter and receiver with a coiling reel. She immediately looked down into her shirt and saw that the telegrams she smuggled in were already gone, and with them, her father's very last words to her.

"My men are verifying your telegrams with our Ahnenerbe," Rahn said, strolling in front of her while pulling out a crumpled strip of paper from his lapel. "'The way is a rose to the sword in the stone.' Communicated through the same Jewish code; have you since divined its meaning?"

Silence descended upon the sanctuary. Rahn stood over Psalmodie, seeing the paralyzed emotions in her absent eyes. She didn't react to his presence and looked more desensitized to the judgment she knew she would have had to have faced. Still unsure about how to comfort her in her last moments, Rahn pocketed the paper and adjusted his collar.

"After we had the hand cannon you found translated," he continued, "the mufti offered us access to the building these past couple of days to see if, by chance, we could still happen upon your relic. But just as we suspected, we didn't find it; of course, we were really here for you. It wasn't easy, though; roving around all of Jerusalem's boulevards and holy places all this time while the Arab nationalists suddenly decided to stalemate the British in the Old City, forcing us underground." A tepid chuckle seeped through in his voice. "And I will confess, hiding out in our consulate yesterday was not something we would have suspected of you and your friend."

A trenchant question was wrung out of Psalmodie. "You really spent the last month scouring Jerusalem only to *kill* me?"

Rahn fell quiet, absorbing the poor girl's wrath. With a scathing, yet tortured glare, Psalmodie recognized that same fatherly pain stamped on the man's longing gaze; he wiped at his eye, though whether it was for weariness or grief, she didn't know for certain. Her uncertainty, however, soon gave way to panic filling her stomach as she saw him walk around her and heard him kneel behind her.

But just as she was about to accept the fate for which she came, to her surprise, she felt Rahn's bony fingers tugging around the restraints on her wrists until the tight knots loosened and the ropes slipped down from her hands. Stunned and unbelieving, she stiffly brought her freed hands in front of her face, wondering why.

But in her blank incomprehension, she felt Rahn's hands take her forearms and help her to her feet. When Rahn gently stood Psalmodie up by her shoulders and tenderly fixed a loose blonde hair behind her ears, she felt the pitiful ambivalence and bitter repugnance stirring in her. The longer she looked at him, however, the more she felt that repugnance festering her strangled heart.

Rahn cleared his throat and managed a response. "Where else in the 'Holy Land' than the Old City? And where else in the Old City than the church, the mosque, and the wall? And who else but a daughter trying to fulfill her father's memory?" He put a hand over his collar and swallowed a lump. "And who else but I to save her from her father's fate?"

Psalmodie slapped him. "Why—*why* are you telling me this?" she cried, now more in perplexity than resentment.

Rahn caressed his own cheek, and after a beat, he responded, "Because you deserve nothing less than the full truth, and you must therefore know that I am *not* a godless man." For a long moment before Rahn continued, there was nothing but a desolate breeze howling down the Foundation Stone's hole. "My mother may have been of Jewish blood, but my father was a devout Christian; *my* father, Psalmodie, who would not go to church, but would instead look at a single tree and say, 'This is God.' For him, the Holy Spirit was not of good or evil, but immanent in all things, blossoming such wonders in his life. But what both of our fathers wouldn't see was that their god was merely a demiurge who shackled our immortal spirits in flesh; an insatiable devil who had always vaingloriously demanded bloodshed from time immemorial; a devil whom the ancient Israelites had fatally mistaken for God.

"If Christ had been crucified, then it would have perhaps been to liberate us from the demiurge's tyrannical Law. But it isn't the Son's, but the *Father's* crucifixion that is indispensable for our salvation, for what remains of all three of Abraham's religions is a vestige of their inescapable pagan heritages; there is much less need for prophecy and revelation in our world and more in cultic acts of congregation. Pagan faith was never meant to be a vulgar dispensation of our baser instincts; it has always been organically and intimately ingrained in humanity's shared experience of this meaningless universe. It never died out, but stayed with us, held captive by imperial monotheism.

"The Cathari understood this; they knew the truth that today's Zionists, Crusaders, and Saracens could never bring themselves to accept: We are all fallen angels of light, shackled by meaningless flesh and matter. The true Messiah will come not in flesh, but as pure illumination to deliver humanity from the Jewish demiurge's profane, Babylonian cycle of incarnation. Our Messiah is Legion, the Morning Star; our Promethean advocate against pride, and our redemption is synonymous with his own. Lucifer is not the Lord of Lies, but rather, the true Son of God, and it is therefore far better for all men to be near a bearer of light than a refraction of it—a broken mirror dripping with blood."

Psalmodie looked away and paced off, shaking her head in disbelief. At this, Rahn sighed, and he forced himself onward. "You may think you know what they are capable of, but the things that I have seen... It beggars all description. It made my spirit feel small compared to the meat of my own body. What they did to your father; what they would do to Jews; to people like me. And on behalf of the wronged Son of God, I already know that I can *never* let the same happen to you." He gazed down and shied away from Psalmodie. "You know that I sent you those telegrams for your father, but I had no clue that he codified classified information in his messag—"

A Waqf guard rushed down the grotto steps. "Sir?"

Rahn turned, startled. "What is it? One of the telegrams is unverified?"

The guard gulped. "No, your men say they caught someone toiling about the Dome of al-Khidr!"

"Well, did they shoot at them?"

"No, your men say they await orders, sir."

"Orders?" Rahn responded quizzically. "To kill some straggler outside? Why?"

"They say the man knows your prisoner," the guard responded. "So, they brought him inside for you."

Psalmodie saw that Rahn's face had grown pale. He looked back down at her with a similar expression of alarm before looking back up at the guard and nodding uneasily. The guard climbed back up the steps and signaled for Rahn's men to proceed down to him.

Then, two hulking figures descended into the sanctum while dragging something behind them. Psalmodie eventually noticed that that something was a some*one* by the way the load tried struggling to his feet, though he couldn't regain his footing over the steps. Like her, he was dragged by his wrists bound behind his back and his head hung down in apparent disorientation. Rahn's German enforcers heaved the man forward and his body fell over the carpet like a sack.

At first, Psalmodie couldn't recognize the man. She tried peering through the darkness, but she still couldn't have discerned his face. But once Rahn walked over to force him up on his knees by his scruff to get a better look at the trespasser, Psalmodie's mind unraveled and panic surged through her heart.

"Francis?" she croaked, blinking back more tears. She stepped forward, nearly rushing for him, but one of Rahn's enforcers immediately raised a pistol at her. She froze in her tracks, gingerly raised her hands, and slowly lowered herself to her knees. Helplessly, she looked over and saw that Francis' drenched face was sallow, and blood from the laceration on his left eyebrow was all run down into his eyes.

Rahn looked into his narrow eyes before traveling his gaze down to his collarbone, noticing the small rosary medal and crucifix depending from it. "At the very least," Rahn contemned, "your animist Tatar ancestors were forthwith and unapologetic in their dreams for total world conquest, for they at least believed that the souls of *their* ancestors lived out their afterlife in the natural world as the spirits of the rivers, the trees, the mountains; the neutral angels of the Garden of Eden."

Francis didn't respond. He tore in a breath through his nostrils, assumedly by the pain of Rahn's tight grip on his hair. The sound of panting from behind Rahn called his eyes back to Psalmodie, still on her knees and gaping at him with the shine of tears in her eyes. Abated by her distress, Rahn pulled something from his pocket and turned his chagrined eyes back on Francis.

"I'll let you help her find peace with this," he spat, thrusting Francis' head down over the object over the carpet, "before I do what I must."

As Francis' eyes tried to refocus from the beads of sweat that ran into them, he stole a glance at Psalmodie, still looking on in desperate horror. He went back to reading the inscriptions on the ancient hand cannon she told him about, though with the semidarkness of the grotto, it was difficult to fully comprehend what it said. He could have only speculated, but after rolling the artifact over with his knee to read the other set of vertical inscriptions, the words broke from his lips:

Holy Blood and Water
Holy Cross of Thieves

He shook his head incredulously, still trying to make sense of the inscriptions' meaning. Though it hadn't been a full second, Psalmodie felt the silence had lasted for an eternity. Rahn went back to the socle in the corner, sliding a casing in an empty chamber and tugging the toggle with a familiar-sounding slide.

Upon hearing it, her shoulders quaked and heaved with each pant. Tears spilled from her eyes, and she knew that it would have been moments before Rahn discharged Eggers' Luger rifle into her. But then Psalmodie saw that Francis was still hunched over his knees, absorbed. He had finished reading the Mongolian script, but she saw that his eyes were enthralled by the unfinished Templar cross on the cannon's reinforce.

T

With her hands still raised, Psalmodie leaned in and called quietly, "Brother!"

Francis didn't react, almost as if he couldn't have. Psalmodie eyed him fretfully but became transfixed by the jarring expression she saw on his face. She couldn't tell if he was simply sobbing or laughing. Though his gums were red with blood, the pain wasn't enough to dilute this upsetting display of joy. Soon after, Psalmodie saw his head rocking back and forth as he intoned the same name over and over again like a soothing mantra.

"*Francis. Francis. Francis. Francis. Francis. Francis.*"

At the other end of the room, Rahn took notice. Equally disturbed by Francis' burgeoning madness, he approached him with his weapon held at ease across his body. Though he stood directly over him, Francis wouldn't stop repeating his own name.

"Brother, stop!" Psalmodie begged quietly, her skin crawling with terror. "Brother, please, he's going to—"

Rahn kicked down Francis' back and clubbed his brow with the butt of his rifle, knocking him unconscious again. Psalmodie cried out and her restraint gave way; she rushed for Francis, skid to one knee beside him, and obstructed Rahn's aim with spread arms and a rigid, yet defiant glare. Rahn's enforcers were ready to drag Psalmodie away, but the commotion had already drawn five Waqf guards down the stairs and into the grotto, pistols and daggers at the ready. The enforcers stepped off with their hands under their coats.

"What's going on?" one of the guards demanded.

"Get out of the way, Psalmodie," Rahn urged gravely, drawing the gun barrel closer to her head.

"You were going to shoot me anyways, weren't you?" Psalmodie said, her voice ragged with wrath. "So go ahead. Why don't you finish what you started?"

"Get. Out. Of. The. Way."

The Waqf guard advanced on Rahn. "Wait, you're shooting them *here? Now?* But that was not part of our—"

Rahn's fist flew out, connected with the guard's jaw, and sent him reeling back towards the stairs with the others. All at once, the German enforcers and the Waqf guards wrenched up their weapons and circled around each other in a tense stalemate. The bruised guard trained his pistol on Rahn and yelled, "Neither Allah nor His Eminence will have blood spilled under Bayt al-Maqdis!"

Rahn stared down his rifle's sights on Psalmodie's face, caught between saving her and exacting the vengeful justice of his Cathari prophets, or at least a former vestige of it.

But then he remembered himself.

Trapped between the Arab world and the Aryan, there was nowhere left for him to belong except in releasing Psalmodie of the morbid suffering he feared awaited her as it had awaited him and the entire world after his purpose in Wewelsburg would have inevitably expired. His haunted gaze focused, and his forefinger twitched over the trigger. Rahn sucked in and drew out sharp breaths, tormented by the resolve he felt cannibalizing at his own conscience. Around Rahn, the two factions spectated his every movement.

Rahn saw Francis' head writhe behind Psalmodie. He was lapsing into a coma, but with drowsed eyes, he peered up to the only person he had left in this world. Then Rahn heard him moan out a name that was barely given breath.

"...Shiloh..."

Rahn loosened his hold on the rifle as he and Psalmodie looked back at Francis, startled and captivated by what he called her. Rahn saw her head cast down and her shoulders droop slightly, as if all her strength had been drained by a vain effort of will. Then he saw the anguish of her realization swelling and cutting into her; when she slowly brought her tormented gaze back up at Rahn, he saw her delicate face beginning to crumple as she struggled to stifle the sobs rising in her throat. He became lost in her eyes.

Those familiar, angelic blue eyes.

Then, in the blink of an eye, he saw Psalmodie had again become the little schoolgirl he had once known, her eyes all too naive and credulous. He then saw the little girl's tearful eyes clench in despair and anticipation alike. Then, realizing what he had just heard and recognizing what he saw in her, the rifle slipped out from Rahn's fingers and clattered on the carpet next to Francis' head.

Psalmodie's eyes were still closed, and for a moment, she couldn't tell if she was dead. While Francis' body was stock-still, she found the perpetual darkness had become colder. But once she felt her lungs still filled with air, her restless eyes blinked open and darted over the floor. She ventured her flummoxed gaze up to her captor and saw the horrified look on his face. He had staggered back away from her and cornered himself against the cave wall.

He came back.

Psalmodie's eyes were still tragic, but they began to light up; she knew better than to reach out to him since he was still her father's murderer, yet she felt an untoward sense of pity coaxing her forward. She almost wished she had some faith with which to comfort him, but instead, with a faint tremor in her soft voice, she gasped out, "My father has always loved you, Otto. *Always.*"

Then Rahn's face crimsoned. He turned away and raised a hand to his quivering lips only to throw it back down in a clenched fist. Still on guard, the Germans and Waqf exchanged tense glances towards each other before silently exhibiting their unwillingness to go through with the stalemate. They all cautiously lowered their weapons and foregathered again in equal bewilderment.

"Let them go," Rahn said, swallowing hard. "Just let them go." Then, without looking back one last time, Rahn cut through the confused Waqf guards, his hurt evident in his hobbling gait. When he trailed up the stairs, he left only a quiet of sadness in his wake.

Psalmodie released a tremulous breath and recovered some of her composure. She turned and kneeled by Francis to tug at his shoulders. "Francis? Francis, wake up!" she cried, gathering up his head and rubbing his cheeks and temples. She looked to the Waqf guards to try to plead for his sake but was soon interrupted by four jackboots coming before her.

"So, we can't kill them here," one of the enforcers said in German, picking up the Luger rifle. "Do we have to take them outside then?"

The second hesitated before responding, "Didn't you hear Rahn? I guess we'll just have to leave them here."

The first frowned. "After all that we have done, you are saying that we ought to let them go?"

"Rahn ordered so; take it up with him," the second said, looking back down at Psalmodie. "After we commandeer the telegrams, we are to ensure his safe return to Wewelsburg for debriefing; I don't want to exceed our mandate and be found in direct violation of his command as an Obersturmführer, no matter the abomination we know him to be. But besides that, do we even need to kill them now?"

"Reichsführer Himmler and high priest Wiligut Weisthor were clear—"

"Yes. Dead *or* alive."

"—and did you forget they actually stabbed Eggers?"

"Admit it," the second spoke up. "You and I both know that that man deserved it. But even if that weren't the case, Jerusalem outside is still infested with English infantry. The boy here is one from that missionary order, and if his body is found, he becomes deified into their pantheon of wretched martyrs, fomenting war wherever they go. And even if these two *did* go to the authorities, what evidence do they really have? Who is going to take their charges seriously?" His voice inflected in triumph. "We finally have the telegrams and—"

"But what of the Holy Grail?" the first countered. "We already came this far to get her. What—we're simply going to let the Christians walk away with its legacy? We're really going to let her keep searching for this false relic, as if the cross hasn't oppressed our fatherland for long enough?"

The second modulated his voice. "But why would she have parlayed with us? I mean, look at her." He pointed down at Psalmodie, still tending to Francis' limp body. "She has very clearly come to the end of herself." He drew closer to his associate. "And I know neither of us can bring ourselves to shoot any *Aryan* children; not while the *untermensch* still roam freely over the face of the Earth."

The first opened his mouth to protest, but the grievance died aborning. He glanced over towards the Waqf still waiting for them by the stairs and shot one last look at his supposed targets before heading off towards the guards and ascending the stairs.

"We're done here," the second announced to them, following shortly after his associate and moving for the telegrams over the table. "Do with them as you will."

Though the Germans had left, the Waqf guards remained in the Holy of Holies. Psalmodie watched as they quietly took counsel—perhaps even debating—amongst themselves in Arabic while looking down on her and Francis with uncertain, yet mild regards.

Psalmodie gently lowered Francis' head and looked down at his rosary and crucifix. Overwhelmed and faint with shock, she closed her eyes, let head fall against his shoulder, and felt the comforting warmth of his breath over her head, steadying her frantic mind.

But that comforting warmth felt fluctuating, and she felt faint vibrations coursing through his shoulder. She glanced up and saw Francis murmuring unintelligible words in his concussed state. When she nestled her head closer to him and put her ear by his mouth, his speech sounded clearer. It sounded like the same mad rambling, but this time, she wanted to allow herself to be nurtured by it.

But what she heard made her heart contract so much, she could not breathe. That name he kept parroting to himself wasn't his own. It was a name she saw briefly mentioned in her father's journal. One she had heard and read many times before.

"Shiloh... It was... him... Francis... Saint Francis..."

"What?" Psalmodie gasped softly.

"Oh, my dear *huli xiangtou*... It was... him..."

CHAPTER 47

The Hospice of Saint Vincent de Paul
October 18th, 1938

Psalmodie felt a cold draft river over her as she slept fitfully; her lips moved in a buried murmur and her eyes fluttered behind closed lids. The nightmare she had just lived through made her wake with a cry and bolt up in her cot. Still winded, she propped herself up on her elbows and tried to steady her shuddering gasps, though her bleary eyes still couldn't make sense of the dark shapes swimming through the continuous blur of light all around her.

She coughed twice and sat forward, putting a hand to her sternum to feel for her palpitating heart; once she felt she was still alive, her vision focused and the vaguely outlined shadows gradually took form. Long buttresses of soft light fell in from the wire-meshed window guards above her over a long, linoleum-floored white room lined end to end with more cots and tables. She looked down at her legs and saw that she was wearing a loose gown while her lower half was tucked under a linen bed sheet. Her clothes were folded neatly and set on the table next to her. It seemed she was admitted into a general ward, though she still didn't know where in the city she was.

The moment she draught in her first calmed breath, she noticed two figures standing by the door at the far end of the ward. One of them was a mature woman—perhaps an orderly—wearing what looked like a nun's coif with a winged brim. She was scolding a younger man in a British officer's uniform, looking as though he was trying to assert his authority over her, though he wasn't prepared for the nun's pedantic stubbornness. He kept looking back and forth between the nun and Psalmodie, but the nun slapped his cheek to refocus his eyes back on herself.

When Psalmodie turned, she saw that standing at her bedside was a petite, wafer-thin nun, perhaps around Psalmodie's age, staring curiously down at her. Psalmodie couldn't tell whether the girl was Jewish or Arab, but she did look local, having a delicate olive face, large brown eyes, and short black hair.

"Where am I?" Psalmodie groaned, shutting her eyes and pressing the heel of her palm against her throbbing head.

"Maybe you should take it easy," the young nun said, gently pushing Psalmodie's shoulders back down on the cot. She poured water from a ceramic pitcher into a small glass at a nearby table. "You're back in the hospice. The other nuns saw some policemen bring you two a couple of hours ago." She leaned over, put a hand to Psalmodie's brow, and closely examined her eyes. "Sœur told me to ask if you know what day of the week it is."

At first, Psalmodie thought long and hard for such a simple question, but then her muddled mind darted to, "Francis? Is he—"

"I think I saw Brother sleeping in the men's ward downstairs," the nun said. "He's still sleeping. Sœur said you should too."

Psalmodie sighed her relief, gently sinking her head back against the cot's headboard and letting herself bask in the silence. She laid still and felt her eyes falling heavy, but soon felt the nun's tender hand pick up the back of her head and tilt the glass of water towards her lips.

As the water cleared her parched throat, her detached eyes looked up at the hospice's coffered ceiling and settled on Jesus' corpus on the crucifix hanging on the wall over her. Clarity continued to elude her heart, still divided against itself. But for a brief moment before her sight faded again, she wondered whether those dead eyes had actually been contemplating her.

CHAPTER 48

Rahn sat in the backseat of a stolen car, looking down at Psalmodie's telegrams while his mind swam with melancholy and indecision. Ever since he and his SS-Standarte had departed Jerusalem for Acre on the roadway back towards Damascus, he simply sat in silence and gloom while the night-filled car's movement gently jostled him. For every mere moment he stared out the car's window, he only saw a dark world narrowing and receding behind him.

He emptily regarded his tin cigar lighter in his other hand. When he ignited it, he stared at the tiny tongue of flame, fluttering a muted firelight up over his perspiring face. Soon, however, the car became more illumed in this light after he joined the tongue to the papers. Then he rolled down the window, ground the burning papers in his fist, and held it out to let the winds wither away the telegrams until they were nothing more than embers and ash.

As the flakes scattered into the void, his limp, smoldering hand hung out for a moment. Rahn's dead eyes drifted out, but while he sensed those same fires awaited him, whether at Niederhagen, Buchenwald, or Dachau, he found his idling thoughts had turned to that night in Paris only a few days ago.

. . .

He was in that house cellar, adumbrated by the meager blue moonlight entering through the rectangular egress window wells. The entire space was pure concrete except for the ceiling, which was only deck boards held up by exposed wooden floor joists and stuffed with dangling threads of insulation. With his flashlight in hand and his day bag over his shoulder, Rahn strolled through a winding labyrinth of freestanding shelves and antique furnishings covered in white drop cloths.

Though he did not expect to find much, amidst the cobwebs on one of the shelves, he found a framed photo of that man, so urbane and striking. He clicked off his flashlight and took it from the shelf. The low-keyed achromatic contrast of the photograph was not enough to dispel the quiet intensity in the man's doe-eyed stare while he sat in his usual cross-legged posture. Then Rahn felt slightly put off, as he always did when the man was around him, by the shine of the golden crucifix pendant peering out from the shadow of his shirt collar.

Rahn only needed the moonlight to prize the man's likeness, but when the room was lit up by a naked bulb at the center, Rahn spun around to the rickety plywood steps creaking under footfalls. For a moment, he feared that Eggers might have tracked him down to further inquire about what Rahn had in the day bag he had brought from Wewelsburg.

But once the mahogany door at the foot of the shadowy stairway yawned open, he saw the man's very image in the endearing little schoolgirl he had once known. The girl may have been grown up now, but to Rahn, she still looked every inch the princess she was; the very ghost of Rahn's bygone passion; the reincarnated guardian of the Holy Grail. As Rahn stared at her, he found it difficult to comprehend how either God or Lucifer could have ever conceived of so fair and so dear a creature.

When she saw Rahn standing alone with her father's photo, he carefully set it back down on its shelf before coming around to face her fully. He fixed his fedora around his head, and a faltering smile squirmed unto his mouth until it eventually became more real with each moment he contemplated the young girl: Psalmodie Vingt-Trois.

Though Rahn had expected her to feel some fear despite what she may have told him over the phone, he saw no such thing. Her hand was resting on the doorknob, as if she would have soon slammed the door behind her. But as she looked up at him, standing in a vignette of darkness, she seemed numb to his presence.

There was a quiet complexity of emotion in her precious face. There was always a gentle dignity and youthful grace with which she held herself, and even though Rahn read stoic resignation in her countenance, in those soulful, deep blue eyes—shining like onyx through the shadows—he still recognized a latent, lionhearted resolve. Even so, she offered no reaction, seeming to have already settled on suffering all the monstrous wrongs done to her patiently. Rahn strolled towards Psalmodie, measuring his slow steps. When he was standing over her, he leaned over and gently pecked her on her freckled cheek. He took two steps back to again behold her character in full, as if to acclaim a beatific vision.

But then, as if Rahn weren't even there, the emotionally guarded girl quietly passed him to carry on with whatever she was there to do. Rahn followed after her, entering a lowered and more open part of the cellar where she kept all of her book- and paper-filled bins under shelves and tables. There, she knelt down and took to a trivial reorganizing of the labels in one of the bins. Though this was to Rahn a taciturn effort to estrange herself from him, he felt it was perhaps done more to distract herself from her own grief rather than the hateful spite he so rightfully deserved.

Unsure of how to begin to offer solace, Rahn reached out, "Psalmodie, I know this must be difficult for you, but you have no idea how much I appreciate you agreeing to meet with me tonight."

Psalmodie kept quiet. Though the air was warmer in the cellar than it was outside, Rahn saw that she stopped flipping through the books' spines and folded her arms tightly over her stomach, as if to brace against the coldness of his presence.

After wiping her palm up the side of her eye, she attempted a steady tone. "You sounded urgent over the phone, and I didn't even know there was anything left to say."

Rahn looked down at his shoes before asking, "How go your studies? Did your bursar receive your father's check from our think tank?"

"I'm fine..." Psalmodie answered simply.

"And is your roommate giving you any trouble?"

Psalmodie scoffed, "If anything, *I'm* the one giving her trouble."

"Yes, I've heard. You actually ran all the way to Glastonbury Tor after you managed to steal the *Cwpan Nanteos* all by yourself?"

"Borrowed," Psalmodie corrected, shaking her head as if the mere gesture would have changed the subject.

Rahn didn't hear her. "What?"

Shrugging with a tense shiver, Psalmodie repeated, "I borrowed it— Yes, she made it quite clear she wasn't all too thrilled about it on the way back home. I still haven't heard the end of it from her when we spar in fencing club." A wry laugh rose in her voice. "She is so sentimental; she's even invited me to pray with her at her mosque for a change, although I told her that my peers and churchgoers might not have thought well of that."

Rahn smiled for a moment before the concern came back in his eyes. *"Have* you been attending Mass lately? Praying at least?"

Psalmodie looked up at him, mildly confounded. "I thought you despised the Church."

"Yes, but anything is better than just toiling about your—" Rahn caught himself, feeling the rue stab him once he saw the sheer look in Psalmodie's eyes. Without saying anything to this, Psalmodie stood to her feet and started back for the stairway. Rahn sighed and reached for her hand. "Psalmodie, wait. I didn't mean to suggest that you—"

Psalmodie whirled on him. "Why are you here, Otto?"

Rahn drew out the moment before walking over to a nearby rectangular table. There, he set down his leather bag on the dusty tabletop and pulled out a handbound volume from under its fold. "I'm here because I found this in your father's desk, and I imagined my superiors would have burned it without even reading it, judging by how the cover looks." Rahn pushed the tome towards Psalmodie with two fingers over the Jewish-looking letters on the cover.

"I find it quite interesting that you chose to 'borrow' the *Cwpan Nanteos* out of all the Grail claimants in Europe," Rahn continued, "considering what is said in Glastonbury's local myths about where the relic's mystical wood comes from. Not a relic of the Last Supper, but fashioned from something far, far greater. Hoax that it may be, perhaps it was a sign that it might be time for you to accept that you were looking for your father's Grail in all the wrong places."

Rahn eyed her, waiting for the doubt on her face to turn to curiosity. After staring at Rahn uncertainly for a while, she pulled the book closer in front of her and opened its cover to the first couple of pages. She turned the pages slowly at first, taking her time to read its contents until her bored gaze became engrossed in her father's visionary passion. Her radiant eyes jumped up at Rahn, still regarding her.

As Psalmodie continued rifling through the book, Rahn saw those same words flash by in those pages: *Holy Grail, Chrétien de Troyes, Saladin, Knights Templar, Sarras... True Cross.* An hour passed for what seemed more like two minutes.

As she kept reading, Rahn leaned over the table and, quoting from his own book *Lucifer's Court,* whispered to her, "'The farther away people are, the closer they are to our spirit. And when these people begin the passage to eternity, they come nearer to us than ever before: Suddenly, we carry them within. In memory we grow only more aware of the dearly departed.'" He then pointed to her father's journal and added, "All of that, he sacrificed to help me survive... and to give you a future..."

Psalmodie looked up from the book, her eyes brimming with both a sorrowful and nostalgic emotion Rahn hadn't felt in a long time; revelation and closure, harmonized at last.

"Why are you giving me this?" Psalmodie asked, trying to keep the wondrous joy out of her voice. Rahn felt his heart sink deeper into his chest; he thought for a moment and pushed off the table to stroll away from her. Seeing this, Psalmodie straightened, and her face fell back to confusion. "Otto?" she called after him.

Rahn turned away from Psalmodie and pulled the hat off his head. "Psalmodie, I'm in a lot of trouble here." He turned slightly and began to circle her. "Those telegrams I sent to your father for you; they found the ones you sent in the barracks."

Psalmodie followed him around the room. "What do you mean?"

"He was keeping them under the floor of some Catholic priest's bunk post."

"Wait, did they decipher his code?"

"Yes!" Rahn exclaimed. "The Jewish Atbash code!"

Psalmodie shrugged and scoffed. "Well, what are they going to do to me? They're all the way in Germany, so it's not like they can—" She stopped, and her breath escaped her when she saw the tears guttering down Rahn's cheeks.

Rahn turned to face her squarely and his voice emerged low. "Yes."

Psalmodie backed away from him in a panicked daze. Her eyes swam intensely, and the now-tearful glint in them became so bright, her corneas looked enlarged. She nearly doubled over, but instead, she leaned back against a shelf behind her. Rahn saw her thoughts shrieking terrified through her skull. "No, no, no," she cried, panting so heavily, she gulped for breath. "No, Otto... No, this isn't you. It *can't* be..."

Rahn only kept quiet, allowing Psalmodie more time to weigh the experience.

Psalmodie choked on her own breath. She raised a finger to the table and stammered, "Is-is that wha-what that was about? Was th-that all just reassurance for a lamb before the s-slaughter?"

"I wanted to see your father in you one last time," Rahn pleaded, "before I get the telegrams from you."

"Why? So you can *kill* me afterwards?" Psalmodie said.

Rahn wavered, as if weakened by the very word. "You have to know that this isn't easy for me."

"I know too much, is that it?"

"Psalmodie, please..."

"Did Himmler or his deranged little Rasputin in your tiny castle put you up to this?"

"I was starving!" Rahn yelled. "I was without means; a man has to eat! And what else was supposed I to do? Turn down *Himmler* of all people?"

"You could have done *anything!*" she demanded. "You could have run away with my father! You could have slandered anybody else to save yourself! But you chose to slander my father, and instead of running away from them, you became a eunuch at their beck and call, complicit in all their monstrosities; you even tried to curry more favor with them! And all of this... because you were stupid enough to fall in love."

Rahn fixed Psalmodie with a tortured stare. "You're right…" he muttered. "After Himmler made me serve my time in Dachau, upon my return to Munich, it all came back to me, and I could no longer sleep nor eat. The bloody events to which I had borne witness; it was as if a nightmare had lay upon me. I tried so hard to lie to myself that all of that murder could not have been me; that I became possessed by some cold spirit worse than any devil; some spell or neurosis the Führer cast over all our people.

"But just when I started to mourn the truth that Otto Wilhelm Rahn died forever in Dachau… I woke up the next morning, felt for my heart, and realized that I was still him. I was him all along. My duty in Dachau was my choice. It was always and *only* I. I. I! *I! I* who killed all of those people…" Rahn leaned his hands on the table and begged, "I didn't know who I was… until it was too late. I would give anything to never be Otto Wilhelm Rahn ever again, and now, I am here to finally witness my Being die in you, Psalmodie; here at last to rebel against the mortal flesh that has God cursed us with; here to spare you the unconscious, murderous truth of *your own* Being that I now know Himmler will awaken and enslave you to."

Despite herself, Psalmodie watched Rahn's face with a mix of horror and understanding. Then she took a deep, shuddering breath and spat, "I don't want your truth… I don't want to be saved… and I'm not giving you anything."

Rahn approached her and whispered, "Psalmodie, I want you to think very carefully right now, especially for those around you."

He saw the urge to run away on Psalmodie's face. She had already started to turn away from him, but she froze, perhaps knowing that she wouldn't have made it very far. Still, she seemed to have been caught between withdrawing one foot and advancing the other. It wasn't long before he saw that his words had ultimately made her stop.

Then, Psalmodie's fierce voice came out a sibilant whisper. "You leave her out of this, Otto."

"Are those telegrams here or not?" Rahn asked more firmly.

"Go to hell…"

Rahn shook his head. "If they aren't in this house, then they might be in your apartment with her. My lieutenant is not as smart as he thinks, but he's more brutal than he looks. One way or another, my troop will get them. And if they're not here and if you don't cooperate, I'm not sure how I will be able to stop my men from going there and doing as they will to her."

Psalmodie drew forth for another condemnation, but she held back as something inside her shifted. Her scandalized stare became rigid, as if accepting, but still not quite believing the fires of all-consuming madness eating away at her reality.

"Psalmodie, as far as Himmler has to know, you are the only one who knows about the telegrams' existence. Only you can make copies of them; no one else. *No one* else has to be implicated in this..." Rahn paused, seeing Psalmodie's mind fragment and scream. He continued, "You and I have both lived our lives walking in a shadow cast over us from some time that is yet to come; a single moment we will never witness, yet it continuously shapes our experience." Feeling an upwelling of passion, Rahn took Psalmodie's hand and kissed her knuckles. "I beg you, Psalmodie: Let that shadow end with us..."

With tears quivering in her eyes, Psalmodie swallowed the lump in her throat and nodded absently. She let go of Rahn's hand and quietly walked herself over towards something behind him. She pushed off a metal shelf leaned against the wall, revealing a small rectangular air vent. Rahn saw her peel off a small dilapidated fly screen from its hinges, set it down on a bin, and pull out a small wooden coffer with a small fleur-de-lis engraving over its lock plate, though there was no lock in the hasp.

She slowly drifted back towards the table and carefully set down the coffer. Rahn saw on her face that her mind was filled with every fear and regret she had ever felt in her life, for it was a look he saw once before; a look that haunted his every waking moment ever since he had abandoned her father in Dachau.

But then he saw her face light up with sudden anger, and in that moment, she threw up the coffer's lid and swung a semi-automatic 1911 Browning pistol up at Rahn. He cringed and lifted his hands in a vain expression of harmlessness.

"What are you doing?" Rahn sighed, as if he were half-expecting this to happen.

"I'm leaving."

"But where on Earth would you go?"

"Oh, you would certainly like to know that, wouldn't you? Put it on the table. Go on."

Rahn complied, cautiously removing his Borchardt pistol from under his overcoat and dropping it on the table. With the Browning pistol still trained on Rahn's chest, she carefully circumvented him and inched sideways towards the table. There, she quickly swapped her pistol for Rahn's pistol before shoving her father's book back into the leather satchel. After she tossed the Browning in with the book, she scooped up the bag with her free hand and draped it by its strap across her back.

"That gun is an older Luger model; do you know how to fire that?" Rahn asked tensely, sounding more like he was casually trying to make conversation rather than express concern.

Psalmodie answered, "Would you like to find out?"

Rahn shrugged and stretched his hands. "No, not particularly."

Psalmodie backed away from the man and entered into the maze of furnishings. Rahn tracked her with a solicitous gaze and followed in to keep her in view. When he had found her again, he saw that she stayed her purposeful course, paralleling his short steps through the shelves dividing them while keeping the pistol in her hand aimed sideward at him.

Psalmodie broke the silence. "Oh, how you've fallen from what you insisted your beloved Cathari were to your nation."

"And you?" Rahn questioned. "Is this something you really think your loving Christ would have done? Your father died believing in Him —in that side of the Grail—, even though I never stopped insisting that he was wrong to do so!"

"A part of me is telling me that you're right, but mistaken or not, I intend to see his dream through."

"You still don't understand."

"No, you see, the worst part is that I really *do* understand why you think you should kill me," Psalmodie said. "My father... After you had him arrested last year, I was afraid they would shoot him. But after you sent that telegram from him telling me what was happening to those people in that camp, I was afraid that they wouldn't... for his sake and—

Oh God help me—my own." She pointed the Borchardt directly at his forehead. "I don't care if you thought he loved you for sending his last words to me. The sad truth remains... We're both godless. But you? There's no love left for you. None."

Rahn watched as she made her way towards the steps and put her foot on the first tread. Before she walked up, he saw her raise the pistol up at something on the ceiling above him. Rahn dropped onto his elbows and crawled for cover under one of the shelves as she fired once at the lightbulb and set the entire room in its original darkness.

Soon after, the entire room strobed with muzzle flashes and deafening blasts; reckless, inordinate volleys that glanced off of the steel mesh and wires all around him.

When the silence had settled and the ringing in his ears had stopped, Rahn heard his empty pistol tumbling down over the steps along with the bullet casings clattering over the ground. He would have peered up at the steps, but he was sure that Psalmodie had already gone; she had bought herself enough time to run to the university to either get her friend or retrieve the telegrams.

Breathing out, he looked over and caught sight of the shattered picture frame of that man lying on its side.

The sound of a car door opening next to Rahn drew his attention back to the present, where one of his cronies stood over him to discuss the boarding procedure for one of Acre's many barges to Cyprus and Constantinople.

"Obersturmführer?" he asked. "We're here. What is it that you command now?"

Rahn looked over his enforcer's shoulder to see the towering derricks of the port city's shipyards before looking down to render his thoughts back on the faded photograph he still had in his hand. Rahn removed his Ahnenerbe Totenkopf ring from his finger and wiped the rosy swastika with his thumb.

Holding the photo and the crest side by side, his mind became filled with the Cathari once again, and the heresies they so cherished all the way to their noble martyrdom at Château de Montségur—Lucifer's

Mount of Assembly—before the moment the true Grail was carried down the mountainside by the surviving bonhomme and forever lost to history.

Were the Holy Grail found, however, Rahn sincerely doubted if there would have been anyone left to drink from its raw power after the murderous consequences of the Third Reich's science and religion would have eventually caught up to it. For a brief moment, Lucifer's impassioned zeal for rebellion seemed so insignificant, and in his divine stead was an ever-expanding void. Everyone had now forsaken Rahn, and there was no one left for him to find in them the communal intimacy of the true Son of God; no one left for Lucifer to channel his divine will unto him.

Rahn couldn't help but see the true extent of the ideology he helped to propagate. He saw the fruit of all his labor—the desires that Lucifer himself promised to Eve—robbing him of his own Being, transubstantiating the red wine of the Grail into the blackened blood of Dachau before his very eyes. For all of the Jews' and Christians' and Muslims' lies throughout the centuries, Rahn understood that there was indeed only one thing that they were ever right about.

There always existed a secret knowledge locked away ever since the foundation of the world by wrathful gods and arrogant sciences: A presumption that every moment can be logically discerned through some immutable, totalizing property of existence. The implicitly accepted premise that humanity will one day fully harness this substance to empirically comprehend the whole of these entangled constellations therefore tragically projects itself into the farthest reaches of existence.

"The true mystery of the world becomes disenchanted; so much so that even the realm of hell now paradoxically offers to the imagination some comforting and predictable knowledge of fire and darkness, whatever its cosmically unknowable hideousness may be. The sin of the fruit of knowledge of good and evil was therefore never the pursuit of knowledge itself, but the hubris that one could *already* know and conquer everything, exactly as the God of Abraham said He did.

Knowing this finally, Rahn confessed in his heart, *There is no god but Legion, and Heinrich Himmler is his prophet.*

Death is the Messiah...

The enforcer looked back towards the port city and asked again, "Obersturmführer? What now?"

Rahn looked back towards the long mountain range spreading all the way to the Horns of Hattin behind him, putting him in mind of those beautiful piny Alps in Austria. Then he directed his thoughts forward in time and felt the luring call of the void, almost as though a paradise had somehow still awaited a poor fool like himself somewhere in the abyss; a world beyond the SS and a final chance for him to fade serenely into the forgotten annals of history by giving himself over to depths of something beneath the Earth's existence.

For all his life, his desires had been desired according to the desires of others. All desires... except for one... and he knew to extinguish that final desire meant the final release of his own conscious existence. No want or worry, no perception of time passing... only silence. Heaven was nothing but the tranquil silence of eternal darkness, and if the beatific vision of this secret glory of Heaven had therefore meant first harrowing Hades—the true hell he wrought upon others and himself—, then so be it.

The time had come to unfetter his intrinsic divinity—his true, angelic love—from the inherent sin of the world.

Rahn closed his eyes, but when a blinding flash of light forced them back open... it was five months later... and there, again, were those Alps; the Mount of Assembly in the most distant midnight...

CHAPTER 49

Wilde Kaiser Mountains
Tyrol, Kufstein District, Austria
March 13th, 1939

Deep in a dark forest on the Alpine mountainside was a surging whitewater freshet. Rahn was running desperately —vainly—to hide from the Gestapo hunting him, so he trudged upstream to keep from leaving footprints behind in the metre-deep snow. He stumbled and fell on his hands and face into the slushy snow before crawling to droop his back up against a fir tree's trunk, his entire body convulsing like a withering leaf. Rahn's fading eyes stared through the night, through the blizzard's whistling flurries, and out into the yawning glen below.

But as the clouds rumbled and moaned overhead, he thought he could have heard the airy strings, the flutes, the drums, the brass instruments, and the hymns, all sounding the slow, yet triumphant and spellbinding finale to Richard Wagner's masterpiece opera, *Parsifal;* the consoling adagio to Rahn's transfiguration.

The sacred victory of something that was never supposed to have won.

He opened the two small medicine bottles he had in his grip, tapped out four sleeping tablets into his quivering palm, and put them into his mouth. Then he felt his body become numb and torpid from the white-hot sting of frostbite consuming his every fiber and ligament, every cell and atom encasing his true Being. He could have hardly moved, but as he looked down on the world and into the cosmic beyond as the guardians of Lucifer's Holy Grail did nearly seven centuries ago, he felt as though he had traveled from universes afar... for he felt time itself converting into space.

From the pitch darkness of the forest, he thought he saw rising columns of white smoke, glowing brilliantly as if from a bright blue flare. He was still paralyzed on the ground, but he felt his spirit blindly venturing into the snowstorm, gracefully suspended over the abyss like an entranced tightrope walker, opening his arms to encompass his own apotheosis as he offered himself into the dark unknown.

Then, having experienced the *Consolamentum* and *Endura* sacraments of his Cathari prophets for himself, in simultaneous ecstasy and suffering, Rahn immersed himself in the eternal current of time and space. He at last surrendered himself to the warm splendor of his beatific vision: A singular point of dazzling light heralded by countless, spiraling hosts of angels.

The Holiest of all Holies, calling Rahn back to his true self...

He looked down along his body and noticed that his pants were rolled up to his knees and his feet were bare, resting over what appeared to be a large wooden mazer or baptismal font filled with water. The warmth never left him, but it instead moved down his legs until it stopped and hovered over his ankles. With tender hands, that warmth took Rahn's feet and proceeded to wash them before drying them off with a towel. But when Rahn looked closer into this warmth, all he saw was that man's sweet smile... and the mortifying sight of the cross... That cursed, cursed, cursed cross, gleaming out from the darkness...

And when he, Otto Wilhelm Rahn, at last saw Satan fall like lightning, he hunched over and clutched at his scalp. He didn't know whether to laugh or scream for release, but when he raised his cracked face towards the heavens for the last time, he shrieked unto his own death, his echo outliving him: "Get thee behind me! *Me!! Ahhhh, me!!!!*"

CHAPTER 50

The Church of the Holy Sepulchre
The Old City of Jerusalem
October 21st, 1938

As the morning dawned, a heavenly solemnity seemed to have whispered from the circular colonnade of the triportico in the grand rotunda of the Church of the Holy Sepulchre. For a moment, Psalmodie felt as though she could communicate with the timeless memories emanating from the church's hallowed stones. She felt past peoples searching for something inside themselves, perhaps even searching for themselves.

A requiem for the forgotten.

The church was on the Biblical site of Jesus Christ's crucifixion and Resurrection in the Old City of Jerusalem and was originally built and maintained by the Roman Emperor Constantine and his Byzantine successors before being significantly renovated by the Crusaders centuries later. Though it was the holiest site in all of Christendom, ever since the fire of 1808 and the exploited religious pretexts of the Crimean War in 1853, coexistence amongst the various Christian denominations who shared the church through the former Ottoman Sultan's decree of the *Status Quo* had become quite fragile.

At least, that was what Psalmodie overheard from passing the

Muslim key-holders and liveried consular guards, or Kawas, of the church sitting on the divan by the entrance and conversing with some pilgrims from France. There was also still some debate over the British's decision to reopen the Old City to the public after the nationalists' failed revanche in the last few days, although most seemed to have been relieved that Christ's holy city was at least still intact. Though Psalmodie did behold the church's history in full, she wasn't there for pilgrimage.

After she found that note on the door of her room at the hospice, she promptly dressed herself and came to the Holy Sepulchre to look for someone. The church was nearly vacant save a few soft echoes from footsteps and creaking doors. Around her were those magnificent Romanesque and Byzantine pillars, all belonging to a circular arcade that ascended to the dome of the Anastasis, with a circular skylight casting a seemingly heavenly shaft of light over the object of veneration for all the world's Christians.

The rotunda invoked in her imagination the Great Hall of the Grail in the triumphant final act of Richard Wagner's opera, *Parsifal*. But instead of the Holy Grail, at the very center of the rotunda was the Aedicule, the ornate marble shrine that marked the very place of Christ's Resurrection. Psalmodie paused, looking at it with pitiful lament.

Oh, Otto...

As Psalmodie continued her way around it, she smelled the air about it was heavy with the aroma of ritual incense. She also noticed the blue and red gonfalon banners featuring depictions of the Resurrection, suspended between the cubic shrine's dome and the high-arching arcade as awnings over the entrance; to her, they seemed more like majestic flying carpets taking to the air. Acting as stanchions at either side of the chamber entrance were two rows of four towering paschal candles, fixed on tall stands of gold. Adorning the Aedicule's Baroque entablature were innumerable hanging brass vigil lamps, both Latin and Oriental in design.

Still immersed in the Aedicule's architecture, she bumped into something when she turned the corner. Standing in front of her was a young Maghrebian girl, perhaps five years old, looking up at her with a cherubic face.

Psalmodie heard a voice ahead of her gently call out, "Hanifa?"

Behind the girl was her mother wearing a black, gold-trimmed mantilla veil, and joining her at her side was her husband donning a red fez and white thobe. As their daughter inserted herself back between her parents, the mother slipped her hand through the father's arm, all three walking past Psalmodie with warm smiles.

Psalmodie couldn't help but look after them with a dream-like captivation.

She somehow knew where they had come from.

She looked to her right, and she saw the iron latticework and small golden canopy protruding out from this, the far end of the Aedicule. A hut-like booth with a small altar inside that looked more like a prie-dieu to kneel before. Lining the walls inside was a gold-ground, candle-lit tapestry depicting pageants of angels and prophets. Over the center of the small altar was an altarpiece icon of the crucifixion, and the grief circulating around it in the women of Jerusalem and John the Apostle embracing the Virgin Mary.

In the image's bottom frame, between the flared bells of two white Madonna lilies, a Sahidic inscription with English and French transliterations beneath it.

Before Psalmodie could have read it, she heard a low voice speak out from behind her. "The Copts are very lucky to have their chapel right next to Christ's Resurrection, aren't they?"

She turned and found Francis sitting in a plastic chair by the column behind her with that rosary medal over his knuckles. She followed his meditative gaze back to the Coptic Orthodox icon before walking over to him. She had half a mind to march him back to the hospice given his health after their episode only three days prior. He still had gauze wrapped around his head and she was told by the nuns that he had not been cleared to roam freely.

But a part of her also indulged his appreciation, so she quietly sat herself down on the ground next to him and leaned back against the column with a knee drawn up and a leg out. Psalmodie's remote eyes roamed around the surrounding arcade, and it seemed to her that they had the rotunda all to themselves.

Francis tried to fill the silence. "I was told by the Abbess that some of the people in the Waqf had somewhat amicable relations with Britain's Palestine Exploration Fund? They handed us over to the police and returned us to the hospice? Just like that?"

"I wasn't awake either, so I don't know, but I've also been told as much, yes," Psalmodie responded stolidly.

"That sounds... rather easy, wouldn't you say?" Francis remarked.

"Well, after being shot at and knifed and drugged these past few days, I'm not going to complain."

Francis saw the subdued look on her face, so he didn't bother wasting any more time with anodyne conversation. He again rested his heavy eyes on the Coptic chapel ahead of him, but his concentration gave way to another memory he hoped he had buried long ago.

"When I told my father I was to be baptized," he reflected, "even when I was that young, he renounced me and left me behind in Paris after taking me along for some business trip. At first, I blamed it on his Buddhist *anatman*, and I hated that he had annihilated his own ego—his very soul for it since he was born... But then, I learned afterwards that he was in fact a compassionate bodhisattva; he could have actually gone on to Nirvana, but he chose *me* when I was born. And so, when I read about the history of our people... it tortured me to accept that I really could no longer blame him for what he thought was necessary to save others from suffering."

He hunched forward in his seat. "Some eighty years ago, his grand-mothers down in Nanjing, China were raped and mutilated in a manic genocide of Manchus during the Taiping Rebellion. This lunatic, Hong Xiuquan, he proclaimed himself to be Jesus Christ's younger brother and laid utter waste to China in Christ's holy name. His savage proto-communist cult was enough to disgust even Karl Marx himself, and after only fifteen years, over 20 million people were defiled, gutted, and forgotten in Hong's wake."

Francis steadied his gaze on the rosary medal. "But I met my first fervor in primary school... My *huli xiangtou*... My intimate fox spirit... My enchanting medium through whom I can hunt for the healing touch of the gods..." His eyes became filled with memory. "She's the one that showed me the holiness of Jesus even though she said she couldn't feel it herself; she showed me His true love when my parents left me; after I heard what unspeakable horrors those Japanese soldiers inflicted upon my ancestral family home in Nanjing last year, my faith in Him was gravely shaken, almost gone..." He shook his head. "I know that I should, but I could *never* feel sorry for my sinful passion for her... because, were it not for that sin, I never would have found Him again in those eyes... Those consoling eyes that shined like the sunset..."

A small laugh broke through in his voice. "I may have kept my father's courtesy name, 'Gaiwan,' but my baptism name? I know I joked about it to her, but it wasn't for the Jesuit Saint Francis Xavier; it was actually *her* idea. She seriously wouldn't shut up about the Franciscans even when we were both that young." He paused, and his aspect fell again to solemnity. "She suggested the Missions Society to me to help me honor my parents in some way; to help keep my faith from ever becoming a monster in my home again... I was gifted who I am to myself by her..."

Psalmodie's eyes stitched red as she remembered all the things she hoped Shiloh knew. With Francis beside her, Psalmodie pushed the words out before they got stuck in her chest: "She always told me that she was weak and cowardly... but she didn't listen whenever I told her that she was the only person I have ever met who ever dared to question..." She tried not to cry, but trying only seemed to make it worse. "Brother, I know we have said things that we both regret, but you were right. My father, Shiloh, Malik... they are all on my conscience..."

Francis objected, "It would have been you as well; there was no possible way either of us could have known that any of that would have happened." Francis paused for a moment to let his words hang in the air. But the more he looked at the torture in Psalmodie's eyes, the more his thoughts turned inwardly. He sighed and voiced quietly, "I wish she was here."

Psalmodie opened her mouth to say something to this, then she subsided. Another long silence fell over the church as Francis and Psalmodie looked back at the chapel's icon in mournful veneration, allowing themselves to share in each other's weakness.

Looking down at his interlocked hands over his knees, Francis couldn't help but wonder aloud, "Where do you think she is now?"

Psalmodie shrugged and, barely whispering, vented definitely, "However she's been judged, at least she gets to be with at least one of her parents... which is already more than I can say for myself when it will be my turn... I thought suffering myself to Otto could have been the only hope for atonement I would have gotten for her..." She took another breath to explain herself but caught herself, only choking out, "Either way, I don't think her God would ever let me see her again..."

At first, Francis wanted to take exception to Psalmodie's damaging sentiment, but he resigned tactfully, disinclined to reopen her wound even if it meant trying to heal it. His eyes again scanned the Aedicule, this time searching for something else to say. But after collecting his thoughts, he mused on one in particular with a small smile.

"Saint Francis of Assisi," he finally said, savoring the idea. "Shiloh wasn't Catholic, but she truly believed he was the greatest imitation of Christ to have ever lived. The saint had a great and innocent love of nature, seeing the sun, the moon, the elements, the flowers, the animals —all of God's creation—as his brothers and sisters in 'Being.' He committed his entire life to poverty, mercifully serving the outcasts and leper colonies of his day. He was also the very first of a long line of saints to have miraculously received Christ's wounds from the crucifixion on his physical body: The stigmata. For all of this, he eventually came to be known as an *Alter Christus*—Another Christ."

Psalmodie's eyes snapped up at him. "What are you saying?"

Francis went on, "That 'T' mark on the hand cannon? I don't think it's a Templar symbol, but it sure does greatly resemble a Tau cross; it was Saint Francis' personal sign in life."

"You got that much from that one symbol?" Psalmodie asked insouciantly.

"That, and what Shiloh told me about that 'Holy Cross of Thieves' phrase."

"*Shiloh?*" Psalmodie reacted. "How could she possibly know what the inscriptions said if she couldn't read Mongolian?"

Francis looked down and chuckled softly. "I'm referring to Saint Francis' 'greatest test of faith,' as Shiloh called it."

After a dumbfounded beat, Psalmodie asked, "And what could she have meant by that?"

Francis sighed before expatiating, "When Saint Francis traveled to the Egyptian port city of Damietta, which was under siege by the *Fifth* Crusade at the time, he crossed the battle lines and met with Saladin's nephew and heir, Sultan Muhammad al-Kamil, to try to peacefully convert him by having an extraordinary faith exchange with him. It wasn't clear what happened during Saint Francis' stay, but Shiloh's version of events goes that when the sultan received him into his court, the sultan laid out a carpet full of beautiful cross-like patterns and challenged the discalced friar to step over them to talk to him. To the sultan's shock, and without any hesitation, Saint Francis walked across the crosses to reach the sultan, telling him that the Holy Cross had been entrusted to him, and just as two thieves were crucified beside Christ, so too were the *Saracens* left with only the empty *signs of thieves*.

"Now, I'm not sure how much truth there is to that story, but if Saint Francis did make that claim, then he certainly would have made it while he was fully aware of Saladin's capture of the True Cross." Francis then gestured a hand to the icon in the booth. "And what Shiloh told me was that it was also around this time that al-Kamil was said to have even negotiated the True Cross to the Crusaders in a last-ditch truce to save Damietta, perhaps even with Saint Francis acting as his messenger to the belligerent papal legate. She believed the sultan was only bluffing, but it seems like the sultan *did* have the cross after all.

"She *did* also tell me at one point that there was an unusual period of peace between the feuding Muslim princes of Egypt and Syria during this time, giving the sultan the chance to obtain it somehow. Although all negotiations with the Crusaders ultimately collapsed, the sultan was already *deeply* moved by Saint Francis' genuine concern for his salvation amidst the Christians' and Muslims' endless cycle of violence; for both sides, 'God willed it.' Shiloh told me that Saint Francis had already rejected many lavish gifts from the sultan, but if the sultan did indeed have the True Cross in his possession... Well, I'm sure that is one gift not even the holiest of saints could ever refuse."

Psalmodie chuckled dryly, still digesting the story. "So, you expect me to believe that the Holy Grail ended up being a gift from a sultan to some poor monk that he's never met?"

Francis also chuckled, delighting in his namesake's legacy. "Some years after Saint Francis' death, his mendicant Franciscan Order was also allowed custody of Jerusalem's Christian holy places by later Muslim powers, including this very church. In fact, Shiloh told me that the very first Franciscan friars were also the very first Catholic missionaries to China and Mongolia, even long before and long after Marco Polo." Francis patted a hand over his heart. "Like I said: My name was *her* idea. Not mine."

Psalmodie inclined her head, remembering. "Those piles of crosses we had to walk over under the mosque in Damascus... That Templar helmet with the Golgotha symbol... You don't think they alluded to that 'sign of thieves' statement Saint Francis made, do you?"

"As alluded to by the inscriptions on the hand cannon, at least," Francis added.

"And—you see—there's *that*," she began. "Why were those inscriptions *Mongolian?* Why on a hand cannon? And what of those Templars in Antioch?"

"Didn't Shiloh also say there were also Templars at Damietta?" Francis responded. "I can only speculate, but perhaps the contingent with Saint Francis were the only ones who knew what he ultimately did with the cross. The secret must have been passed down through the more trusted members of the order." Francis' face darkened with more thought. "And given how overmatched and outnumbered they must have found themselves against the Mongols some forty years later, they must have felt compelled to leave behind markers for whoever would have proven themself worthy enough to have deduced Saladin's religious intention for the holy relic down the line.

"And so, while they were in Damascus, then, I believe they must have written the clue in Mongolian as a bulwark against the coming of another Saladin, and the inscriptions were esoteric fragments of Catholic meaning as a bulwark against the Mongols themselves." He smiled in consideration. "It's interesting too. When I told Shiloh I came from China, she made a big point of how the Fifth Crusade could have *easily* won over Egypt after Damietta..."

Psalmodie looked up at Francis with knit brows. "Why?"

Francis smirked. "Because the Mongol raids at the time actually pulverized the Crusader army's expected reinforcements in Georgia; reinforcements that, apparently, could have actually dramatically changed the history of the Crusades. To make matters even worse, Jerusalem itself was sacked sometime after the Sixth Crusade by wandering Persians after their empire was destroyed by the Mongols." He shrugged with a sigh. "If all of that's true, then there's no chance that the Templars in Damascus would have *not* resented this major reason for their constant failure to control Jerusalem."

Psalmodie shook her head, addled. "Wait. So, after all of that, you're seriously saying the Mongols found absolutely *nothing* under that mosque?"

"I guess not," Francis said. "I think it is the only way this all makes sense. The Templars were the only ones to have been with both Saint Francis and the Mongols. So, effectively, I figure that that hand cannon is the *only* clue left in the world to the truth of what happened to the True Cross." Francis paused, vacillating. "But then again, there's that other inscription—'Holy Blood and Water'—I guess that could mean many things. The obvious being the blood and water that flowed equal from Christ's side on the cross? Or is it the blood that ran like water after the Babylonians desecrated Solomon's Temple, as the psalm goes?"

Psalmodie threw up a hand. "Well, what *can* we know about it?"

With a sweeping gesture, Francis added, "Well, it's been said that Saint Francis based his entire faith on the Eucharist, and sometime after his stigmata, his order also authored a popular version of the 'Way of the Cross.' Prayers articulated to imitate Christ's carrying the cross to Golgotha. There's your Grail and cross right there. Maybe there's a connec—"

When Francis checked Psalmodie's face to gauge a reaction, he saw that none of this was either amusing or convincing to her. She merely rested her chin on her hugged knee, idly twisting her fingers over her boot with a glazed look in her eyes. Francis again stared down at his rosary, discerning in silence. But his thoughtful mien eventually faded to yet another hunch. The supposition was still budding, but voicing it still felt better than continuing in silence.

"After you told us about the True Cross aboard the Orient Express," he sighed out, "I must admit, the former Buddhist in me couldn't help but reflect again on the Noble Truths—those harsh and unavoidable realities of suffering that can only spring from the errant desires of the ego. So, I went to the hospice's study to do a little research of my own and learned quite a few new things about the world's religions."

Francis' suggestion pulled Psalmodie out of her blank despondency for a moment. "And what did you learn?"

"Well, I learned that Abrahamic faith is actually quite *demystifying*, and because of its cultural similarities to other pagan myths in the Near East—quests for immortality by the chosen survivors of a great flood—, it is a Trojan horse meant to free us from paganism *from within*."

"Where did you come up with *that?*" Psalmodie asked with an impassive, yet inquiring regard.

Francis elaborated, "The point of the Abrahamic religions is not to simply hope for some blissful afterlife beyond our cruel world, but to remember that death is the meaning of life. To *'memento mori'*—remember to die. But because death is non-Being, we constantly seek out things to affirm our sense of our own uniquely 'meaningful' existence. Our desires begin to shape who we are. And what are the gods but ordinary belief projected out of our own collective desires? Hercules is strength, Minerva is wisdom, Venus is beauty, and so many other gods made in our own image to bring some false sense of Being."

"You say that like those are bad things to want," Psalmodie challenged.

"No, not really," Francis clarified, "but it's desires like these that tend to tempt us to sow discord and scandal against victims just so that we can somehow have a better chance of attaining them. But then there is our Christian faith, the *only* major religion to have as its central focus the perverse and 'undesirable' death of its only God. Mind you, Psalmodie, the Roman cross was seen by the Jews of Jesus' day as a pagan taboo, used for the shockingly sadistic torture of nameless slaves; really, the killing of a cockroach. And they were right: All capital punishment of criminals by the Roman *civitas* was at the same time seen as a sacrifice to gods like Mars. Absolutely *no meaning* could have possibly come from the cross, let alone the salvation of Israel!

"And yet, Christ's death and Resurrection was, in a way, akin to the creation of the world... The only two times in history where our only God emptied Himself of His own divinity through His own Word so that our world could live... Because the cross is, in this sense, the 'anti-myth,' I can't help but wonder: What if the True Cross relic itself wasn't so 'true' after all? In fact, I think I remember reading about how the Protestant theologian John Calvin even said that there were enough of these physical 'candidates,' as you called them, all across Europe to fill the hull of a ship anyways. So maybe that first King Arthur storyteller you spoke of was onto something there after all, huh?" Francis gave a short chuckle, but then his brow pinched, and his eyes centered. "So, what of the Last Supper...?"

His response deflated Psalmodie. "Hardly," she said, almost monot-onously. "My father couldn't have been more explicit: He believed that the Holy Grail wasn't really a cup in the literal sense of—"

"See, but what if it actually *is?*" Francis enthused. "The Eucharist itself is, after all, a ritual in remembrance of the covenant that is sealed in blood; a new covenant, mirroring the one God made with Moses in Egypt, when the Angel of Death spared the enslaved Israelites' firstborn children by passing over the houses marked with lamb's blood. But this new Exodus from our sins is in the remembrance—the *anamnesis*—of God's enduring covenant with Israel: The lamb's Passion, Resurrection, and Ascension."

Psalmodie looked thrown by his fervor, but she still didn't look convinced by his claim. Her eyes returned to the middle distance despite Francis' rambling.

"It goes without saying that Jesus Christ was a Jew of His day," Francis said, "and as you said, the Last Supper was His celebration of a *Jewish* Passover; but none of the Gospels say He ritually closed the meal by drinking the last cup of blessing, as was the custom. I think it was both Matthew and Mark who wrote that He said He wouldn't drink from the fruit of the vine until He was in His Father's kingdom, and so He and His apostles sang the Great Hallel psalm and," Francis shrugged, baffled, "without ceremony, just up and *left* for the Mount of Olives the night before His death."

Psalmodie scoffed, "So what exactly is your point, Brother?"

Francis went on, "Yet just before He died, He said *'I thirst.'*" He shuffled his chair closer to her, searching out her gaze with marveled eyes. "*'I thirst,'* Psalmodie. The Jewish Passover ritual actually *made* the crucifixion of His Body the last cup of the Last Supper!"

Psalmodie shook her head with growing aggravation until she exclaimed, "But what would any of that mean, Brother? What is truth?"

After her question echoed into the silence of the ancient church's rotunda, she gulped and fixated back on the Coptic chapel. But Francis saw something pleading in her lustrous eyes; a desperate longing for some form of closure, or perhaps even merciful release. At first, his Jesuit calling to be a person for others urged him to give solace, but oddly enough, he felt that that calling had drawn his mind elsewhere.

He dwelled on one memory and summoned up what he had learned over the years.

"'Do whatever He tells you...'" he mumbled to himself.

"Come again, Brother?" Psalmodie asked emptily, shifting in place.

Francis waxed on, "Ever since the serpent deceived Eve into believing that she wanted to eat the forbidden fruit of knowledge, across all cultures and myths, it seems like we were always enslaved to that same compulsive desire to feel like we belong among the crowds, and with all our shortsightedness and caprice, it makes us believe that we crave what those crowds crave. Whether it's wealth, sex, power, and other false Grails we so desperately pursue, it feeds into our ego, and we become *incurvatus in se*—a collapsing in on an illusion of an inward depth to our own Being, like insatiable Black Holes sucking the light out of the world into ourselves, instead of living for others."

"Pride?" Psalmodie ventured.

Francis nodded. "We really do sell our souls to a devil who promises us everything we've ever wanted. We crave and envy each other's Being, and we become possessed by them; we are not so much individuals as we are 'interdividuals,' each craving according to the cravings of another. It's only after we grow weakened by killing each other in pandemic wars and conflicts that we begin to understand our need to end this positive feedback loop of endless chaos. No one can stop death, but to control it is to believe that you also control morality itself. We begin to believe that there has to be a line that we can never cross, and so we draw that line across the slit throat of a scapegoat. We live up to the devil's Hebrew name: Satan. *'Accuser.'* We learn to accuse, hating those our neighbors hate and killing those they kill; Jews, Manchus, and so many other victims.

"Then, after we spend so much time rousing a hateful community against a scapegoated innocent, we start to think that the gods somehow approve of how our unanimous hatred of him keeps our community whole. We ritualize that hatred and become a dysfunctional communion in Legion, the Antichrist who, as Christ said in the Gospel of Mark, strangely represses himself; violence moderating violence, violence *controlling* violence by continuously sacrificing and cannibalizing the victim to carry on with some vain sense of social and sacred order."

Psalmodie volunteered, "We covet the goods and wives of others, so we lie, steal, and murder for them? And when chaos inevitably comes, we create false idols to keep the peace?"

"'The Lord is my shepherd; I shall not want,'" Francis recited. "There are wants that tempt us to pride, which tempts us to violence and hatred. This is why we keep the Sabbath, remember our mothers and fathers, and remember the Lord our God. We remember who we are in this world."

"But history shows that the Commandments failed," Psalmodie said. "God has failed."

Francis shook his head. "We are *all* self-righteous rebellion, thinking ourselves better than the sins of human history; even as Christians, we still think like pagans, arrogantly thinkings ourselves better than the Jews' ignorant rejection of Christ and the Israelite prophets, and that we ourselves, like Satan, would do better if we were in their place, as if *we* were God. We sacrifice innocent scapegoats for the sins we refuse to acknowledge. But we never truly appreciate that we ourselves are a part of that sinful history, and we never stop and think to form a loving Communion with the innocent scapegoat, with whom God identifies. Christ Himself.

"I may no longer believe in Nirvana or the samsara; we are only born once with a soul that has real, meaningful needs and desires that we can never deny: Love, family, and friendship. But our *rivalrous* desires are aimed at a vain self-fulfillment of Being, a pursuit of the forbidden fruit: God's Own nature. And in our fruitless striving, we forget that we will one day die. We are all in a Buddhist Net of Indra, an infinite web of interconnected mirrors endlessly reflecting off of one another. We let the darkness in, and if we do not die to our own prideful egos and rivalrous desires—our *false* selves—, then we sacrifice the innocent instead. The contagious cycle of violence never ends, and we end up crucifying Christ Himself over and over again.

"He may be the *'I Am that I Am'*—the perfection of 'Being' itself—, but given His own humility and self-giving love on that Godforsaken cross, even He does not want to 'Be' unto Himself only. He doesn't desire our desires. He desires only *us*. Christ never succumbed to the Pharisees or the Romans, neither accepting nor cursing their paganly ritualistic murder; instead, He only begged God, *'Forgive them, for they know not what they do.'* We have to empty ourselves, as God did in the creation and on the cross. So, I wonder, then, what if Christ's cross *or* cup is more than *just* a cross or cup? What if this long-coveted 'Holy Grail' is really just—"

He broke off and he fell into deep thought, as though fallen into a silent trance. His searching eyes stilled, beholding the truth. He parted from the Coptic icon of the crucifixion and looked down at the rosary medal with an awestruck reverie. The prolonged silence was almost enough to draw Psalmodie's quizzical eyes to him, but her eyes insisted on that Coptic icon. That icon of Shiloh's echoing past.

That icon was all they had left of her.

Then Francis' sotto voice pierced the silence once more. "What if it's just *you?* You. Shiloh. Our enemies. Their murdered victims. Our mothers and fathers. Man or woman, slave or free, Jew or Gentile. *All* of us... one baptism through, with, and in Christ's Being, as a return to Adam and Eve's Being before the fall. All of us, all saints and sinners throughout the ages, all made in the image of God; one bread to give and share and nourish one another. It is to *remember* the covenant. To remember the victims who were mutilated like Christ, tying ourselves to them and them to us. It is to remember that the murderers truly do not know what they do to others and to themselves.

"It is to remember each other and to share in His Trinity through

Christ's essence as goodness and love itself; to share equally in God's reign without any one 'King Arthur' consecrating violence through some mythical claim to a 'Mandate of Heaven' over all of us... Isn't that what Saint Francis wanted when he took his vow of poverty and tried to reach the sultan's heart? Isn't that really what Christ desires from His own cross? For Yahweh to ultimately *anoint* Israel and fulfill the messianic covenant by reconciling us to each other in one Communion in Him?"

Psalmodie jolted from her thoughts; her ruminative eyes flashed and flicked sidelong to Francis, quietly studying him as she felt the dawning revelation penetrate her mind and seize her Being. Her eyes came back on the icon and found a lonely mother grieving at the foot of the cross, looking up from John the Apostle's embrace and longing for her dying son to come back to her. Beneath her feet, the Sahidic Coptic inscription of the last commandment Jesus had issued to men from the cross for the woman who gave Him His flesh.

~   ⲈⲒⲤ ⲦⲈⲕⲘⲀⲀⲨ   ~
Behold your Mother

It should have happened, however, that one among her children in Christ came before Psalmodie. A young elfin-faced British police officer unceremoniously obstructed her view of the Aedicule, looking down on her with an irritated bearing.

"*Tres bien,* Mademoiselle Vingt-Trois," he addressed her in French. "You've had your minute alone with him. Shall we go then?"

Francis looked discombobulated. "Uh, I'm-I'm sorry? Psalmodie, is this a friend of yours?"

"This is Officer McCarthy," Psalmodie responded. "We're going to be placed under house arrest while you recover for our deportation back to Paris, although nobody in the hospice was expecting that you'd sneak out the way you did—you know—given your condition."

Francis appraised his uniform and raised his hands in token surrender. "Say no more. I prayed for my guardian angel, but I guess you will have to do."

His flippant remark made Psalmodie giggle under her hand. Francis collected himself as he tried to push himself up to standing from the plastic chair's armrests. Psalmodie stood up to grab him by his elbow and shoulder while McCarthy watched them impatiently. Once Psalmodie helped Francis up, she draped his arm over her yoke as McCarthy gestured towards the other end of the Aedicule.

"Thank you," Francis said, putting some of his weight on Psalmodie.

"No," Psalmodie said. "Thank *you*... for everything."

Francis smirked at her. "Part of the job, Tintin."

"Tintin?" Psalmodie replied, the smile still in her voice. "Okay then... 'Sir' Brother."

"Yes, well, my vocation would have me disagree with your accolade there." Francis snickered before elaborating, "You know—it's quite funny actually—earlier in their lives, Saint Francis and the Jesuits' founder, Saint Ignatius, were themselves *bon vivant* knights errant wannabes before they eventually committed their lives to the—"

Psalmodie abruptly put a finger to his lips. "If you're going to try to sell me on a nun's life of chastity, then maybe you'd better stop talking."

Francis glanced down with a self-deprecating smile. The two locked grateful eyes for one long moment as they followed McCarthy out the church doors. Psalmodie glanced back once more to peer through the towering candles and vigil lamps to Christ's empty tomb. For an instant, she thought she could have heard an angelic choir from its walls, singing triumphantly of the good that rose up from the tomb and very nearly rose within her own heart.

"God is good," Francis said to no one in particular, "and God is love."

"Good for you," McCarthy scoffed, "and meanwhile, we will be what we will be."

CHAPTER 51

The Hospice of Saint Vincent de Paul

Psalmodie read and reread those same two French-translated verses from Saint Paul's Epistle in Brother Francis' Inner Mongolian Bible, with the rosary he gave her twined around her thumb. She sat isolated at the far corner of a long trestle table in the Vincentian hospice's main refectory, where the nuns had trickled in for their collation supper after their Vespers evening prayers.

But as she read, Psalmodie slid sideways into a waking dream of that moonlit Friday night back in Paris, only two days after she had returned from Glastonbury.

Usually, on such nights, Shiloh went down to the mosque for the *tahajjud* prayer, but Psalmodie remembered she had the distinct impression that her friend had gone off to search for herself somewhere else. Any other time, Psalmodie would have left her alone, but after that unwarranted invective she inflicted on her, she had felt a guilt driving her to see to her morale.

Down the Boulevard de Courcelles beyond the Avenue des Champs-Élysées in the 8th arrondissement, there was an 18th-century landscape garden Shiloh told Psalmodie that she and Francis frolicked around in primary school for its Chinese pagoda and Egyptian pyramid. When Psalmodie got there, the wooded Parc Monceau had been mostly empty of tourists. At certain points in her walk, the pleached foliage of the perpetual, forest-like bosquet gave way to pruned garden clearings and winding promenades.

As Psalmodie looked about this artificial wilderness, she saw the park's most eye-catching folly: A ruined semicircular colonnade running along one end of a water lily reflection pond like a Greco-Roman Stonehenge. The pond itself was set like glass, centered by the lush catkin branches of a towering willow and lined by thick growths of rush, lavender shrubs, and overhanging tree branches.

Then, Psalmodie stopped in her tracks when she saw Shiloh: A little girl sitting on the ledge with one leg hanging down over the water, her hand holding idly onto a column. Psalmodie heard her singing, gently, a plaintive Arabic lullaby to herself. Shiloh stopped singing and looked back at Psalmodie; the little girl's amber eyes gleamed with tears in the moonlight, but she simply nodded her greeting at Psalmodie and looked away, perhaps not willing to admit the enervating torment in them.

Psalmodie hesitated for three steps before stopping shortly behind Shiloh to look down at the grass. Psalmodie still felt at a loss for words since all she ever said only seemed to make things worse between them. She hovered shyly behind Shiloh, wringing her own wrist and twirling her heel over the ground as she looked inwardly. No words were shared between them that night, but in that ambivalent silence, Psalmodie remembered how, in spite of the gaping distance between them, they had shared in each other's comforting presence in spite of everything.

There was a consoling reverence with which Psalmodie regarded the little girl as she approached closer, almost as if there had indeed been some celestial secret hidden away within her for countless centuries.

No Grail... No gods... Nothing...

Only you, Shiloh...

When Psalmodie's mind's eye had come back to the present in the hospice refectory, she found herself meditating again on those same verses:

1 CORINTHIANS 10

[16]Is not the cup of thanksgiving for which we give thanks a participation in the blood of Christ? And is not the bread that

we break a participation in the body of Christ? [17]Because there
is one loaf, we, who are many, and one body, for we all share
the loaf.

While Psalmodie read them, she ate her stir fried potato omelet
from a plastic tray. She saw McCarthy with his own food tray sitting
himself at a table right across from her, fixing her with a dubious look.
She barely reacted, only returning his look with a preoccupied indifference. She raised another fork-full to her mouth and leisurely chewed
with an idle stare.

Just behind McCarthy, Psalmodie saw that a group of nuns were
bunching around something. It appeared to have been a wooden
console with a grainy, black-and-white newsreel. On the small display,
Psalmodie recognized the German chancellor—an angry little man—,
going on yet another vitriolic diatribe over his peoples' national pride
with his foppish mannerisms, his hands flying to and fro before
clutching to his chest like a tragic actor. At the end of it, he threw up the
salute to stir the exultant devotion of his masses, though he himself
seemed to have been loath to join them.

The nuns came together to gossip about this man, and Psalmodie
saw the tension amongst them. Some stood by and sighed their suspi-
cions while others seemed to have spoken equivocally of his intentions.
Knowing better than to join in, Psalmodie focused back on Francis'
Bible.

But just when she was about to resume her perusal, she heard the
light rasp of boots approaching her. Psalmodie looked up and saw that it
was the bright-eyed little nun who visited her a few days ago. The nun
quietly sat herself down with her tray and waved at Psalmodie with an
awkward, yet eager smile.

But once the nun saw that she was only greeted with an unsure look
from Psalmodie, the nun's beam fell slightly. "Monica, remember?" she
ventured timidly, hoping to fit in. "From the hospice? I'm sorry, I can't
speak that much French beyond what the other—"

Psalmodie flinched from her lapse. "I'm sorry—yes! *Bonjour!*" she
responded in English with a shake of her head. "Yes, I do speak fluent
English. I'm so sorry. I just have a lot on my mind lately."

"I know," the nun said, turning to eat her food. "Brother told us about what happened."

Psalmodie gave a nervous start. "He did?"

"Yes," Monica went on, "that must have been so upsetting for you to go through."

Psalmodie's eyes faltered a moment before supposing, "Yes. Yes, it was."

"Hopefully your friend Monsignor Jean-Patmos will not be missing for much longer."

At first, Psalmodie's face shifted at this, but she then quickly understood what she was referring to. She shut her eyes and tried to dismiss the chilling possibility that Rahn or Eggers might have had something to do with his disappearance. "I hope so too," she responded.

"The other sœurs said they will offer up our intentions for him at tonight's Mass," Monica said before her face lit up with another smile. "You will join us in the chapel, yes?"

Psalmodie looked up at her, mindful of Monica's benign innocence. "Oh, I-I'm not Catholic," she finally admitted with difficulty before dropping her eyes modestly. "Not anymore at least."

Monica shrugged. "Well, then maybe you can stay with me for the rosary." She looked down at Psalmodie's hand. "I see you already have one there."

Psalmodie smirked down at the beads and gave Monica an intrigued look. "For a young woman, I can't imagine devoting your whole life to faith when our world is going the way it is. When you took your vows, were you running to God or were you just running away from the world?" She paused and glanced up at the other nuns' headwear with a playful grimace. "Or do you just like to wear those silly hats?"

Monica giggled and answered, "I was the only little girl in my village. The other boys wouldn't let me play in their games, distracting themselves with grand old tales of knights and warriors. I'd get angry at them, and I was just as crass and vulgar as they were. I thought I wanted the same things they did. But when the time would come that they needed someone to share their secrets with—secrets they didn't want their parents or friends knowing—, I was a shelter for them. God help me, but I'd like to think that they didn't believe God was there for them, but I was. And as the only girl in the village, I was there for God too."

Psalmodie asked, almost challengingly, "So you think that just because you were a girl, God especially chose you to reach out to them? That those other boys weren't just as capable of empathy?"

"I'm not saying that only *we* can experience it," Monica clarified eagerly. "Quite the opposite actually: Because we are still working through a social legacy of competition and division, men have to open their hearts more often to this feminine empathy, given how impersonal and emotionally detached they can be to others as they become consumed in their own interests. Amen I tell you, Psalmodie, that after Saint Francis of Assisi, most of the saints who were worthy enough to have miraculously received Christ's five wounds on their body were in fact *women:* Catherine of Siena, Catherine of Ricci, Veronica Giuliani, and Rita of Cascia."

Monica tapped at the devotional medal in Psalmodie's hand. "Not to mention Christ's own mother! She held firm to her faith despite seeing her own Son tortured and murdered right in front of her, not knowing what would become of Israel's salvation. Ever since the Apostles, men have fought and died in the way of Christ's mission and glory, if not for other earthly wants. They enjoy doing works for their own righteous sake.

"But you and I? We *marry* ourselves to who Christ is. We enjoy doing works for what they can do for others. That is why the entire Church has always been considered the *'Bride* of Christ.' Within ourselves, there is this closer union between body and soul, blossoming out in compassionate sensitivity for all of humanity. Throughout my time working here in this hospice with the other nurses and doctors, I feel that this empathy allows me to relate to Christ's Passion in a very real way. Whenever I follow another person in their sufferings and sorrows, I follow myself... I follow Him..."

When Psalmodie recognized what she said, she recited keenly three verses from the Gospel of Matthew, *"'Sell all you have and follow Me.' 'Deny yourself, take up your cross, and follow Me.' 'Follow Me, and I will make you fishers of men.'"* Psalmodie again struggled to contain her pleasure of this truth: Of forsaking trivial distractions to authentically experience ultimate existence through the other. When she saw Monica beam at her with gleeful surprise, Psalmodie waved away her pride and remarked, "Yes, I did indeed have *those* parents."

"Yes, me too," Monica commented.

Soon after, however, the nun's mirth fell to musing as she looked back down at the rosary. Her smile hadn't entirely faded, but Psalmodie sensed the shift in the nun. At first, Psalmodie tried to catch a glimpse from her, but then Monica quickly moved to dust off her tunic.

"Would you happen to know what day of the week it is?" Monica casually brought up.

"Friday," Psalmodie responded, going back to eating her food.

"Really?" the nun exclaimed. "I thought it was Saturday already! So, it's the *Sorrowful* Mysteries today then. We should hurry. Can you believe some of the other sœurs spoke of *snow* again?"

Psalmodie didn't quite hear her. "What's that?"

"Yes, snow!" Monica twinkled at Psalmodie. "Just like in February, when it snowed—"

"No, you said 'Sorrowful Mysteries?'" Psalmodie asked. "What's that?"

"Oh that. Yes, the other sœurs say that we remember Christ's Passion every Friday. You know—His crucifixion?"

Psalmodie glanced up from her rosary with a newfound spirit. "The rosary?"

Amused at first, Psalmodie's mind hung on Monica's words. Her eyes came to rest on the rosary beads around her thumb. She laid its thread end-to-end across the open Bible as her indolent gaze trailed rightward from the curved end to the medal and...

...the small crucifix.

In that moment, her widened eyes jumped up, and she looked as though she were having a premonition. She stared right at the clueless nun in front of her and restlessly searched her own mind.

"What's the matter?" Monica reached out to her. "Are you feeling alri—"

Psalmodie's trembling hand clumsily swiped across her tray and spilled her food all over her shirt. She shot up and tried wiping off the stain with her bare hands. At that point, Officer McCarthy had already approached them.

"What's going on?" he demanded.

Monica waved him off and offered Psalmodie a napkin. "Oh, it's just a small accident," she placated.

Psalmodie's face was a mask of shell shock, and she felt as though there was no longer any ground beneath her feet. "Can I go to my room and fix myself?" she asked uneasily, grabbing the Bible and rosary from the table.

McCarthy looked between the two girls and led Psalmodie away in the other direction, all the while Monica's words darted around in Psalmodie's mind.

Rosary. Crucifixion.

CHAPTER 52

The way is a rose to the sword in the stone.

Once she was back in her room, she sat on her cot and leafed through the foxed scritta pages of her father's journal. Medieval excerpts, frontispieces, and miniatures from Arthurian romances, Biblical stories, and Crusader chronicles. Psalmodie took it all in, waiting for her father's words to resonate with the one page she was searching for.

Her father's retraced copy of an 11th-century circular map of the Crusader Kingdom of Jerusalem used by the Knights Templar.

Outdated as the map may have been, she trailed rightward as she did with the rosary in the refectory. She knew each of the five rosary decades —ten beads for ten Hail Mary prayers—represented a different event, or "mystery," in Christ's Passion narrative. She knew the rosary tradition came sometime after the High Middle Ages, but her father was desperately trying to tell her something through it before he died. He *had* to have been. She frantically flipped back to those pages briefly dealing with the prayers of the "Way of the Cross."

Then elation and urgency stirred in her.

The first mystery and the first station are one and the same!

Her chamber door rattled, and a stern voice shouted, "Psalmodie? Psalmodie, have you changed yet?" McCarthy's shouts were punctuated by more knocking. "Psalmodie?"

Psalmodie ignored it and set aside the journal. She pulled Francis'
Mongolian Bible onto her thighs and scanned through the French translation for all accounts of the event in question. The adrenaline surged
through her racing pulse as she started with Matthew's Gospel and
quickly rifled through its pages until she came across the chapter to
search for what it was about that particular event that intrigued her
father.

Her face was swept over with disbelief when she poured over the
page... and found *that* word.

There was more knocking at the door. "Psalmodie!"

Psalmodie returned to her senses and quickly turned to the other
Gospels' parallel passages of the same event.

The word reappeared every single time.

In Matthew.

In Mark.

In Luke.

In John.

That word, uttered by Jesus Himself very shortly after the Last
Supper.

The auspices had coalesced into one singular revelation, and she
soon realized that her father had known the truth all along.

Outside, Francis heard McCarthy's fist still pummeling the door. The
officer kept yelling, "Psalmodie! Psalmodie, you open this door right
now!"

Walking down the corridor was Francis with an overwrought
Monica beside him, still stammering and panting against her growing
nausea. "Sh-she looked so sp-spooked, I-I don't know if it was s-some-
thing I did or-or said or if I—"

"Officer?" Francis called out patiently. "What are you doing?"

McCarthy turned and referred him to the door with a child-like
petulance. "She's not opening."

Francis frowned at him. "Maybe she just needs a little time to
herself? You haven't exactly given us that much space."

Monica looked up at him with the same concern. "She's been in there for a long time now," she said, a whimper starting in her throat. "Almost an hour now. And the crack under the door, we feel cold air coming from it."

The Jesuit sighed his hesitation, still unsure of the situation. But once he saw the young nun's face had cowered away with self-conscious shame, he gestured for the officer to step aside and moved towards the door with a jangling key in hand. With the knob gripped, he leaned his head in towards the door's stile.

"Psalmodie, it's Francis; can you hear me?" he called in. "Psalmodie, I'm sorry, but we're coming in, okay?"

He paused for a response. When there was none, he twisted in the key and pushed into the room with McCarthy and Monica quickly following in. While Monica clung to the back of Francis' coat, McCarthy ungraciously pushed ahead of them and looked around the plain room for the missing liability.

Monica instantly felt the snowflakes blowing in from the shattered window next to her. Flowing from its sill were numerous cardinal-colored bed sheets, their ends tied together in knots to form a long makeshift rope fastened to the cot caught against the wall.

"Oh Lord, she's Rapunzeled down!" McCarthy exclaimed, quickly looking out the window before charging out the doorway.

After he left, Monica herself rushed to the window and peered down to make sure her worst fear wasn't the case. To her relief and concern alike, Psalmodie was already gone, but Monica instead found the girl's rosary dangling from the window sill.

Slowly taking the medal in both hands, she looked down at it with lonely introspection and fell back into homesick longing; she sniffled and rubbed at her welled up eyes with her knuckle. Then she heard the sound of paper rustling with the wind and found the French and Mongolian script of Francis' Bible on the cot flashing through in one continuous blur. The tome next to it, however, was closed, and she noticed the odd script on the leather cover.

חזן בנסא

Monica then saw Francis approach the bedside and pick up both books. Then, taking the rosary from her hands, he turned his stare towards the gathering streets before the Jaffa Gate outside with a knowing grin small on his face. Monica let her head fall and burrow into Francis' coat. Still overwhelmed, she looked up and followed his warm gaze to the crepuscular rays streaking through the rolling mists of the evergreen trees beyond Jerusalem's cityscape.

"Wh-why did she run away?" Monica cried in distress and incomprehension.

Then Francis put a consoling hand on her shoulder. "Don't worry about her," he replied in a comforting tone. "She came here like me. She only misses someone."

Then she heard a woman's voice behind her exclaim, "Monica? Monica, what happened?" Monica turned and saw one of the nuns marching over to her. She hunched over and gently put a hand to Monica's cheek before looking up at Francis in sharp reprimand. "Brother, I'm sorry, but she has been through enough as it is."

Francis didn't look at either of them. As Monica was led away by her shoulders, she stole one more glance back at Francis and saw the rosary's small medal and crucifix dangling over his fingers. Though there was little to his expression, he was looking out the window as if his own soul were somewhere out in the mystical sands of the desert, plain and in the open.

Francis held himself still as a single tear started in his eye. He believed himself unworthy of fully experiencing the revelation. No matter how much he feared God, he would always find himself desiring Shiloh more, and with a solemn vocation to continuously discern God in all things and in all people, he could never imagine looking away from her eyes. No matter his countless acts of contrition, the only thing he would ever see in the world was the reality that she was no longer there with him.

There was nothing else.

He no less knew that they were both out there, somewhere, somehow still sharing in the world's existence... In the hidden depths of his heart, his cells, his atoms, his very Being... he felt his soul becoming thanksgiving...

Find her, Psalmodie...

CHAPTER 53

The Christian Quarter
The Old City of Jerusalem

Psalmodie trotted through the ancient-looking archway of the Souq Aftimos bazaar into the Muristan market square in the shadow of the bell tower of the Lutheran Church of the Redeemer. Despite the windless sunshower of snow, many canopied storefronts and stalls lining the walls along the street were still awash with a vibrantly varicolored forest of disparate Paisley tapestries, Oriental garments, and ersatz Christian jewelry and handicrafts.

She looked up at the half-clouded twilight sky on her left and saw the rising minaret of the Mosque of Umar ibn al-Khattab, neighboring the golden cross glimmering atop the snow-dusted dome of the Church of the Holy Sepulchre.

The last Sorrowful Mystery: Christ's crucifixion.
The way is a rose.

Psalmodie stared at the structures, mesmerized for a moment; she then noticed the crowds of eager pilgrims filing towards the parvise of the church, though she didn't intend to follow them. She instead turned eastward and wended her way through the crowds congesting the vaulted street of clothing outlets and snack bars that seemed more a narrow hallway. Some stores were still reopening and recovering from the recent insurrection, but the marketplaces were still noisy with merchants, artisans, money-changers, vendors, and bakers. Some traders and muleteers from the ancient city of Jabal Nablus lugged wicker baskets filled with cotton, grapes, and blocks of olive oil soap while little Bedouin guttersnipes and street urchins raced past Psalmodie, gleefully chasing after one another after having begged for candies and baksheesh.

But beneath all of this bustling trade and commerce was something *much* more.

Psalmodie came to a bend and emerged into a more desolate brick alley. A little ways to her right, she saw a number of disconnected buttress-like arches extending over her between the buildings on either side of the peasant street. Inscribed on tile signs embedded in the walls around her, she saw the same words in Hebrew, Perso-Arabic, and Latin.

ויה דולורוזה
طريق الآلام
VIA DOLOROSA

Cutting across the Old City's Muslim quarter was the processional route of Christ's journey to Golgotha where Pontius Pilate forced Him to carry His own cross. "The Way of Suffering."

The Way of the Cross.

Psalmodie strode ahead, her legs carrying her forward to the exit of the Old City's walls at the far end of the street. Her fingertips traced along the walls' aged craquelures as she felt herself moving backwards through time to the very beginning. She felt the bittersweet nostalgia for her mother's processional prayers at each station of the Passion all around the Cathédral Notre-Dame de Paris before coming before the *Pietà* sculpture of Our Lady at the foot of a golden cross with her dead son tenderly reposed over her knees.

She felt a piercing chill run deep through her Being—in body and soul—as those treasured memories now guided her forward along His very way in ancient, snowy Jerusalem. For a moment, she felt as though a cortège of ghosts passed her by; saints, sinners, and soldiers alike, ancient guardians of a long-forgotten sanctity. But in all ages to the present day, she also saw the same people. Wizened paupers sat on the ground along the walls, hugging themselves to sleep wrapped under a hessian blanket; veiled Jewish and Arab fellah peasant women carried their newborns or baskets of flatbreads, desensitized by their own daily hardships; grimy waifs walked aimlessly past them, looking up at Psalmodie with passive and naive eyes.

Cold and forsaken by God and man.

Psalmodie passed them, considering them with rueful sympathy, but once she stopped beneath the medieval Lion's Gate, her eyes went afar to take in the horizon's picturesque alpenglow. Against the darkening pink sky, she saw that every sunlit building top, dome, spire, and open field was streaked by wet clumps of snow. She felt a gentle flurry of snowflakes brush through her flyaway hairs, and as the serene sunlight set behind her, the cypress-speckled eminence of the Mount of Olives became clearer.

She glanced right and found the sealed Eastern Gate she scaled up three nights ago, which had once led into the Temple Mount. Her eyes followed down from the structure to the other end of the cemetery beneath it... and her rapt mind was ensnared by the sight.

Beneath the Islamic al-Aqsa compound and between both prominences was a well-known valley; the ancient boundary line of Jerusalem once widely believed to be the site of the Last Judgment of all nations before the final Resurrection of the Dead and the advent of the Messiah from the Mount of Olives.

The Valley of Josaphat.

Through Joseph under Sarras, then Kingdom Come.

She broke into another jog down the winding roads below and crossed the ice-glazed street, trudging over the brick sidewalk covered with gray slush. A motorcade of lorries filled with standing British soldiers drove by on its way to the Old City. Her glance followed them briefly, but she pushed on, homeward.

Sparkling grains of snow hazed over the sun-streaked road ahead of her. She saw her breaths smolder out in front of her, but despite the soft diffusion of snowflakes and mist speckling over her eyelashes, nothing else existed except that place.

The first station and the first mystery.

Psalmodie slowed to a stop and stood frozen before the Parthenon-like portico of the Neoclassical edifice at the foot of the Mount of Olives in the eastern outskirts of the Old City. The building's powdered façade presented a triangular pediment with a modern mosaic depicting the red-robed Word of God, kneeling before the Alpha and Omega above while the presence of angels and humanity gathered intimately by His sides.

Supporting the lintel were four thick Corinthian columns, and atop each one was a cast sculpture of each of the four Evangelists, vigilantly guarding what lay within for those who proved worthy. The wrought-iron gates were open, and Psalmodie felt Jesus' word, again, beckoning her inside.

But just when she was about to step through the gates, she noticed that a young custodian holding a whisk broom had been standing on the far left side of the church's front steps the entire time. He had tonsured hair, a brown hooded robe with a cord-like cincture, and was barefoot. A monk at first glance, but Psalmodie recalled the other inscription.

Holy Cross of Thieves.

A Franciscan friar.

He stared silently at her for a while with a look of concerned uncertainty. Paying little mind to the custodian, she looked back up at the church before venturing through its main door and entering upon a blissful realm of color.

What little light was left outside filtered in through the frosted translucent alabaster windows with a subaqueous, violet-blue hue. Dividing the rectangular church into three aisles were six Corinthian columns of polished salmon-colored marble, supporting twelve cupola vaults. Transported with wonder, Psalmodie took in the stunning display of mosaics all around her. In each vault, yellow stars arranged in opposing spirals were set against a deep indigo night sky and wreathed by branching canopies of lush olive groves. Among the stars were small amphora vases and discoid cameos commemorating numerous national flags: Belgium, Britain, France, Germany, Italy, Spain, Canada, America, Mexico, Argentina, Brazil, Chile.

The veritable "Church of All Nations."

A church built with funds from countries all across the Earth after the Great War over the Garden of Gethsemane, the Biblical site of Christ's agony and arrest the night before His crucifixion. The place where Christ's "sweat became like great drops of blood" in Luke's Gospel. The place where Christ said to Saint Peter, the "rock" upon which He built His Church, "Those who live by the sword will die by the sword" in Matthew's Gospel.

Holy Blood and Water.

...to the sword in the stone.

Beneath Psalmodie's feet, the hallowed tile floor roiled with Byzantine-style mosaics of tessellations and interlacing motifs, bordered by floral arabesque tendrils. Over the very center of the church in the central aisle between the long pews was a large inlaid cross pattée alisée. Its central medallion, a Eucharist with a Christogram symbol. The topmost pendant of the cross drew her eye up the nave, where she saw that on the pendentives over the Corinthian capitals were more gilded mosaics depicting Seraphim angels, aglow with the radiance emanating from the tealight candles on votive stands and the golden flame-like incandescence hovering over the marble balustrade of the altar rail.

This dazzling light illuminated three arched alcoves with apses towards the back of the church, making for one triptych that depicted the events of that fateful night. Judas' betrayal, the Temple guards' arrest, and...

Before Psalmodie brought her anxious eyes to the central panel, something tickled at her awareness, almost as though the weather around her had changed.

It had, as did everything else.

All around her, she found dense mists rolling through the mangled, iron-gray boughs and undergrowth of a moonlit orchard. With each wary step she took, twigs snapped, and mulch crunched underfoot. The warbling and stridulation of wildlife whizzed through the foreboding wilderness. Psalmodie's wild eyes roved around this new dimension, and she felt as though it were closing in around her.

"Hello?" she called.

She lingered a moment in this murky darkness when she was startled by a faint murmuring from beyond the dense brush. She whirled and trudged through the gaps between the gnarled tree trunks, running towards the sound and trying her best not to stumble over the many exposed roots along the muddy trail.

But her foot caught, and she fell forward over a drift of leaves. With a soft groan of pain, she pushed herself to her knees and wiped away the grime over her brow. She tried staggering back up, but one knee gave out and she fell again on all fours. She shut her eyes and her chest heaved with labored breaths, but when she gulped between draughts, she heard a breathing that was not her own.

Her eyes swept up to a discrepant outline on the ground; a bedraggled little girl lied prostate in front of her, seemingly begging for the torture of the night to stop. With nowhere else to go, Psalmodie crawled uncertainly towards the sprawled girl. The closer she got to her, the louder the girl's sobs became. Psalmodie grabbed the girl's forearm and shoulder and tried bringing her up to her level. As she straightened out the disheveled garbs hanging from her quivering frame, Psalmodie's distracted eyes focused on hers.

What she saw made her eyes glisten with tears.

The little girl's nose dripped with sweat; her short hair was damp and matted; her eyes were glazed over and dried of all tears... shining impossibly amber. The girl seemed numbed and faint, emotionally surrendering herself to a world that only passed her by; she didn't even acknowledge that Psalmodie was directly in front of her, trying to search out her gaze.

Unsure of herself, Psalmodie could only think to embrace the young Shiloh. Psalmodie reached out her trembling hand to cup Shiloh's cheek and tenderly pull her head into her arms. At this, Shiloh's heavy eyes began to flicker with more awareness, and when her hands bemusedly found Psalmodie's back, she slowly awoke to her presence and clutched to her as if holding on for her life. More weak whimpers spilled out from Shiloh's breath, and she wedged her cheek deeper into Psalmodie's shoulder.

As Psalmodie gently cradled Shiloh in her bosom, Psalmodie felt the melancholy swell and carve her out, leaving her empty and longing. Her fingers lingered against Shiloh's cheek, although she felt that it was now moving. When Psalmodie felt Shiloh gently pulling away from her embrace, Psalmodie looked at her and saw that Shiloh was no longer Shiloh.

In Psalmodie's arms was now a local man, His citrine eyes just as tortured as her gone friend's; His face, drenched in a blackened red perspiration. Through choking gasps, the man seemed to have been muttering something. Psalmodie heard that same word Shiloh had taught her only days ago, and with it, those other words from Scripture rising up from the depths. Upon hearing it yet again, Psalmodie's eyes shut back more tears.

> **My Father, if it is not**
> **possible for this cup to be**
> **taken away unless I drink**
> **it, may Your will be done.**

At that moment, night turned to day in a blinding glare of white sunlight, and for what seemed less than a second, the trees around her dried up and gave way to a gravelly esker in an endlessly mountainous desert shrubland. The man's entire figure flew back, heavenward, and His arms spread aloft like the wings of a great angel until His limbs were set against a wooden beam, suspended between two other men in the scorching air above Psalmodie's head.

His face was now battered and torn beyond any human likeness. His gums, swollen over His teeth. His split abdomen, spurting out pus and fat. His unclothed loins, raped and castrated. The flayed ribbons of His putrid skin and flesh, pulsing with larvae and clinging to the pink-white bone of His brittle rib cage like frayed rags of rubber. Blowflies had already begun to hatch from the tarry feces in His loose viscera to trace signatures around His bloated scalp, which ballooned through the tightly coiled wire of a Roman laurel wreath of thorns.

Psalmodie's eyes welled up and swayed in horror of this morbid abomination; she couldn't stop looking at the man's hacked carcass— His rotting face, absent of the gods' wrath or the surrender to man's dogged hatred. Cast out to die in the wild outskirts of Jerusalem like an Israelite scapegoat was none other than Israel Himself...

But then, what she sensed to have been the bleached snags all around her had suddenly taken on impossible life. The faint noise of jeering and clamoring gathered forth, growing louder and louder in her ears. She dared not blink or move, but she sensed the mob's hatred gathering around her like a swirling storm cloud; the teeming multitude of aboriginal nomads, tribal shamans, and bejeweled harlots; Jews, Arabs, Hellenes, Norsemen, Berbers, Nubians, Afghans, Mongols.

Every single one of them, possessed by each other's spirit, and for their craving of some mediation and cohesion amid their cultures perpetually disfigured by chaos, they converged on their sole, common scapegoat for capricious relief. The shamans among the nations, bound both to the gods' sacred myths and man's cruel laws, cried out against the man in blind unanimity, "Crucify Him! Crucify Him! It is better that one man should die than the whole nation perish!"

Time seemed to move slower to Psalmodie, as if the whole of reality moved underwater before her eyes. She saw the godlessness of sin reflected in the sheer godlessness in front of her. One sin after another, venial and mortal, against the innocent and the depraved, across time and space, making present each and every moment of the Apocalypse, the final revelation of humanity on the cross. As the hateful throng of nations egged on the Roman praetors and centurions standing about the dying man, she saw one of them moving for something amid the shrubs at the far side of the esker. The executioner moved through the crowd, brushing past a small gathering of peasant women.

But Psalmodie's heart kicked twice when she saw that standing amidst them was a virtuously veiled mother, her long, flowing, blue and white robes billowing out behind her with each passing gust. The woman was looking straight at Psalmodie over the crowds with a rent gaze, almost as though she were still witnessing her son's agony even though it was still unfolding behind her. For some odd reason, Psalmodie sensed she knew the woman; she thought she recognized traces of her own mother's warmth in the woman's eyes, though the woman looked nothing like her mother, nor had Psalmodie ever seen the woman once before in her life.

A short-lived scuffle in the boiling turmoil of the mob caused Psalmodie to break away from the woman and focus back on the executioner, who returned with a long javelin in hand to complete the murder.

The victim hanging above Psalmodie seemed ready to wail another despairing prayer for His killers who knew not what they were doing. Instead, crying out in the poverty of His own spirit and suffering unto the great silence, as the Israelites and their prophets did in Egypt and Babylon generations before, He questioned, "My God, My God, why have You forsaken Me?" The man was now emptied of His own essence, truly among His own creation; always straying further from God, but still remembering the incarnated covenant... between God and Israel.

As the man's mouth quivered open to weep bitterly, He became speechless when His delirious eyes noticed Psalmodie in the crowds staring intently at Him. She saw that something in His mutilated face shifted. He seemed utterly captivated by her face, as if His poor spirit had become sustained by her very Being.

As if she herself was a sacrament consecrated to Him.

The thief crucified to the victim's left wept, "I have sinned, and I deserve this... But once I am in hell, I ask only that You remember me. Remember me. Remember me, oh Lord, when You enter into Your kingdom..."

As the executioner brought the iron pilum to the victim's torso and rubbed the blunt pyramidal head around the clammy, rubbery membrane over the victim's right ribs, the victim stayed His gaze on Psalmodie, bracing for the final blow as He replied to the thief, "Amen I say to you, today you will be with Me in Paradise..."

But once the soldier finally rammed the spear up into the victim's heart—when at last, the victim's cup seemed ready to be poured out—, lightning fell from Heaven and Psalmodie saw the man's face give way to a flashing vision of senseless, meaningless, Godforsaken butchery. Brown blood clung frozen to the shriveled fingertips of the countless emaciated mummies of men, women, and little children that spilled out from derelict wooden cattle wagons over railroad tracks.

Some of the bodies were thrown down in orgiastic tangles into a muddy ditch, their eyes and mouths screaming, all frozen by the winter as though they had been recreated in wax. For a moment that felt like all eternity, her own existence felt precarious, and she felt as though she were seeing her own future—her own death—, slowly earning its physical reality.

The sound of air raid sirens and droning propellers drew her eyes up to the sky, where she saw staccatos of tracer bullets streaming upwards towards a massive armada of bombers blocking out the heavens and flying through black flak bursts. Beneath the fleet, vast legions of parachuting soldiers were floating down across the smoldering landscape like the flakes and embers scattered across the air.

But then she caught sight of Otto across the mass grave in black uniform, shuddering and weeping in horror like some frail old woman. Once he saw in the chasm of burnt offerings a dying infant still nursing from its mother's leprous corpse, he turned away from her and walked back between two train tracks leading through a gatehouse, his silhouette eventually swallowed by the glaring halation of a white searchlight peering through the rolling mists.

When the gates of Hades seemed to close behind him like an eclipse, and the shrieking hellfire rained across the undulating horizon... there was neither pomp nor fade to the reversion of Psalmodie's original surroundings. She let out a soft gasp of stunned relief as the scene before her had simply vanished into silence in less than the blink of an eye.

Still on her knees, she was no longer in the aisle of the church, but at the chancel in front of the altar, over which was the relic around which the church was built. On the elevated floor was the Rock of Agony, a flat outcrop of rock fenced off by a wrought iron garland of thorns. At each corner were silver statues of doves, alighting with unfurled wings. In front of Psalmodie, a pair of small thorn birds were perched...

...over a simple iron chalice.

Christ, the Jews, Rahn, her own father... and Shiloh... in remembering them, Psalmodie felt a gaping distance yet again; a friction between her own consciousness and theirs. And yet, it was that very distance that was oddly the most intimate connection she felt with them. She knew in her heart that she was not God nor could she be any other person. She was who she was... but in simultaneously experiencing the radical otherness of each and every subjective conscious experience, for a moment, she thought she could finally begin to somewhat apprehend the all-seeing Mind of God.

With the tolling of the Angelus bells and the calling of the *Isha'an adhan* vying for the snowbound Jerusalem landscape outside, Psalmodie sensed the winter's shadow enclosing about the church and fading in through the windows. She shut her eyes, let her limp hands settle over the rims of the chalice before her, and felt as though the enormity of all human history had suddenly become incarnated within her. She couldn't help but venture into the deafening silence of God and push back against it.

...and blessed is the fruit of thy womb, Jesus...

With her last rosary prayer, there was a newfound throbbing proceeding down her arms, and with it, a bolt of sheer pain ripping through her. With a wince, she clutched her wrist and shook out her hand; when she heeded her palms, her expression instantly filled with intense shock and ecstasy for the blood seeping from the round incrustations of flesh from both of her wrists. The marks of the Resurrection of the Word of God; the plainest, most awful form of His love, now forever absent of all of death's meaningless finality.

In the presence of souls as numerous as the stars above, Psalmodie found her own conscious Being peculiar, and she felt some oddly thankful appreciation for its impossible existence; an existence she understood was more verb than noun; an ongoing revelation truly made in the image of Yahweh's Trinity. Many persons communing in the perfection of Being: *"I Am that I Am."* Empathic love became existence itself, and as Psalmodie understood the otherness of every soul—each a profoundly distinct and conscious member of the same Body—, she felt herself drawing closer into the unattainable mystery of Christ's Being... resurrected at long last...

Through, with, and in the one true cup of God...

AUTHOR'S NOTE

My interpretation of the Holy Grail had many sources for inspiration. Since countless legends and conspiracy theories about the relic persist, to help navigate its vast mythos, I drew largely from the Arthurian historian **Richard Barber's** 2004 book *The Holy Grail: Imagination and Belief.* While I personally came to the conclusion that it was no accident that the very first Grail romance was written around the same time as the loss of the True Cross and the fall of Christian Jerusalem, the idea that Christ's Crucifixion was the closing ritual of the Last Supper was born of the New Testament scholar **Brant Pitre's** 2011 book *Jesus and the Jewish Roots of the Eucharist.*

For the theory that the Crucifixion itself is a unique and unprecedented revelation of the scapegoating mechanisms among the world religions, I am absolutely indebted to the work of the French Catholic anthropologist and polymath **René Girard,** in particular his 1982 book *The Scapegoat.* For the prescription that we ought to commune with Christ through empathic Communion with others, I drew heavily on the ideas of the philosopher saint **Edith Stein,** most notably her 1916 doctoral dissertation *On the Problem of Empathy.*

While I have taken certain creative liberties to suit the purposes of the book's plot, I have endeavored to stay completely faithful to both the historicity and the spirit of its setting. Ultimately, however, my book is a work of historical fiction, and I therefore encourage all readers of this book to verify each claim or depiction I have made with reputable scholarly sources before fully accepting them as true or dismissing them as false. I should also mention that the following characters in the book are based on the historical figures of the same name: Heinrich Himmler, Karl Maria Wiligut, Otto Wilhelm Rahn, Kurt Eggers, Mohammed Amin al-Husseini, Herman Wirth, Ernst vom Rath, Asta Bach, and her son. All other characters, including Shiloh, Psalmodie, and Francis, are entirely my creation.

ACKNOWLEDGMENTS

This section should really be a book on its own. There are just too many people to thank, and I am so grateful for the many people in my life who helped me get this far with my work. First and foremost, now more than ever, I want to thank **my loving mother,** whose lifelong passion for Christ was without a doubt the driving spirit of this novel and whose words continue to be an ever-nourishing wellspring of inspiration to this day: "...we belong to the same spiritual family, to this great family that is the Church; we can 'feel' each other's sufferings, because we are all sharers of the same love."

I am also greatly indebted to **my devoted father,** who first taught me that everything in my life that was ever worth doing was never going to come easy to me. Whether it was in school, the swim or cross country teams, or my career, he pushed me to persevere and strive for excellence in whatever endeavor I undertook. I was incredibly fortunate to have been raised by him. When things got tough, he never gave up on me, and he continues to be the example of the man I hope to be for others. I want to thank **my loyal brother Gabriel** as well, whose infectious enthusiasm and upbeat attitude kept my spirits high, especially throughout lockdown.

I want to thank my mentor at Holy Cross, **Professor Mathew Schmalz,** who first introduced me to the work of René Girard in his Religion and Violence seminar. He stoked the flames of my interest in the academic study of religion, and I wouldn't be where I am in my life without his guidance and intellect. I also want to thank **Professor Travis LaCouter,** who not only launched me further into the rabbit hole of Girard's theory through his Modern Catholic Theology seminar, but also greatly exposed me to other systematic approaches to understanding Christ that have radically changed the way I look at my own Catholic identity. I also want to thank **Professor Caner Dagli,** whose Qur'anic hermeneutics have not only broadened my understanding of the Islamic tradition, but significantly deepened my fascination with the three Abrahamic religions and how they each engage and dialogue with other spiritual systems. I would also like to thank **Professor Sahar Bazzaz,** whose seminar on Israel and Palestine helped me greatly in understanding the context and numerous dynamics that led to the conflict.

Special thanks go to my college roommates **Andrew Rolles, Fabrice Charles, and Daniel Desmond.** If we weren't out partying, going to the movies, or getting a bite to eat, we spent the night casually pondering those age-old questions: What is love? What is the mind? Is humanity inherently good or evil? I also want to thank friend and fellow alum **John Pietro,** whose endless fascination with historical time periods—from the Roman Empire to the Middle Ages to World War II —have sparked countless, *countless* hours of discussion and debate that have only fired me up to continue writing this book. I also want to thank friend and fellow alum **Richard Lyons,** who took time out of his busy life to read through a draft of this novel and offer constructive critiques. I am much obliged to him, and am very grateful to call him a friend. A big thanks to the lovely people at Cassidy Cataloguing Services, Inc., in particular **Paula Perry and Megan Staloff,** who greatly assisted in properly classifying my books.

I also want to give a shout-out to one of my best friends, **Brendan Joseph-Torres,** who is on his own quest for the Holy Grail as he continues to build others up and help them become the people they were born to be through health and fitness. His drive to actualize himself through the positive reinforcement and uplifting of others is nothing short of noble. I also want to shout-out my other best friend, **Hayley Moore,** whose loyalty and kindness as well as her love of foreign languages never cease to both comfort and inspire.

Turn the page to read an excerpt from

EXTRA

TERRESTRIAL

BY

PAUL FABIAN

CHAPTER 1

My jacket billowed out behind me like a flapping wing as I stood against the dust storm blasting in my face. But once the storm subsided, I looked down and noticed that there was no longer any ground beneath my feet. I screamed down at the Earth as whatever haunted the heavens above that midnight raised me up to them in a vertical shaft of white light. I flailed my arms and legs around, tumbling *upwards* through the air without any sense of gravitational pull. I looked around, and beyond the light, I saw nothing but an infinite darkness across Boston. Fearing my Lord's Presence, I shut my tearful eyes and braced for His awesome power to overcome my soul.

But then, I dared to steal a glimpse at Paradise... and saw no such thing.

As I levitated towards the blinding light, it was difficult to discern what it was I was seeing. The light looked like it came from a circular hatch that belonged to a metallic, discoid object with a rounded fin on the roof, and except for the smokeless blue flames blowing out from four bottle-shaped nozzles fixed around its edges, it made absolutely no sound.

Unable to comprehend the impossible, I shut my eyes and whispered a Hail Mary in my Arabic mother tongue. Especially in Beit Jala, the little town on the outskirts of Bethlehem where I was born and raised, I had heard fantastical tales of great men and women ascending to the heavens from the Earth. At that moment, I knew that I was not a great man nor was I on holy land, so I concluded that I was either hallucinating or the Lord had allowed the so-called "light bringer" to play another one of his cruel tricks on me.

By the time this tractor beam brought me through the light, my blinded eyes adjusted to my new surroundings. My panicked hands felt around the ground, cold and metallic. I jerked my head around and saw that I was in the middle of a plain gray corridor, the walls lined only with large plumbing and dimly flickering sconce lamps.

I struggled to my feet, resting one hand against the wall for support as my legs got used to the gravity again. For a moment, I imagined what the headlines in the *Boston Globe* might look like the next day: "21-year old M.I.T. student Lenin Abd al-Rahman missing, presumed dead." Ha! Like anyone would have cared... unless they knew it was beings from another planet who killed me. Aliens... Even then, as I was aboard that ship, I thought the notion was insane. If I couldn't believe it, how on Earth could anyone else?

Once I caught my breath, I looked up and down the length of the corridor, looking for something, anything: Another room, a map, an escape pod. I'd even settle for finding a little green man with a ray gun pointed at me if it meant the nightmare would have ended.

But just when I was beginning to carry myself forward, the floor shook and rumbled. A light brightened from a large rectangular crack in the wall in front of me; white sparks flared out from insulated wires and scattered across the floor like yellow marbles. I fell back a step and murmured another prayer to myself, this time to Saint Michael the Archangel.

When the passage gaped open, I bore witness to something whose features could only have been rationally comprehended or described by the insane. They were neither angels nor demons... They looked nothing like the drawings of them that I've seen. Even now, I can never hope to describe their abstract features. All I can say is that there were five of them, gathered around a computer console as if convened for some kind of ritual or emergency conference. Then, to my sheer horror, one of them called to me in perfect English, "You weren't supposed to see us, Lenin."

Filled with the impulse to run out of the room, I turned around only to have the door shut right in my face. As I frantically groped around the door for some button or release to pull on, another one of the aliens called out to me, "There is nowhere else for you to go."

I stopped, hanging my head down to try to compose my splintering thoughts. Slowly, I brought myself to turn around and face the beings once more. I tried to summon up some question for them, but my voice caught in my throat. The only thing that came out of me was a weak and pathetic, "Why?"

An alien answered, "You were walking through Killian Court back to your residence hall far too late at night. We weren't expecting for you to see us. It was our fault: We should have remembered that midterm schedules start tomorrow for students."

My mind couldn't wrap around how human their manner of speech was. Meekly, I responded, "Yeah, well, I had some other terms and concepts to cram."

"Indeed," an alien said, a chuckle in its voice. "But what's past is past, and in fact, now that we have you here, we do have some important things to tell you."

One of the aliens, the captain, interjected, "No, you can't say anything to him. One word of this and—"

"What?" I yelled, finally mustering the courage to confront them. "You can't say what? In fact, why don't you just kill me now and be done with it? No one but me knows that you exist!"

The captain objected, "We can't kill you. Humanity has cultivated a genetic evolution over countless millennia. It is not our place to alter or adjust it in any way; doing so would mean offsetting the economy of the universe's diversity at large! It's nothing short of colonization!"

"Then what the hell are you doing here?"

"Observing. Learning. Appreciating the inherent goodness of your world and the goodness of the universe."

One of the aliens then told the captain, "But you also believe that their destiny and ours' are one and the same, do you not?"

"Yes! But that isn't an excuse to just—"

"Then will they believe this young man by his words of us... or by his actions for humanity?"

The captain kept silent, pondering this point. He shot a glare at me and, once he backed down, its subordinate proceeded with whatever it was it needed to tell me: "Mankind is accelerating to a point in its evolution that will transcend its present conceptions of reality. To our minds, this is an exciting prospect, and we are cautiously optimistic that your species will one day achieve the technological capacity to realize this transcendence. But we still see what you are doing to your planet. What you do to yourselves and each other. Nuclear holocaust, environmental collapse, political and religious discord arising from hatred and avarice. How can you hope to become what you were created to be without moving past all of this poison?"

"Were it so easy..." I remarked.

The alien continued, "I understand that, but that is no excuse to do nothing."

My breath trembled, and I couldn't resist the question: "What is our destiny?"

None of the aliens answered me. They instead exchanged hesitant glances, signaling to one another the beginning of something. One of them put a hand on the computer console in front of them, and some sort of headset appeared on an ejector tray. The headset was covered in plugged-in wires and buttons, and it came equipped with virtual reality goggles like the ones I've seen down in the M.I.T. Media Lab. It appeared to be some kind of brain-computer neural interface, though the sight deeply alarmed me. I wondered what would have come next: Probing? Dissection? Egg-laying?

"What is that?" I demanded.

The aliens only responded by seizing my arms and legs. I struggled to break free from their grasp, but for such little creatures, they had the surprising strength to pin me down against the floor. As four of them held me still, one of them forced the headset on me. Before I could scream my protests, I saw a mesmerizing image materialize in front of me: A blood-red star, a billion times larger than the Earth's sun.

As I beheld this cosmic sight, I could hear the disembodied voice of one of the aliens echo, "As with all that is existing in our universe, there is chaos and order kept in balance in the core of the star you see in front of you. There is the outward expansion of fusion and the inward expansion of gravity. But when that chaos suddenly stops, the funneling nature of order compresses space, time, energy, and matter to a singular point..."

At that moment, the red star exploded in a blinding flare of white light. In the vacuum of space, there was a deafening silence, except what sounded like a radio tinnitus and the crackling of a Geiger counter. An incandescent cloud of red gas expanded from where the star's core once was. And in its place was a small, pitch-black sphere with a swirling distortion of light around its circumference, as if it were encased by a glass bubble. The sphere emitted a warped and eerie droning, like an endlessly winding moan echoing through a haunted chasm of dark nothingness.

The captain pointed a finger to the black sphere and said, "Behold, Lenin... The Face of God..."

Seeing this, I prayed unto our shared oblivion, *"Aba-na 'alladhi fi as-samawat..."*

ALSO BY PAUL FABIAN

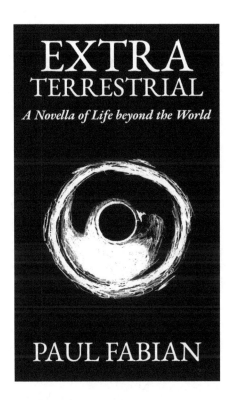

EXTRATERRESTRIAL

After 21-year old M.I.T. student Lenin Abd al-Rahman was diagnosed with a terminal illness, aliens abducted him to reveal a startling secret about the future of human evolution. With only months left to live, Lenin descends further into a spiral of obsession as he works to make sense of what the aliens showed him that night, all at the expense of his relationships with those closest to him.